INSURRECTION

POWERS LEGACY BOOK 3
STARR Z. DAVIES

CHARACTER ASSASSIN BOOKS

Insurrection: Powers Legacy Book 3

BOOKS BY STARR Z. DAVIES

For everyone who has hit rock bottom, feels alone, and can't see the light.
Sometimes it's easy to lose focus and consider giving up.
Sometimes it's hard to find the strength to say enough is enough.
Sometimes, you just need someone to reach out a helping hand. A friend...a stranger...or even an enemy.

No matter what, don't give up. You matter.

Author Note

W ELL, YOU MADE IT this far, so I can only assume you are okay with a lot of the sensitive topics included in this series. Insurrection continues exploring these issues including: same-sex couples, alcoholism, emotional and physical abuse, atypical behaviors, science versus religion, torture, entrapment, depression, and thoughts of suicide.

I am adding one more sensitive topic to this list. Sexual slavery. While this isn't explored in depth, the topic is touched on. If this is a trigger for you, please know that it only plays a small role and I in no way glorify this practice. In fact, my character condemns it very openly.

The purpose of these topics is not ever meant to excuse some while invalidating others. Sadly they exist as part of the human experience.

Cast of Characters

Elpis

Paige Powers — Somatic Muscle Memory; Psionic Precognition/Dreaming (and more to come...)

Gavin Powers — Psionic Perfect Memory & Psychic Navigation; Naturalist Matter Manipulation, Mutation, Environment Creation, Electromancy (and more to come...)

Easton Sinclaire — Somatic Strongarm; Kingdom recruit

Harper — FlexVision; returned to Elpis

Doctor Adams — Healing Hands; returned to Elpis

Olivia — Tracker; died in the Battle of Old St. Louis

Ugene Powers — Powerless; Paige/Gavin's dad; current Minister of Elpis

Enid Powers — Environmental Creation; Paige/Gavin's mom

Aron — Visual Linking; data analyst & Gavin's co-worker

Tudor — Parabolic Hearing; Department of Security Specialist; Paige's ex

Higbee — Natural Mutation; Gavin's boss

Bianca Pond — Super Somatic; Department of Security Colonel; Paige/Gavin's adopted Aunt

Director Levi — Levitation; Director of Department of Security

Alex Miller — Electromancy; Paige/Gavin's adopted uncle

Councilwoman Howser — Telekinetic; councilor of Elpis

Director Perlberg — Psychometry; Director of Department of Science & Technology

Captain Wilson — Department of Security Captain
Mat, Carlos, Nate, Sam, Benny, Elly, First Sergent Camden
  — Specialist training team with Easton/Paige/Tudor

The Haven

Drake — Silencer
Emil — Lie Detector
Minister Charles Garraty — Influencer; Senior Elder
Carmen — Matter Mutation; Resource Elder
Ally — Strongarm; Guardian Elder
Luke — Telepathy; Education Elder
Julia — Healing Hands; Medical Elder
April — Wind Dancer
Dani — Transmutation Conversion
Pippen — Powerless
Mrs. Garraty — Powerless
Ajax — Strongarm acolyte

The Kingdom

Alric Strong the Third — former king; deceased
Alric Strong the Fourth — former Crown Prince; deceased
Queen Elena Strong — Lie Detector; mother of Alric the
  Fourth, Bronwyn, Cypress, and Dominic
Lady Emry — Blood Cleansing; former king's consort; Zephyr's
  mother
Lord Baron Strong — Elemental Control; Admiral of Tides;
  brother of Alric the Third
Bronwyn Strong — Telepathy; princess; second-born child
King Cypress Strong — Item Tracing; third-born child; King of
  the Kingdom of Tides
Dominic Strong — Influencer; forth-born child; Keeper of
  Tides

Zephyr Strong — Power Negation; only child of Lady Emry; Captain of Tides

Lord Vincent Greene — Operator; oversees horse breeding and sales

Nat — Energy Absorption; friend to Zephyr and his First Mate

Ingrid, Mariah, Helen, & Maddy — Paige's maids/stylists

Officer Cante — Hematology; Zephyr's friend; Easton's trainer

Officer Ody — Scopic Vision; Zephyr's friend; Easton's trainer

Finrik — Operator; mainland recruit

Ian — Aurology; mainland recruit

Jeff — Stealth; fort guard

TRIBUTES

Alice — Environment Manipulation; mainlander

Bella Greene — Nature Manipulation; islander; Lord Greene's daughter

Everly — Telekinesis; islander

Holly — Futuresight; mainlander; left behind her one true love

Ivy — Mimic; mainlander

January — Cellular Manipulation; mainlander

Layla — Psychic Navigation; mainlander

Maeve — Organic Mutation; islander; father operates farmlands on the island

Nora — Hematology; islander; formerly engaged to Alric the Fourth and close with the family

River — Shriek; mainlander

Summer — Sound Amplification; mainlander

THE HAVEN

EXCERPT FROM THE JOURNAL OF AIREN MOSHEYEV

T HESE GIFTS WE WERE given do not make us superior. They make us accountable toward the Inferiors who survived the fallout against all odds. They don't have the same gifts as us to create a safe water or food supply. They make us accountable toward the world, which cannot be born anew to bring future generations into days of glory if we do not nurture the earth to prepare it for the new world.

Crow was wrong. Closing the borders and putting up barriers was wrong. Shutting out the world was wrong. We should not be cutting off those who need us most. We are responsible for their survival, and answerable to it. I tried to explain this, but only a few would listen. I tried to fight against the rampant hate against outsiders, against Inferiors, but I was shunned.

So we fled. If only they could see us now.

This new home will be called the Haven, because that is what it will become: a place of safety for *everyone*; a stable home for the gifted and giftless alike; a refuge against those who would attempt to oppress or control us.

But for the Haven to survive, I must continue the research I started years ago. Power stones are not what we thought. Deadly, yes, but a tool to use efficiently if we learn to understand them, respect them. In the Haven, I will have everything I need to continue my life's work.

The Haven will not only protect those who cannot protect themselves. It will change things. I've seen it.

This is where the end will happen.

This is where the future begins.

This is where the new world is born.

1

GAVIN

EVERYTHING HAS CHANGED.

I don't like change. Especially when it comes with so much attention.

Drake reclines back on his bed in his cramped little apartment, hands folded behind his head on the pillow. "I still don't understand why you would choose the floor here instead of a bed in your apartment."

I moved out of the Minister's house after the incident at the temple. The invasion in the Garraty home became too much for me. The acolytes took Mr. Garraty somewhere deep in the temple's belly. I hate admitting that I haven't had the courage to confront him. After everything I suffered at his hands, I'm still terrified of him. How much can I trust him, let alone trust his acolytes not to turn against me? I considered asking to move him somewhere else—somewhere I can monitor him. But that would require talking to him, seeing him.

I'm a coward. I know it. My reasons for avoiding him are entirely selfish. Not only do I fear what power he may still hold within the temple, but the thought that he might blame me for his daughter's death, even if it was his fault, haunts me. I may not have loved Pippen, but I cared about her. Would Mr. Garraty blame me for what happened to her? I would be a fool to think he wouldn't be at least a little justified. My arrival here, and my Powers, made me a target. After I rejected her advances, she volunteered for the horrible experiment. If I hadn't rejected her, would she still be alive? She would be if I had never come here. I know that for certain. While Mr. Garraty is responsible for the experiment that killed her, he certainly could blame me for creating the series of events that took her life.

Mrs. Garraty has been lost in grief over her daughter's death and her husband's imprisonment. The acolytes still won't let her see him in his cell somewhere below the temple.

Looking at her fills me with shame, so I avoid her. The words she said to me as I moved out of their apartment—a spoken verse from the *Book of the Prophet*—still haunt me. *"Loved ones will be broken, their faith deceived by dark spirits."*

I roll on my side. For the past couple of nights, I've slept on Drake's floor. "My new apartment is big, empty, and lonely," I reply.

The new place is bigger than I deserve or need. It's one of the largest in the Haven. For over a week, I've avoided the new accommodations. The space is just too much. It has a massive living room with a full kitchen, three bedrooms, and two bathrooms. I hate it.

Drake pops up, grinning down at me. "Well then, we have a simple solution."

"What's that?" I love that grin.

"I move in."

My stomach flips madly. My cheeks heat. I hope he can't tell. "Move in." I feel like an idiot, parroting his words back to him, but I'm too stunned to formulate a response.

"Sure." He shrugs. "There are three rooms, right? Let's get my stuff together and I'll move into one of the spares."

Excitement mingles with terror and disappointment. The idea of having Drake living in the same space fills me with a thrill, but at the same time, I don't want him in a spare room. The proximity will be a sure test of my will. Until he makes it clear what he wants from me, if anything, I can't make a move. Not that I would know what to do.

That settles the matter, though. I don't have the courage to question his suggestion aloud, nor make any other suggestions. So, we do as he suggests and gather his belongings. It doesn't take long before we are in my apartment, parting ways at our doors. When I close myself in my bedroom, I lean against the door and press my face into my hands.

I'm such a coward.

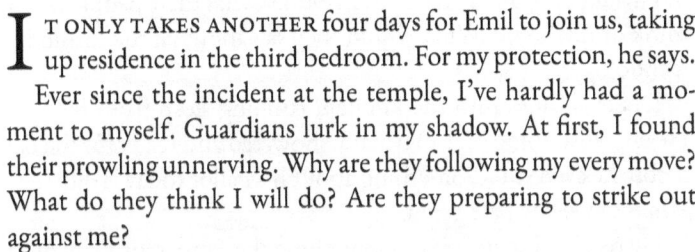

I T ONLY TAKES ANOTHER four days for Emil to join us, taking up residence in the third bedroom. For my protection, he says.

Ever since the incident at the temple, I've hardly had a moment to myself. Guardians lurk in my shadow. At first, I found their prowling unnerving. Why are they following my every move? What do they think I will do? Are they preparing to strike out against me?

But as the surge of Havenites congregates outside of my apartment and trails my every move around the halls with disturbing reverence, I swiftly realize the Guardians are *protecting* me from the Havenites, not spying on me or preparing to attack.

Acolytes flood my apartment with offerings. Trinkets from a world long lost. Baskets of food in all varieties. Trays of dinners and breakfast feasts the likes of which no one else in the Haven sees. I suspect that Emil only moved in to get access to the food.

I don't leave the apartment often. The crowds overwhelm me. Everyone wants something from me. Everything from petitions for new apartments for larger families to a simple touch—like a blessing. It makes my skin crawl that they think touching their hand or arm will make any difference in their lives.

I'm also avoiding the Elders. They have sent several requests to meet, but I've found excuses to worm my way out of all of them. Again, I'm too much of a coward to face the very people who tried to burn me alive—who *did* burn me alive. I should be furious with them, want to bring my wrath down upon their heads. That's what Paige would do. But that isn't me. *No, unlike Paige, Gavin Powers hides in his comfort zone and avoids conflict.*

Like every morning, I open the door to pull in the gifts and food left outside my door. Wreaths and bouquets of flowers line either wall outside the door like a shrine to someone missing or deceased. The lights flicker, as they often do. A small push of my Power steadies the glow. A few people linger near the door, their jaws dropping in awe at my small display of strength. It makes me uneasy.

I retrieve a basket of fruit and kick the door shut without a word, eager to cut myself off from enthusiastic faces. What I just did would be ordinary in Elpis. I wonder what these people would think of my home. What would they say about all the forbidden technology?

Drake shuffles into the kitchen, rubbing sleep from his eyes. He enjoys sleeping in. I'm usually showered and ready for the day before he even stirs. Something about his pallor today is different. *Wrong.* A sickly pale green.

He reaches for an apple—something they apparently can grow in abundance here. I make note of the tremble in his hand. When he takes a bite, I study him. It takes far too much effort to carry out such a simple task. He even chews it slower.

"You feeling alright?" I ask, setting the basket on the counter-top.

Drake grunts. I'm uncertain what to make of the response.

Then he collapses on the floor, shaking like he's having a seizure.

"Drake!" I rush around the counter to his side, too slow to break his fall.

Drake's head hits the concrete floor. His eyes roll back in his head. Every part of me trembles. What is wrong with him? I roll him on his side, afraid he's about to choke on his own saliva, and make sure his airway is open.

Emil steps out, asking about the commotion. When he sees Drake, he pales.

"What do we do?" I ask, too panicked to think straight. "He was pale this morning, then he collapsed completely."

Emil rushes over, nudging me out of the way. I don't fight him. The terror in me overwhelms logic. I can't lose him. Drake is the only thing keeping me sane.

As Emil checks Drake's vitals, I pick up the apple rolling across the floor and sniff at it. But it smells like an apple. I don't even know what I'm thinking. Drake didn't look good from the moment he stepped out his door. It isn't poison.

Emil curses under his breath. "Something is draining him." He's shaking, too.

Draining...? My gut sinks. I riffle through the baskets on the counter and uncover not one, but four different Power stones in various baskets, buried beneath the food. Is someone hoping to incapacitate me with these again? I learned my lesson the first time and know how to protect myself from them now.

Gingerly, I gather the four small stones in a fist, wrapping my Power around them to protect myself and, hopefully, Drake and Emil too.

This isn't the first time acolytes have left Power stones outside my door. It's the tenth. *How many do they have?* I've destroyed all of them. These stones are too dangerous to leave lying around. Drake's reaction is precisely why.

Are the acolytes trying to hurt me? Is someone else? Or is this a test to see if I can do what I did in the temple that horrifying day—to destroy them with my bare hands?

Regardless of the intentions toward me, the proximity effect these stones have on Havenites with Powers is dangerous.

Anger builds in my heart, spreading through my body with each thump of my heartbeat until the ferocity of it makes me tremble. I clutch the stones in my fist and storm toward the door.

"I will take care of this," I growl. "Help him. Get a doctor if you need to."

Emil knows what to do. Drake is in excellent hands. But unless I put a stop to this, they could suffer much worse.

Hiding is no longer an option. Not if it puts the lives of those I care about at risk. Whether or not I like it, it's time to step forward and wield whatever measly sense of power these people give me.

And it starts with these acolytes and their twisted sense of purpose.

2

PAIGE

THE PALACE FEELS EMPTY without Zephyr's presence. It isn't until he's gone that I realize how much I had grown used to the feel of his Power pushing against my own, like a dance between the two of us even when we aren't together. I sit by the window in my room, peering out at the lake, missing his snarky wit. I'm stuck on this island until spring.

Princess Bronwyn and Prince Dominic have helped me pass the time, but I suspect their appearances are more about keeping tabs on me than anything else.

The princess is far wiser than anyone else seems to realize. She is quick to laugh, to share her knowledge of the island and the people who control it. Something tells me she would make a fantastic queen, but she cannot rule the Kingdom of Tides just because she is a girl. It's infuriating the level of sexism in this place, but she doesn't seem to mind being overlooked.

Once King Cypress has made his selection—as if none of us girls even have a choice—he will arrange for the princess to wed next. I prod her for information about who catches her eye, but she just shrugs. Apparently, the men on this island are arrogant—big surprise considering the overwhelming patriarchal society they have here—and Princess Bronwyn can't stand being around most of the men long, even if some are nice to look at.

Prince Dominic is so much like his sister that I sometimes wonder if they should have been twins. But where she is shy and reserved, he makes jokes and bends over backwards to make me smile. As long as I don't mention Zephyr. Just saying his name creates lines of sadness around Prince Dominic's eyes. The pain is still raw for him. Does he blame me for Zephyr's fate? Does he hate me for what happened to his brother?

No doubt the prince and princess report to King Cypress and his mother, Queen Elena. What does the royal family think I will do? Maybe they are worried that Zephyr will try coming back to see me. It's still winter, so he is on this island somewhere.

Zephyr hasn't come back. I can't even locate him in Dreams anymore. If I can reach Gavin hundreds of miles from me, I should be able to find Zephyr. Wherever he has gone, he doesn't want to be found. That causes me immense pain. I try reaching out to Easton in Dreams a few times, but something blocks me.

The ease with which the rest of the Tributes move on from Holly's suicide makes me sick to my stomach. Holly was like most of us, ripped away from her home, her family, her love, and forced into this ridiculous pageantry. How would her boyfriend feel if he knew how little these people cared about her? I don't even know what they did with her body, and I'm ashamed to admit I don't have the courage to ask. There's no funeral or memorial for her.

Life simply goes on.

A few days after Lady Emry's funeral, King Cypress beings calling on each of the girls for one-on-one time. I can't help but worry about the odds I will regain his trust. With Zephyr in the wind, the king is currently my only hope of getting out of here. According to Prince Dominic, no matter what their mother decrees, King Cypress is the only one who can order my release from the island. The only one who can force me to stay.

And he's avoiding me.

Not that I can blame him. If he really developed feelings for me, regardless of whether I share them, knowing that I nearly kissed his younger brother probably cut him deeply.

I still hold out the hope that we can open some sort of diplomacy between Elpis and the Kingdom of Tides, even if he's lost interest in me. Why I still want it, I don't fully understand. These people are callous, sexist, and authoritative, bordering on tyranny. Why should we want any sort of diplomacy with the Kingdom?

Nora is the first girl King Cypress calls on—not that I'm surprised. He starts with the native girls, taking them out every day or so. The girls are all closed-mouthed about where they go and what they do. I think they are afraid that comparing notes will set one of them above the others.

Weeks pass and he still hasn't called on me. If King Cypress has already organized us into some sort of prioritized rank and he is working his way to the bottom, I'm the sludge at the bottom of the barrel.

I've been counting. The two remaining island natives—Nora and Bella. Then January, Layla, Summer, Alice.

One morning after breakfast, when we all return to our rooms to "freshen up", I hear another knock. I peer out my door down the hall as River receives her invitation to join him later in the day. My heart sinks.

Only I remain. While I don't care about marriage or love, I *do* care about convincing him to let me go home in the spring. Perhaps with the promise of future diplomatic relations. If he thinks so little of me already, the hill I must climb is much higher than I anticipated. My only hope may be to play to his pity. But considering what he did to his own brother, that hope is miniscule.

No matter what I do to pass time—observing guard rotations around the palace, poking around for every conceivable exit from the building, talking to servants to get a feel for how they feel about the Kingdom—I can't seem to focus on any task for long. My mind drifts to King Cypress. To Zephyr. One whose attention I need. The other whose attention I want. Both have vanished from my life.

The kiss that never happened haunts me. Zephyr was punished for it—exiled. If I could change that moment, seize it, I would. That night, I felt like Zephyr and I had found a common ground, bonding with one another. He opened up about his mother, which I'm sure he didn't enjoy talking about. I bared my deepest fear to him.

Without him nearby, my nightmares have returned. I can't be sure that his exile and my worsening nightmares are linked, but considering how his Power inhibits my own, I can't help connecting the two things together. His presence gave me shelter. Now that shelter is gone, and the storm is rolling in with ferocity.

In the nightmares, I stand alone at the end of the world, consumed by mysterious red Power. Then Zephyr appears. He holds me tightly and helps bear the burden of the overwhelming Power until we both die, clinging to each other. Unlike the other dreams I had with him before the exile—dreams that felt so real and shared—this one is surreal. And it plays on repeat, night after night, though some of the smaller details change.

Why, when I have such horrible dreams with him beside me, do I even want him near me? Shouldn't I want him to be far away, where that horrible fate cannot come true? Is it even an inevitable fate, or just my inner fears coming to life in my dreams?

I wake up in a sweat most days. I gather myself and get showered before the maids come to clean me up and dress me for the day. Not that it matters. King Cypress won't show his face.

Bella graces me with a visit after the King's daily invitation has been delivered—once more, not to me. She lets herself in while I sit near the window, then glides toward me like a panther stalking its prey. I want to push her out of the room, or maybe off the balcony.

"You are failing, Paige." Her voice grates on my nerves. I clench my jaw. "I told you to get close by any means necessary."

"He won't even show me his face," I mutter. "I don't know why you care. Why do you want me to get cozy with him, anyway? I thought *you* wanted this."

"He's hurt." She runs her fingers over the top of my dresser, giving a casual shrug. Her Power-dampening bracelet dangles around her thin wrist. "Not that I can blame him, I suppose."

How does she *know?*

"Stop waiting around. Go to him. Grovel. Beg his forgiveness. Give him a reason to *want* you close again."

I tear my gaze from the lake beyond the windows and gape at her. Grovel? No. I won't do it. Her threat toward Easton has me worried, but Easton is a big boy. I can't imagine Bella can do anything to him that he can't handle. There is no way I will grovel at the king's feet. And her implication on *how* I should throw myself at him isn't lost on me.

"Why should I?" I snap. A wave of fiery anger rushes through me. The nerve of this girl! "You haven't told me anything."

"Nor will I." Bella puts her hands on her hips. "It isn't for you to know why. All you need to know is that I have access to your friend, should you refuse. Go to King Cypress. Throw yourself at him. Get his attention."

I can't nail down Bella's motives. Her first warning had been clear. Stop hogging the light and keep my distance from the King. But something changed. The exile of a prince. What benefit did Zephyr's fall play in her plans? Or did it force her to change everything? *What* are her plans?

I glare at Bella, itching to throw her over the balcony rail to her doom. I won't let a bully push me around. "No."

Bella's jaw tenses. "I will give you a few days to reconsider and plan your advances. Fail, and I will have pieces of your friend delivered."

She pivots toward the door.

She's bluffing. There's no way she has that kind of access. Certainly not while we are all locked up in here.

I surge to my feet, clenching my hands into fists. "Why? Why do you need me to do this? I want answers, Bella."

She ignores me, closing the door behind her.

Somehow, I need to learn more about her. Nora knows her. Would she have any further insight? What will Bella do if I bring Nora into this? There's a chance it could put Nora in danger. I can't do that to her.

For the moment, I need to lie low and monitor Bella.

3

GAVIN

THE MASSIVE DOORS OF the temple remain open all the time now. I stroll through, hands clenched into fists at my side and my Powers wrapped around me like a protective blanket. My mind won't stop spinning through scenarios. What the acolytes will say. What Powers they will use against me. What kind of fight I might be facing. It's hard to get a handle on my whirling worries, which only fuels my confrontational anxiety.

Every part of me trembles with both anger and anxiety. I hate confrontation. It rattles my nerves, makes me sick to my stomach, and just makes me utterly miserable. But I can't avoid this. Not when it affects the people I care about. Not when no one else can do this but me.

Overhead, the open ceiling of the temple reveals a gray pallor in the sky beyond the snow-capped oak, maple, and pine trees. The color reflects my mood.

I climb the stage stairs, marching over the restored wooden planks—planks I had only weeks ago transformed into wooden acolyte protectors. Now, there are no signs of the struggle that took place here. The acolytes fixed everything. Everything except the giant hole in the ceiling and the new position of the Idol statues.

At the door leading to the Minister's office and the belly of the temple, I pause and take a breath to steady my frayed nerves. It doesn't work.

The door opens without my touch, moving at my will alone. The Power stones in my hand pulse against me. While they may not affect me as they did before, the sensation they leave behind still causes queasiness.

A handful of acolytes in their pale robes move along the hallway in their own business. What they are doing without the Minister guiding their hands, I can't be certain. When they spot me shuffling toward them, all five freeze mid-task, clutching books, trays, or foods.

I'm losing my nerve. It slips gradually from my grasp as confrontational terror slows my steps. *I can do this. I must do this*.

One acolyte passes a notebook to another, then steps forward. He's a sturdy man of about twenty with features that give away his Somatic strength. I recognize him instantly. He's the one who knocked me out the last time I was down here. He's the one who gave me to the Minister to drain, then burn. Seeing him makes my knees weak. The others quickly defer to him. Does that put him in charge?

"Idol Powers," he says in a deep voice.

The title makes my queasy stomach even more uneasy. Heat climbs to my cheeks. But the awkwardness is nothing compared to the mortification that floods through me as he drops to a knee and bows his head to me...like I'm a king or something.

"How may we be of service to you, Your Grace?" he asks.

Grace? I lick my lips, tightening my grip on the Power stones. He either notices them or feels them. His eyes dart to the stones. Sweat prickles along his hairline.

Just rip off the bandage, Gavin. I raise a trembling arm and flip the stones up so everyone in the hallway can see them clearly. They all flinch back. The Somatic kneeling in front of me shifts like he wants to run.

"Why do you keep leaving these at my door, hidden in baskets of food?" I ask.

He frowns, staring at the stones. Confusion wrinkles his forehead. "In the baskets?"

My stomach sinks. "Who is in charge of leaving the baskets at my door each day? Who puts them together? Who delivers them?"

I try to make my voice authoritative and confident like Dad, but a quiver punctuates each word. Hopefully, they don't notice.

"W-we have a small team that has organized to bring you offerings of peace. Food and whatever else you might need." His sweat rolls down his temples. "Perhaps the stones were placed in them as part of the offering. We saw what you did with the last one. It...was a miracle."

I shiver, remembering how I ground it to dust.

"How many of these are there here?" I ask.

"Your Grace?"

"Stop calling me that."

He flinches.

"Just answer my question."

"How many do you require, Idol Powers?" he asks, careful to avoid the forbidden title. Not that I like the replacement any better.

His response incites immediate curiosity in my mind. Curiosity and fear. That he needs to ask implies far more than I would like.

"All of them," I say.

He gulps. "All? But sire—"

"These stones are dangerous, and you know it," I snap, irritated that he could pull yet another title out of the air. "The sweat on your brow tells me you feel the effects of them and understand what will happen—what is probably happening to you right now. The sickness in your stomach and weakness in your limbs. It starts slowly, and it's horribly painful. Next will be your mind. You won't be able to think straight, then lose control of your own limbs. How long must we stand here and have this conversation before you tell me what I want to know?"

A bead of sweat rolls down his temple. He dips his head as if ashamed. The other acolytes in the hallway at some point kneeled as well. All of them stare at the stones in horror.

No one speaks. They don't even seem to breathe, as if just the act of drawing in air allows the stones to affect them.

I close my fist around the Power stones. They pulse with sickening delight in my palm.

"Why do you need all—?" He cuts off as I use my newfound Power against the stones, as I did weeks ago in the temple. They don't just shatter in my fist. The stones dissolve into a fine powder. I open my fist and tip my palm toward the floor, brushing my hands together.

To his credit, the Somatic leader doesn't move despite how uncomfortable the dust makes him. His face reddens.

I've never called on fire before, but it seems appropriate in the moment to try. It's a dangerous element without proper control—something I've never really learned. But I need to make the acolytes recognize I mean business. The heat rushes through my veins before streaming from my fingertips to burn the powdered stones.

This moves him. The Somatic draws back, covering his nose and mouth with the sleeve of his robe to avoid breathing in the fumes. From what I've read in the lost journal, which they call the *Book of the Prophet*, smoke should not have any adverse effects.

"Is my intention clear enough now?" I ask.

He nods, eyes wide.

4

PAIGE

THE GIRLS HAVE TAKEN their placement in the line with King Cypress as a sign of his preference. Each day they offer me consolation, which only infuriates me. The pleasant smiles and reassuring pats on the arm or shoulder. The sickeningly honey-sweet reassurances of, "I'm sure he will call on you soon." I want to punch each of these girls in the face.

No doubt they assume I will be the first to go. It wouldn't bother me if I knew I had a chance at getting home. But Zephyr thoroughly destroyed that hope when he told me the shores are frozen until spring.

I've watched the water from my balcony for weeks. If even one boat goes out on the water, then being dismissed wouldn't be so bad. I could find my way across the massive lake to the mainland and find my way home.

Not a single ship leaves port.

After River's date with the king, I wait in my doorway for the inevitable invitation.

The butler reaches the top of the stairs beside my room and gives me a polite bow. I straighten.

Then he passes and knocks on January's door.

Each rap of his knuckles against her door knocks more air from my lungs. I stumble backward into my room and close the door, pressing my back against it. Not only am I his last choice, but he thinks so little of me he is making rounds *again*.

How I wish I could rip off this bracelet locked on my wrist and seize my Powers. While I don't understand them, or what I can do with them, maybe they could help me escape this place.

I probably deserve the cold shoulder. Queen Elena all but told me King Cypress wouldn't choose me, so why waste time on me? I tried to kiss his brother, after all.

After dinner, I return to my room to find a small package neatly tied with red ribbon sitting on my pillow. Hoping that it's a gift from the king, and maybe he is changing his mind, I rush to the small box and untie the ribbon.

The lid lifts without trouble.

I gasp, gag, and stumble back the moment I see the contents of the box.

A pale pinky finger rests in black crushed velvet inside the box. A male finger. A small note is tucked in the box.

Shaking, I reach for the note.

By any means necessary.

Bile climbs up my throat. I slap the lid back on the box. Someone needs to see this. Bella *can't* be that powerful. And there's no proof that this finger belonged to Easton. *Why is this so important to her?*

Whether or not this finger belongs to Easton, I have to do something. He is my last link to home. I don't have deep feelings for him, but I do care about him. The only way we will make it home alive is together. I feel it deep in my gut.

The last thing I want is to touch the box, but I can't leave it on my pillow. If Bella is threatening me, Easton, or even the king, someone else needs to know. I can't show this to the princess. She's likely to faint in shock. But the prince will know what to do.

I scoop the box off the bed and rush out. As I close my door, Bella watches me from her own doorway, smirking. How I would love to beat that girl until she's incapable of smirking again! I swallow the lump of bile in my throat and duck my head toward the elevator. Whatever game Bella thinks she's playing with me, I won't be used. And I won't be intimidated.

Prince Dominic's room is on the top floor. I've had lunch with him and the princess in the room before.

In just a few minutes, I'm knocking on his door, shaking with fury from head to toe.

He pulls the door open, frowning when he sees me. "What's wrong?"

I thrust the box toward him. "We need to talk."

———— ⬦ ————

P RINCE DOMINIC SITS AT his desk near the bay of windows, the box closed and pushed away from him. I spent the last half hour spilling everything I can remember about Bella. Her original threat the day the dome collapsed, then again at the funeral. How she warned me to try harder with the king just a few days ago.

Prince Dominic shakes his head, running his fingers through his curly locks in distress. His face has taken on a pale pallor. "Why would Bella do something like this? She isn't asking you to back off, which is what I would expect the girls to do. It doesn't make sense, Paige."

"Does she have access to Easton?" I can't help the heat rising in my voice, nor the fear.

"Not that I know of."

"Well, that finger came from someone!" I pace the carpeted floor, unable to stay still for more than a few seconds.

"It did. But this, what you are telling me about Bella... I've known her for years. She can be arrogant, but she isn't vindictive." He leans forward, arms resting on his knees, clutching his hands together tightly. "There must be some mistake."

"Is that her handwriting?" I snap, stabbing a finger at the note.

Prince Dominic blanches, peering at the floor as if unable to look at the "gift" left for me. "I don't know."

I huff. Irritation coats my insides, burning like fire. My hands clench and unclench in fists as I continue my agitated strides.

"I know what she said. He would be delivered in pieces if I didn't do what she wanted. Which I didn't. And look." I wave toward the box. The floor trembles with each step.

His gaze flicks at my feet, a curious expression on his face. "I saw." Something else has distracted him. What could be more important than protecting his brother? And why isn't he more incensed about this? It happened right under their noses!

Prince Dominic rises, striding toward me like an orderly would an unhinged patient, hands raised in supplication. His gaze flicks to my wrist. To the bracelet locked on me like shackles wrapped around my Powers. "Paige, I need you to calm down."

I stab a finger at the box. "How can I?"

He puts tender hands on my shoulders. "You're agitated, and your magic is fighting to break out. You need to calm yourself before something happens."

Despite the fear and anger coursing through me, Prince Dominic's words stop my pacing. My heartbeat slows. Tears brim my eyes.

"You need to dismiss her," I say, pressing urgency into each word.

"I can't. Only Cypress can dismiss any of the girls." I open my mouth to argue, but before I say a word, he holds up a hand to quiet me. "I will talk to him, but the ultimate choice is his."

Of course. Hopefully, Cypress will listen to reason. Prince Dominic probably stands a better chance of convincing him than I would.

"I will investigate all of this," he reassures me, gaining confidence now that I've calmed down. "For now, just to be sure we don't accidentally warn anyone who might be helping her, let's keep it between us. If you can find hard evidence against her, something Cypress could not ignore, bring it straight to me."

Hard evidence? What more does he need than a severed finger? I understand his logic, but meanwhile, more pieces could arrive in my room. "What about Easton?"

"I have a man I trust in the fort. I will ask him to keep an eye on your friend." His voice is soft, reassuring, a soothing balm on my burning insides.

The rage subsides. I nod. I trust the prince to investigate this and monitor Easton. Without Zephyr, what choice do I really have?

5

GAVIN

LAST TIME I PROWLED the halls of the acolyte section of the temple, I had broken in to find the *Book of the Prophet*. It was dark and quiet, and I had followed Emil's directions to the letter. But the halls are very different during the day. Lights shine brightly—far brighter than the rest of the Haven, and not even one malfunctions—young men and women of varying ages hustle about to carry out their daily duties. Every one of them bows out of our way as we pass. I would like to think they are deferring to Ajax, the Somatic guiding me along, but I know better.

Ajax calls another acolyte forward, a young woman named Viola. As we walk, she offers insight regarding the inner workings of the temple and the acolyte education as if she believes I'm there to take over. What she tells me shines further light on what Emil had already mentioned from his two years living among the acolytes.

The temple teaches the *Book of the Prophet* to children with the potential to develop "gifts" from a young age. Education begins at six. Children are divided into groups by age until their gifts manifest. At that time, the groupings are reassessed by the acolyte teachers and children are divided into additional coursework that focuses on developing their gift.

"What age are children brought down here?" I ask Viola.

She and Ajax exchange confused glances.

"Brought down?" she asks, as if she truly does not know what those two words mean.

I pause, forcing the entourage to stop as well. Ajax crosses his arms and takes up a position behind me. Viola licks her lips. I may not be good at reading people, but discomfort is something I learned to identify quickly. It's a feeling I often give to others.

"Yes, the children who are identified to have the potential to develop," I clarify. "What age are they brought down from the Haven?"

Viola opens her mouth, but no words come out.

"The Minister can explain all of that to you," Ajax says. His voice vibrates against my nerves. "We divide the children into their classes at six."

"So, you bring them down at six," I say, hoping for further clarification.

Neither gives me a straight answer. Why?

Viola shakes off her discomfort, picking up steam as she explains their education—learning to hone their gifts, to read and write, to study the *Book of the Prophet*. Besides their education, acolytes maintain the temple and organize the educational materials given to the other Haven children.

"Where are all the older teenagers?" I ask, eyeing the children and pre-teens following along with older acolytes in their early twenties. I make a mental note that I have seen no acolytes older than Ajax. "And older adult acolytes?"

Once more, an uncomfortable silence settles over Viola. Her gaze darts to Ajax.

We turn out of the hallways and begin moving along a downward sloping tunnel. Powers or age wore the basalt walls smooth. In the luminary lights along the tunnel floor, flecks of green shimmer. My fingers twitch toward the wall, sensing with my Powers. *Not Power stone.* I breathe a sigh of relief. Part of me worried they lined this path with the dangerous stones.

"At age twenty, acolytes are assessed for Guardian or medical service," Ajax says, once more covering for Viola. "They leave the temple to serve the Haven."

But they aren't out there. Not all of them. Sure, the Guardians prowl the halls. And yes, the medics work in the clinic. But that can't possibly make up the entire aged acolyte population. There are nearly as many acolytes as Havenites down here.

"But not you," I note.

Ajax grimaces. "My assessment has been postponed...indefinitely."

It only takes a second for the implication to settle in. The Minister performs the assessments, and with him imprisoned, there is no one to continue the process.

"And the teens?" I press.

Ajax glances at Viola, then raises his chin as the tunnel curves left. "I suggest you talk to the Minister, sire."

"Don't call me that." Why can't they answer my questions without directing me to Mr. Garraty?

Ajax grunts. "What would you like to be called, if I may not use your titles?"

"I don't have titles." We stop near a cavern entrance. I meet his gaze, hoping to appear far more controlled and commanding than I feel. "I'm just Gavin."

"'He will reject worship, for all men are equals'," Viola murmurs the verse I recall all too well from the *Book of the Prophet*. "'His humble grace will guide faith'."

Stop quoting scripture like I'm fulfilling another dumb prophecy!

"All due respect, sire," Ajax says, "but you are not *just* anyone. If you require answers, the Minister can answer all your questions to your satisfaction."

I'm sure Mr. Garraty would do no such thing. I brush off my doubts and nod toward the cave entrance. "The stones are all in there?" Why does this feel like a trap? A horrible sinking sensation presses down in my gut.

Ajax nods. Viola has gone horribly pale.

I step toward the entrance, expecting the two of them to flank me like they have done all the way down here. After a few steps, it becomes clear they have no intention of following me.

This close to the entrance, I can sense the Power stones within like a fog slowly settling over my body and smothering me. I gulp. Do I really have the strength to walk in there and destroy all of them? Knowing they are already affecting me clouds my mind in doubt. My fingers twitch.

"Sire?" Ajax calls.

I groan, turning to him with a glare.

He flinches but doesn't back down. "Please don't destroy them all."

"And why not? They could kill you."

"We know that." He swallows, making his thick Adam's apple bob. "But without the Power stones, the Haven could collapse."

I cock my head. "Explain." I should walk in there and destroy every one of them. But Ajax has just given me an excuse to chicken out and I'm well aware of my weakness.

He shifts feet, eyeing the cavern with obvious discomfort. I sympathize. If it feels like fog to me cloaked in my Power to protect me, what must it feel like to him right now?

"We have several educational programs that depend on the stones," he says. "But more than that, or perhaps equally important, is the defense of the Haven. The stones protect us from outside forces with...more gifts."

"Like the Kingdom." I nod, understanding the implication. "Do you know what these stones can do to people like us over time?"

"People like us," he motions between himself and Viola. "Not you. But yes. Maybe that's why you cannot find adult acolytes. Either way, we're all aware of the risk and will make the noble sacrifice to protect the weaker citizens of the Haven."

This admission sends a jolt through me. They *know* that the stone slowly steals Powers and makes Powered people sick until they die, yet they are willing to die. Paige didn't make the Kingdom seem *that* horrible. But as memories of the battle against their military resurface, I turn my gaze to my boots. Do I have the right to strip away the protections these people covet? Whether Paige thinks the royal family is bad is irrelevant. They still captured her and forced her to go with them. And they would do the same thing here if they found this place. My gaze darts to Viola. She would be there with Paige if the Kingdom found the Haven.

"Decisions made in haste often lead to unfortunate consequences," Dad once told me. *"You're smart, Gavin. Smarter than*

anyone I've ever met. It's easy to jump to conclusions. It's harder to step back, look at the data, and make the right choice." He had been talking to me about the incident with Liam years ago, worried that I would do something hasty to retaliate. But those words have shaped my life.

And Dad's right. I could go into that cave and destroy every Power stone, but what effect will that have on the community? If my actions put them at risk, I need to step back, analyze the data, and find a better solution.

Which means right now, I need to walk away from this cave.

"No more delivering them to my apartment," I command. "I don't want them out of this place at all. Not until I know what to do about them." Remembering what the Minister did to Pip sends a chill down my spine. These stones won't just harm the acolytes. They're a danger to all the Haven. "They're too dangerous for everyone."

Viola glances at Ajax, her wide, questioning eyes fixed on him.

He seems just as stunned by my command. Will they obey?

6

ZEPHYR

WIND RIPS AT THE tails of my overcoat like a living thing trying to drag me down to the earth. And I'm tempted to let it, to not just fall to the earth, but tumble into it, become part of the dirt. But the stubborn Strong blood won't allow me to give in. Strongs don't need pity. They don't feel despair or defeat. They stand, as the surname implies, strong against all tides that hammer against them.

Even if I'm not the King's son, I am still a Strong. Unyielding as the earth. Persevering as the tides.

For weeks, I have come to this spot. To the rocks where King Alric the Third and his first son, my brother Alric, the Crown Prince, died.

No. Not my brother. My cousin.

All my life, they led me to believe the king was my father and the princes and princess were my brothers and sister. But just before she died, my mother confessed the truth. The king was never my real father. His brother, Baron, is.

Baron, who helped raise me. Baron, who turned a blind eye while the king beat me. Baron, who gave me my first drink to dull the aching pain. He made me who I am. Broken and alone.

I can't stop staring at the boulders that took the lives of my uncle and cousin. The rocks that upended my life. If these rocks hadn't killed them, I never would have gone looking for Tributes. I never would have found Paige. I never would have committed treason against Cypress, the man who is like a brother to me.

I never would have been exiled.

My jaw twitches as frustration takes hold, squeezing me in a vise. Cold air nips at my face like a hungry beast.

"Do your worst," I mutter, then raise the bottle clenched in my fist.

My reserves of alcohol are running dry. Nat, my First Mate and best friend, was nice enough to take me in when my brother—*no, my cousin*—kicked me out of the palace. My money will only go so far. Not that it will be of use on the mainland, anyway. I can't ask Nat for much more than I have. It's enough that he gave me a couch to sleep on.

I lost everything because of Paige. My title. My job. My home. But I still can't blame her for my ill fate. I knew what I was doing. And I would do it again...but better. If exile would be my fate, I would have been bolder. I would have breathed in her scent, drank my fill of her umber gaze, run my fingers through her wavy dark hair.

I wouldn't have hesitated to kiss her and hold her. If I would suffer exile, I should have taken everything she was willing to gift me.

Instead of being angry with Paige, I spend my waking hours daydreaming about her and my evenings drinking myself into oblivion just so I don't have to dream of her. She consumes me wholly.

Once more, Mom's voice haunts me. *"When the right girl comes along, she will slip through the cracks in your walls and see you. She will draw you in, consume your every waking and dreaming moment."*

Grief clenches my throat. Tears well in my eyes, but I blink them back. No amount of alcohol can erase the shame of my last memory with my mother. The anger. The monster that emerged from me. She died with that image in her mind.

I shuffle a step closer to the edge of the rocks, peering at the dangerous fall beneath me.

Every day I come here thinking of Paige, of Mom, of the end.

But that Strong blood won't let go.

The wind pulls at me, and I let it.

It sways me like tall grass on the breeze, like a ship in choppy water.

I hold my arms out and give in to the flow, clinging to the bottle in my hand like a life-preserver. Then the world lurches as something hammers against my temples.

My boot slips on the slick boulders. I don't tumble down the rock face. Instead, I lean back and slide down. It isn't until I hit the bottom that the full scope of what happened hits me. My back hurts. My hands throb. *How much did I drink?*

Frowning, I search for the bottle. *Where did it go?* I must have dropped it when I slipped. I close my eyes and lie back on the rocks.

The gash on my palm pulses with life, reminding me I'm still here. My heart still beats.

SOMETHING POKES AT MY ribs. I groan, shielding my eyes from the blinding light.

"Get up, you bum." Nat's sharp tone slowly pulls me out of my haze.

At some point, I found my way back to his apartment and passed out on the couch. I plant a palm over my face as my head hammers.

"You're bleeding," he snaps, "on my sofa. Get up."

Bleeding?

Before I can move, he grabs my legs and throws them off the couch, forcing me to sit upright.

Nat's apartment is a tiny one-bedroom with a kitchenette that offers little more than a small fridge, stove, and sink. It's cramped with both of us living here. Nat, of course, gets his bedroom—he pays the rent, after all. I get the couch. The small living room is immaculate, aside from the blankets I leave strewn about the space—blankets Nat always folds and stacks on the end of the couch each day when I leave.

I've been imposing on his goodwill and friendship for weeks. My money helps a little, but it only goes so far. The set of his jaw as he looks at the blood on his furniture tells me that his goodwill is ending rapidly.

But Nat doesn't complain. Not much. Mostly, he mutters under his breath.

"What happened?" He huffs as he kneels on the couch to inspect my injuries.

I don't really feel them. Not over the hammering of my hangover.

"I was on the rocks," I grumble, leaning forward so he can see my back.

"Again?"

"Then the earth moved, and I fell." I press my fingers into my eyes.

He pulls out his first aid kit and sets to work cleaning the cuts on my back. "An earthquake. The entire island felt it. You're lucky you didn't die up there."

"Luck and I aren't really friends anymore."

"You and I won't be, either, if you can't get your act together." His hands work expertly over the injuries, but not without some malice. "Doesn't look like you need stitches."

I hold out my injured palm to him. He sets to work. "The whole island..." My muscles tense. "It was her."

Nat scrubs the dirt out of my palm, then bandages it. "You have *got* to let go. That girl ruined you. Instead of wasting your days drinking, why don't you take advantage of the time you have left on this island?"

I flex my fingers around the bandage. "How?"

"Talk to your father."

I flinch. He may as well have slapped me.

After arriving on his doorstep, I poured out my whole sad story. What I did to earn my exile. What my mother told me about my father before she died. Nat had been so sympathetic to my plight that he insisted on taking me out to see some of our friends for drinks and distractions. That distraction became more of a burden to him after about a week. Apparently, he thinks there's a limit on how long I'm allowed to grieve over everything I've lost. And that was only one week.

But one week wasn't nearly enough for me. I'm not sure how long will be. If ever.

"If Baron gave a crap, he would have come to see me by now." I suspect Baron is happy to have me out of the picture. A strong instinct tells me he is up to something, working against the crown, for reasons I don't fully understand. Maybe vengeance for being kept from marrying the woman he loved—or for being forced to watch his brother with her instead. Did he kill his brother because of Mom? Maybe he had enough and snapped.

Pain clenches my heart. At least I won't be forced to watch Cypress with Paige—a small mercy. I won't be allowed within fifty yards of either of them.

"The Admiral's been asking about you, Zephyr," Nat admits as he packs up the first aid kit. "He cares, but I think something is preventing him from coming here. He won't say as much, but something is off. He's been on edge since Lady Emry—"

Suddenly, he cuts off, gaze flicking to me. Mom. Another touchy subject.

"What time is it?" I ask, pulling away and shutting down the conversation before it goes any further.

"Just past dinner. Some officers and I were planning to meet at the inn."

"Perfect." I slide on my coat.

"Zeph." Nat surges to his feet, then shuffles them, unable to meet my gaze. "You need to take the night off."

The words draw out of him painfully. Nat means well. I know he does. He would do everything he could to help me. Hell, he gave me free use of his couch. But I've overstayed my welcome. He probably expected me to get a job by now. But who will hire the exiled not-a-prince and risk the king's ire?

Maybe Cypress thought exile was a mercy. He doesn't understand the world beyond his palace walls. He left me destitute, with little more than the savings I squirreled away over the last two years.

Were it not for Nat, I would be homeless. None of the property managers would give me a room, even with a generous deposit. This temporary couch situation has become a wait-until-spring-to-leave situation. Then I'm on a boat for the mainland to scrounge like the rest of the mainlanders.

Nat almost looks sorry as he slips his coat on, then pauses in the doorway to peer at me. I wave him off. I won't be a further burden on him. Let him have a night without me.

Nat gives me a small, apologetic nod before closing the door behind him.

Leaving me utterly alone.

7

PAIGE

THE DAYS CONTINUE TO bleed past. January. Layla. Alice. Nora. River.

The only invitations I get are for tea with Princess Bronwyn or an afternoon with Prince Dominic. Neither of them ever mentions Zephyr. No one does. He is little more than a ghost that haunts the halls.

Lord Baron hates me. I see it in every passing interaction. Hard, calculating examinations from across the breakfast hall. Observing my passage in the halls from the corner of his eyes. The way his jaw tenses every time he sees me. He blames me for Lady Emry's fall, for Zephyr's exile. The only thing keeping him from throwing me in a prison and locking me away forever is the king. Not that King Cypress has done more than pass me without a glance.

No more pieces of Easton arrive as a warning. Prince Dominic reassures me that Easton excels at his training in the fort, impressing even the Admiral. No missing digits as far as anyone can report. But I still receive warnings. No more body parts. Instead, she sends pieces of Easton's Specialist uniform. Something just about anyone would have access to. The badge of Elpis of the crow in flight, along with a warning. *Talk to anyone again, and we will see if this crow can fly.*

The warning is clear. She knows I told Prince Dominic. She knows he went sniffing for answers. Maybe she can't get close to Easton now because the prince has someone watching Easton? I can't make any assumptions. And I'm not sure if she would know if I shared this new threat with anyone. For now, I will keep it to myself.

What does Bella even want from me? Her commands have been conflicting, and I can't make heads or tails of her plans. One thing is clear. Whatever Prince Dominic told King Cypress was not enough to dismiss her.

Bella spends more time with King Cypress than I do. I don't understand why she can't do whatever needs to be done on her own. *Unless I'm a pawn.* That thought terrifies me. Bella is playing a different game than the rest of the girls. Not for the king, but for something else.

River is gone. Apparently, she and King Cypress agreed that there was no spark between them and parted amicably. Prince Dominic helped load her into a carriage to take her to her new accommodations in town. No one has seen her since. Summer was miserable after River left. It was only a matter of time before she was gone, as well. I hope the two of them are happy together wherever they are.

More dates with the king, then more girls leave. Alice. January.

I can't stand it much longer either. Only Layla, Bella, Nora, and I remain. It's agony watching girls escorted away by Prince Dominic, knowing that those girls can move on with their lives while I'm stuck here. While King Cypress continues avoiding me.

I can no longer convince myself that it doesn't matter. I've been ripped away from my family, my life, for nothing at all.

With my back pressed to the closed door, I hyperventilate. I fold at the waist, hugging my stomach tight as silent sobs crush all the air from my lungs. The agony is overwhelming. The loss is unbearable. I'm a prisoner dressed like a princess.

And they are all toying with me.

The bracelet burns against my skin, a timeless reminder of the chains the Kingdom has bound me in. As if the jewelry is responsible for my inability to breathe, I dig my fingernails under the band, tugging, yanking, fighting with the unbreakable locking clasp. Fury and grief and loneliness overwhelm me. I howl at the wretched band.

"You will never leave this island." Queen Elena's declaration echoes in my mind.

I had hoped that if I could just get the king to see reason, her words would be worthless. But I can't even get him to see *me*, let alone reason! Heat pulses through my veins as panic claws at my throat. I yank at the bracelet as the heat in my veins becomes unbearable. Tears blur my vision. Then the bracelet grows hot. The lock breaks as hidden gears splinter into a thousand pieces. I yelp in relief as it tumbles to the carpet at my feet.

Power. Glorious, warm Power envelops me. It rushes through me like fire through a tunnel of fuel, igniting everything in its path.

Screw King Cypress.

Screw the Kingdom.

Screw Zephyr and Princess Bronwyn and Queen Elena and this entire charade.

Holly deserved better.

I deserve better.

A cry, a scream of fear and frustration and anger and sorrow and grief, rips out of me. The mirror over the dresser shatters, glass raining down on the white surface, speckling the rug. The entire palace quakes under the force of my wrath. Alarms wail somewhere in the distance.

I stumble to the bed and collapse onto the mattress, burying my face in the pillow. The sobs are wretched, raw, chaffing. My entire body burns red hot as my tears soak into the pillow.

A gentle knock on my door is followed by the click of it opening.

"Paige?" Nora calls inside tentatively. "Oh, Paige, are you alright?"

She rushes in, her shoes crunching on the broken shards, and settles beside me on the bed. I continue crying into the pillow, unable to control myself any longer.

I've lost everything.

For nothing.

Nora curls up next to me, pulling a blanket over my dress. For a while, she just rubs my back while I cry. Her touch sooths my aching soul, calming the inferno in my veins. At one point, I think

I feel her shaking her head and waving a hand. I don't care. I let the sorrow pour out.

Once the tears slow and I can breathe again, I roll over to face her.

Even laying on my bed, her head on the other pillow, Nora is stunning. But she doesn't look at me like the other girls often do, with skepticism and fear. Instead, she reminds me of my brother, eager to help make everything better. She brushes my mess of wavy hair back away from my face. Her touch is comforting. It's a cool balm against my aching soul.

A lump the size of the planet seems caught in my throat.

"I can't even imagine what all of this must be like for you," she says. There is no judgment or arrogance in her tone. Only pure, unfiltered sincerity. "To be taken away from your family and brought here for this. And how different it must be from what you're used to. But I've known Cypress all his life. I can tell you with certainty that he isn't cruel."

I shake my head. When I speak, my voice is strained, as if the earth is still trying to prevent me from speaking. "I've done...something."

Nora smiles. "What do you imagine would make him hang you out to dry like this?"

I swallow hard. I can't bring myself to tell her the truth. That King Cypress kissed me, and I felt nothing. That Zephyr didn't and I feel everything. I bury my face in my hands, flooding with regret.

Her warm hands slide into mine, easing them back from my face. Again, as her warm hands hold my own, the storm within subsides. My gaze flicks to her wrist. No bracelet. At least I'm not the only one who rebels and takes it off.

"I assure you, it isn't that bad." Her voice is gentle.

"I...danced with Zephyr." My voice catches.

"So? I have as well."

"That night. The night Holly... We stepped outside. He gave me his jacket, and we talked and..." I squeeze my eyes shut, too embarrassed to see the shock in her eyes.

"Did you kiss Zephyr?" She giggles, which draws my eyes reluctantly from behind my shield.

"No. Almost. We were interrupted when..."

Her eyes widen. "Ah. That explains so much. I guess I could see how that might upset Cypress. Are you sure he knows?"

"No. But Zephyr is gone. Would Zephyr tell him?"

Nora falls silent. Her sharp eyebrows draw together as she considers the situation. I can almost see how hard she is thinking this over. Each moment that passes has me even more worried about the answer.

"I...don't know. I would be inclined to say no. Zeph is very guarded." She chews her thick lip. "But somehow, Cypress must have found out the truth."

"But we didn't actually kiss."

Nora sighs delicately. "The Strong boys are a strange bunch. The boys often had brotherly fights over the most ludicrous of things. And Alric was always the one to smooth things out."

I can't help but laugh at this. Imagining the two of them each wanting their own way when at odds with one another is amusing. It conjures an image of puppies playing tug of war over a squeaky toy. *Am I the toy now?*

Sadness crosses her face and vanishes in a flash, killing my amusement. "Alric was always going to be king. Then Dominic was named Devotee of Tides, training to be the next Keeper. Once their father named Zephyr Captain of Tides, a title Cypress had been expecting, where did that leave Cypress? He had no role to play in the family. No reason to toe the line. Cypress was often overlooked."

My heart goes out to King Cypress. I can understand the feeling. Gavin was always so incredible that I felt overlooked, like I had no clear role in my family, either. Maybe the king and I aren't so different.

"He watched all his brothers step into their roles and had little more to do than while away the time. With Alric gone, the burden of ruling fell on Cypress' shoulders, and they didn't train him for this. Not really. Without Alric here to smooth this out...no doubt

Cypress and Zephyr butted heads. They have *always* competed for the same things. In this case, when they butt heads, Cypress wins because he is the king now."

If King Cypress really had been interested in me and he discovered he lost me to Zephyr, it probably brought up feelings of inadequacy that I can also understand.

"Please don't tell anyone else about this, Nora," I plead. "It really was nothing at all and I don't want the other girls to use it against me." Especially Bella.

She quirks a brow and smirks. "How do you know *I* won't?"

"Please." I roll my eyes. "You don't need any help."

The moment of open honesty between the two of us creates a bond, something warm and comforting.

We lie there on the bed, talking. I tell her about Tudor and how he dumped me because he was envious that I outranked him, then about Easton and how much we fought right until we kissed in that carriage. How worried I am about him now because I don't know if he is well. I don't tell her about the finger or the threats to his life. Some things I can't share.

Nora tells me about her family. Her parents died of an illness when she was young. Her father runs the docks—a fact I file away for later use—or he did until he died. Nora's older brother took over, but the two of them don't' get along often. He's put a lot of pressure on her to become the queen. If she doesn't succeed, he intends to wed her to one of the island lords. Something she isn't looking forward to.

She also tells stories about Alric, who was supposed to be the next king before he died in a rockslide. They were promised to be wed, and she thought he was the most beautiful, warm, wise boy she had ever met. He didn't want to bother with the Tributes. They fell in love when she was only twelve and that was it. He knew there wouldn't be anyone else for him. Except her Bloodmagic, which I can only assume is Hematology, developed late. The king allowed Alric to wait until she was fourteen before drawing up a formal agreement, and if it didn't happen by then, he intended to force Alric to choose from Tributes. And it didn't. Nora was a late bloomer.

Nora stares at her fingers, flexing them. "I was seventeen."

So late!

"I think the king planned on forcing Alric into the Choosing anyway," Nora says softly. Tears prick the corners of her eyes. "But Alric fought him every step of the way. He promised he would marry only me. Still, no matter how many kisses we shared or how many times he made the promise, his father hadn't drawn up the betrothal agreement with my brother. Then..." The memory of Alric's death brings her to tears, but she recovers quickly.

"Do you even want to marry the king?" I ask.

Nora sighs. "What do you do when your soulmate dies, Paige? No one will ever compare. But Cypress reminds me of Alric, sometimes. He has these moments where I can see the good, wise king in him. Or when I see Alric in his smile. I'm not so different from Holly. I can never have what my heart truly desires. But I'm not one to give up. And I think Cypress could make me happy. Maybe I could make him an even better king."

I sit up, tucking my legs under me and adjusting my skirt. "You know, where I come from, some women never marry. They are content to pursue their own desires. Or find their own way when they lose what is dearest to them." I pick at the hem of my skirt. "It's a personal choice."

A choice I've considered for myself. I'm not sure if I believe in soulmates like Nora. I'm not even sure if I could ever find genuine love—certainly nothing like Mom and Dad have. Desire and passion, sure. But real, deep love? I don't think it's possible for me.

Then what is Zephyr to me? I shake off the thought.

Nora pushes herself upright as well. "That sounds nice. I'm not sure I could live like that, though." She shrugs. "What about you? Do *you* even want this?"

I swallow. "I want to go home. My family must be beside themselves with worry."

She places a hand in mine and squeezes it gently. "I'm sorry. I can't even imagine."

That one slight gesture accompanied by the heavy conversation seems to settle it. No matter what happens, I have a friend in Nora, if no one else.

8

GAVIN

*T*ALK TO THE MINISTER. Everyone keeps saying it, and I know they are right, but I just can't muster the courage. Thankfully, my new status in the Haven gives me a little wiggle room to slip out of some of the more uncomfortable situations. But not everyone in the Haven is pleased with the new status I've attained as the revered Idol.

Julia and Carmen have given me the cold shoulder, ignoring me as they carry on running the Haven without the Minister. Luke and Ally have attempted to invite me to meetings among the Elders. Meetings I have avoided. Because I'm a coward.

Emil advised I find replacements for all of them; that my new position as the Idol of Creation should allow me to pick my own Elders. But there are so many problems with that suggestion. Mainly because it would create a sense of permanence here. And I don't plan on sticking around much longer. The Elders also know how to run the Haven, which they have continued to do even without the Minister among them. I don't know how to do any of this, and I don't know who else does. Replacing them will accomplish little more than insurrection. Against me. I shudder at the thought, remembering some of Dad's stories from his own youth and revolution.

It's never pretty.

Neither Emil nor Drake understands. In their eyes, I have complete authority over the Haven. Or I could, if I wanted to exert it, but I don't. What I want is for the people here to live their lives as they deserve, with no one lording over them with prophecies and firm hands.

History teaches us a lot if we pay attention to the lessons. I see several moves ahead. Removing the Elders leads to resentment. Some might even call me a tyrant and question if I'm a false idol. In no time, they will turn against me with the backing of any who doubt my position—which could end in another burning. I didn't come here to shake up their world. I came to reach out the hand of peace. Then go home.

It's hard to forgive the Elders. They allowed the Minister to burn me alive, to kill Pip. Especially Julia, the Medical Elder. She shoved that pill down my throat to awaken my senses but keep me weak just before they tied me to a wheel to burn. It still gives me nightmares weeks later. I'm not sure that will ever stop.

"Writing again?" Drake shuffles into the living room, rubbing sleep from his eyes.

I look up from my notebook. One of many I own now. My shelf is stacked with notebooks.

Drake's hair is tousled from sleep, but the look still heats my blood. It's been a couple weeks since I visited the Power stones cave. He looks better. I mean, not *better* better, but better. He still looks...

Living with him is a mistake. I jerk my gaze away and return it to my notebook. The forced proximity makes the air thick with tension I can never relieve. For a moment in the temple, as the chaos died down, he looked at me in a way that ignited something inside. But ever since, everything between us has been painfully friendly. Whatever I thought I saw in that moment was misread. It isn't the first time I've done it. But I won't make the same mistake I made with Liam. My first crush. My first kiss. My first horrifying rejection.

"I think it's important to capture everything," I say as he shuffles past me toward the kitchen.

Drake pats my shoulder, hand sliding off as he moves away. That one touch makes my stomach writhe madly.

Stop, Gavin. It's nothing. We're friends.

"I would expect no less from you." Drake opens the fridge—another luxury most Havenites lack—and retrieves a piece of fruit. "What's this?" He runs a thumb over the skin.

I turn on the sofa to watch him. The movement of his thumb over the fuzzy skin fills me with a yearning so intense it provokes a fire inside my veins. What I wouldn't give to have him touch my skin like that. "Kiwi. Not native here. It was in an acolyte basket. I don't know where they grow them."

"They're holding out on the rest of us," he mutters, then sinks his teeth into the juicy fruit. He moans in delight, a sound that sends my head into a tailspin. "This is my new favorite thing."

He moves toward me. I avert my gaze, certain that my face is burning. *Can he tell?*

Drake holds the fruit to my lips. "Try this."

I want to refuse, pull away, create as much distance between us as possible, but when I look up at his eyes, I'm drawn in. I can't do anything but comply. I've had kiwi before. It's harder to grow in Elpis, but our gardeners create enough to keep the stock going.

Eating food that he holds in his hand feels deeply personal. But I sink my teeth in, aware of how his knuckles graze my cheek.

He lingers for a moment, watching me with a grin. "Good, right?"

I nod, wiping the juice from my chin quickly. Then I notice his hand drop. For a moment, something flickers in his eyes. He turns away, headed back toward the kitchen.

"What's the plan today, boss?" he asks, tone changing as quickly as the subject.

"I'm not the boss."

"Tell that to the people crowding outside the door." Drake chuckles. "The Elders are frothing like a rabid dog to get you in a meeting with them. You know you can't avoid this forever. Not after what you did."

"Not all of them are eager," I grumble.

He grabs a glass of water and drops into a chair at the table. "You have to face this, Gavin, hard as it might be."

Drake is right. As usual, he sees me more clearly than anyone else. He might be the only person who sees *me* and not the Idol. Drake and Emil both.

I've done my best to ignore the summons from the Elders. Eating meals provided by the acolytes has helped me avoid going out at mealtime where I might encounter the Elders. A few times, I pretended not to be here when they came knocking on the door.

But the Haven is small. I started this chain of events with my display at the temple, fulfilling several of their dumb prophecies to save myself and Pip.

I wince. I couldn't save her.

Dad would do what needed to be done, face down the Elders, and maintain the upper hand. I must be like him. Somehow.

Heaving out a sigh, I push off the sofa. "Fine. But it will be on my terms."

I want to trust the Elders, but I know they aren't as happy about my "coming" as the rest of the Havenites.

I am a threat to their positions. Like all leaders throughout history, they will tear me down to preserve their power.

Unless I outsmart and outmaneuver them first.

9

PAIGE

"Y OU KNOW THIS IS for your protection as much as ours." Prince Dominic glances up at me as he uses the key to lock the fixed bracelet back on my wrist. He flashes me his kind smile.

I just roll my eyes and shake my head with a grimace. He can convince himself that's true, but he won't convince me. This bracelet is prison bondage, cutting me off from my Power. Well, not completely. I can still Dream with the bracelet on.

Prince Dominic finishes and slides back in the chair, relaxing. He rests his arms on the chair. While he oozes kindness and compassion, his eyes are piercing. Like King Cypress', they are blue, but with a deeper hue, richer and darker. The resemblance between him and the king is remarkable. And I can see Queen Elena in both as well. But not Zephyr. No matter how many times I search his face for traces of Zephyr, I find none. How can brothers look so different?

"Roll your eyes if you like, but you lost control of your magic and created an earthquake. That's no small thing." The level of calm patience in the prince unnerves me. No one should be so cavalier. But I've learned that's just Prince Dominic. He's relaxed no matter where he is.

"I didn't—"

"Paige, it's alright." He reaches over and pats my knee. "No one is angry. This time. But you didn't just shake the palace and set off all the alarms. It was the entire island. That level of magic is..." He emits a low whistle, shaking his head. The movement makes his curly locks wave. "I'm envious. I can't do much more than persuade a few people not to hate me."

Who would hate him? Prince Dominic is one of the nicest people I've met on the island.

"What you can do is dangerous to all of us," he continues. "Especially without control. The bracelet will protect you. It will protect us all."

I turn the thick band of gold inlaid with green gemstones around on my wrist. I still don't understand how these bracelets work. If these are Power stones, they should be too dangerous to wear. Unless something in the metal prevents them from harming us. Our knowledge of Powers stones in Elpis is still new. It's possible the Kingdom has had longer to understand them.

The first bracelet they gave me didn't work well to contain my Power—plus I took it off several times—so Prince Dominic came to me with this new one. A stronger one. The rest of the girls still wear the old ones. I'm the only one who needs something with more containment power.

"The entire island?" I murmur in disbelief.

Caught up in my rage and grief, raw Power had consumed me, exploded from me. I hadn't realized the extent of it.

"No one was hurt, were they?" Maybe he's right. Maybe I need to wear this to protect the innocent people on this island. It isn't like I know how to control these strange Powers.

Prince Dominic offers a sad smile. "No. I hear some people had a couple of scrapes from stumbling, but nothing more." He rises from the chair, languidly stretching his arms over his head.

I hadn't realized before just how tall he is compared to the other royals. Prince Dominic must have several inches on both of his brothers and sister. Despite his position as Keeper of Tides—the king's right hand, a desk jockey—Prince Dominic's lean form is toned. He brought me to the workout room a few times over the past weeks, racing me on treadmills and rowers, challenging me to power lifts. The bracelet inhibited my ability to use my Muscle Memory to beat him. He grinned at me and called it a fair game. There's a competitive playfulness to the prince that I find endearing. Gentle as a lamb, with the grace and strength of a panther.

"Has your brother said anything about me?" I ask, trying not to pick at the skirt of my dress.

Prince Dominic pauses at the door, raising an amused brow. "Which one?"

I flush a brilliant shade of crimson. "The king," I say flatly. *Wait, has he seen Zephyr?* "How is your other brother faring?"

He stuffs his hands into his pockets, a guarded posture he frequents. "You flipped that coin quickly."

Nothing I say will redeem me, so I tug my shawl tighter around my bare shoulders. These dresses are impractical.

"The king trusts my confidence," he says at last. "I won't break that."

King Cypress *has* said something about me, but his brother won't divulge.

"As for Zeph... I haven't seen him for a while. Probably drinking too much whiskey if I know him at all. I hear he is staying with his friend, Nat."

The unspoken words hang at the end of his sentence: *until he is exiled to the mainland.* Zephyr lost everything, and it's my fault. I would willingly trade places with him in a heartbeat, which is probably why we were put in these positions. Zephyr is exiled to the mainland. I'm trapped on the island. Both of us would be happier if the roles were reversed.

"I'm surprised he has friends," I say, making a lame attempt at a joke.

"He has trust issues. Can you imagine?" Prince Dominic's normally friendly tone takes on a sarcastic touch. "But he and Nat served together for years. They trained together. Nat won't turn him away."

I take a moment to recall Nat. The friendly First Mate on the ship. The one who often consulted with Zephyr on the way to the ship. I'm glad Zephyr has someone to lean on. *For now.*

"That's a dangerous look for you," Prince Dominic says, drawing me from my thoughts of Zephyr. He shakes his head at me. "If you ever want to get on Cy's good side, you need to learn to use a poker face, because your emotions are clear as day. And Cy's not blind."

I swallow, rising from the edge of the bed to move toward the prince. "I just want to see my family." Switching gears might help me. "I wish I were exiled, instead."

Sorrow crosses his face. "I understand. And I'm sorry, Paige." He squeezes my arm in reassurance. "You know, maybe it's a good idea if we learn a thing or two about how your magic works. For all our sakes. Let me talk to my brother and I'll see if we can arrange some lessons. We have a few talented trainers on the island."

IT DOESN'T TAKE PRINCE Dominic long. After lunch, a servant retrieves me and escorts me to the lobby. Prince Dominic escorts me to a carriage.

We load into a carriage where an older man waits on another bench. I've seen him before but can't quite place where. His plain clothes and the way he slouches aren't like anyone I have seen here before.

"This is Vincent," Prince Dominic explains. "He taught all of us kids how to control and use our magic. You will be...a new challenge for this old man."

Training kicks in at that moment. I take in Vincent's lithe frame, bald head, and peppered beard. There's a hardness in his eyes as he studies me.

Then he harrumphs. "Interesting girl."

Prince Dominic grins from ear to ear, winking mischievously at me. I fight off a smirk.

Houses and the palace fall away from sight as we venture into the woods deeper into the heart of the island. Snow smothers everything in a heavy white blanket, making tree branches bow under the weight.

My stomach twists with worry. Leaving is punishable as treason. What will happen to me if the king finds out? After everything else I've done, he will probably kill me this time.

"Don't worry." Prince Dominic leans close and whispers conspiratorially, as if he can read my worry. It's probably etched all over my face. "He knows where we're going. No need to bare your sins and confess to him. He agreed to training." He sits straighter in the carriage beside me. "We decided it's best if we take you to a training ground further from the palace. Just in case."

In case I lose control again.

Vincent observes everything about me with keen interest as we ride. It doesn't take long before the carriage pulls into a massive gray hangar. Inside, old airplanes from before the collapse wait in disrepair.

"Do those still work?" I ask, pointing at one of them.

Prince Dominic shakes his hand back and forth. "Sort of. They fire on, with the right people to get them started, but we can't get them off the ground."

My heart aches. If I can get these going, I can fly out of here. No ship necessary.

But I don't know how to fly. The closest we have to planes are DS riot shuttles. They can only fly over rooftops and can't go very far. And I don't know anything about the controls. Does Easton?

"Your magic is not the right kind to get them off the ground," Vincent says as he marches across the hangar. "Nor could you without royal dispensation."

Royal dispensation be damned. If I can figure out how to get this thing going, I'm leaving this place and taking Easton with me. Maybe Zephyr, if he will come.

Vincent snorts, as if he sees what I'm thinking. *Can he read minds?* Not that he could read mine. Gram put walls around our minds to protect us. No one can get in without permission.

We step outside, away from the planes and horses, into an open airfield. Prince Dominic removes my bracelet, then steps out of the way as if he expects my Power to explode out of me.

I rub my naked wrist. The thick layers of my coat ward off the cold from the winter air, but ice still settles in my veins. "Is this safe?"

"That depends on you," Vincent replies.

For the next hour, we work on drawing out my Power. First, Vincent guides me through meditative focus techniques, followed by light combat. We try object focus, to no avail. The fire that burned in my veins is gone. Only the familiar feel of my Muscle Memory works. I drop into the old habits from training as my Muscle Memory kicks into gear, stretching itself out like a cat stretching in the sunlight.

Vincent is sweating despite the cold. Prince Dominic watches everything in amusement.

When nothing extraordinary happens, Prince Dominic kicks off from the ground where he had lounged watching us.

"May I?" he asks, raising his hands toward my temples.

"With what?" I ask hesitantly. He mentioned making people like him, so he must be an Influencer. Can he Influence my Powers to the surface? Do I want him to? Recalling how my anger caused the island quake, I know I have little choice. He's right. If I don't learn to harness this Power, it's dangerous. I bite my lip and nod.

His fingertips are cold against my temples. His blue eyes pulse with a light I've never seen before. Prince Dominic isn't just looking at me. He's seeing into me. That should unnerve me, but it's a comfort. Maybe he will finally understand my need to get home.

Sweat beads on his brow as his focus intensifies.

Something presses against my mind as he seeks the key to unlocking my dormant Powers. I close my eyes, but he gently whispers for me to keep them open.

Open the door to the part you are willing to share, Gram had said, *and they can walk through*. So, I do. I open the door for Prince Dominic to find what he is looking for. I can't do this alone.

A moment later, a small smile curls up the corner of his mouth.

Power races through my veins like fire seeking oxygen. It burns through me all the way to my fingertips. I try stepping back to avoid hurting the prince, but his fingertips hold fast to my temples, eyes distant.

The heat intensifies, molten hot, ready to erupt from my limbs. "Prince Dominic, let go," I whimper, afraid of what I will do.

"It's wild, Paige." His breath is ragged. "Tame the beast within."

Tame the beast. I don't know how. It's like trying to control a raging wildfire with a thimble of water.

"Box it in." Vincent stands at my shoulder. His words are firm, commanding. I want to obey, but I can't.

I shudder, eyes wide as the red mist from my nightmares rolls out of my fingertips. Terror grips me as I recall the image of Zephyr and me clinging to each other as we die.

Prince Dominic is no longer holding me with his fingertips. His palms are flat against the sides of my head, firm and unrelenting. I will kill him. This raging fire is eager to consume everything.

"Let go," I whimper. "Please. Dominic let go."

"Focus, Paige," Vincent croons at my shoulder. "Box it in." And I try. So desperately, everything in me aches to do as he commands. But I just can't do it. It's like trying to contain flowing lava with a tiny paper box.

I'm crying, shrieking soundlessly, certain that I'm burning from the inside out. It's too much. It pulses with untamed life.

"I trust you." The prince's voice penetrates the screaming in my head, soothing and patient. "Keep your eyes open. Keep them on me."

The red mist winds around my arms like serpents, then spins down my body into the earth. "No..."

"Box it, Paige," Vincent says again. Something about his voice is hypnotizing.

How? I flinch, but keep my gaze locked on the blues of the prince's eyes. They glow like sapphires in the sun, sparkling brilliantly.

The ground beneath us cracks. Red rivers glow in the thin fissures. This Power is dangerous. Too dangerous to control. Too dangerous to let loose. I don't want to box it. I want to destroy it.

"No more," I whimper, but can't stop it. The Power has a hold on me now. Just like it does in my nightmares. My bones tremble in terror at this horrible Power.

Prince Dominic's heartbeat pulses in his palms against my head. I can feel it like my own. With a thought, I can stop it. I don't know how, but I'm certain that I'm capable. My entire body is on the verge of giving out. Winter-bare trees near the airstrip burst into flame. The hangar doors creak on melting hinges.

Unable to keep my eyes open, unwilling to witness the prince's certain doom at my uncontrolled hands, I squeeze my eyes closed with a whimper.

The Power winks out of existence. I collapse as every muscle in my body gives out. Vincent catches me, easing me to the cold ground. Blood thumps loud as my heart beats like a drum in my ears. The prince and Vincent exchange a few words, but I can't hear what they are saying.

The next thing I know, I'm in the carriage, leaning against Prince Dominic as we lumber back toward the palace. I shift, rubbing my eyes. A hammering headache beats against my skull.

"What—?"

He hushes me, glancing at Vincent knowingly, then turns those ever kind eyes on me. "You did beautifully, Paige."

"I almost killed you."

"No. You controlled it to protect me. Just like I knew you would." He gives me a brotherly hug and kiss on the top of my head. "You did beautifully. And next time you will do even better."

Next time? I barely controlled it this time. Did I control it at all?

My fingers brush the bracelet, which just this morning I considered prison chains. Now I'm reassured that it is keeping this Power leashed. Or at least under some level of control.

I don't want there to be a next time. I don't even understand what the Power within me is. It's nothing like anything we have back in Elpis. It's fire and rage and destruction.

And I can never let it out again.

10

GAVIN

T HE CARVED WOODEN WALLS of the elder chamber glow warmly in the dim lights that ring the room. Some lights have burned out. I arch my fingers outward at my side. Power pulses out of me. Then the lights are back on, burning as bright as new.

The room isn't large. Seven carved wooden high-back chairs occupy the space behind a semi-circular table. The space is comfortable and inviting. Yet a coldness presses down my spine as I step over the threshold.

Four Elders sit in their high-back chairs. They shift when I enter flanked by four Guardians. The statement I've made by bringing them along is clear. The Elders hold their seats, but I hold the power—at least, according to the people. I can't afford to have the Elders attempt undermining my goals. As much as my insides are writhing in a mass of nerves, I cannot show them weakness. Experience tells me they will chew me up and spit me out if I appear weak.

Last time I entered this chamber, there were five Elders and the Guardians at the door were there for the Elders' protection. The tables have turned on them dramatically.

Each of the Elders eyes the Minister's vacant seat, marked out with a six-spoke wheel with a six-pointed star within. No one has seen him since the incident at the temple. He's alive, but the acolytes have him well guarded somewhere in the bowels of the temple. Likely in a Power-dampening cell like the one they trapped me in recently. Except the acolytes can't be using a Power stone on him. He would be dead by now if they did. They must have other technology the Havenites don't know about.

These leaders expect me to take the Minister's seat.

I don't. I have no intention of assuming his position. I have no intention of staying in the Haven for long. Not that I can tell them. Not yet. I intend to use this newfound position of influence to help the Havenites, then get out of here and head home for help for Paige. With any luck, the Haven will talk to the Council of Representatives to negotiate an alliance.

But step one is securing a few more Elders who will listen to me. Luke and Ally might. Carmen is unpredictable. Julia definitely won't support me. But there are now three empty seats—two if I can keep the Minister position vacant.

Instead of sitting, I stand in front of the four of them. They watch me uncomfortably, waiting for me to say something. My gaze falls on the other empty Elder seats. Positions no one has had the right "gifts" to fill. That's about to change.

"It seems you have been running the Haven without the full capacity of necessary leadership," I say, forgoing greetings and pleasantries. They wouldn't buy it, anyway. I hope they can't hear my voice shake. "We need that to change. You can't expect to grow without the right seeds in the dirt."

Julia, the Medical Elder, is the first to break their silence. Her tone is sharp and angry, which matches her angular face. "You can't waltz in here after ignoring us for weeks and expect to change things. We have been holding this place together with hopes and prayers ever since your *display*." The emphasis on the last word makes clear what she thinks of my Powers. To her, I'm a threat.

But her opinion bears the least weight on me after what she put me through. Not that the rest of them weren't complicit.

"I would expect a powerful group like yourselves capable of holding things together," I say just as sharply. *What am I doing picking a fight with them?* "You've done it for over a century. And with dwindling numbers. One less can't have made matters so difficult. Especially not with Ajax holding the acolytes to their structure."

They flinch. They must know by now that I visited the acolytes.

Luke, the Education Elder, shoots a warning glare at Julia. "I think what Julia is trying to say is that you have changed everything already, just by doing what you did. The people are restless now, eager for the Days of Glory. Yet we remain down here—"

"By your own design," I can't help adding the jab.

He concedes with a nod as he continues. "And the one person who was ordained to help these people, to lead them to this glory, has been hiding in his luxury apartment."

Ordained. I fight off the wince. I knew what I was doing when I used my Power and fulfilled those prophecies. I knew the people would respond dramatically and look to me. But the weight of that expectation is too heavy for me to bear alone. And I won't.

"Which brings me back to my first comment," I say. My hands are shaking, and I clasp them behind my back to hide my fear. "These chairs need to be filled."

Carmen, the Resource Elder, leans forward in her chair. "But no one has the gifts to—"

"You don't need *gifts* to lead." I straighten my spine. *This* is the part I was ready for. I expected resistance and prepared for the battle. "The purpose of these seats is to help the people, to take charge of certain necessities for the benefit of everyone. To work toward creating a better life for the people of the Haven. I know first-hand that you don't need gifts to lead. My father is Powerless, just like most of the people in your community. He has dedicated himself to helping people and has made life better for everyone in our community. There is no reason you cannot do the same here."

"But didn't you tell us that your community is full of gifted people?" Carmen asks. "That gives your people more flexibility in leadership."

I shake my head. "You're missing the point. We aren't talking about who can do what with gifts. We are talking about who can help the *community*. Your *gifts* have nothing to do with it. You've made it this far on a skeleton crew. Imagine what you could do if you had more support, Powerless as it might be."

Julia clenches her teeth so tightly I can hear her jaw clicking. For a medical professional, she certainly has little regard for the welfare of others. If I could remove her from her position, I would. But I need their knowledge and experience to get this rolling. Then the people will remove her for me.

"Who are we missing?" I ask, eyeing the empty chairs. "The Organization Elder. But there is one more seat."

"Two," Julia corrects tartly.

"One." I meet her hard gaze without flinching.

Silence falls over the chamber as the implication of that one word settles over the four of them.

"Expansion," Carmen says in a small voice.

"*You* will take over the Minister's duties?" Luke asks me. His lips thin. "Do you even know the scope of what he was responsible for, son?"

"Please don't call me son." Steel laces through my voice, just as hard as my gaze. "I have a father, and he isn't any of you."

Somehow, that minor act of rebellion has given me courage. It pulses in my veins as surely as my Powers. "If your people are going to get what they want, these so-called Days of Glory, then we need to make changes." I summon as much of my father's poise as I can, but I'm nowhere near as confident as him. Can they tell?

"What do you propose?" Ally breaks her silence. As the Guardian Elder, she controls the military here. From what Drake told me, Ally grew up as an acolyte. If anyone will be in my corner—judging by how quickly the acolytes all bowed to me—it'll be her.

"I will organize a small team to choose two or three candidates for each of the vacant seats," I say. "You are all welcome to make suggestions."

Carmen taps her fingertips on the arm of her chair. "And who makes the final selections? You?"

"No. I shouldn't have that authority."

Julia snorts. "For once, we agree."

"Nor should you," I shoot back at her. I carefully outlined all of this in my notebooks. This proposal had to be bullet proof to keep the Elders from tearing me apart or undermining me. "The new Elders will be selected by the majority."

Majority vote is the risky part of this plan. If the Elders have enough influence with enough people, they can sway the vote in whatever direction they choose.

"A vote." Luke's voice is flat. "That's what you are offering."

"A vote, yes, but not among the five of us. The people will choose, as they should."

Julia gapes at me. Carmen taps her fingers on the arm of her chair again.

"Do people vote for their leaders where you come from?" Luke asks.

"Not until recently," I admit. "And before, the system was...flawed." *Corrupted* is the word I wanted to throw at them, but that wouldn't have gone over well. "But now that the people get a choice, life is better for everyone."

The four Elders exchange glances. Entire conversations pass in those looks. I don't have to read minds to know they are already plotting against me.

Carmen speaks for them. "We agree."

Julia glowers but doesn't argue. Clearly, she *doesn't* agree. *She will be a problem.*

I dip my head in thanks. "Submit your candidates to me by the end of the week. Next week, I will have the final selections, then we can begin their outreach campaigns."

"How do we know you will seriously consider our candidates?" Luke asks.

"You are a telepath, right?"

This alarms him. He probably thought keeping it secret would give him an upper hand against me. He nods.

"Then you will know."

"I can't read you," he grudgingly admits.

"You can read enough when I allow it. And I will. Transparency is critical to this process. For all of us." Which brings me to my next order of business. One they will not appreciate nearly as much. I clench my hands tighter behind my back and steel my nerves against the oncoming storm. *Face it. Don't back down.* "In the spirit of transparency, I believe each Elder, current and new, should work with an outreach assistant. Someone who will be the bridge between the Elders and the needs of the people. None of the Havenites can tell me exactly what any of you do, aside from keeping the community going. Blinders will do no one any good."

Julia scoffs, slamming her fist down on the table. "No! You are accusing us of being underhanded but masking it with kind words and spies."

I throw a verse from the *Book of the Prophet* back at her. "'Those who lack faith will scoff at any truth that challenges their own evil desire'."

"Evil!" Julia chokes on the word, eyes wide in shock.

I expected at least one of them to resist. No surprise that it's her. I was also prepared for resistance and came prepared. "Very well. Answer a couple of my questions honestly, and I will rescind this proposal."

"It isn't a proposal," she snaps.

"I'm being perfectly reasonable and patient." Thank goodness, my voice doesn't shake, even if my bones do.

"Ask your questions," Ally says, glaring at Julia.

"How does one become a Guardian?" Even as I ask, I watch each of their reactions. It's a mixed bag. Julia continues clenching her jaw. Carmen glances at Ally, who stiffens. Luke's eyes widen ever so slightly. "I hear we might have more capable fighters here who would be interested in protecting the Haven, even without *gifts*. So how can we make that happen for those who wish to volunteer?"

I already know where Guardians come from. Ajax gave me a brief insight, but their honesty at this moment will speak volumes. They don't know what I know, and right now, that's my best weapon. This is a test to see if they will tell me the truth. They chose acolytes with the right skill sets for training. None of the Havenites are selected for service. This gives the Minister and the Guardian Elder complete control. *Dangerous territory.*

"Guardians are specially trained acolytes with adept gifts for their jobs." Ally's tone is utterly flat, monotone.

"Then how does one become an acolyte?"

They all flinch.

Luke steps in, and Ally nearly sags in relief as he speaks for her. "We select acolytes as children. Those whose gifts and temperament make them a good fit for training."

An evasive answer. Luke is telling the truth, but only part of it. I've been doing my homework. And Perfect Memory makes it impossible for them to hide the truth for long. I learn. I process. I see the cracks in their foundation. "No one in the Haven seems to know where those children come from."

"It's better that way," he says calmly. "Parents can have a hard time with separation from a child. Family and friends volunteer for Erasure."

My heart stops. That word tells me everything I need to know, but I can't help asking. "What is Erasure?"

Julia's face softens, an odd look that makes me even more uncomfortable than her usually bitter expression. "When a child is selected, the family and friends often find it easier to allow us to remove the memory of them. It's voluntary, but no one refuses."

A lump lodges in my throat. Tampering with memories is a soft spot for me. Aunt Bianca had much of her childhood erased from her memory by her own brother years ago. She recovered none of it.

I croak, "That's horrible."

"It's a mercy."

The nerves that were twisting uncomfortably in my gut have turned to lead. Do they really believe it is mercy to erase a child from memory?

"What about the children? How do they not remember?"

Ally licks her lips, glancing at the others before speaking. "They are young. It's easy to forget as time passes. Children forget on their own."

The story doesn't make complete sense either. Even if parents choose not to remember, what about the surrounding community? Surely, others would remember something.

I clear my throat. "One more question." Julia glares at me. Ally stiffens. Luke clasps his hands tighter in his lap. Carmen is the only one unaffected. "Why have non-Haven-born community members never held a seat on this council?"

Stillness. That is the only word I can think of to describe the eerie feeling settling over the room. No one moves. No one breathes. It's as if time itself has stopped. It stretches on for so long I worry no one will answer me.

"Gavin, we haven't had any from the outside who qualified for a seat." Luke's voice is so soft, like a calm breeze before a storm blows in.

I don't flinch. "Emil is qualified."

"Emil has a one-track mind. And he is a Lie Detector. His gift doesn't fit in any of these seats."

"We are not limited by the gifts we are given, but by the lack of opportunities taken." Dad's words spill from my mouth. "Our Powers don't define us. They don't make us one thing and nothing else. We are each unique, multi-faceted, multi-functional individuals with the capacity to expand ourselves beyond limit. Small minds accomplish small feats."

Jaws drop. I hear every ragged breath they draw against the hammering of my heart.

Ally's voice is meek. "Are you suggesting we allow Emil to have a seat?"

"I'm suggesting you open your minds beyond gifts to see what *all* these people can achieve. Stop putting people in boxes and sealing them in. Your Days of Glory can't arrive if you cut off your nose to spite your face."

Julia's face contorts, as if I've insulted her. Maybe I did.

"As long as we work together openly and honestly, maybe we can hold off on the outreach assistants," I say. Not that I believe they have been fully open or honest, but to them, this is an olive branch. If it extends peacefully, fantastic. If they go behind my back, I will know where they truly stand.

I offer each Elder a respectful nod, then pivot and march out. My knees shake like crazy.

11

DRAKE

THE HALLWAY ACROSS FROM the elder council chambers isn't comfortable. I'm sure this is by design. Anyone who has to wait out here has to suffer and know they are at the will of the Elders, not the other way around. Maybe I can suggest Gavin install comfortable seats set up in the hallway or something.

The Guardians never made me uneasy before. But ever since the incident at the temple, I'm now wary of everyone. Guardians had blocked the doors that day to keep anyone from leaving once the sermon had started.

And the Minister had spoken at length about the coming, false idols, and the potential for anyone to be an Idol. "Maybe even someone here, under our own noses, could rise," he had said. A sense of dread had filled me the moment he had first mentioned false idols. Gavin had been missing all morning. It took me a while to get Emil to confess that Gavin had broken into the temple to read the *Book of the Prophet*.

Gavin is too curious for his own good. That curiosity ended with him burning alive. The terror and heartache and pure loneliness that consumed me as I watched helplessly, pinned to the temple floor, only solidified what I already knew—and denied.

I would do anything for him.

When he rose from the dead, nothing could explain the wonder and relief that had rushed through me. But then the Minister used me against Gavin. The memory of the Minister forcing my actions still leaves me feeling dirty.

Between Gavin trying to convince me my faith is a lie and being used by the very Minister who holds my faith in his hands, I've been lost and conflicted. Is everything I thought I knew a lie?

No, not everything. Gavin isn't. He's real. He is what we were promised, even if he denies it. Even if the Elders hate him for it. Gavin *is* the Idol of Creation. Whether or not he likes it, he continues fulfilling the prophecies we were all warned to watch out for. He is real, and above all else, above the Haven and the temple and the *Book*, I believe in *him*. I will fight for him. I will stick by his side through everything that comes his way.

Gavin needs me because he can't always see what's right in front of him.

I close my eyes, allowing my mind to drift just for a moment as I wait for the doors to open. To a perfect world. A new world. And at the center of it all is him and me.

It's a sinful dream. Forbidden. But I can't stop these dreams from invading my thoughts, no matter how hard I fight to suppress them.

The doors open and the two Guardians in the hallway with me stand at attention.

This is it.

Gavin's not always easy to read. He thinks so much that it gets in the way. But the light in his eyes shows the success of his meeting.

Yet that's only the first step in his outlined plan.

12

Zephyr

This is a problem. I know it, but I can't stop. The whiskey bottle warms quickly in my palm. Without this, the sorrow pulls me under like a sailor lost in the tides. It's a crutch. A life preserver.

My eyes blur as I pour another into the glass on the counter nestled between my fingers. *Stop!* The voice in my head—the angel on my shoulder—screams at me. But the devil's voice is louder and much more seductive. *You need this*, it tells me.

I nod to myself, agreeing. *I need this.*

I stumble toward the couch with the glass in my hand, sloshing amber fluid. I sink into the stiff cushions, then lick the whiskey off my hand.

A hammer of magic slams against my chest. Raw. Intense. Overwhelming. Blinding like the sun. *Paige.*

Fear clenches my stomach. This is it. She's lost control. And I'm helpless to do anything but sit here and accept the end.

The hammer strikes again and again. It beats me into submission like a helpless child—a sensation I'm all too familiar with. My eyes burn. Tears slip down my cheeks. But I can't see. Not the floor or ceiling. Not my hand. The raw intensity of her magic blinds me and renders me utterly and completely vulnerable. I can't even draw air into my lungs.

I'm drowning.

S OMEONE PULLS MY EYELIDS open, flashing a narrow light in my eyes. I groan, still aching from the hammer of Paige's magic. It leaves me in agony as surely as if it had beaten me with real fists. My hand twitches against the rough wool blanket.

"Zephyr?" Baron's voice presses through the fog on my mind.

"I came home and found him like this." *Nat*. He sounds worried.

I groan, creeping the heel of my palm against my chest, right over my heart.

"Thank goodness." Nat's relief makes me wonder what state he found me in.

I blink, my vision gradually coming into focus on Baron kneeling beside me where I lay stretched out on the couch. Baron, my father. Baron, the man I suspected of treason not so long ago. But I found no evidence to prove it. Now, I don't care.

"What happened?" Baron asks, concern shining in his dark eyes. I don't want his fatherly worry now. *Too little, too late*. His fingers press firmly against my wrist, checking my pulse. I try to shake him off, but he's stronger. Or I'm too weak. Or both.

My eyes sweep the floor, searching for my glass. It lies on its side. A wet spot has soaked into the rug. *Pity. That's a waste.*

"Your heart rate is wild." Baron frowns as he says this, as if he cares. I don't need his concern. Not anymore.

"Get off me," I grumble.

This time, he doesn't resist when I jerk my arm away. Baron sinks back, resting his arms on his knee. Nat paces the small floor like a caged animal, rubbing his hands anxiously. I grimace at the sight of the two of them. This place feels very cramped with the three of us crammed into it.

I reach for the empty glass on the floor, glowering into it.

A snort of disgust from the kitchenette draws my gaze to the left.

Easton leans against the counter, arms crossed over his barrel chest, eyeing me in utter revulsion.

With an eyepatch.

"What the hell happened to you?" I snap.

"I could ask the same of you," he sneers, his gaze sweeping the mess on the floor, then eyeing the bottle on the counter beside him. In seconds, he has deduced the truth for himself. He mutters to himself. "I don't get it."

"Why are you even here?" I shift my attention to Baron, jaw twitching. "Why is he here? He should be at the fort." As I sit up, my head swims and everything goes dark. I rub my forehead, trying to brush away the nausea building inside.

"We'll get to that." Baron rises, looming over me in a way that reminds me a lot of his dead brother. But I don't cower like I did from my uncle. I won't cower to anyone ever again. "This has to stop, Zephyr."

"Agreed." Easton's voice is flat, angry. Something splashes. He's upended the bottle of whiskey and pours it into the sink. "You're weak."

"Stop!" But my protest is lame and late. Already, my hands are trembling in fear of withdrawal. My mouth waters as my throat dries. Anger burns in me, directed at Easton. "You have no idea what I've suffered."

"I know what *I've* been through," he says sharply, setting the empty bottle on the counter with a heavy thump. It's a little too close to the edge. His depth perception must still be off. "Captured. Imprisoned. Tortured." He stalks toward me, which only takes a few steps in the small apartment. My gaze is drawn to the eyepatch. It gives me chills. "But I don't drown myself. I don't wallow in self-pity." He bares his teeth in a nasty grin. "I guess my people are made of sterner stuff."

My hands flex in angry fists. I growl at him, wishing my body wasn't still so weak. I would love to see which of us could win a fight without one eye and his muscle magic to help him. "I didn't pass out drunk. It was Paige."

Baron frowns. Nat groans and rolls his eyes.

"It isn't what you think, Nat!" Heat floods my cheeks. I know exactly what he thinks. That I'm obsessing over her. But my magic tells a different story. I glance up at Easton, who lingers near Baron's shoulder. "Remember what I told you in the carriage?"

When my men mutinied against me, I confessed the truth about Paige to Easton. That the scale of her magic compared to ours is through the roof. An understatement if there ever was one.

Easton nods.

"I felt it. But more so."

"How much more?" he asks.

I swallow, meeting his gaze unflinchingly, hoping he can read the truth in that one look. How much will Baron glean from this conversation? What does he already know about her? I told Dominic. Would my cousin have blurted it to Baron? Even now, after everything I lost because of her, I can't help but protect her.

Easton curses under his breath. Apparently, he doesn't need my answer. He understands enough. "I asked you to do *one* thing. One Godforsaken thing! I was handling my situation thinking you were holding up your end." Frustration pours off him like fire. When they arrived on the island, Easton begged me to protect Paige. I tried. And that brought me closer to her. Close enough for the king to exile me out of jealousy.

"What is he talking about, Zephyr?" Baron asks, his voice laced with worry. "What have you done this time?"

My jaw twitches, but I ignore him. All my focus, all my anger, centers on Easton. "And look where it got me, doing your *one* favor." I try to rise, but my legs give out and my head spins wildly.

Easton sneers again, "Get over yourself."

I'm getting sick of that sneer. If I could stand, I would launch myself at him.

"If I had known I was putting my trust in an alcoholic, I never would have asked." Those words are a punch in the gut. Easton selected his fighting ring well.

Nat looks like he wants to melt into the wall.

Baron glares at Easton, his eyes just as deadly as his own elemental magic. "Watch your tongue, boy." His fingers flex like he is reaching for his magic, but nothing happens. Not with me in the room.

Easton's stance firms, bracing himself for a fight. His own muscle magic bucks against my magical block as he tries to grasp it.

"I thought you weren't fighting my battles anymore." My words are sharper than I intended, but the meaning is clear. Baron warned me after my return from the mainland, after I disobeyed the command to return to the island, that he was getting sick of cleaning up my messes and fighting my battles. I didn't understand why he even bothered. At the time, I thought he was my uncle, not my father.

Baron winces. His shoulders sag, and sorrow creases his features. "Zephyr..." But either he can't finish whatever he wanted to say, or he won't. Instead of pressing the issue, he switches gears. "I—we have noticed a few things. Things that aren't normal."

The muscles in my back tense. I meet Baron's gaze fearlessly, then flick past him to Nat, who hovers near the door, agitated.

"Like Easton's eye?" I ask. "What happened?"

Easton growls. It's a menacing sound not meant for me.

"Among other things," Baron replies, interrupting before we can lay into one another again. "We are still looking into it. He didn't see who ordered it taken."

I almost snort at the irony of that phrase. After training with Easton at the fort, I don't believe for a second that he didn't memorize everything for future use. He doesn't *want* to share. Either he doesn't trust us, or he plans to exact his own brand of justice. Or both.

"Even in the fort, I have noticed strange behavior," Baron continues. "Nat brought it to my attention. Longer training hours for recruits. Officers have altered guard shifts in certain places around the island. I started checking records against supplies. Swords. Shields. Battle gear. Logged for transfers. Not all of it. Not even enough to notice were I not paying close attention. The numbers are so small I missed them. I feel like an idiot."

I gape as it hits me. "Shipments of supplies meant for the mainland... But who, besides us, has the power to move that kind of material without notice? Cypress wouldn't. He wouldn't need to."

Baron shakes his head. "That's the question, isn't it? And why? Which is why I recruited Easton's help. He can hear and see things we can't around town. Besides, they have done something to him, and for some reason he can't tell us what."

Or he won't.

Easton snorts, drawing our attention his way. His lonely eye darts from one of us to the other, as if he expects us to put the pieces together. Finally, he drops his arms to his sides, exasperated with all of us. "You have led sheltered, privileged lives here. That or your training sucks. The answer is right in front of your faces."

We continue staring dumbly and he grunts. "You have a new, young, inexperienced king who was never meant to take the throne. Zephyr already experienced a mutiny." He waves a hand toward me, and I notice a missing pinky finger. A wound healed over with smooth skin. "Someone isn't happy with how things are run and sees this new king as a chance to nurture insurrection."

Baron scoffs at the idea. I admit I find it hard to believe as well. Who on this island would have enough power to carry out something like this right under our noses?

But I have suspected this for months now.

We have a traitor in our midst.

13

PAIGE

A KNOCK ON ANOTHER door halts me in my tracks as I pace the rug in my room. A moment later, I race to the door and glance along the hallway. Layla quivers as she takes the invitation off the silver platter. The butler bows and marches stiffly away.

Layla meets my gaze. There's excitement and terror in her eyes. Until recently, an invitation meant the king was still interested. Now the reality of our situation is hard to ignore.

Not every invitation arrives with his affection. Some end in dismissal.

I try not to think about any of this as the day wears on. Prince Dominic and Vincent take me out for another Power lesson. When the prince prepares to unlock the latch on my bracelet, I jerk my arm away and step backward. Vincent looms behind me and my back smacks into his chest.

"It's okay, Paige." Prince Dominic offers his softest, more reassuring smile. The memory of that horrible, destructive Power still haunts me. I don't want to let it loose.

"What if something goes wrong?" I whisper.

"Until you learn to control this, it's dangerous. I think this bracelet can only contain it for so long, and we can't give you anything stronger." I tremble in fear as he removes the bracelet, resigned to my fate. "Paige, if we don't do this, something much worse could happen. I know that's not what you want."

I bite my lip and shake my head. "Why hasn't the King dismissed Bella?"

Prince Dominic stiffens, glancing past me at Vincent. There's something guarded about the look in his eyes. As he touches my temples, he leans closer and whispers, "Turns out it's harder than we thought to get rid of her."

Does he not want Vincent to hear him? Why is he acting like we shouldn't trust the man who is supposed to help me with training? I try to sneak a peek at Vincent, but Prince Dominic gives a subtle shake of his head.

"Let's begin," he says just loud enough for Vincent to hear.

Who is this guy?

I open the door in my mind for Dominic, wary of Vincent now. Can I selectively lock anyone out for good? I've never tried.

"Before, we were concerned with boxing the magic inside of you," Vincent says from behind me. I'm startled at how close he is to my shoulder. "This time, I want you to focus all your energy on harnessing it. Think of your magic like an unbroken mare, bucking for control. You are the horse mistress, Lady Paige."

I am the horse mistress. I repeat the words as the fire burns through my veins. Prince Dominic doesn't flinch as he holds my head in his hands. His touch is soft and cool.

I try heeding Vincent's advice, but the heat, the Power, overwhelms me. My breaths come in ragged gasps. I imagine myself riding the wild Power, attempting to control it, but the fire continues consuming me, burning me. I moan in misery. Red mist glows in my palm, curling around my hand and up my arms. I press down on the Power, hoping to slam a lid over it.

"Don't box it this time, Paige." Prince Dominic's voice is distant, patient. Somehow, he knows what I'm doing. "Grab it. Guide it."

His voice repeats on a loop in my mind, as clear as if he says them aloud. Our gazes are tethered, and his sapphire eyes glow with hungry life.

My heart races wild like a galloping horse, but the harder I try grabbing hold of the Power, the harder it becomes. My fingers slip through it like a hand through water. Comparing this to mastering a horse is all wrong. It's more like trying to doggie paddle in raging waves. The rush continues flowing over me, pulling me under, threatening to drown me.

"No more," I whimper, unsure if they can even hear my voice over the raging hammer of my heartbeat.

Guide it. The prince's voice resounds clear as a bell in my mind.

I shake my head, but the movement is stifled in his firm grasp. I squeeze my eyes closed; my hands clench into fists.

"No more!" The words erupt out of me like a geyser, echoing off the nearby hangar walls.

Prince Dominic staggers backward, stunned and blinking.

Vincent has turned and heads back to the awaiting carriage, each step stilted as if some invisible force pushes him onward.

The prince's chest rises and falls in rapid breaths, and he clutches at it. Clearly, his heart is racing. "What was that?"

I collapse to the ground in a heap, tears streaming hot rivers down my cold cheeks. "No more," I whimper.

He kneels next to me, stroking the hair away from my face. "No more. For now."

I'm too weak, too battered by this Power, to argue as he locks the bracelet back on my wrist.

Unlike before, the current of Power remains, moving through my veins slowly, a babbling brook compared to the tides of moments ago.

The bracelet no longer keeps it away. I should use that to my advantage to learn more about control, but the prospect is far too terrifying.

———※———

THAT EVENING, THE WALLS of my room are so confining I can't breathe. When I step into the hallway, a guard is posted near the steps. That's new. Is that because of what I did earlier? Do they fear me now?

I smile at him and close my door again, then head to the balcony.

The air is frigid. I gulp it down, relishing the way it burns my lungs. Despite the numbness creeping along my bare arms, I perch on the edge of the rail carefully and stare out at the lake, remembering the raging waters of my Power. It's still there, taunting me, reminding me it can break free.

The trickle of my new Powers remains there beneath the surface. I close my eyes and try to focus on it, probing for some way to grab hold of it or follow the flow of the current. Warmth spread through my body, chasing away the winter chill. When I open my eyes, everything looks different. Desolate or rotting. It's a putrid vision of the world. But it isn't real. It's like looking at the world through a dirty filter. Tears well in my eyes and I blink them away.

Some areas are worse than others. The garden across from the palace is dead from the winter, but still has less of the desolate filter than the lake beyond. What does it mean? What am I seeing? I don't understand, and I don't like it.

I want to wipe it clean but can do little more than prevent the decay on my own balcony when the wood beneath me pops like it's about to give out. Sickness surges in my stomach. I lean against the rail for support as I clutch my gut. When I open my eyes again, everything has returned to normal.

What Power is that? Can I see what the world was like just after the Collapse? Or is this a sign of what's coming?

Exhaustion and nausea tug at me. I press my hands tight against the balcony rail for stability as my hungry Powers pull at me like an eager puppy.

Distant voices draw my attention toward the red carpet steps leading into the palace.

Or in this case, out of the palace.

Layla clings to the king's arm in a stunning green dress, pleading with him. I can't make out her words, but the intention is clear enough. She doesn't want to leave. I can't see King Cypress' face as he eases her tight grip off his arm. Then Prince Dominic places his hand against her back, turning her away from the king. All the fight goes out of her as the prince escorts her down the red carpet to the waiting carriage. Then he climbs in after her and it rides away into town.

King Cypress' breath rolls out in a cloud. He shakes his head and marches back inside, shoulders curled inward.

We are down to three, and I still haven't said more than a few words to King Cypress.

I should feel bad for Layla. She wanted to stay. All of us know she adores the king. She wanted this, unlike me. So why do I get to stay when she must leave?

"You are never leaving this island, and he will never choose you." Queen Elena's warning makes my heart ache. Perhaps my isolation from him is her doing.

I climb into bed, pulling the blankets up tight to my chin, and cry myself to sleep.

I'm never getting home.

———❈———

I BLINK, DISORIENTED BY my change in surroundings. I've never been here before. Where am I?

Small café tables line the outer edges of the small space. In the center of the bar, a wide opening offers a view of the dance floor below. Pristine white rails guard the opening alongside more tables. I edge toward the rail and peer down at a tiny dance floor and bar below. A curious space. We seem to be at the top of the palace, judging by the view out the windows. It's beautiful up here.

The plush carpet beneath my bare feet is deep blue and covered in stars. I dig my toes into the fibers, relishing the soft texture, then make my way around the outer edge of the room. Blue cushioned benches line the outer walls, kissing the ledge of the windows on three sides.

King Cypress reclines against a pillar on one of those benches. One foot is propped up on the bench and he rests his arm on his knee, carelessly swirling a glass of white wine. King Cypress gazes out across the water, lost in his thoughts.

Seeing him like this disarms me. The few times I've seen him, King Cypress has been collected, immaculate, confident, and charming. Slouching on a blue cushion with his sleeves rolled up makes him appear almost...normal. He draped his jacket across a chair on the other side of the table.

His blue eyes turn my way. I tense, worried about what he will say when he catches me spying. But he peers straight through me. Can he not see me standing ten feet away?

He draws in a breath, then huffs it out. "Imbecile," he mutters to himself, shaking his head. He takes a drink, then resumes staring out at the water.

I edge closer, observing him in this moment when he believes no one is around. It's the first time I've really seen him since the ball. There's something very real and vulnerable about him at this moment. Sadness encircles him like a cloud raining only on him. So many people surround him, care for him. He rules everything and everyone. What does he have to be sad about?

"I thought I might find you up here."

I jump and spin around, worried I've been caught spying.

Prince Dominic strolls around the bar and sits in a metal chair, facing the king. He is just as oblivious to my presence as King Cypress is.

"That was wretched," King Cypress grumbles into his glass. He's about to drink, then sighs and lowers it. "How is she?"

"Settled and resting soundly."

Who are they talking about? Layla or me?

"It took you a while to return this time." King Cypress sets his glass on the table and straightens. "Did Layla resist the whole way?"

That answers that question.

Prince Dominic straightens his cuffs, then checks his fingernails. "Yes. In the end, she gave in, just like the other girls. I made our position clear. She will keep her distance. You need not worry about her causing trouble."

King Cypress heaves a sigh. "I didn't mean to hurt her. There just wasn't...a connection. And she talked too much about nothing at all. It was exhausting." He shakes his head and leans back again. "No point trying to force it."

"So, who are you favoring right now?" Prince Dominic asks. "There are only three girls left."

King Cypress shoots a grimace his way. "I'm aware."

"And?"

"And what?" He peers into his glass as if he can pull an answer from it. "You already know the answer to that question." He swirls the glass, then takes a sip. "How is training progressing?"

My heart beats harder. I'm not supposed to hear any of this. Why am I here? *How* am I here? And how are they *not* seeing me so close to them?

"It's extraordinary what Paige is capable of. If you want a queen with raw power, she is your obvious choice. None of the other girls even come close. But she's terrified of it."

"None?"

Prince Dominic shakes his head.

King Cypress sighs heavily. "Then I guess time is up."

I need to leave before they finally spot me. I rush to the door and down the stairs, running in a direction I hope leads to my room.

I BOLT AWAKE, DRIPPING with sweat. What happened? One moment I was running to my room, then suddenly nothing. At all. It was a dream. It must have been.

But it felt and sounded so *real*. The plush rug. The conversation seemed too intimate to have been created by my mind. *Can I Dreamwalk?* It's a Power kids joked about, walking through reality by dreaming of it. But no one has ever actually *done* it before.

I throw off the blankets and shower. By the time I emerge, my maids are already in the room with a crimson dress laid out on the bed.

Over breakfast, Bella and Nora murmur about Layla's dismissal.

I repeatedly draw my gaze to the head table where the king eats. On one side, Queen Elena picks at her meal. On the other side, Prince Dominic enjoys a drink of juice. He catches me staring and the smile that spreads across his face is encouraging. He leans toward the king and whispers something in his ear.

King Cypress draws away, picking up his coffee cup. Those cool blue eyes peer into my soul. Then the corner of his mouth tips up in a smile.

My breath hitches and my stomach drops. I glance away. Does he know I was listening last night? Is he smiling at me now because he sees me as his only choice? I want his attention so I can get him to send me home. So I can get back to Gavin. Not because I want to be his queen.

Breakfast doesn't end quickly enough. I'm the first out the door. The first to the elevator. The first to my room. My palms sweat like mad. I try wiping them off on my skirt, but the sheer layers upon layers of crimson material absorbs nothing at all.

I rush to the bathroom and wash my hands.

A knock on the door stills my hammering heart. I freeze, gazing at the closed door. A moment later, another knock.

Swallowing the lump in my throat, I shuffle to the door, every muscle in my body protesting the movement. I take a breath to steady my breathing, then open the door.

The butler waits patiently outside my room with the tray containing a single sealed envelope. He bows, holding up the tray for me to take the invitation.

Nora lingers in the hallway near my door, an encouraging smile on her face. It should excite me to receive the invitation. It's been a long time coming. I convinced myself that, when this envelope finally arrived, it would bear bad news. After what I saw last night, I no longer know what to think.

Unable to calm my nerves, my hands tremble as I take the envelope and murmur my thanks.

Dearest Lady Paige,
Please accept my humblest apology. I'm sure the wait has been difficult to bear. Understand that I had my reasons. And sometimes, it's best to save the finest for last.

Miss Ingrid will escort you to the lobby shortly after lunch for an afternoon together.
Dress warmly. Wear pants if it pleases you.
Yours,
King Cypress Strong

Despite my stress over why he is now suddenly interested in taking me out, his permission to wear pants is endearing. At my very first breakfast with the royal family, I asked him why women didn't wear pants here and he called it unusual. At least he has a sense of humor.

14

GAVIN

TRUSTING THE ELDERS TO keep their side of the bargain is not an option. I knew it when I offered to rescind the need for outreach associates. The moment I leave, I expect them to undermine me. But I'm already ahead of them. After all, they agreed to this plan to a vote for the Elder seats.

While Drake sent the Elders the message that I was ready to meet with them, I had Emil quietly gather the Havenites with the help of Ajax. I can't say why I trust Ajax, but he seemed sincere when he walked me through the temple tunnels—even if he obviously refused to answer some of my questions.

As soon as I step out the door, my Guardians in tow, Drake kicks off the wall across from me.

"Everyone's eager," Drake says, falling in step beside me. The Guardians eye him suspiciously, but Drake is the one person here I trust without a doubt.

"Good. Let's keep the Elders on their toes."

Public speaking is one of my greatest weaknesses—aside from reading people's emotions—but someone must do this and the Havenites will listen to me. They might ignore Emil and dismiss Drake. But me... I hate how these people hang on my every move, every word. However, if I want to help them, I have to play their game.

Drake takes my hand. I startle, gazing at his hand in mine, cool and comforting. He gives me a reassuring squeeze. "This will be fine, Gavin. You can stop fidgeting."

What was I doing? My nerves are wound up tight, but whatever he caught me doing with my hand is beyond my recollection. I take a deep breath to steel my nerves, but that fails miserably. My other hand uncurls and sweat coats my palm.

Drake's face heats and he drops my hand, stuffing his own deep into his pockets. "I have faith enough for both of us."

Well obviously, that's true. I'm not a man of faith; I'm a man of science. But Drake believes I came here for a reason. I promised him I wouldn't attempt to steer him away from his religion again, but it doesn't mean I understand.

We stop at a bend in the tunnel leading into the underground square. Drake had wanted me to do this in the temple, to remind the people what I did and who I am, but I had steadfastly refused. I don't ever want to stand on that stage in front of all these people again as long as I live. I *won't*.

The chatter of hundreds of Havenites pours into the tunnel where we stand. I scrub my hands against my pants, hoping to rid myself of the sweat and smooth out my shaking nerves.

Ajax pops around the corner, pulling up short when he spots us. "Good. They're ready."

I nod, straightening my spine and raising my chin in what I pray is a mirror of Dad. I could use even a fraction of his confidence right now.

Drake subtly clears his throat, tipping his head toward the corner. Then he disappears around it. He and Ajax are part of my newly forming entourage, but neither of them wants to stand at my side when I enter the room. Drake seems to think it's best if I don't look like I'm leaning on them for support—even if I am.

I give them a moment to enter the square, then force my feet along the floor in their wake. The four Guardians move behind me like my shadow.

The square slowly falls silent as I cross toward the platform. I feel a thousand eyes trailing me like a thousand needles against my skin. It takes everything I have not to scratch my arms.

Two Guardians peel away and take up corner positions with a clear line of sight in the room—as if they think someone will attack me. The other two accompany me to the announcement platform reserved for the Elders. They assume positions at the back of the small platform.

The moment I stop on the platform, all whispering halts. My stomach twists in painful knots. I hope I don't get sick.

Channel Dad's voice, his confidence, his leadership. I'm his son. This shouldn't be that difficult.

I clear my throat. "Thank you all for coming on such short notice. I know this is…unorthodox, and you are not used to hearing from me." My voice shakes a little at first, but steadies as I gain momentum. I must get this started before the Elders enter to stop me. They won't be far behind once they hear about this gathering. No time for preamble. "First, I would like to announce that anyone who wishes to volunteer for training to become a Guardian is welcome to do so. You can petition Elder Ally with your request. The days of depending on gifts alone to protect the people of the Haven are behind you."

I'm careful not to include myself in that statement. Once I settle things here, I will leave with a promise from the full council of Elders to open an alliance with Elpis.

This announcement sends a ripple of excitement through the crowd. I can already identify several of the younger Havenites whispering their interest in volunteering. *Good. It's what these people need.*

"Two empty seats have remained open among the Elders for years," I continue. "They say it is because no one with the right gifts has come along to fill those seats, which may be true."

A few people murmur and nod, understanding why those spaces are vacant and accepting it as a matter of course.

"But it is no longer necessary to *keep* those seats open."

The Elders slip in from the tunnel on the other side of the Haven square, making their way toward the stage. Havenites eye me curiously, whispering speculations about who would now fill those seats.

"The Haven will hold an election for anyone with the knowledge and skills to fill those seats," I push the words out, watching the approaching Elders. They freeze in a small cluster.

And the Havenites notice. They eye the Elders curiously.

"Applications for these positions are open to any citizen, whether or not one has a gift to match the seat," I continue, worried the Elders will interrupt before I can finish. "From those, a committee will select the top candidates, who will spend the next few weeks campaigning for their position, working to convince the rest of you why they should be chosen for the position."

The whispers become a muted din of noise all around the square. People crowd around tables in conversation over the news. A few of the older Havenites frown at me, but in general, the news seems to be received well.

Mrs. Garraty elbows her way toward the platform. Her skin is gaunter than the last time I saw her, but anger burns in her eyes. "Is this true, Luke?"

A hush falls as everyone awaits Luke's response.

He squares his shoulder, then hesitates a moment before joining me on the small platform. "Yes. We only minutes ago convened on the matter." He shoots a glare at me.

I purse my lips but refuse to back down. I am my father's son. I refuse to be pushed around.

"But how will these elected Elders know what to do without the gifts necessary for the position?" another man asks.

"An excellent question," Mrs. Garraty says sharply.

Julia approaches, patting the Minister's wife on the shoulder, but Julia doesn't step on the platform. Instead, she stands directly in front of Luke and me. "We are still sorting out some details. This announcement might have been premature."

"No." I snap the word out. Most of these Elders scare me, but Julia is nothing more than a bully. And I have a lot of experience with bullies. Before she can interject, I press on. "You have all waited long enough for a properly established and well-rounded group of leadership. When was the last time you had all these positions filled?"

Everyone exchanges uncertain glances.

"It has been far too long, because the necessary gifts protect us from danger," Julia says. The woman practically preens as if she has bested me.

I smirk. "Intelligence is far more powerful than gifts and works just as efficiently. Perhaps more so." I step closer to the edge of the platform and try to speak loud and clear so that everyone hears me. *Time to play to the crowd.* "I've walked the surface for hundreds of miles. I've studied the former dangers on the surface extensively. If you want the Days of Glory to come, you need to prepare for what comes next, which begins with a *full* council of leadership. It's time to step out of the shadows."

A few people scowl at me, but more murmurs of agreement and approval ripple through the crowd than opposition. That's a good start.

"We understand your concerns," I continue, "but I can assure you only those with an aptitude for these positions will be selected for election."

"And if there is no one?" asks a young woman I remember as a friend of Pip's.

"We will post the requirements so that you all know what is needed and expected," I say. "And I have every confidence there will be more than enough of you who qualify."

Julia crosses her arms, standing aside so she can glare at me openly. She wants everyone to know she doesn't approve, and that she doesn't like me. What would she have to gain from such a display? And how many of these people would follow her lead?

"And what of the other positions?" asks a woman with long black hair braided over her shoulder. She shoots a dirty look at Julia, making it clear even to me what she means. "What if we are eager for new leadership in *all* positions?"

Julia deflates at this. "Becca, I did everything I could for your sister. But she lost—"

"My sister hated you," Becca snaps. "She was a threat to your position. And when she needed your help, you conveniently couldn't help her."

Interesting. Dissention among the people toward the current Elders hadn't even crossed my mind. It should have. And it could be dangerous to the process.

Julia shakes her head, but before she can open her mouth to defend herself, I barrel over them both. "I think we need to take this one step at a time. Let's fill all the seats. Then we can discuss future elections."

"What?" Luke gasps at my side.

I seek a familiar face in the crowd and land on Drake. He is beaming at me, then gives me an encouraging nod, signaling a subtle thumbs-up. We scattered him and Emil among the Havenites to listen for any danger to our proposal.

"You said there are only two positions," says a man with an ugly scar on his chin. But as he stares at me, the puckered skin around the edges smooths out. "Are you taking the Minister's position?"

The very notion makes my Powers pulse beneath my skin. The string lights around the room brighten slightly. Mrs. Garraty's eyes widen as she gapes at me. Before I can get in a response, or even think, a barrage of questions and comments assault me from all sides.

"Where is the Minister?"

"Please guide us to the Days of Glory!"

"Is this why we haven't had Mass?"

"Will you be leading sermons?"

I can't even think straight as the noise rises. My head spins. Weight presses down on me from all sides, closing in like I'm a cube being compressed into a smaller space. Is this what Paige's claustrophobia feels like? Sweat beads on my brow.

A woman drops to her knees, hands folded together in prayer. My stomach curdles. Her words are soft-spoken, but they send a shockwave of wonder through the crowd. "In His divine knowledge, He will give strength to the weak, power to the deserving."

A murmur of approval follows her prophetic words from the *Book of the Prophet*. And just like that, the people have opened themselves to this change.

Whether Luke means to end this gathering, or he has some sympathy for my plight, is irrelevant. I appreciate his gesture as he calls for the meeting to end.

Drake, Ajax, and Emil move around the room, encouraging everyone to review the posted requirements and apply.

Luke places a hand on my shoulder. "You are certainly a bold one, Gavin."

I flinch at the touch, eager to pull away but remain rooted in place. *Bold*. Not a word anyone has ever used to describe me.

Julia turns, glaring at me as the crowds disperse behind her. "This isn't over, Gavin."

"Julia." The warning in Luke's tone makes me shrink back. "What's done is done. Let's find the best way to move forward." He steps between the two of us, dropping his other hand on my other shoulder.

The wooden platform creaks as the Guardians shift, preparing for a fight.

Luke only glances at them before he continues. "Be careful how fast you run. I'm not sure how things are done where you come from, but we have rules here that are necessary to maintain our tenuous balance. Changing that system will be a delicate matter. You can't run in headfirst."

A chill runs down my spine. Mr. Garraty said those exact words to me about rules, in that precise phrasing. I don't believe this is a coincidence.

"Noted." I shrug out of his grip, taking a step away. The heat from my Guardians is close enough to feel even a single step back. "Just know I won't be pushed around."

"Noted." Luke nods.

The Elders march off together, with Julia shooting glares at me over her shoulder.

Mrs. Garraty approaches, arms crossed over her chest. "I want to see my husband. They won't let me see him." Her angry glare turns to the Guardians, though I doubt it's these two specifically.

"I'll see what I can do," I reassure her. "I never intended to have any of this happen to your family."

She huffs and marches away.

It isn't until she and the Elders leave the square that I finally relax.

"Julia wants to kill you," Drake notes as he joins me.

"She already tried. I hope she learned a lesson."

Ajax strolls over, each step silent, but when it hits the floor, it gives me a sense that Ajax could smash the earth. How strong he is, anyway? He's certainly one of the biggest men I've seen around here.

"You *need* to speak with the Minister," he says.

This isn't his first request, and it won't be his last. But I'm still too scared to face Mr. Garraty.

"I know."

"*Soon*, sire."

I wince. He won't stop with the honorifics, no matter how many times I insist on it. "What's the rush?"

"These people are not used to having no religious sermons, no sense of order."

"Why not you?" I ask. "You could lead them."

Ajax pales and shakes his head. Seeing such terror and humility on his face is at odds with those muscles. "It isn't just about that. If you intend to fill these positions, but do not choose a new Minister, even some acolytes might question you. The Minister has been asking for you. I think he's ready to talk."

I look to Drake for support, but his compressed lips and nonchalant shrug only support Ajax's statements. "Look, I heard some people talking. They don't think it's right that the Idol of Creation would not take up where the Minister left off. This election might show them some signs of change toward the Days of Glory, but it won't last nearly as long as you need it to." Drake glances at Ajax. "I think he's right. You need to talk to Garraty."

But I can't.

Drake nudges my shoulder. "I'll go with you, if it helps."

"There will be Power stones on his cell, I assume," I say.

Ajax nods.

Drake pales a little, then straightens.

15

PAIGE

INGRID ESCORTS ME TO the main lobby parlor, then directs me to a plush red velvet chair. A musician plays a beautiful rendition of some classical song on the grand piano nearby. The small round table beside me has a tray of hot cocoa and cookies that smell heavenly. Does the King know I have a horrible sweet tooth? My Somatic muscles eagerly eat up the sugar and calories from the sweets. I'm unsure if I should wait or if these are for my enjoyment while I wait.

The main lobby is a comfortable space. Sofas and plush chairs gather in organized clusters along the long lobby space near the windows. I can't help but peek back out the windows as I wait. At the bottom of the red staircase, beneath the shelter covering the road, a black horse-drawn carriage awaits. What is the carriage for?

Even if I wanted to eat the cookies, my stomach wouldn't be able to handle the sweets—something I usually love. After what I overheard between King Cypress and Prince Dominic, I assumed this would be a normal date, or maybe he might even work doubly hard to impress me because now he sees me as his only real choice. But King Cypress only brings out the carriage when he sends girls away.

I was so sure of myself coming down here. I'm not wrong. *I can't be wrong.* I know what I heard. And it can't possibly be a coincidence that King Cypress chose me for the afternoon after what I overheard. No. I'm not being dismissed. Not yet. Though this might be my last chance—my *only* chance—to earn his trust and get a ticket home.

I've already broken down my options to get back to Elpis. I can be dismissed, though Queen Elena seemed determined to keep me on this island no matter what King Cypress chooses. I can take my chances and flee across the lake with Easton, and maybe Zephyr. Nora's brother controls the docks. There's a chance I could use that to my advantage, though I haven't worked out how yet. According to Nora, fishers are allowed out on the open water during the summer months, but they are forbidden from crossing to the mainland without a royal declaration.

Which means I need the king. Every path I've taken leads back to him.

I study the black carpet's repeating squares of green leaves housing bouquets of red petunias. It's worn from age, but clearly well cared for.

"I imagined I would arrive, and this tray would already be empty."

King Cypress' arrival startles me. I was so absorbed in studying the pattern, lost in the repetition and my own thoughts, that I hadn't even noticed him settling into the red chair beside me. Unsure what I should do, I press my hands against the arms of the chair to rise.

"Don't get up on my behalf." He waves me back.

Uneasy, I remain frozen in that position.

He picks up a cup of cocoa and nods to the other. "I hear you have a sweet tooth. I thought this might be a good way to prepare for our afternoon."

I ease back, smoothing my hands over the red chiffon layers of my palazzo pants. My maids outdid themselves with this outfit. The top hugs my curves and glitters with sequins around the low bust line, but the inside is lined with the softest fleece I've felt in my life. The long sleeves stretch and move with ease. Beneath the red chiffon, a flexible, fleece-lined pair of leggings hug my skin in a warm embrace. The elastic waistband shimmers with matching sequins. Even the coat and gloves they provided fits the ensemble.

His gaze sweeps over my clothes as he takes a tentative sip, then licks his lips. "I'm surprised you aren't in pants."

"I'm surprised you can't tell I am."

He chuckles. The sound is warm. Then he glances at my untouched mug. "Do you not enjoy cocoa?"

I swallow, absently fiddling with the bracelet. "I don't mean any offense, Your Highness—Grace?—" How do I not know which way to address him? My cheeks heat. "But it's been weeks and you've not said a word. I've watched most of the other girls leave. I would prefer knowing where I stand now than waiting until the end of the day."

What I actually want to ask is if he set this date up because of what his brother said about me, but I hold that back. For now.

He squints slightly, a twinkle of amusement in his blue eyes. "Direct. I appreciate that." He sets down his cup and rests his arm on the armrest, leaning closer to me. That crooked smile he flashed at me the day I arrived in the palace lights up his face. "Lady Paige, I'm not sending you anywhere. And you can call me Cypress."

It takes a moment for his meaning to sink in. A few seconds later, I sink back against the chair. He thinks I believed this would lead to my dismissal. Maybe I can work with that.

"I have to ask," I say carefully. "Why has it taken so long for me to get an invitation? The other girls have all spent time with you at least twice now."

"Keeping score, I see." He winks.

I flush and avert my gaze. "It's hard not to notice when you're feeling ignored."

King Cypress leans back and picks up his mug once more. A shadow of doubt crosses his face. "If we are being honest, I'm a little worried. Consider my position here, Lady Paige. I welcome eleven girls into my home and must find one to fall in love with and marry. As if that's not enough pressure, on the same night, one of those girls chooses death over me. Another..." He turns his gaze up to meet mine, exposing the vulnerability in the depths of his blue eyes. "...chooses my half-brother."

My heart stutters for a moment as the air rushes out of my lungs. I try to formulate some line of defense, but my mind fails me utterly.

He shakes his head. The charm has vanished. King Cypress sags. After a moment, he sighs and shrugs. "I just needed some time to figure out how to approach you."

My voice is thick with worry. "Why exile him? Why not just send *me* away?"

"I don't know. The fancies of a hopeless romantic? I can't say I blame Zephyr. The moment I saw you climbing those stairs that first day, I knew you were special."

Special because of my Powers. But that's not fair. He didn't know at the time just what I could do. *I* don't even know what I can do.

King Cypress takes a sip, then sets his cup down and waves as if trying to wash away his answer. "No. No, I have a better response." He turns to me. "A stubborn refusal to give up a fight."

That *is* a better answer. I'm not one for romance, but I respect determination.

I pick up my mug. The cocoa is just warm enough to take a long drink without burning my mouth or throat.

"I didn't choose anything," I admit. "And nothing happened."

"*Something* happened."

We lock gazes. His is firm, unyielding while also displaying his fear.

I nod. "Nothing of importance happened."

"So hope is not lost?"

I smirk over the rim of my mug. "Not yet." Though even as I say it, I know it's a lie.

"I can accept that."

Agreeable silence settles between us as we drink our hot cocoa and snack on the cookies. The musician continues playing the piano nearby. In a matter of minutes, King Cypress has eased my anxiety about the incident with Zephyr with so much effortlessness. I envy his tenacity.

We make small talk about the palace, and the weather. Such a natural air of calm surrounds him. It makes me comfortable.

As we finish our snacks, he rises, then offers me his hand.

"I danced with all the girls that night except you," he says. "I would like to make up for that, if you don't mind."

Not that it's a choice. I need his help. I can't refuse.

I slide my hand into his. The warmth of his smooth hand is welcoming. He pulls me to my feet, then steps closer and slides an arm around my waist. There in the lobby, where anyone passing by could see, he guides me through the steps as if they're second nature. The embrace is intimate, but not so much that it makes me want to pull away.

His cheek nearly brushes mine as he curls closer to my neck. The move doesn't feel intended as anything more than a desire for more proximity. His warm breath sweeps down my skin.

Even if all I get from him today is a brief conversation and a dance, it's enough. For now, at least.

"You're light on your feet," he murmurs near my ear.

I tilt my head enough to see the profile of his face. King Cypress certainly is strikingly handsome. "I was a champion dancer back home. Were it not for this bracelet, I would be even better at this."

As if to punctuate the point, I step on his toes and wince. He either doesn't notice or has the grace to ignore it.

"I would love to hear more about your home, if you will share." His eyes glimmer in the lobby lights. So close, I can see the layers of blue bursting outward from his pupils, dark to light. I've seen nothing like it before.

Our steps slow gradually.

"I'm not ready to talk about home just yet," I whisper.

His eyes fixate on my lips.

Suddenly, he turns his gaze away and steps back, releasing his hold on my body. I'm surprised that it disappoints me a little. Not that I wanted him to kiss me. *I certainly didn't!* I resent being ignored and locked away for weeks. I resent what he did to his own brother over nothing. Based on that conversation between him and Prince Dominic, I can't only assume he is toying with me right now, trying to get close enough for me to let my guard down. He doesn't really have an interest in me. He wants my Powers.

"Whenever you're ready to tell me more, just let me know," he says. In a few strides, he retrieves my coat off another seat. "We are nowhere near done with our afternoon, Lady Paige. I have a few more things I want to share with you."

I slide my arms into the coat he holds up for me, then I set to work fastening it closed.

In short order, we descend the red staircase and climb into the carriage. There is only one bench inside, and we settle side-by-side. Excitement pulses through me as I realize we are leaving not just the palace walls, but the grounds as well. It will be my first actual glimpse of life on the island since arriving months ago.

As the carriage rolls along the plowed streets, King Cypress offers historical facts about the buildings we pass along the way. Only two windows expose the outside world—one on either side of the carriage.

Snow sparkles in the sunlight as it tumbles lazily to the ground. There's something magical about the blanket of white that covers everything. Even the trees, which are barren of leaves, bow their branches under the weight of the snow covering them.

"We don't get this much snow where I come from," I admit as the carriage turns along a main road. Offering him a small piece of information about home might help him feel like I'm opening up to him. "It caps the mountains nearby, but never reaches us."

"I've never seen mountains." King Cypress peers past me out the window, a whimsical smile gracing his face. "When I was a boy, my brothers, sister, and I would build snowmen in the tea garden and place them like guardians around the fountain."

He continues giving me the highlights of the main streets of the island. I file all the information away for later use. I will dissect everything when I don't need to worry about keeping him talking.

Based on what I can see, the population of the island can't be more than a few thousand. When I ask, he boasts nearly a hundred thousand. But where do they all go? There can't possibly be enough homes for all of them.

The island is bigger than I expected. While Elpis would still dwarf the island, it isn't by nearly as much as I thought.

We stop along the main road, amidst dozens of cozy shops. The door opens and King Cypress steps out first, then offers his hand.

I step carefully, worried about slipping in the snow.

People walk around on their daily business, carrying baskets and bags of various goods. The smell of fresh bread from a nearby bakery invites passersby inside. No one steps in our way, giving us space. I watch them move. They aren't scared or intimidated by their king. The distance clearly displays their respect for him. I file this away, as well. It's good to know how his people see him.

16

EASTON

THE CAPITAL REMINDS ME of newer sections of Pax, back in Elpis. Dusted off and made pretty on the surface to cover the poverty lurking beneath the whitewashed walls and carefully arranged homesteads. I grew up in neighborhoods just like the one Zephyr and I now snake through in the shadows. A governmental promise of prosperity and equality that isn't truly equal.

Zephyr dips his head and turns his back as a pair of guards march down the street. I tug my cap tighter over my face. Not that I'm nearly as recognizable as him.

Zephyr has to see the cracks in this beautiful façade. The broken promises of the ruling class. It's blindingly obvious to me. The hungry. The homeless.

Baron promised me more freedom in exchange for my help, sneaking me out of the fort. I still have to report back regularly to avoid suspicion, but now I know how to get in and out. That information is worth far more than he realizes. But he was desperate. And desperate fools do foolish things.

Something foul is afoot in the Capital. Baron needs me to help ferret out answers. I warned him he may not like the truth. Unfortunately, he hitched me to the disgraced prince to help me get around without notice. Zephyr hasn't told me why his brother exiled him, but I have a few guesses. And they all lead to Paige.

While I don't mind life in the fort much—the other recruits are friendly and there's a familiar sense of comradery—I also spent a lot of time looking over my shoulder, waiting for those horrible blue eyes to find me again. I still don't know who he is; the man responsible for instructing the physician to torture me with testing

Elpis gave up two decades ago. His cold blue eyes were unforgiving when they took my finger. Then the healer patched the wound to remove my agony. As if that makes up for cutting off my pinky.

Losing my eye was far worse. No healer can cure the trauma of having my eye surgically removed while awake. I still have nightmares about it, weeks later. Those cold blue eyes, devoid of emotion. Those sharply chiseled facial features that watch my torment impassively. I shudder just thinking about it, even for a second.

Zephyr and Baron have asked me repeatedly about what happened, but I divulge nothing. Nor can I. Even giving away the one descriptor I have renders me mute. Not that it matters. I will find Blue Eyes myself and remove one of his eyes as he watches. And I won't be delicate about it. I clench my hands into fists, unable to feel the flex of my Strongarm Power in Zephyr's cloaking presence. He will have to be far away when I get my hands on Blue Eyes. I will dig my fingers into his eyes, make him feel true terror and agony.

Paige is safe for now. I need to focus on this task so I can learn enough to get into the palace to help her escape. Then we can head home. She will never return my feelings. Not if she still harbors feelings for the alcoholic prince. While she may not have seen it, I did. Even from a distance. A few stolen glances in his direction on the way to the island. And he shares those feelings, even if he is in deep denial. It's as plain as the nose on his stupid face. That moment we shared in the carriage will be our first and last. *She has terrible taste in men.*

The disgraced prince glances at my fists and grimaces. Does he know when I reach for my Power? What would he do if I punched him in that perfect nose? *I need his help. I can't afford to make an enemy of him.*

We hide together in the shadows of an alleyway. This mission has one purpose. To show Zephyr just what is hiding beneath the glittering surface of this city. Poverty. Anger. Insurrection just waiting to bubble to the surface as plainly as those men who mutinied against him. What better time to revolt against the royal family than when the young king is distracted by a bunch of pretty girls?

I don't want Zephyr to see it. I *need* him to see it, to acknowledge that all of this, his entire way of life, is corrupted at the core. A glittering crown of ash.

Because until he sees it, he won't help me get Paige out of the palace. He will continue hiding in his hole, throwing an endless pity-party.

Across the street, a man glances up and down the street before ducking through the door of a shop displaying a "closed" sign. He flips the lock behind him.

Zephyr makes some noise in his throat. We remain where we are, hiding in plain sight. As per usual, we wait in agreeable silence. I hate talking to him, listening to his whining arrogance.

The longer we wait, the more his hands twitch in his pockets. No doubt he kept flasks there everywhere he went. Ever since I showed up in Nat's apartment, I've kept him dry. He's drowning himself in alcohol. Someone had to do something and I'm not about to risk everything on one drunken idiot. *What does she see in him?*

I used to resent Paige for her perfect life built on the bones of my family. Her dad incited the revolution against the Directorate that cost my mom her Powers—and eventually her life. Dad wasn't far behind her. Grudgingly, I admitted to myself that it wasn't her fault. It isn't even her dad's fault. I can't say I would have done what he did, but I wouldn't have stood by while people were oppressed either. And he didn't fire that bullet that took Mom's Power. Letting go of my anger took time. And as I let go, I saw the girl beneath. There's something special about Paige. But just as I had to accept that what happened to my family wasn't her fault, I have to accept that she may never be interested in me the way I want her to be.

The poverty on the island isn't easy to see if you don't know what to look for; it's been masked so well by the image of a perfect city. But I grew up on the streets of Elpis without parents. I know what hungry looks like. I know what cold and lonely feels like.

No orphanage could protect me from the brutal reality. I had to protect myself, look after myself, and rise above my circumstances.

Maybe that's why I resent Zephyr so much. He had everything handed to him and would rather drink himself to an early grave than grow a pair and man up.

The women and children who loiter near our hiding place are hungry. Their eyes are sunken, faces gaunt. They huddle close to one another near the door of a shelter, asking for entry.

"All full," the man at the door says. His broad shoulders mark him out as a Strongarm like me. He crosses his arms. "Sorry, but I can't let you in."

"The children..." The woman eyes the four kids huddled close together.

The Strongarm's expression wavers. He doesn't like this any more than they do. After a glance, he mumbles something to them and disappears inside. A moment later, he emerges with a small basket of stale bread.

The woman falls over herself in gratitude. "Do you have any spare blankets?"

He grimaces and shakes his head.

"Do you see it now?" I hiss at Zephyr.

The prince's scowl deepens. "There's no reason for people to be turned out or left hungry. We—the King and his council work to ensure there is enough food on the island for everyone before sending anything to the mainland. And the shelters..." His gaze darts around at the surrounding buildings as if looking for something. But he says nothing more.

The shop bell rings across the street. A dozen men and women pour out as the shopkeeper glances in all directions through the window, flipping his sign to "open". *Nothing suspicious about that at all.* The man we watched lock the door holds something in his hand out toward a woman. She nods grimly.

"What...?" Zephyr squints toward them. "Is that...?"

The rumble of wheels along the roadway draws our attention up the street. A red and black horse-drawn carriage stops. Zephyr retreats further into the shadows of the alley. Then his lips part slightly.

"What is it?" I ask.

"Cypress." Sorrow bleeds from his voice.

The carriage door opens and a man about my age steps out, crown perched on his perfect, curly dark hair. He holds out a hand.

Then Paige emerges. Just the sight of her takes my breath away. It's the first glimpse of her I've had since they separated us months ago. Her finely made clothing is warm against the cold. She flashes Cypress a sweet smile. *That can't be real*. She wouldn't betray her people or herself like this. Paige is playing a game with the king.

Her gaze sweeps the street, calculating everything, just like we were trained to do. I fight off a smirk. *Good girl*. For a moment, I think she sees us in the alley. Her eyes lock on our location. But she isn't looking at us, she's looking at the woman and the children.

The compatriots from the shop freeze in the street, glaring at Cypress and Paige. They probably weren't expecting the King to show up as they concluded their clandestine meeting. Paige's eyes lock with one man, and they all quickly return to their work, parting ways and carrying on with their day.

This place is a powder keg.

Cypress slides his arm through Paige's, offering a charming smile as he escorts her into a shop.

Beside me, Zephyr has turned to stone, staring at the two of them. We must be far enough away that his Power doesn't touch them.

I tap his arm. "We need to go."

He breaks away as if shaking free of a spell, and we slink away through the alley.

17

GAVIN

IN MANY WAYS, I'M so much like my dad. This is *not* one of them. As Drake, Emil, Ajax, and I march toward the cells beneath the temple, I worry I'm about to be sick. Nausea curls my stomach. What will Mr. Garraty say when he sees me? Will he blame me for his imprisonment? For the death of his daughter?

It isn't that I like the Minister. He orchestrated the events leading to me being burned alive. Were it not for these Powers I still don't fully understand, I would have died a horrible death. I *did* die, but somehow came back. While I know a lot about various Powers and their potential, resurrection is not one of them. Was it a fluke? Was it even my doing at all? What if an acolyte did it to me with no one noticing?

Drake continues casting furtive glances in my direction as we follow Ajax's lead. What is he thinking? Is he worried about the situation or about me? It's impossible to say.

Two acolytes push off from the wall beside a steel door, hastily coming to attention when they see our meager party approach. Ajax gives a quick command, and they open the door without hesitation, holding it for the four of us. When I pass through, they dip their heads.

Ajax waits for us to all enter the bright white hallway, then he nods toward a cell at the far end. "That's him." He shifts feet, massive shoulders hunched over. "If you don't mind, sire, I would prefer waiting here while you speak with him."

No! I want him there with me. I need all the emotional support I can get, and the Minister terrifies me. Instead of insisting Ajax come along, I nod and swallow thickly.

"Don't open the door, or he will be able to reach his gift again," Ajax warns.

Again, I nod. How strong is the Power stone holding him captive? It can't be as strong as the one he used on me, or he would be dead by now.

Drake and Emil wait for me to steel myself, following my lead. I would much prefer it if Emil took charge of this situation. Instead, he offers a silent stoicism.

Emil doesn't treat me like other Havenites—mostly because he isn't a fervent believer in the *Book of the Prophet*. He still defers to me in most situations. His faith in me is based on respect and not a religious ideology. It's a distinction I appreciate.

My feet feel like lead bricks as I shuffle toward the door at the end of the hall. Each scuff of my boots across the smooth stone floor matches the hammering of my heartbeat—quick, clipped, and erratic. Sweat beads on my forehead.

If I were like Dad, this wouldn't scare me. I would stroll up as casual as an ordinary day, engage in conversation, dig out the information I need, and never once let him crawl under my skin. But I'm not like Dad. Not in this. Everyone tells me to talk to the Minister, but I don't know what to ask him. What information do I even need or want from him? Would anything he tells me be true?

Trying to draw on strength like my sister, determination like my mother, and confidence like my father, I straighten and stuff my hands in my pockets. Dad does this often to make himself appear casual and non-confrontational. Hopefully, the same trick works for me.

"At long last, the Savior has graced me with his divine presence," Mr. Garraty says. His voice is sharp as a knife, but there is a weakness in it that tells me the Power stone affects him.

I pause at the thick window of his cell. Somehow, they designed these cells to contain the strength of the Power stone inside, without allowing it to leak out. The man perched on the cot is a shadow of the man I remember. His hair has thinned, complexion paled. He lost weight, as well, even though I know the acolytes feed him.

Ajax informed me that, for the first few days after his confinement, the Minister had refused food. Hunger broke him eventually, but even then, he didn't eat much. It shows on the sunken cheeks and pronounced collarbone. I suppress a shudder and force myself to meet his gaze.

Despite the weak appearance, hatred burns in his brown eyes. Were there no walls between us, he would attack. How would he try to kill me? With his hands around my neck? By gouging out my eyes? Or by trying to scoop out sections of my mind with his Influence? I fight off a shudder and raise my chin.

"You forced this on me, Charles," I say. Using his first name is a conscious decision, a way to remove his titles and authority. I need every edge I can get in this conversation. "I didn't want it, and you knew that. But you set me up, and when I didn't fall into place as you wanted, you ripped me down and forced my hand. We are where we are because of *your* choices. Not mine."

His lip twitches. For a moment, he bares his teeth. I can't help wondering how thick the glass is, how breakable. Could he break it if he were determined enough?

"False Idol," he hisses. He stalks toward the window like a starved mountain cat, emaciated and eager for a meal to sate his appetite. "The End of Times, verse seven. 'Loved ones will be broken, their faith deceived by dark spirits'."

Mrs. Garraty said those same words to me, accusing me of being a dark spirit. It gave me chills then, but it no longer does. I refuse to take the blame for their actions. This is their faith. They can make of it what they will. And I will use their own arguments against them if need be.

"'Upon his rise from death, the proof of his place will be ir- refutable'," I say, quoting a verse from his precious book back at him. "You condemned me, burned me, and watched me rise. Yet still you deny the words from your own faith. I came asking for peace, and you rejected it. Instead, you allowed your own evil desires to overtake reason. I know of men like you, Charles. You crave power and will go to any length to hold it. My dad fought men like you when he was my age. And he won."

Charles sneers at me. "Is that a threat? My daughter is dead because of you!"

Drake tenses at my side. Pippen was his best friend when I arrived. He saw what her father did to her. Does the Minister's accusation anger Drake?

"I tried to save her." My eyes burn, but I won't let him see me cry. I carry the blame for Pippen's death. But only because I couldn't stop them from killing her. What happened to her isn't my fault. I'm coming to terms with this, and I knew Charles would blame me. The only fault was my inability to save her *before* they killed her.

"We have a few questions for you, Charles," Emil interrupts our quarrel. Can he tell how much the Minister's words hurt me?

"I don't answer to the likes of you," Charles snaps.

Emil clenches his jaw and steps close to the glass. I notice his clenched fist. They must have some feud that goes beyond my days here, some dark secret between the two of them. Perhaps it has to do with Charles forcing Emil to live among the acolytes for two years instead of letting him search for his sister.

I can understand Emil's anger, but I don't need to search. I know where Paige is, and I can't wait to reunite with her. But I can't leave this mess behind when it's my fault. I have to help them fix it, *then* I will leave.

"It's fine, Emil," I say, hoping to sound patient, or even cunning. I don't know if it works. "Charles is having a hard time coming to terms with his predicament, so he will blame anyone but himself. Even if it was a mess of his own making." I don't break my gaze on the Minister as I say this.

His brown eyes flick from Emil to me with just as much fury. Something in Charles snaps and he lunges at the window, throwing a fist into it. I jump back, startled by the sudden outburst.

The corner of Charles' mouth twitches up in pleasure. He wanted a reaction and received his reward. I curse myself for the show of weakness. No one else in my family would have moved. They would have been secure in their position and their safety. *Why can't I be like them?*

I pause to collect myself. "The Haven is preparing for elections to fill the open Elder seats." I curse the tremble in my voice. "Your help could go a long way to improve this situation." I nod at his cell. "What can you tell me about the use of Power stones in the Haven?"

Charles' frail shoulders rise and fall with angry breaths. He no longer looks like a starving mountain cat, but a raging bull. His pointed nostrils flare with each exhale. His brown eyes study me, calculating the situation, sizing me up. The silence becomes so long and deep I doubt he will say a word to me. I do my best not to flinch under his glare, to hold my ground even if my insides are chewing me up from the inside out.

Drake turns his back on the Minister and leans close to my shoulder. "Gavin, let's just go. He won't tell us anything."

I step around Drake, pulling a sweaty palm from my pocket and placing it against the glass. Emil hisses a warning, but this won't change anything. It won't give Charles access to his Power or let him harm me. "Charles, I will make a deal with you."

"Don't," Emil growls, edging closer to me.

I ignore him. "Your wife is desperate to see you. She's overwhelmed with grief over Pippen—"

"That's your fault."

I continue as if he said nothing, even if the words cut at my heart, "—and she needs her husband. Answer my questions, help me, and I will have the acolytes bring her down to visit."

Something flashes in Charles' eyes. Grief? Fear? Sorrow? I can't be sure, but it isn't a positive emotion. I know that much for certain. I've struck a nerve.

"I've heard the acolytes at the end of the hall talking about you," Charles says, his voice hushed. "You refuse your Call and it worries them. They question your true divinity. How long, I wonder, before they believe you are a false Idol? How long before the acolytes and the Elders rise against you again?"

A chill rolls down my spine. While I don't see myself as divine, I know that the faith these acolytes and Havenites have in me centers on their beliefs. I hate to admit that Charles might be right. I cannot hide from this forever or I could end up on that wheel, burned alive once more. Or worse, they will slip in and rid themselves of me while I sleep.

I press on, hoping to force something useful from Charles before my fraying nerves consume me and I run. "The Power stones protect the Haven from outside invasion. They shelter the people from the Kingdom and the acolytes from service to the Kingdom. But how does it work?"

Charles cocks his head, pressing his palm against the glass opposite mine, as if he wants to scratch my skin. "Naïve boy. You don't have the *stomach* to do what needs done for these people."

I swallow hard. "Try me." My voice gives away my fear, cracking over the words. A single, massive Power stone fueled the barrier around Elpis. To keep it going, it slowly leeched off the Powers of those around it. But to truly fuel the power of the stone, people had to sacrifice their Powers to it. My stomach twists in sickening knots, worried that he is about to tell me the same thing.

"No. I think you should go see for yourself why those stones are necessary, what they do for the Haven."

Charles slides a finger so hard along the glass it squeaks beneath his reddened fingertip. The knuckle turns pale white. I follow the movement, curious.

"He's toying with us," Emil grunts. "The stone has driven him mad."

But it isn't madness. Not completely. Charles' movements aren't random.

They're a map.

I pull out the notebook folded in half in my back pocket and quickly sketch out what he has drawn, showing it to Emil.

Charles laughs. "Let's see how you do when the truth of the Haven confronts you."

The words turn my spine to ice.

Drake huddles close to the map, studying it with Emil.

"'When the end comes again, there will be earthquakes, famine, war, and all forms of natural disaster'," Charles says, speaking loud and clear, as if giving a sermon in the temple. "'Brother will betray brother. Greed, pride, vanity, and lust will consume the weak'."

Drake gasps behind me. I glance at him, noting the flush on his face. Curious.

"'Children will defy or betray their parents. Some will be put to death'." Charles' voice reaches a crescendo. "'Trucebreakers will come. Kingdoms will clash. Traitors, tyrants, and treason will cast doubt on the hearts and minds of all. Only those of faith will survive!'"

While the words rattle Drake to his core, and Emil grumbles about madness, I recall the verses from the section of the *Book of the Prophet* titled "The End."

Then I peer once more at the map I've sketched in my notebook.

18

PAIGE

THE CLOSER I LOOK, the more I can see the cracks in this perfect city. The people aren't intimidated by the king, and not all the distance is out of respect. A few people keep their gazes averted; faces set in grim lines. *They* aren't happy about something, and it's easy enough to deduce it is the royal family.

Some girls point at the two of us and whisper or giggle to one another. I step closer to King Cypress.

"How many other girls have you brought to town?" I ask.

He slides his arm through mine and escorts me to a door. "None."

I stumble a step. Not *any* of the other girls? I don't understand him at all. He ignores me—for reasons I understand—then the first time he takes me out he is showing me off to the people? The truth smacks me in the face with certainty. He agreed with Prince Dominic. If it's the strength of a girl's Power he's after, my Power makes me his obvious choice.

But I don't want him.

Zephyr's smirk flashes through my mind. I shake it off. I don't want him either. I don't need a man to make me whole. Still, I sense the familiar push and pull of Zephyr's Power. *Wishful thinking.* I check the street but don't see him anywhere. Maybe he lives in a nearby apartment for now.

King Cypress tightens his grip when I stumble, catching me easily. A guard holds the shop door open for us.

The window boasts fudge in elegant painted lettering. The moment we step inside, the scent of vanilla punches my senses. It's so sweet and strong I can taste it already.

King Cypress leads us to the counter, where a portly woman bows eagerly and motions to a tray atop the counter. *No, not eagerly. She's anxious.*

He's oblivious to her anxiety as he encourages me to choose my favorite flavors—as many as I want. The two of us sample Red Velvet, Rocky Road, gingerbread, sugar cookie, and a dozen more. In the end, we walk out with two pounds of a variety of my favorites. The shopkeeper's shoulders sag in relief as we turn to the door with our prizes.

Next door is a specialty chocolate shop, where the process begins anew. He's really leaning into my sweet tooth weakness.

With our sweets packaged, we continue the tour of the island. Past more shops. Through a park beside the docks. I make a mental map of everything.

King Cypress leans across me, pointing up hill at a white wall with matching buildings and towers. "That's the fort where we train our recruits."

I speak without thinking. "Is that where Easton is?"

He drops his arm and sinks back so suddenly that it brings me to my senses.

I shift to peer at him, daring to take his hand. "I didn't mean to upset you, Cypress."

He draws in a breath so deep in makes his chest puff, then he releases it in a huff. "He's the recruit who volunteered with you."

I nod. I've just put my foot in a mess again. He must know at least as much as Zephyr. And Zephyr definitely knows about my make-out session with Easton.

"Yes, he is there." King Cypress turns his attention out the far window. "The recruits all live in a barracks together during training. Baron has taken a special interest in him lately."

His thumb absently caresses my hand. His grip tightens a touch.

"Zephyr told you." I don't bother asking. It's obvious.

"He did. I shouldn't be surprised that so many suitors are interested in you, Lady Paige."

I bark out a laugh, then slap my free hand over my mouth.

He turns his head toward me, hurt in his eyes. "I'm glad I amuse you." But there's no humor in his tone.

"Sorry. I just..." I turn fully on the bench to face him, sliding an arm across the back of the bench. I want so much to slide my fingers into his curly hair. Not intimately, but out of curiosity. It looks so soft. Besides, a little seduction to soften him up wouldn't be so terrible. It's what Bella wants, anyway. Does he know that, though? How much did Prince Dominic tell him? I should ask.

"I don't have suitors," I say. "What happened with Easton wasn't based on genuine feelings. More like...like an act of desperation. They locked me in that carriage with him, unsure if or when I would ever see my family again, knowing he chose to be there to help me. I just needed that closeness at that moment. Believe me, there is nothing between the two of us."

He studies me in silence. "Then why ask about him?"

"Because we have worked together for years. I may not have a romantic interest in him, but I still care about his welfare. He's my only connection to..." I pause, peering down at our hands as my palms sweat. "...to home." It's the most honest I can dare to be with him.

King Cypress bites his lip, then slides his arm around my shoulders and pulls me against his side. "I sensed the good in you." His breath ruffles my hair as he leans his cheek against the side of my head. "I will talk to Baron about him."

I lean my head on his shoulder. King Cypress is not at all what I expected. Charming, yes. But also open and vulnerable. And I'm using him.

We remain snuggled close to one another as the carriage returns to the palace. The sun sets quickly and by the time we reach the red carpet, it's dark. The butler, Alfred, opens the door and reassures me that my purchases will be sent to my room.

"I have one more thing to show you." King Cypress takes my hand and guides me upstairs.

Up one flight, then another. By the time we round the fourth floor, I realize where we are going.

The same room where he and Prince Dominic were talking about Layla and me.

"Here we are." He opens the door and bows, motioning me inside.

At sunset, the bar has an ethereal glow. The white walls, rails, and pillars glow in the fading sunlight. The blue carpet and benches are deeper, like the night sky.

They draped one table in a navy-blue cloth. A single candle flickers in the center, just like all the other tables. I slip out of my coat and wrap it over a nearby chair. King Cypress motions for me to take a seat on the bench.

Once we are settled, a host of servants enters with covered plates. They pour a glass of white wine for each of us, then set the bottle in a bucket on ice and disappear. I notice it's the same wine we shared when we first met in the library months ago. The King didn't seem to miss any details, and there's no doubt that the wine choice was his. No one else knows about that night.

The food smells amazing. Citrus herb-crusted whitefish with the smoothest mashed potatoes I've ever seen in my life. King Cypress continues telling stories about his childhood. His eyes brighten as he recalls the memories, but each time he mentions Zephyr, sadness presses down on his features. As he talks about his older brother, Alric the Fourth, a deep grief settles over him. The animation that had accompanied his stories becomes more somber.

I reach across the table and brush my thumb over his hand. "I can't even imagine what all of this must have been like for you. Losing someone so dear to you and being forced into this new position." I shake my head, thinking of Gavin. "If anything happened to my brother, it would devastate me."

Tears unexpectedly well in my eyes. My hand trembles as I consider that something could have happened to him. We haven't Dreamed together in some time now. What is he doing? Is he still okay? As the ache in my chest intensifies, my chin quivers. My vision blurs. Hoping to cover the sudden tears, I bury my face in my hands and focus on taking slow, careful breaths.

King Cypress slides on the bench beside me and wraps his arms around me. "You miss your family."

"I do," I moan pitifully into my hands. "And I don't know if I will ever see them again."

King Cypress eases my hands away from my face. He hooks a finger under my chin and tilts my face up to his. I should hate him. The entire Tribute pageant is the reason I am here. It's the reason his men attacked us. It's why my brother and I were separated. But seeing my sorrow reflecting from his own eyes makes it impossible to be angry with him.

Somehow, in just one evening, King Cypress wormed his way into my heart. It's not love. Nowhere near that. But I can't deny I feel some affection for him.

"No matter what happens, I'll help you reconnect with your family," he whispers. He strokes my cheek, then tucks my hair behind my ear.

He agreed! Overwhelmed with joy, I grip his arms. "Really?"

"I give you my word."

The hairs on my neck rise at the whispered vow.

He smells of fragrant spices, nothing at all like Zephyr. I nearly pull away at the ruinous thought. He just agreed, he promised. If I'm not careful, I could destroy this chance.

Any means necessary, Bella's voice croons in my mind. I need to secure Easton's freedom as well, but pushing that far tonight seems ill-advised. I don't want to press my luck.

He slides his hand along my cheek, then his thumb touches my lips. "Can we ignore that first horrible kiss and try over again?"

No. No. No! But what happens if I tell him no? What will happen to Easton if I say no and he pulls away? I already know how this will go, but I can't refuse. Not if there's a chance it could help Easton. I need to fake it for now, at least.

Despite my mind screaming refusal, I nod stiffly. It's just one kiss. One kiss to protect Easton. One kiss to secure our freedom. A fair trade.

King Cypress leans in tentatively, then decisively presses his lips to my own. He tastes like he smells, like spices and wine. He isn't hesitant, nor is he anywhere near as aggressive as Easton had been. It's slow. Deliberate. His lips aren't just tasting. They're exploring. And I let him. I return the kiss, needing him to at least feel a spark of hope for what could be. One kiss for the night. Then another day, I can vie for Easton's freedom as well.

When he pulls back, my heart is hammering against my ribs. Not from excitement, but fear that he knows the truth. Nothing happened for me. No sparks. No stirrings of any form of desire. But could he tell?

"Tell me honestly, Paige," he whispers. "Is there a chance you might want me as much as I want you?"

No. *Play the game, Paige.*

I swallow thickly. King Cypress has been kind and honorable so far. I hate using him. He deserves my honesty. But if I give him the truth, could it hurt Easton's chance at returning home with me? Bella's warning resounds in my mind. I can't tell him the truth, but I can't give in either. The agony of this makes me want to scream.

King Cypress reads something from my hesitation. He pulls back, a sad smile on his face. "Nothing still." He isn't asking. He already knows. King Cypress withdraws his arms, sliding away on the bench. "Did you feel something with him?"

My heart twists, and I open my mouth instinctively to tell him no, because I'm terrified of what he will do if I say yes. But nothing comes past my lips.

He nods sadly, then rises, taking his jacket off the nearby chair.

Terror grips me. I can't let him leave. He just promised to help me get home, no matter what. Will he rescind that offer? Have I ruined Easton's chances? I reach out to him, but the table isn't the only barrier between us.

"Goodnight, Paige."

19

ZEPHYR

P^{AIGE.}

Paige.

The feel of her is as intimate and familiar as my own flesh. I knew she was in the carriage before she even stepped out. Did she sense me nearby as well? The thought of her and Cypress together has sent me into a tailspin.

I storm through the door, shucking off my coat and tossing it aside upon entering the small apartment Baron rented for Easton and me. Nat deserved his privacy and life back, and if we need him on an inside circle sometime down the line, association with me could hinder that.

My hands shake like mad. I stomp toward the kitchen and rummage through cupboards. There must be a stray bit of alcohol here somewhere. I had tucked an emergency stash of shot bottles behind dishes, inside unused pans.

But there's nothing. All of them are gone. The familiar, overwhelming sense of thirst accompanied by a dry throat seizes me.

"You're welcome," Eason snaps.

I round on him, teeth bared, ready to beat *something* into submission. "You dumped all of it?"

"Every. Last. Drop." He enunciates each word sharply, like deadly knives.

"I hate you," I mutter under my breath, sinking to the floor and pressing my back to the cupboard doors.

"I don't care." Easton drops on the sofa. It creaks under the density of his body. He leans his head back, running a hand through his short, dark hair.

"Do you think she's happy?" I can't mask the agony in my heart.

Easton snorts. "No, it's an act. No doubt she is trying to drag some sort of promise from your king to return her home. Your king is a means to an end. Nothing else."

I consider this. Easton is probably right. Paige has never masked her desire to go home. *Poor Cypress.* But how far will she go to get her way?

"Forget about Paige," Easton huffs. "You saw what I was trying to tell you, right?"

I wish I could forget about Paige. But forgetting her is like forgetting to breathe. Impossible. And deadly. "What were those people doing in that shop? They didn't look happy with Cy when he and Paige emerged from the carriage."

Easton shifts forward on the couch, hands clasped together over his knees. Urgency bleeds off him like a personal wound. "They are fed up, Zephyr. Hungry. Cold. Ignored or suppressed by their leaders."

It doesn't make sense though. We have shelters for the homeless. Food reserves stored up to distribute. Job fairs to help people improve their lot in life. "Are the shelters all full?" I mean the question for me, but Easton latches on.

"Shelters aren't the same thing as a home, believe me. A roof can only protect you from the cold, but it can't do any more than that. These people need a better king. One who really sees them. And clearly, your brother isn't who they're looking for. You saw the way those men glared at him, didn't you?"

Brother. That word opens a wound that will never heal. "He's not my brother," I mumble.

If Easton heard me, he gives no indication. Instead, an air of excitement pulses around him. His magic pokes at mine like an elbow in the ribs.

"These people are preparing to force change," he announces.

"Insurrection..." I say, remembering what he told Baron.

Easton nods.

Alcohol would help me in so many ways. Easton assumes it dulls my wits, but it dulls my pain and sharpens my wits. Without a drop to drink, I flounder like a beached fish gasping for air. The shake in my hands is so bad I rub them together in a lame attempt at regaining control.

Only one explanation for the hungry families makes sense. Wherever the shipments to the mainland have vanished to, the supplies for the lower-class islanders have gone as well. This is no minor operation, but I can't wrap my head around the details when all my mind wants to focus on is a drink.

Drink. Drink.

I close my eyes and concentrate on my breathing. Instead, a vision of Paige wrapped around Cypress clouds my mind. Fury and jealousy pulse like fire through my nerves. My heart hammers against my ribs, a rhythm calling out to her.

"You may not like it, but having been expelled from the royal family and exiled from the island, you've become a potential ally to the insurgents." The sound of Easton's voice grates my nerves.

I snap my eyes open and glare at him. "I won't help them overthrow Cypress." Regardless of our differences, I love him like a brother. My situation results from my own stupidity.

"You could infiltrate their ranks, learn more about their goals, and help prevent a massacre."

Massacre? "It won't get as bad as that."

A haunted cloud looms over Easton. He eyes his hands, deep in thought, then raises that one hard eye to mine. "I know what revolution does. It ends in lives lost. There's no way to avoid it. Unless you stop them."

How does he know all of this? The somberness surrounding him, the slope of his broad shoulders, makes it seem as if he has suffered through something similar. "Did this happen in your community?"

"Yes." The word is strangled from his lips. "Before I was born. But it cost my mother her life. Paige's dad led the charge. They call him a hero now. The man who led the people to freedom from oppression to equality. But I grew up without my parents. I've seen the cost of insurrection firsthand. Equality isn't truly equal."

Paige's father was the leader of a *revolution*? I'm uncertain why that surprises me. After knowing her as I have, seeing that open defiance burning in her eyes, her roots should be clear.

Maybe Easton is right. Maybe if I can worm my way into the inner circle of this insurrection he believes looms on the horizon, I can stop it. I can learn who is pulling the strings.

Because someone must be. The mutiny. The missing supplies. The sheer scale of it all... If Baron isn't the one pulling the strings, who is?

I have to find out.

20

GAVIN

A JAX GUIDES US TO our destination without the need of a map. He leads our quartet with purpose and pride in each step, as if he holds an honored position. Perhaps to the acolytes, he does. Drake and Emil trail close behind us. Emil's boots hammer against the tiles like he's ready to destroy this entire temple.

That is not my intention. I promised Drake I wouldn't try to turn him away from his faith. Even now, after all that's happened, he clings to it. Will the truth ahead of us break that faith? Perhaps that's why he drags his heels with each step.

Most of the younger acolytes are in their afternoon courses. We pass the classrooms where they study under the direction of the twenty-year-olds. Few notice our passing, except for a little girl with wide-set eyes and big teeth. As we pass her classroom, some unexplainable force draws her gaze toward us. Her eyes fall on me and widen. Her thin lips part, exposing those large teeth. She doesn't even blink as we pass the window, tracking my movements in shock. Or I assume it's shock. When we pass out of sight, I swear I can still feel her eyes on me, as if she can see me through the walls. *Can she?*

I follow the map in my notebook as Ajax turns a corner and leads us down a flight of stairs. We're close now.

After a quick glance ahead once we reach the bottom of the steps, I add a few notes to my map. Where I recall entering the temple in relation to where we are now. Where the *Book of the Prophet* is, and the prison cells, classrooms, dorms. As I make the notes, I recognize a pattern in the chaos of the Haven hallways above us.

The Haven was built directly over the top of these acolyte sub-levels. While at first, I couldn't understand why a planner would set up the halls far above our heads the way they did, now it becomes obvious. Power and water. The Elders don't control these necessary resources. Acolytes do. They directly linked the electrical grid and water treatment above to the acolyte halls below. Everything is set up brilliantly to control the Havenite resources.

I reach a hand toward the floor, twitching my fingers to feel the electrical pulses. The electrical is clean, free of obstructions from this deep level all the way up. They aren't sent through the walls in conduit tubes, as is so often done in construction in Elpis. These are wires veined into the walls themselves. Why does the Haven above struggle when the acolytes can perform whatever skills these people need? Why don't they use the acolytes to expand?

Power. Anger burns inside my gut. It always comes down to the same thing. The Elders hold power over Havenites if the people depend on them. Control, too. By controlling the population, they can hold on to their power. It turns my stomach, seeing just how much the Elders—the Minister—keeps from the people.

Ajax stops at the end of the long hallway. I nearly bump into his shoulder, lost in my own thoughts. He motions to a set of large doors. I touch the metal, reaching out with my Powers, and sense the tungsten. It isn't just metal. The doors are reinforced with Powers to be unbreakable. Why would they need unbreakable doors?

To hide their secrets from outsiders.

Beside the door, a keypad hums with electrical life.

"Have you been here, Ajax?" I ask, stalling to avoid the inevitable a few moments longer.

He nods. "Many of us have."

"Then why the locks?"

He shifts uncomfortably. "While many of us have spent time behind these doors, they grant access in and out to only a few. It protects those inside."

I'm getting sick of that answer. It's evasive, textbook avoidance, or blind ignorance to the truth.

"Why are many of you sent in here?" Emil asks, eyeing the doors with intense suspicion. He shifts closer to me and hisses in my ear. "I've seen this door before. I told you acolytes disappeared behind it. I didn't see some again."

Ajax frowns. Did he hear Emil's warning? "I don't understand why it matters."

"It doesn't," I say quickly, shooting a warning look at Emil. *Yet.* We can't afford to give away too much until we know what's behind these doors.

"Without the code, we can't go further," Ajax says. "They give only the Chosen access."

"Chosen?" Drake's brows lift.

"Those the Minister selects to help manage the activities beyond," Ajax says, as if it should be obvious.

Activities... That word unsettles me for reasons I can't pinpoint. Drake senses it, too. He shifts feet, arms crossed defensively.

I lick my lips and raise my trembling hand to the keypad. Charles' final rants ring in my head, and I recall the verse numbers from his *Book* quotations. 6-8-2-4.

I punch in the numbers, holding my breath. The keypad beeps, then turns green. The lock on the door clicks.

"How did you do that?" Drake asks.

"Charles told me the code." Did he mean to? He must have. He wants whatever hides behind these doors to make me give up the fight, tuck tail, and run. Which means it can't be good.

Ajax's jaw slackens as Emil eagerly moves forward to thrust the door open. He steps in, followed by Drake. Ajax shakes his head in awe at me. "You will never cease to amaze me, sire."

"I hope I do, actually." I edge around his massive body.

My gaze sweeps through the small lobby. Clean white walls and polished tile. Everything looks and smells sterile. Hallways branch off the small space—one on each wall—and several office doors sit ajar.

I edge further inside, curious about this new place, when a woman steps out of one office and gapes at the four of us. She is older than any of the acolytes by far, with long gray hair drawn back in a tight braid that hangs all the way down her back. Her cool eyes match her hair, but cold and unforgiving.

"May I help you? This area is restricted."

"Not anymore," Emil says flatly. He moves toward one hallway, but a man roughly the same age steps out of another office and cuts him off.

The elderly woman eyes Ajax, and her puckered lips drawn into a tight line. "Ajax, I never thought you would return here. Why do you bring outsiders?"

"He is not an outsider, Madame Christiane," Ajax says. I wince before he even says the next words, knowing what he is about to reveal. "He is the Idol of Creation."

Madame Christiane eyes me just as critically as my teachers used to do in high school—like I think more of myself than I should. I don't. "I saw what he did."

Ajax beams. "Then you know."

"I know nothing," she says sharply, pivoting to face him, hands on her plump hips. "And neither do you."

My heart sinks. Not because I want the people to see me as their savior, but because her words remind me of Charles' warning. Some acolytes doubt me. Worse than the doubt is the fear of what that doubt will drive them to do to me.

"We all did," the man blocking Emil says. There's a sharpness in his tone that sends a chill down my spine.

"The Minister sent me," I say. Something about this woman makes me uneasy all the way to my marrow. "What is this place?"

"If he sent you, then you should know that already," Madame Christiane responds tersely. "Why are you here?"

Sensing my unease, Drake steps up beside me and meets Madame Christiane's gaze without flinching. "To learn the truth so that we can appropriately help the Haven." His gaze flicks at me as if seeking confirmation. He's spit balling.

She shoots a stern glare Drake's way. He swallows, but doesn't back down. I can't help admiring his determination and strength. "I found it interesting that he sent you when we weren't allowed to speak with him since the incident." Her lips curl around the last word with distaste. She already doubts me. I wouldn't care, except she terrifies me.

Her sharp eyes turn to me, calculating this situation. What does she think she sees in me? I try my best to appear confident, but I'm certain it fails. Confidence has never really been my strength.

When she breaks her silence, she doesn't break her stare, calling to the man over her shoulder. "His Grace would like to know what we do here, Brother Gram. Please give our esteemed visitor a tour of your sector, will you?"

It requires all my willpower not to wince when she calls me *His Grace*.

Brother Gram raises a brow but doesn't question her orders—and there is no doubt it was an order—as he dips his head and motions to the hallway to his left. "Of course, Madame. It would be my honor to show him. Though many of the acolytes are currently engaged in their required activities."

"If he wants to see, show him."

Something about that statement doesn't settle well with me. Especially not after I watch Ajax pale and shuffle a step away from the hallway. His gaze meets mine for a second before dropping to the floor. What does he know about what we are going to encounter here? Why didn't he tell me already?

"Let's go, Gavin," Drake mutters, so only I can hear. He nudges my shoulder subtly to break me from my trance.

I swallow and step forward, following Brother Gram into the hallway. The other three fall in behind us with Ajax trundling at the rear of the group. Emil mutters to himself, but I can't make out anything he is saying. Drake remains perfectly silent, as if he's wrapped in a cocoon of his Silence Power. When I glance back at him, he gives me an encouraging nod, but his eyes are stormy.

The hallway is short, then turns abruptly to the right where a series of doors lie closed tight.

"What activities are the acolytes participating in behind these doors?" I ask.

"I can show you," Brother Gram says. "It's unorthodox to interrupt. We find that privacy is more conducive to success, and it helps the acolytes become more comfortable performing the required activities. We handpicked partners based on gifts and their strength."

"Partners?" Drake asks. I glance back at him, and his face has gone pale. *Why?*

Brother Gram stops outside one door for only a moment before opening it.

Inside, a young couple sit on opposite sides of their cramped apartment. They both jump to their feet the moment they see Brother Gram. The girl flushes a brilliant shade of crimson. The boy works his jaw like he wants to say something but can't get any words out.

Brother Gram frowns at the two of them. "What are you doing?" He glances at his watch. "We discussed optimal propagation times based on your cycle. You are within your window."

The girl's eyes widen. She shakes, eyeing the boy as if asking for help. He offers none.

Emil curses, not bothering to hide his anger. "I knew it."

I'm ashamed to admit I take too long to catch on. Everyone else already knows. By the time the pieces click into place, all four of them are staring at me, expecting me to say something. Partners. Propagation. Her cycle. My knees weaken. *"Between the age of sixteen and eighteen, they select acolytes for a secret program,"* Emil hinted at this, but I never guessed the extent of what it could truly mean. Brother Gram had no problem walking in when they were supposed to be mating...

I have no clue how to respond. It's horrible and wrong. They wanted to shock me by witnessing it in action. My gut writhes.

"You did this?" I ask Ajax, my voice just as weak as my knees.

"It's an honor to be chosen for this program," Ajax says, but he doesn't sound honored.

"Honor..." *How brainwashed* are *the acolytes?* My gaze falls on the girl hugging herself and visibly shaking. It makes me think of Paige stuck in that pageant in the Kingdom, forced to perform for the king. What would I do if I found out they forced my sister into this sort of act?

Fury replaces my shock, melting away the inability to move or speak. It pulses through my veins. Without meaning to, I clench my hands into fists.

"Yes, Ajax was very productive during his time in the program," Brother Gram says, oblivious to my growing rage. "I was sad to see him leave."

I flick my glare at Ajax. But his discomfort has nothing to do with me. He didn't enjoy his time here.

I stride deeper into the small apartment. There is no privacy anywhere but the tiny bathroom. No kitchen. A two-person sofa and a two-person table occupy one side of the room. A full-size bed consumes the rest of the space. The boy lingers near the bed, watching me as I move toward the girl.

She flinches, eyes wide as she looks to Brother Gram for guidance.

"What's your name?" I ask her, using a far gentler voice than I have with anyone else here. The poor thing is terrified of all of this. Even I can see that.

"P-penny," she says. The stuttered letter "p" makes my heart stop, thinking once more of my sister.

I hold out a hand to her, allowing her to move toward me like I watched Paige do with the doe our team encountered in the field. "It's alright. I promise not to hurt you."

Her clammy hand slides into mine. It trembles terribly. I encourage her to settle back in her seat at the table. Penny obeys, once more seeking some approval from Brother Gram. I don't bother looking back. The last thing my anger can do right now is to see his expression.

"Penny, forget him. Forget all of them." I kneel, cradling her hand in my own. I lower my voice for only her. "Have they hurt you?"

She swallows. "It's an honor to be chosen for—"

"I'm not asking what they want to hear," I whisper. "I'm asking how you are feeling."

Tears brim in her eyes. Her voice is so weak I can barely hear her response. "I don't like him. He calls me ugly and tells me he thought it would be an honor to participate in the program, but had he known he would be stuck with me..." Her tears spill out. "I didn't have a choice. He makes me cover my face."

I pat her hand, sympathy for this poor girl making my heart ache. It fuels my anger. Penny isn't the most attractive girl, but she isn't *so* bad, I suppose. I would put her on the same level with Pippen. Plain, but pretty in her own way. That this boy treated her so poorly increases my adrenaline. My Powers pulse with wild life, eager to let loose. "You don't need to worry about him any longer, Penny."

"But I've not been successful," she whimpers. Then she breaks down in sobs, as if her failure has finally broken her.

Drake steps up beside me. Our eyes meet and I see the same anger—and disbelief—in his dark eyes. The storm has become a tempest. "It's okay," he says, kneeling beside me. He pulls her into a gentle hug.

I rise slowly, turning toward the boy. His sharp features become more pronounced as he senses my anger. Were it not for his ugly words and horrible treatment of Penny, I might have considered him attractive. His ugly words and horrible treatment of Penny revealed the monster beneath his handsome surface.

All the bullies from high school are him. The ugly words. The abuse. The self-importance. My jaw twitches as I stalk closer.

He senses something in me and shuffles backward, but his legs hit the edge of the bed and he sinks down. I tower over him, hands clenched into fists at my sides. I'm not sure how to deal with this. What sort of punishment is appropriate in this situation?

"You are not *entitled* to anything," I growl. Maybe I can remove his Power. Is that even possible? Without a Power, he isn't worthy of the acolyte program. I raise my hand, staring at the pulsing blue energy. When did I call on that?

My mouth goes dry. *Many of the acolytes have been here.* That's what Ajax said. Emil told me that acolytes disappeared for a special program between the ages of sixteen and eighteen. No one could tell me how they selected the babies for the acolyte program. *No one* would *tell me*, I correct myself.

"They lied to me," I mumble to myself. The Elders said the families gave up their children, but Ajax and Viola couldn't tell me at what age or where the children actually came from. Or they wouldn't.

They knew and so did the Elders.

The temple is corrupt to its core. Is it my duty to take that power away? To change this system? Someone has to do something. The blue Power pulses with excited life in my hand, and somehow, I just sense what to do with it...how to use it.

The boy shuffles back across the bed as I reach out for him.

"What are you doing?" Brother Gram asks. Even his voice shakes.

Words that Havenites said to me rise to the surface. "Give strength to the weak, and power to the deserving."

"No," the boy whimpers as I lay a hand on his ankle.

I feel it in him. The Power raging in desperate life. Telepathy. Realizing what his Power is only fuels my anger toward him. He *knew* how his words hurt Penny, as well as his actions. But he did it anyway. His back arches in a silent scream as I pull on an invisible thread wrapped around his mind.

"Gavin..." Drake's voice is muffled by the hammer of my pulse in my ears and the Powers surging through me. "Stop." He appears beside me, resting a hand on my shoulder. Sorrow shines in his eyes. Sorrow and fear. "This isn't you."

I hesitate with the edge of the boy's Power in my grasp like a thread tied to the end of my finger ready for me to unravel the weave. The fear stabs my heart. He's afraid of me, of what I'm capable of. I ease back, holding his gaze, tethered to it like a lifeline.

Drake eases the hand I had used on the boy away, wrapping it in his hands. "This isn't his fault." He swallows hard and tears shimmer in his eyes. This revelation has shaken his faith.

My Power wanes in his hand, then winks out, leaving me cold and terrified of myself—of what I was willing to do and what this place is turning me into. I was ready to take away his Power. "I have tolerated a lot of things since arriving here, but this is too much. It goes against everything *I* believe in."

Charles' mocking laughter haunts me. *Let's see how you do when confronted with the truth of the Haven.*

"I know," Drake says softly.

"It has to end, Drake. This is wrong." My voice trembles.

"I know."

When I snuck into the temple to read the *Book of the Prophet* weeks ago, a young couple had slipped into a room together, worried about being caught. The girl, in particular, seemed terrified of what might happen if they were discovered.

Emil stands beside Penny, offering awkward reassurance and steadfast protection. No one responds.

I face Ajax, clinging to Drake's hands like salvation. "You didn't tell me. I trusted you, Ajax."

Ajax has gone sickly pale, staring at me as if I were some strange creature. "I told you to talk to the Minister."

"You could have told me yourself. And you did this?"

Ajax shifts feet.

"He did quite well at it," Brother Gram adds. Brother Gram clutches his hands in front of himself so tight his knuckles are white.

"Silence." Drake glares at Brother Gram, waving a hand toward him.

Brother Gram's face turns beet red as his lips move, but no sound comes out. Drake Silenced him. *Good.*

All of this is so corrupt. So *wrong*. I imagine my parents. The absolute devotion to one another makes my heart ache. These acolytes don't know what it even means. They are indoctrinated from birth to believe in this system with absolute faith.

"Do you not feel love?" I ask Ajax.

He blinks, dumbfounded or confused by my question.

"I've never understood emotions very well, but I feel them all the same," I say. "The desperate need to be around someone, the absolute loneliness when they are gone. The feeling of acceptance and understanding and...faith." My throat clenches as I realize what I'm saying, who I'm referring to.

At first, I thought of my parents and sister and the love I have for them. But it isn't only them. These feelings are very different, even if on paper they sound the same. This awareness hits me like a hammer. I struggle to avoid staring at Drake. "Have you ever felt a connection with someone, like they are the one place in the world where you feel completely safe, and when they are gone, even for a minute, you can't breathe the same?"

Drake stiffens, drawing away from me. He hugs his arms over his chest and studies his shoes. The withdrawal hurts far more than I can ever tell him. I mask the pain by pressing on. If I have any authority in this place, I will exert it here.

I turn to Brother Gram. Drake seems to pick up on something, because he waves a hand, dropping the Silence around the older man.

"The acolytes can choose their own partners, just like anyone else," I say. For a moment, I hear Dad's confidence in my tone. "Or no partner at all if they prefer it that way. This program is done."

Brother Gram works his jaw, summoning words and struggling to summon a rebuttal for a moment. At last, he says, "This is just one part of a much bigger puzzle. You don't have the authority to stop it."

I flex my fingers. The blue Power doesn't return, but Brother Gram's gaze flicks to my finger as if it did. He pales.

"Would you care to challenge me, Brother Gram?" I stalk a few steps closer to him. He retreats toward the door. "Show me the rest of the puzzle."

21

PAIGE

I've made a terrible mistake. Again. These mistakes continue mounting to the point where I've lost count.

After the disastrous end to our date, King Cypress renewed his efforts to avoid me. The next morning, I expect to receive a notice that it's time to leave. But it never comes. Nor does he. All I want is a chance to explain myself, perhaps redouble my efforts to invoke his promise for Easton and me both. Will he keep his word? I realize I don't know King Cypress well enough to be sure if he is a man of his word. *Zephyr would know.*

Just thinking of Zephyr hurts. A pain I push away. I don't need them. I'm highly trained.

I'm a Powers.

It's time for me to put this dumb pageant aside and use the knowledge I've gathered to my advantage. I know where Easton is. I know how to get there. I know who runs the docks. Once Easton and I are far enough from the island, we should be clear of trackers following us back to Elpis.

The first time Prince Dominic arrives at my door, I'm certain this is it. He escorted all the other girls away. Now he has come for me. Not that I care any longer. I don't need the King to get out of here anymore.

But that isn't his intention at all. After leading me to a carriage, he reassures me we will continue the training.

The days bleed past. I spend my morning planning my escape from the island, plotting a cautious course home, and talking to Nora about her family. She's pretty open with me and doesn't seem to realize I'm fracking for clues about how to get off the island via the docks.

After lunch each day, Prince Dominic and Vincent escort me to the training grounds, where we hone my skills until dinner. The tidal waves are just as strong as before, but somehow Prince Dominic has helped me move with the flow of the current. Instead of being dragged into the undertow, I can predict the waves well enough to avoid being pulled under. After two weeks, I can select my targets with dedicated focus, as if riding the surface of the waves. But I still cannot control the flow of the tides.

The Power is foreign to me. Unknown. I manipulate nature to destructive ends. While I can move objects, unearth trees, sense the ebb and flow of the world, the Power is unlike any other Telekinetic or Naturalist I know of. The strength that pulses through me does not engorge my muscles like it does Easton. Yet I feel the sheer power of that strength all the same, intoxicating and overwhelming.

My focus isn't for Prince Dominic's benefit. The sooner I learn what I'm capable of, the sooner I can use that to help Easton and me get home. My Powers must be the key.

The first time I Control Vincent, Prince Dominic practically whoops in glee. I release the hold immediately, hating the way it coats me with filth. But the Prince won't be deterred. He encourages me to try again; over and over until Vincent's blue eyes glaze over; until his strides no longer appear forced, as if he moves of his own volition and not at my will.

Though Vincent is open to my Control, a willing participant, his mind and body resist like someone suffering abuse. I want to collapse in a heap of tears. Control is an ugly thing that makes me feel like I've abused someone on the deepest level.

"Prince Dominic, I don't like this," I say, fighting off tears. My throat constricts. "Can we just harness it? Lock it away? I don't ever want to do this again..."

He pulls me into a warm hug. "No more Operator magic, Paige. But the rest... I don't think it can be contained. If we don't learn how to deal with this, now, it could be catastrophic later."

Tears well in my eyes, and I blink furiously to fight them back. None of my Powers create. All I can do is Control and destroy. It's invigorating and horrifying. The thrill that it generates throughout every fiber of my being terrifies me to my deepest core.

Muscle Memory is the weakest of all my abilities. How I came to be a Somatic in Elpis when all this strength and these abilities rage inside, I cannot understand. All my life, I wanted more. To be more. To live up to expectations. I am no longer inadequate.

I'm a weapon. Lethal. Destructive. Now I understand why Dad says there's nothing wrong with being ordinary. I always took it as an insult, an unintended slight for being less gifted than Gavin. Now I wonder if I would give this Power up.

Prince Dominic steps back. Each day, he uses his Influence to help me control this tsunami within. Today, a sheen of sweat beads on his forehead despite the cold air. A gleeful smile lights up his face. Those sapphire blue eyes sparkle with invigorating light.

"You, my lady, are a marvel." He takes my head in his hands and places an affectionate kiss on my forehead. "Beautiful!"

His elation is contagious. Despite the discomfort I felt a moment ago and the way my stomach continues writing, I can't help but grin back at him.

He practically bounces back to the carriage, dragging me along with him.

Vincent waits inside, seated on the bench across from us where I commanded him to go. "Success?"

"Resounding." Prince Dominic settles beside me.

We return to the palace, Prince Dominic reveling in our success. Vincent praises Prince Dominic's efforts to teach me—as if I had nothing to do with it. My insides are churning madly. They call it a victory, but none of this feels like one. These Powers are sickeningly sweet, curdling my stomach while seducing me with their draw.

This is all wrong. I can't stomach another one of these training sessions. I feel beaten by the tides like worn rocks along the shore. And I'm eroding away.

It's time to leave.

22

ZEPHYR

THE HAMMER OF PAIGE'S magic returns every day at the same time with a vengeance. Someone is training her to use that destructive force. Why would Cypress allow it? Why wouldn't Dominic stop it after the warning I gave him?

The first time it happens, the force of her magic knocks me out cold again. I wake to find Easton crowding over me, concern lacing his hard features.

"Paige again?" he asks, but he already knows the answer.

I only nod.

After the fourth day, Easton and I have fallen into a routine. I black out. He wakes me with smelling salts, then gives me water and painkillers for the pounding headache. We become so acclimated to the timing of her brutal, swift attacks that we plan our days around it. Go out early. Contact the people, starting at the homeless shelters and food banks. Return home for a quick lunch, prepare for her assaults, then spend the night reviewing our progress.

After two weeks, I've learned to brace myself for the shock, cocoon myself protectively in my magic to remain conscious. The familiarity of her strength against my own becomes a comfort, a way to keep her close. I hold on to her magical grip as long as she allows it, like a fiercely intimate, doomed embrace. Does she know how it affects me? I've tried opening myself up to her Dreaming, but so far, nothing.

The attacks become less vicious as the days go by as well, though no less powerful. Whoever is training her is doing something right.

Easton and I make our way back to the apartment from the food kitchen, where we volunteer our time hoping to contact the men and women opposing Cypress. One day, I recognize a man from the shop that Easton and I had been watching. He eyes me up and down, his lips thin and bitter.

"Heard you earned a banishment from our little king," the man says.

I pause, glancing along the line behind him. Only two others, both of whom appear to be companions of his. "Yeah."

"What'd ya do?" he asks.

I decide to lean into the truth. Easier to keep my story straight later. "I didn't think it was fair he got all those girls to pick from like a herd of heifers." I mentally wince. Paige would punch me for that comment for certain. And I would deserve it. "So I made a move." Not the entire truth, but not a full lie, either. I give a casual shrug. "He found out. One of the other girls tattled."

They study me for a moment, then grin wickedly. "You sleep with her?"

Anger and heat pump through me. I need to play their game, but I don't want to do this. *Paige, forgive me.* "Nope. Didn't get a chance to get that far before the other one jumped to her death. Interrupted our private moment."

One of his friends chortles. "A girl would rather kill herself than marry him. What did I tell you?" He eyes his compatriots.

They shush him before their leader nods to me. "Didn't hear about the death. Good day, black sheep." They wander toward a table before I can ask further questions.

As I continue serving people and making small talk, Easton wanders the room doing the same with the people. A reassuring hand on the shoulder with some words here and there.

Watching Easton work with the homeless is inspiring. He has a knack for relating to them, a skill which I lack. And he smiles—actually, genuinely smiles—at the people he engages with. I don't understand why he enlisted in military service when he clearly has a calling for social welfare.

That night, we walk the alleys before returning to the apartment for our usual daily breakdown. As usual, Easton says nothing. Every word he choses is carefully crafted to serve a purpose. Easton doesn't waste words, a fact I humbly respect. He is a better version of me in every way. Stronger, smarter, humbler, more compassionate...

This calling of his has garnered the trust of the people as well. The old and young. The bitterly resentful and guarded. He's a natural-born leader.

I stuff my hands in my pockets and try to remain small. Easton makes me feel insignificant in every way. I hate the envy that burns in me.

Instead of turning up the street toward our apartment to close the loop on our walk, Easton continues along the main road. I hesitate at the corner, jogging a step to catch up.

"Where are you going?"

"The Windsor."

A curious choice. The Windsor is one of the upper-class apartment buildings, owned by the crown and operated by the Greenes as one of their many properties around the island. Lord Greene's daughter currently lives in the palace as a Tribute. They gave each of the girls Cypress dismissed an apartment in The Windsor until they either marry or find work on the island. By my count, six of the girls should live there now.

"Why?" I can't help asking. Easton has puzzled out something and I hate not knowing.

"I was talking to a few people today. Eight girls dismissed. Only two of them have been seen around the island. No one has seen the other girls. Nor have we."

We stop across the street from the large evergreen building. The sun has set, and streetlights cast an ominous glow from their solar lights over the structure. The Windsor is four stories tall, with a hipped roof and dormered windows overlooking the street from the top floor. Only a few lights glow inside, but electricity shouldn't be an issue in The Windsor. So why are so few people inside?

"Maeve and Everly would have gone back home to their families," I say. "Not here."

"Two girls seen around the island."

A chill runs down my spine at the implication. "What happened to the other six?"

Easton nods grimly. "Do you think you can get us inside?"

I shake my head. "It isn't a guarded door, but it locks at night to protect the residents." I stride across the street, checking the names on the apartment buzzers for any of the girls. My jaw twitches, finger sliding down the panel. Finally, I shake my head in denial. "It doesn't make sense. They should be here."

"Any chance no one added the names?" Easton looms near the door behind me.

I feel like an idiot, unable to do much more in this scenario than shake my head. *Probably look like an idiot to Easton.* When I glance over my shoulder at him, Easton has a hand around the doorknob, turning it and fiddling with the lock. By the time I realize he has a lock-picking tool in his hand, the door is already swinging open.

As I slip through, I gape at him. "I won't even ask where you learned to do that."

"I have a bit in common with some people here." He leaves it at that as he follows me up the hallway. "You can sense Powers, right? Can you feel any of the girls here?"

I climb to the second floor, hand sliding along the whitewashed banister. Easton's on my heels, making each step creak beneath his density. I reach out for something, anything. When I feel nothing but Easton, I climb to the third floor and try again. Then the fourth. I stop at the top, dumbfounded. We are surrounded by green painted, wainscoted half walls, smooth laminate wooden tiles, white rails, and apartment doors.

And nothing else.

Easton waits patiently, a knowing expression in his eye, hands tucked in his pockets. My face must give away the truth, because all he does is nod as if he already knows the truth.

None of the girls are here. *Someone* should be. The odds of all six girls finding another placement already is incalculable.

"This is impossible," I whisper, worried that the ordinary occupants might hear us.

"Are they always brought here?"

"Since the first king."

Easton turns and gallops down the winding staircase. I follow without a word, trying to puzzle out what all of this means—and if it means anything at all.

23

GAVIN

THE NURSERY ISN'T SO bad. I should have expected it, considering the breeding program in place to produce more little acolytes. At least the infants and toddlers are cared for by the young women who give birth to them for the first year of life. After that, the toddlers are kept together with a handful of older women and men who focus on toddler development. From age one until five, they are kept in these care centers, unaware that a whole other community of people live above them.

But I learn the hard way to stop asking questions—not that I ever will—when I question Madame Christiane about the acolytes who don't develop gifts. "What happens to them?"

And she shows me. A few serve in the labs that focus on understanding the benefits of Power stones. The labs remind me a little of the stories Dad told me of Paragon. Maybe not as bad or extreme—no one seems to get hurt—but something about what could be happening that I don't yet see leaves my stomach queasy.

Drake has fallen silent behind me, hands in his pockets. A sickly pallor has replaced the normal flush of his skin, though his eyes remain clouded by dark thoughts.

And then she shows us the mine. I've been here before, a few weeks ago, but I used a different entrance than the one we stroll through today. The air is stifling. Drake wheezes. Emil's boots start dragging on the ground. Ajax has hung back to avoid joining us.

"You two should go back," I say over my shoulder. "I'll be fine."

"I want to see this myself," Emil says through his teeth.

I pause and peer at Drake. His face sets grimly, and he nods tightly. I'm worried about what this mine can do to him. Seeing him collapse from a Power stone before had been terrifying. And that was only one stone. This is a mine.

Madame Christiane remains unaffected. How is that possible? Surely the woman in charge of all of this has some kind of Power. These stones must affect her somehow.

Our small group carries on. Thankfully, we don't have to go very far before all of us abruptly halt our steps.

The mine shaft opens into a small cave. The strike of metal against stone rings loudly against the walls. The stench of sweat is overpowering as dozens of teens swing their pickaxes against the mine walls, digging for Power stones.

"Slave labor," I mutter. What else could it be? These are the teen acolytes without a Power. They send those who don't develop gifts to the mines to harvest Power stones. "Why do you need so many stones?"

Madame Christiane observes the teens with her hands on her hips. "They offer us protection against the Kingdom. And the more we can understand about them, the better we can protect ourselves."

I glance at Emil for confirmation. He gives a half shrug, as if to say it's partly true. Of course, she won't tell me everything. Not that I need her to. I know that this can't all be because of the Kingdom. "They aren't *this* bad."

Her sharp eyes snap to me. An angry line creases her forehead. "What do you know? Every generation or two, a king takes the crown and becomes a dog with a bone. Finding us would be a crowning victory to whichever king sits on the throne. Some kings have been relentless, and come far too close for our comfort. These stones are all that stand between us and forced service."

I clench my jaw as a chortle climbs up my throat. Does she not see the irony of that statement? "You mean like this?" I wave my hand at the teens. "The deeper I dig into this place, the more certain I become that these elections are necessary, and that the Elder's have harbored secrets for too long."

"What do you suppose would happen if the people found out?" she snaps.

"If these stones can do everything you claim, protecting you from the kingdom, what makes you think some of those men and women wouldn't volunteer to take shifts down here?" I shake my head. Enough is enough. I close my eyes, feeling out with my Powers for the instruments of slavery. Each of the pickaxes transforms. I don't care what they become as long as they can no longer force these kids to break their backs in this mine.

A gasp ripples through the cavern. The Power stones blaze with brilliant green light, reflecting off the crosses in each teen's hand.

Drake edges closer, his jaw slackened in both horror and awe. Before I can speak, he steps toward the teens. "You have been tested. You have suffered. Do you still hold faith?"

"Drake," I hiss.

He holds a hand back to me, signaling me in some way I don't fully understand. Am I to wait?

The teens all shuffle closer together, peering at the glowing stones, then the pickaxes turned crosses in their hands. The oldest steps forward, anxious as he shuffles closer to Drake. My muscles coil.

Then he falls to his knees. "I believe."

The pain in my gut is agonizing as I watch these abused teens follow his lead, one at a time. Emil curses softly behind me. I understand the sentiment, and I need to stop this before it gets out of hand.

I move to Drake's side, shooting him a venomous glare. How dare he pull me into another prophecy. He knows how I feel about this! But seeing the sorrow and pain in his eyes makes some of my anger subside. He's only trying to help.

I kneel beside the oldest boy, placing my hand on his shoulder. "You don't have to do this any longer." I peer past him at the rest of them. "None of you do."

"You don't have the right to come down here and—" Though Madame Christiane's lips continue moving, her words are wrapped in Silence.

Drake sags in relief, but judging by the way he's sagging, he won't be able to handle being down here much longer. Sweat pours down his temples. His face has gone green. Exhaustion bleeds through every part of him. The need for expediency and urgency presses down on me.

"This is no longer your cross to bear," I tell the teens. "Follow me. We will get you cleaned, fed, and rested." I nod for Drake to lead the way.

Madame Christiane continues raging in Silence as we lead the teens out of the tunnel, out of the secret labs, out of the belly of the temple.

24

PAIGE

THAT WRITHING DISCOMFORT FROM training does nothing to help the uneasiness of finding Bella waiting for me in my room upon return. *Why is she still here?* I need to talk to King Cypress about this myself. Whatever Dominic said didn't work.

I hesitate, eyeing her as I slide off my coat and hang it. The floral wallpaper seems sickeningly bright today.

Unafraid of Bella, I turn my back to her as I sit on the edge of my bed and slip off the boots. A trail of dirt has followed me inside. A pang of regret seeps into me. The poor maids will have to clean that.

In a lame attempt to exert an air of calm, even if I don't feel it at all, I meander into the bathroom and wash my face.

Bella leans against the doorframe, scowling. She's pretty when she smiles, but whenever the two of us are alone, that scowl is as firm as any stone carving. Flowers bloom in her idle hand, and her fingers absently stroke the silky petals. My gaze flicks to her bare wrist. *She removed her bracelet.*

"Somehow you continue dipping your toes into trouble, then dive in head-first," she says. Her tone is hard, yet nonchalant as well, as if she believes all of this is ordinary, but necessary.

"What do you want?"

"I think I underestimated you again," she says.

I wipe a towel over my face and turn to face her, hands on my hips. "Good."

"You have a penchant for trouble." Her eyes burn into me. "But it isn't without its merits. You will deal with it. Tonight."

"What are you going on about now?" Though I know. King Cypress ignores me again, after what the other girls assumed was a successful date. Only Bella, Nora, and I remain. Bella must go. I will convince King Cypress to send Bella and me both on our way, and to extend the offer to Nora. I don't know how, but it will happen.

I brush past her into my room, wary of her Power. My training taught me to respect the capabilities of others with deadly precision, and Bella is no exception. Removing her bracelet is her way of flexing her Power over me and this entire situation. *If only she knew I can still use mine with this bracelet on.*

"I spoke with Cypress." Bella follows me slowly, as if the world will bend to her will. I don't know what he said to her, and I'm not sure I want to. "You broke his heart. Poor thing. A father who overlooked him, a mother who prefers his brothers, a girl who prefers his dead brother, another who prefers his half-brother. I should applaud you. Somehow, you have taken that selfish boy and driven in the final knife. Humble is a strange color on him."

My heart clenches for King Cypress. I never meant to hurt him. "Then you should be happy. He's weak and you can move in."

She nods, still fiddling with the small white flowers in her hand. A warning. "I should. But I'm not happy, because even broken-hearted, he is still hopeful. And he is still *king*."

I open my mouth, unsure how to respond. *Still king...* "You intend to remove him from the throne?" *Treason!* My brain is screaming at me. Reflexively, I dig deep to pull at a tendril of my Powers, just in case.

Bella didn't come here to become his wife or queen. *Or maybe she did. Maybe she had hoped to take the crown and kill him on their wedding night.* I sink down on the bed beside a beautiful bouquet of colorful lilies—her creation, no doubt.

Bella stalks closer, moving with terribly chilling steps. "No, I don't."

Panic grips me. My heartbeat increases and my lungs collapse as the walls close in on me. The world around me spins until Bella's face fills my vision as she crouches in front of me. Her hands rest on my knees, fingernails digging into flesh. My mind can't stop screaming *treason!*

"Tonight, after everyone has gone to bed, you will go to his room—I believe you've been there before—and you will convince him it was all a mistake. You will get him to lower his guard."

My mouth goes dry. "I won't help you."

"You will."

"Then tell me what you are after."

A wicked little smile blooms on her face like the flower in her hand. "*That* is not your concern."

"Lies. It is my concern. You are making me an accomplice to treason, Bella." I swallow. "Who would take his place? Bronwyn can't. Zephyr is gone and Dominic is sworn to his position."

Bella tucks the small white flowers behind my ear. "That's also not your concern. Your only concern is that you go to him tonight, get close to him." The flash of amusement in her eyes makes my skin crawl. "Let nature take its course."

Nature... I won't sleep with him. I have my integrity. Handsome as he is, King Cypress doesn't stir any desire in me. "Why don't you do it? You can clearly get closer to him than I can right now."

Bella scoffs. "Also no."

"Have your eye on someone better than a king?" I snap.

Her unruffled demeanor irritates me. "I'm not foolish enough to bare my secrets to you like you've done to Nora."

My heart stills. Nora? What has she told Bella about me? Are they *both* in on this? Both girls are island natives. They stand to gain something from the King, and not just a crown. But what do their families gain from his fall? Nora's brother controls the docks, meaning all means of transportation on and off the island. Bella's father is a horse breeder, meaning he controls transportation on the land. That alone can cripple the island and the Kingdom.

Bella rises.

"If I refuse?" I call after her.

"You won't." She waves toward the bouquet on the bed. "I left you a gift. A reminder of what you have to lose."

My Powers press at the bracelet, attempting to break free. I hold on to just a ripple in case I need to defend myself.

Bella makes her way to the exit as I glide a finger over the bouquet. She slips her bracelet back on her wrist.

Nestled in the heart of the colorful array, a small gift box awaits. Trembling violently, I ease the box out and remove the lid.

One cloudy, sightless eye gazes back at me. I yelp, dropping the box and jumping off the edge of the bed. I rush to the bathroom and vomit into the toilet.

When I return to the room, the eye remains where I left it. Deep, dark brown. Familiar. I know this eye. It has glared at me hundreds of times. It has poured intense longing through me.

Easton.

Shaking, I read the note attached to the top.

The heart comes next.

25

ZEPHYR

EASTON PACES THE FLOOR in our apartment, arms crossed and fingers pressed to his lips. A strange contemplation draws his brows down. One eyebrow creases around the black eye patch.

I perch on the sofa, wringing my hands and wishing a drink was in them. My knees bounce of their own accord.

For two weeks, we have worked closely with the lower-class citizens of the island. What I've learned haunts me. They fear deportation. When the shelters get overcrowded, the crown quietly and discreetly sweeps up the weakest and oldest among them, packs them onto a ship, and sends them across the water to live or die outside the protection of the island. Starving and freezing in the streets of the Capital is a far cry easier than what awaits them on the mainland. Attacks from wild animals, poison from inedible plants, abuse at the hands of the men living on the mainland outside the reach of the Kingdom's protection. No one sent to the mainland is ever seen again. Does Cypress know all of this? Does Dominic?

I will become one of the outcast mainlanders soon. I would like to think I can handle myself, but enough people on the mainland know my face that I doubt they would welcome me anywhere openly.

The news of such duplicity disturbed Easton deeply and sent him into a silent rage for days. With acts of abandonment plaguing the crown, it's no wonder the people have grown disgruntled with their king. Does Cypress have any idea of the trouble he has stepped into? This all reeks of King Alric's heavy-handedness.

At the moment, Easton is focused sharply on the missing girls. He brooded in silence all the way home and now he won't stop pacing the floor.

"Run through it one more time," he says, not bothering to glance at me.

I don't want to. It doesn't make sense.

"When Cypress dismisses one of the girls, she is put into a carriage with enough clothing to get her by for a while, and a generous stipend is set up with the bank to give her spending cash as she settles into her new life." I chew my lip.

"And the Keeper of Tides, your brother Dominic, is the one who escorts them to their accommodations." Easton isn't asking. I've already told him as much several times.

"Yes."

"Always him."

"Yes."

Easton scratches the stubble on his chin, then stops pacing. His one eye fixes on me, flashing some internal war. His lips part as if about to say something, then he presses them together and his jaw twitches.

"Any chance it could be him?" he asks at last, as if afraid of posing the question.

I laugh. It's the first genuine, deep belly laugh I've had in a long time. The idea that Dominic would ever do anything against the tide is the most amusing thing I think I've ever heard. And I can't stop laughing. It brings tears to my eyes.

But Easton isn't amused in the least. The absolute seriousness of his expression sobers me.

"It's ridiculous." Even my voice is laced with amusement, like Easton has lost his mind.

"Is it?" He taps his bicep.

Now I'm not laughing. "Dom is the gentlest, kindest person I've *ever* met, and I've been all around this kingdom. He wouldn't hurt a fly and his loyalty to the Kingdom is without question. If you knew him, you would know how stupid you sound. I would suspect Bronwyn before him."

"Bronwyn...the overlooked princess." Easton squints, as if trying to focus on some distant memory.

I fight off the urge to smack him. Just that statement coupled with that expression makes his implication clear. He wonders if she would be angry that she was overlooked in favor of Cypress After the king and his heir died.

Easton seems to break from some dark spell. "You said yourself that whoever is behind this has to be connected, right?"

I don't like where he is going with this. Not at all. I refuse to provide an answer that will add fuel to his insanity.

"I've seen your king, your Admiral, you, dozens of your officers, a handful of the island lords, but I've never seen the prince and princess. Why?"

My heart races. Some part of my brain is trying to connect these dots for me, making me see whatever he sees. But I block it out by instinct because Easton has clearly lost his mind. The torture and mistreatment he has suffered since arriving has finally taken their toll.

"Why should you?" I snap. "You're no one."

"Not true. I'm the companion of one of the king's Tributes. I'm someone to somebody."

Suddenly, my racing heart stops beating altogether. My gaze flicks to the eyepatch, to his missing finger, to his covered arms where tags of skin have been removed and healed dozens of times by a physician at the fort. I struggle to drag in ragged breaths. Who would have that sort of connection, power?

It isn't Dominic. It couldn't possibly be. He doesn't have the constitution or the stomach for it. There must be some other answer. Someone is setting him up to be the fall guy. *But no one would ever believe it was him.*

"I can list half a dozen lords on this island who stand to gain something if the crown falls," I say sharply. "Lord Greene among them, *and* he is in charge of The Windsor, so he would have access to those girls after they are dropped off."

He nods. "Then let's make the list. We can start with Lord Greene, then we can cut through each of them to get answers.

Once we exhaust them, if we don't find answers, it leaves only one option."

Easton has me paranoid now. I won't suspect Dominic or Bronwyn, the gentlest of the Strong children. But Lord Greene has something to gain, for certain.

"Fine," I mutter, shuffling toward the door. "I need a drink."

Easton seizes my arm so tight it instantly cuts off my circulation and leaves my fingertips cold. I clench my fist as his fingernails dig against my flexing muscles.

"Let go," I snarl through my teeth.

"This isn't about you or me right now. This is about Paige. If Cypress dismisses her, where will she end up?"

Every muscle in my body coils tight. I'm worried I might snap and start throwing punches at Easton if he doesn't let go. I jerk my arm, knowing I won't break his grip. Thankfully, he lets go.

"If Cy knows even a trickle of what she is capable of, he will never let her go." My next words drag out, horribly, brutally honest. I know Cypress well. Better than most. I saw all the signs, even if I wanted to deny them. "Cy exiled me in favor of her. Paige isn't going anywhere." My throat tightens. "He's already in love with her, or the idea of her, at least."

26

DRAKE

GAVIN HAS TAKEN MY world and everything I knew and believed and turned it upside down. He has made me question my faith, but never since our debate weeks ago about religion versus science has he pushed his views on me. All he asked was that I keep my eyes open. And I did, without meaning to. I should resent him, hate him for making me question everything I believed in, but I can't.

Then I went against my promise to him down in that cave. But I had to. I didn't mean to pull him into another prophecy, but something needed to be done. I've interacted with enough acolytes to know they respond best to one thing and one thing only. The *Book of the Prophet*. So I used it—not him—to get them to move.

Unfortunately, when we emerged from those tunnels with nearly two dozen dirty, pale, and starving teenagers, it created an uproar in the Haven square. I should have seen that coming. I'm surprised Gavin didn't.

The Havenites were furious when Gavin told them what we found in those mines. Before he could bring up the breeding program, Emil and I both shut him down. If they reacted this way to a handful of teens from the mines, what would happen if they learned the truth about the breeding program?

I had to grovel for his forgiveness once we were back at home. Gavin wasn't angry with me. My actions hurt and disappointed him. Somehow, that's so much worse.

For the next week, tensions in the Haven coil tight. Though the Havenites were quick to help the teens, taking them in, feeding them, caring for them, their mistreatment has created a fracture among the people. I haven't heard much more than whispers, but I can feel the tension everywhere coiling tighter and tighter. At some point, it will break.

Gavin and I are in our apartment, agonizing over final selections for potential Elders. I watch Gavin pour over final applications for the Elder seats and admire him—in more ways than I should be comfortable with. I also fear him a little. Gavin has so much power he doesn't yet understand how to wield. When we learned about the acolyte breeding program, he nearly unleashed a gift that made my stomach uneasy. He created so much agony in that acolyte boy that the boy couldn't even manage a scream. And it wasn't until I gathered the courage to reach out to him that Gavin realized what he was doing.

He needs someone to balance him. His inability to recognize emotions in others isn't something I'm surprised by or unfamiliar with. I've been trying to work my way past this with him since the boat ride back to the Haven. But the blindness to such pain terrified me. I understood his anger. I felt it, too. But in him, it burned like the sun. Everyone in that room feared him.

We have only returned twice to ensure the acolytes were being released from the program. On our first visit, Gavin had been angry to learn the administrators had twisted his words. Acolytes were not let loose, but were freed to choose their own partners within the program instead. I had waited, ready to stop Gavin from lashing out, when I noticed the vein in his neck throbbing. But he had remained calm—almost robotic—as he made his meaning crystal clear.

And then Brother Gram was banished from any activities behind those metal doors.

Nothing is what I thought. Nothing except for him. Whether or not Gavin accepts it, he *is* the Idol of Creation. I have witnessed the signs for myself. Even if my faith is shaken, my belief in him is not. If he won't hold this faith for himself, I will nourish it for him. Because he needs balance.

Gavin shifts at the table, wincing for only a moment before resting his head in his hand again over the stack of applications.

A few acolytes have left the dorms beneath the temple and live among the Havenites. Gavin thought it was a good idea, but I'm worried. The acolytes are people who live to serve the temple. The whispers started. Rumors about the breeding program. About Gavin. If the acolytes no longer serve the temple and the *Book of the Prophet*, what does that mean for the promised Days of Glory? I haven't heard anyone say it, but I worry the Minister was right when he taunted Gavin about this new position.

If Gavin refuses for much longer, I'm worried people will think he is a false Idol. What will they do this time? Burning didn't work—I still don't understand how or why. Will they resort to beheading, separate his body from his mind so he cannot return again?

I worry about his wellbeing. Something dark is coming. I feel it. I have to remain alert, because Gavin won't notice until it's too late.

As this realization strikes me, Gavin slumps in the chair, then his head hits the tabletop. Did he just fall asleep in his chair?

27

GAVIN

THE MUSCLES IN MY back ache. We have converted the dining table in my apartment into a workspace filled with applications for the open positions among the Elders, as well as positions as assistants. The response from the Havenites has been overwhelmingly positive and excited. This is a change they have been awaiting far too long, though I suspect anger has brought on some of their determination after learning about the mines. Most of them were furious to learn the truth. We still haven't told them about the breeding program.

As I sift through the applications, my eyelids grow heavy. I think about Paige. I miss my sister more than I can find words to express. Her snarky comments and quick smiles are a foundation in my world. Without that foundation, I feel lost.

As if summoned by my thoughts, Paige appears. I blink in alarm, confused by what has happened, and turn slowly in place.

I'm no longer in my apartment. The surrounding room is spacious, but clearly a bedroom. Floral wallpaper. White bed and dresser. Green sitting chairs with a matching bedspread.

Paige is curled up on the bed, eyes shimmering with tears.

"Paige?" I run my hands over my body. Is this another Dream? How did she pull me from my place? Or did I fall asleep at the table?

She sits up, assessing me. When she opens her mouth to speak, a strangled sob climbs up her throat. I'm about to move toward her when she launches off the bed and throws her arms around me. Her hug is so tight it constricts my lungs.

"What's wrong?" I ask, hugging her back.

I expect her to hesitate, to draw back into herself like she sometimes does to avoid expressing her emotions. Instead, Paige shocks me by breaking down and telling me everything. Like, literally everything that has happened to her these past weeks since the last time we spoke in a Dream. I settle on the edge of the bed with her, letting her dump everything out of her system without interruption.

All the news has my head spinning, but I take it in. I don't know any of these people she rambles on about. At least, only what she has told me already. She talks about an incident between her and Zephyr, and his exile. About the king kissing her—twice—and realizing that she didn't share his feelings—twice. About the queen's warning that she could never go home. When she launches into a tirade about some girl named Bella, Paige nearly loses control.

"She sent me his finger in warning, Gav," Paige says. "And his eye!"

"Easton? How do you know it was even his? You haven't seen him since arriving, right?"

Paige mumbles something, then heaves a sigh and flops back on the bed. "I suppose I don't know for sure. But it must be. Prince Dominic says he has it under control, but I don't know anymore."

I lay on the bed with her, and we stare at each other like we always did as kids. I miss her so much it makes me ache.

"So, the Prince is in charge of the military?" I ask. "I thought you said that was this Baron fellow, the Admiral?"

She sniffles and swipes away a few stray tears. "Baron *is* in charge."

"Then why wouldn't the Prince go to the man in charge of protecting and training Easton? Wouldn't that be the Admiral's job?"

She opens her mouth to reply but cannot produce a response. After a moment, she simply says, "I trust Prince Dominic. He's sweet and harmless."

I grimace. "Those are the ones who can hurt you the easiest." Pip's face, her innocence and sweetness, rise to the surface. But she wanted one thing from me, and when I couldn't give it to her, she turned against me. "Paige, in our positions, we can't afford to trust anyone. Don't wait for the prince to placate you. Go talk to the King yourself. Show him the eye. If he really cares about you at all, he will listen."

Easier said than done, I'm sure.

"What about Drake?" Paige asks, raising a brow. In another dream, I spoke at length about him—probably too much. "You clearly trust him."

Something inside of me alights at the thought of Drake. I smother the flame before it can consume me. It does me no good to linger on something I can't have, even if I'm falling for him—especially since I'm falling for him.

I bite my lip as I chew on my response. "When everyone else turned against me, he didn't. He fought for me. He and Emil both."

Paige suddenly pops up on her elbows. The sudden movement makes me flinch. "I forgot to tell you! I found Emil's sister."

"What?" I sit up as well, suddenly alert. "How is she? Where is she?"

Paige bites her lip and gazes at the ceiling. "Lady Emry became the King's consort. She was happy here, in the end, though she still missed Emil. She and the King had a son. The guy who attacked us and captured Easton and me, Zephyr, Captain of Tides, is Emil's nephew and her only child."

Zephyr is Emil's nephew? He will be thrilled! I think... I take a moment to digest the information and process it. Then I realize Paige spoke in the past tense. "She *was* happy? Why isn't she happy any longer?"

Paige drops back on the bed again, gnawing on her lower lip. She puts her hand over mine. Apparently, I was fidgeting again. "She had a Power-related illness. She died a few weeks back. I told her about Emil, and she lit up like the sun."

"And Zephyr is now in exile because of his feelings for you." My brows knit together, eyes darting back and forth quickly. "Wait, that means he is coming to the mainland in the spring, right? Like you said? Maybe I can help reunite them. Uncle and nephew."

Emil has lost his sister, but he still has family. That must count for something. It certainly does for me.

As soon as I have stabilized matters here in the Haven, I'm leaving. The Queen can't keep my sister captive. I will get help and bring her home.

Just as suddenly as I appeared in the room, it vanishes and I'm sitting at my table.

"Thank the Idols," Drake breathes. He is crouched beside me, a hand on my leg. Emil lingers behind him.

I frown and rub my eyes. "Sorry. I must have fallen asleep." My head aches. I rub at my forehead to ease some of the pressure.

"Sure, if you're narcoleptic," Drake snorts.

"What?"

"You were sitting there like normal, then your head just hit the table," Emil reports. "You almost fell out of the chair before Drake steadied you. What happened?"

I glare at the table as if it were to blame. Emil's sister... I should tell him the good news, but the coward in me resurfaces. Telling him Paige found his sister would lift him up, only to be slammed back down again upon news of her death. I can't do that to him. Not that I know how to break the news. How do you tell someone a beloved sister is dead? How would I want to be told? I wouldn't. That's the full truth of it. I wouldn't want to hear it regardless of whether I needed to know.

"Why are you looking at me like that?" Emil asks, drawing back. "It's unnerving, Gavin. Stop."

I swipe a hand over my face, turning attention to Drake.

"Are you okay?" he asks softly, in genuine concern.

I nod. "It...was my sister."

"Another dream?" he asks.

I don't bother affirming that. He already knows. "She's in trouble, Drake. Another girl is threatening her and Easton. The Queen is refusing to allow her to come home. I think something more is happening, but I don't know anyone there or anything about them." A growl of frustration climbs up my throat. Paige needs me and I'm stuck here. Worse, I don't even know what I need to know to know how to help! There is little I hate as much as not knowing something.

"Your sister seems capable," Emil says. "I doubt you have much to worry about. She can handle herself. As can Easton."

"He's right." Drake squeezes my leg. "You can't take on everything. No matter how smart you are, you can't know everything."

I scoff, throwing out a lame smirk in an attempt at humor. "Maybe *you* can't."

28

PAIGE

MY HEART HAMMERS HARD with each second that passes. My fingers twitch to the pocket of my robe where the box containing Easton's eye waits. I want to throw it out, burn it, cast away the image of that one empty eye staring at me. I glance once more at the clock.

"Don't wait for the prince to placate you. Go talk to the King yourself. Show him the eye. If he really cares about you at all, he will listen."

How late should I wait for the palace to sleep? Midnight has come and gone.

Bella expects me to win over King Cypress, play her puppet and possibly be her scapegoat. Her belief that she can bully me into submission shows plainly she has once again underestimated me. I won't throw myself at the king. Gavin is right. As always. I have another plan. One that will hopefully protect Easton and me while getting Bella thrown behind bars. With any luck, it will at least allow Easton a ticket home.

I'm not foolish enough to believe Bella is the mastermind, working alone. But if anyone can follow the threads to who is pulling her strings, it must be the King.

I had considered running, going to get Easton and escaping to the docks where maybe we can find a way across the water together. But the ice is thin, so we can't walk. The water is frigid, so we can't swim. Boats seem to be out of the question if I don't know how far I can trust Nora.

My best bet is to throw myself on the mercy of King Cypress. And if that fails, I will take my chances running with Easton. Somehow, I have to make all of this right again.

I close my eyes and take a deep breath to steady my nerves. The robe acts like a suit of armor over my pajamas. The soft cotton can't protect me for real, but it offers comfort.

Now or never, Paige. Just get it over with.

Steeling my nerves, I creep out the door, glancing in all directions, then tiptoe down the stairs. Remembering which door belongs to King Cypress takes a moment. It's been a couple of months since he brought me to his room. When I find the right door, I hesitate outside. Who will come if I knock? Will it be King Cypress, or a guard on duty to protect the king?

Worrying my lip, I rap gently, monitoring my peripherals, just in case.

Heartbeats pass. I hold my breath, worried he couldn't hear me. My hands tremble violently, and it requires a great deal of fortitude to knock again, a little harder this time.

Someone grumbles from the other side. Fear freezes me in place. I could change my mind and run. But I can't. Not when Easton's life hangs in the balance, and possibly King Cypress' life as well.

A lock clicks. The door opens a crack, revealing striking blue eyes groggy with sleep. "What do you want at this hour, Paige?"

I lose my voice, unable to find the words. All I can do is blink dumbly at King Cypress in nothing but a pair of pinstriped pajama pants that match the blue in his eyes.

His lips thin. He opens the door and motions for me to enter. He's not as muscular as Zephyr, nor as tall as Prince Dominic. If anything, he appears unassuming beside them—small and easily overlooked—but alone, I wonder how any girl could look past him. Myself included.

I step through the door, dipping my head in thanks.

"I came to apologize," I say. My voice sounds so small. "And to grovel."

He closes the door, then moves to the wet bar to pour each of us a glass of water. "Have you changed your mind?"

I settle on the crushed velvet sofa of his parlor, accepting the glass he offers to me. But I set it on the table. "I really am sorry. I never meant to hurt you."

"I'm not sure I can handle more rejection, Paige. And I won't be used."

The words cut my heart. "That's fair. You deserve my honesty. So here it is. When my parents first met, my father never really saw my mother," I say. "Not like she wanted him to, but she stuck with him. It wasn't until he realized what he stood to lose that he finally understood the depth of his feelings for her."

King Cypress settles across from me, resting a hand on the arm of the chair like a throne. His keen eyes watch me, sharpening by the moment.

"And once he realized he couldn't live a breath without her, he never let go again." I can't look in his eyes, worried about what he will see in me. "I never expected I would ever find someone who affects me like that."

"Have you?" he asks.

This will hurt. A lot. *Better to get this over with.* Bella expects me to throw myself at the king. I have no such intentions. I do plan on using him, and he will know it. But with any luck, he will see why I have no other choice...why *he* has no other choice.

"I think so."

King Cypress perks up, drawing my gaze to him. *Oh no.*

"I'm not sure the depth of my feelings, but there is...something. A need I can ignore but not eliminate. It always hovers at the edge of my mind, haunting me in my loneliness moments."

A youthful interest shines in his eyes like the sun off ripples in the cool water. He assumes I speak of him. He hopes I'm ready to give in, but my words aren't about him. Another Strong brother haunts me.

"I'm willing to submit myself to your judgment, whatever that might be, in exchange for two requests." Everything inside of me is twisted in a knotted mess. My Power pulses wildly against the bracelet, but I focus on riding the tides to keep it in check before anything horrible happens.

The interest and hope in his bright eyes wink out as under-standing settles over him. The King knows I'm not speaking about him any longer. Why else would I come to bargain? His shoulders rise with tension. He draws in a deep breath, holding it in his chest, preparing for the final blow.

My fingers fumble around the box in my pocket as I withdraw it and place it on the table.

His gaze flicks to the box, curious. "Why should I agree to any request?"

"Because I can offer you information in exchange."

He sneers, "What could you possibly have to offer me?"

I nod at the box. "Someone is working to remove you from the throne."

Once more, he eyes the box. "Who?" But the tension in his shoulders the moment I said it reveals enough. He already senses as much, and likely has a few suspects.

"Before I say more, I need your word that you will consider my requests."

He shakes his head. "Or I can just fetch my mother to pry the information from you."

"It won't work. You can ask her. She has already tried prying her way into my mind."

King Cypress presses his fingertips into the arm of the chair until the tips redden and the knuckles turn white. All friendliness vanishes from his tone. "What do you want, Paige?"

"A ticket home for Easton."

"Easton." Alarm flashes in his eyes. It takes me a moment to realize why. King Cypress now assumes Easton is the one I spoke of. The one I can't stop thinking about. While that is true, it is also much different from the way Zephyr haunts me. I worry about Easton as I would about my brother. I don't *need* him.

"Yes. That is my first request. I need you, personally, to see that he is free to go home and safe until he can leave the island." I lick dry lips. "The second is probably much harder." I let out a slow breath to steady myself. "Bring Zephyr back to the palace."

"No."

"You need him more than you need me. If someone is working against you, and I'm certain they are, then you need his ability at your side, protecting you."

"I don't need his protection," he spits. "I can handle myself."

I lean forward, imploring with everything in me for King Cypress to agree. "*Please*. I will submit to your judgment, whatever that might be. *Anything*." Tears prick my eyes. "Bring him back to help you."

King Cypress presses his back into his seat, staring at me, studying and picking apart every inch of me. "It's him," he whispers at long last. "He's the one, even after all this time, consuming your thoughts, the way you consume my own." He blinks rapidly, voice hoarse with the final confession.

Something in him breaks before my eyes, as if the last shred of light in his life has finally winked out. An emptiness hollows out his core as I watch. Then his jaw sets and straightens his spine.

"I need to know what you are offering me before I can agree to any of this." He nods at the box. "What is that?"

"A gift, given to me as a warning."

"Warning?" He leans forward, removing the lid. His face pales, but he doesn't show any further reaction. "Whom does that belong to?"

"Easton."

"How do you know?"

I swallow. "Those eyes have shredded me to ribbons enough to recognize them anywhere."

"Why do this to him?" he croaks. "Why threaten Easton?"

"Because he is the one thing here that she knows I will fight to protect, the piece of home I cling to." The surrounding air seems to grow hotter. "This isn't the first piece of him she has given to me, either."

"She..." His blue eyes are ice when he meets my gaze.

"Bella."

King Cypress' lips compress in a tight line. He leans his head forward, rubbing a hand over his forehead before sinking back. If I thought he was shattered before, it's nothing compared to the utter devastation that his entire body succumbs to. He knows something I don't.

"Tell me everything, Paige."

———◆———

T HE NIGHT SKY IS cast in lighter hues of blue as the sun begins to rise, not yet breaking over the horizon. King Cypress
and I spent hours going over the details in painful detail. At some
point, he returned to his bedroom to grab a shirt.

He combs the details surrounding Bella with vicious intent, as
if he's probing for something more. I'm surprised the news about
her duplicity hasn't shocked him more. Especially when he admits
Prince Dominic did, in fact, warn him about her.

"I've suspected her of something for a while now," King Cypress admits. "But we figured keeping her here was safer than
allowing her free domain over the island. Yet you are also right that
she's not the mastermind."

I pick at the hem of my robe. "I admit, I was curious why you
kept her around. I was shocked to see you showing her affection
in the elevator just days after our incident in the dome weeks ago,"
I admit. "I just assumed she had some sway over you."

He frowns, cocking his head to the side. "I never..." But he cuts
himself off. He knows something he isn't telling me. Something
that moves him out of his seat to pace the rug like a caged animal.
"I can accept that she is up to something. What I don't understand
is *why*," he mutters to himself, running his hand through his dark
curls for the hundredth time. "Her father already controls nearly
a sixth of the island, far more than many other lords. What could
they hope to gain, if not the queen's crown?"

"A king's crown."

He stops pacing and blinks at me as if he had forgotten I was
there, lost in his thoughts. King Cypress shakes his head, but when
he parts his lips, nothing comes out.

"Lord Greene?" The pieces of the puzzle begin clicking together for him before my eyes. His stormy blue eyes dart back and forth as if he can see it happening as well. Then his shoulders sag.

I still cannot remember where I know that name from. I've heard it before a few times but can't connect a face to it. *Wish I had Perfect Memory like Gavin right this moment.* It would go a long way.

King Cypress unexpectedly stops pacing and strides toward me. The sudden shift in momentum takes me by surprise. I almost flinch. "I will honor your first request. I will bring Easton here, to the palace, and see to it myself. Baron knows where he is. Once the shores are safe for travel, which should be soon, I will see Easton on a ship toward home myself."

My hands shake in my lap. *Finally!* A victory. "And the second request?"

King Cypress' face contorts as if in sudden agony. "You're right. I *do* need his help. But not here. His presence can be smothering for me as much as for anyone else with magical abilities. Which means he has a place, but not here." He stops in front of me, reaching for my hand. "Paige, I will reinstate him, if you agree to my judgment."

I swallow. *No. I don't want to. What will he do to me?* But it will save Easton and Zephyr. It will protect King Cypress. As much as I don't want to face whatever comes next, my needs are small when it comes to helping the others survive. I can't meet King Cypress' eyes. "What should I expect?"

King Cypress kneels, tilting my chin and forcing me to look at him. "Marry me."

My stomach drops out. My insides curl into a tight knot. This feels like the request of a boy too stubborn to let his brother win, eager to flex his muscles and show that he can take whatever he wants. If I agree with this, I won't be going back home. Any hope of being with Zephyr dies. *But he lives with his family again. Easton goes home, where he might get me help.* I told the king I would give him anything for these two things. He saw the opportunity and seized it. He wants me to give him myself.

His hand, warm and soft, smooths over mine. "I know you don't love me, but my parents didn't love each other at first, either. Am I so terrible that you don't see it as even a remote possibility? Do you think you couldn't wake up one day and see me the way your father sees your mother?"

I want to scream, cry, refuse. Frustration wells deep inside, yearning to spill out. My Power latches on, hoping to ride the waves to freedom. My voice is thick as I ask, "And if my feelings for him never fade? Could you love me knowing that I love another?"

Our gazes tether, and a deep understanding and sadness weaves us, binds us. His words slam the door on my protests. "I already do."

"I'm not worthy of you," I whisper.

He releases a sad huff. "I'm not worthy of anyone."

"But Nora..."

"I am giving up one reflection for another." His certainly firms, unwavering, even if sorrow rolls from him in ripples. "I was never choosing someone who would love me for me. Nora sees Alric, the piece she wants to cling to. Not me. Just as you see Zephyr."

My conversation with Nora, her confession of her feelings for Alric and how she hopes to reshape King Cypress in Alric's image burst forth in my mind. He's right. She doesn't want him any more than I do. She wants to turn him into something he isn't. *Which is what he wants to do to me.*

I shake my head, making his palm slide along my jaw. "Then what difference does it make?"

"To me, all the difference." His thumb strokes my cheek. "I need someone who can balance me. Someone with strength and power to do what is right. Someone who can protect the Kingdom and the throne...and me." He shifts closer on one knee, clinging to me as if I'm all that keeps him afloat. "Coming to me, telling me all of this, being honest with me...all of that tells me you would make a great queen. Someone I can rely on."

Will I sacrifice my freedom for Zephyr's return to his family, his life?

"Paige, if all I wanted was a wife who adored the ground I walked on, I would have chosen Layla or January. I probably could have learned to love either of them in time. But neither had the skills to be my *partner*." He presses his forehead to mine. "It's you. It's always been you."

Tears blur my vision and roll down my cheeks. He tenderly wipes them away. His touch is so gentle. Would this really be so bad? King Cypress is caring and passionate and handsome.

"My family—"

"We will visit. We will invite them to visit. I will open the lines of communication and extend the hand of peace. An alliance through marriage. I will never, ever try to lock you away in this palace and keep you from your family again, Paige. I swear it." His warm breath rolls across my cheeks. "You mentioned they took your brother to the Haven. We will retrieve him. I will send every last man to help your brother. All you must do is agree to be my wife, and I will give you everything I can give."

Gavin! What would he think of this? What would he say? "Can I have time to consider this? It's overwhelming, and not at all what I was expecting."

King Cypress raises my hand to his lips, a sad little smile on his face. "I wish I could give you all the time you need, but we don't have that time. In the Kingdom, the strength of a king doesn't only come from his title. It comes from his partner and what they can do to help the people. It's the entire reason I didn't want to delay this process. And you could do so much for them. I know you could. You aren't just a good match for me, you're a good match for them. We need to consolidate our power before our enemies can move against us."

Do we? I close my eyes and try to focus my reeling mind. I understand the urgency. King Cypress needs my strength, Zephyr's protection, and his own firm stance toward the future. I peer at him, hoping to glean something from those stormy blue eyes. He knows something.

"What are you not telling me?" I ask.

King Cypress licks his lips. "I...need to check something for myself before I cast suspicion further. Agree to marry me, Paige, so we can focus on the danger ahead of us."

Perhaps I can agree, for now, and see if there is another way out of this situation. "Let's just start with an announcement and take our time from there. And I won't do it without my family present." That should buy me some time.

"Of course. I will send word right away."

"Let me send word with Easton. It will be better that way."

King Cypress scoops me into his arms, hugging me tight to his firm chest. His excitement ripples outward. Each breath ruffling my hair. "You won't regret this, Paige. I will spend every moment of my life ensuring that you don't regret this."

I already do. An agreement is not actual marriage.

But what happens if I can't find a way out of it?

29

GAVIN

M Y PROMISE TO CHARLES was to allow his wife to visit. It requires some logistical attention. The right acolytes to prevent him from using his Power the moment the cell door is open. A basket of food brought in by Mrs. Garraty must be inspected for anything that he might use to escape his cell. A female pat down on Mrs. Garraty to make sure she doesn't smuggle anything on her body. The election is close now, and I'm too busy to oversee the visit myself. Besides, they deserve a little time alone.

I don't do this for Charles. I don't like him or trust him. But I've convinced myself that Mrs. Garraty couldn't have known the full extent of what her husband was up to. She doesn't deserve a lifetime of loneliness because of his actions.

The campaigns are well underway. Mostly, I've left the task up to each person. This is their future, and if they want to fill a seat, they need to prove it to others, not to me. I can't win the election for them. Which means I must be careful to make appearances for each of them equally and choose my words carefully. Showing favoritism could sway the vote drastically—something Julia has warned me about several times since the campaigns began.

The people have split into two groups. One group supports change and opposes the systems the Elders had in place—they want new Elders to help make the Haven a better, more equal place. The other group is what Emil has coined traditionalists. They like the way things were working and don't believe the Haven should make drastic changes.

I've stopped by a few of the campaign rallies, which often dissolved into shouting matches. Sometimes, into fist fights. Tensions in the Haven have reached an all-time high—I imagine highest since I've been here at any rate. Menlue, an Organization Elder candidate, has used the mine as one of his campaign platforms, petitioning for reforms and changes that will benefit everyone—Havenite and acolyte alike.

I like Menlue, but I can't tell anyone else that. I think he might be good for these people. He could be exactly what they need. It's hard to stay away from his rallies. I want to see his passionate speeches, listen to his campaign promises. But Julia always finds me when I get too close, warning me that I shouldn't use my influence on the people to get my preferred candidates selected.

The clock is ticking down. It's almost election day. We just have to make it that far.

It isn't just the election that consumes each day. There are a thousand other tasks fighting for my time. I've helped with the crops, turning withering plants into viable produce; improved the purification systems in the water treatment center, and fixed heating systems. The list of demands is so long I end up utterly exhausted by the time I return to my apartment each night.

Tonight is no exception.

Drake and Emil are working on dinner in the kitchen when I enter. Each step is heavier than the last by the time I reach my usual chair and groan, resting my head on my hands. This is all very overwhelming.

Blessing the children is one task I can't stomach, and the line was so long in the square. I refuse to give in to their belief that a simple touch from me will grant their child any future fortune. Not only that, but there is something about infants that makes me uncomfortable. I don't know what to do with them or how to handle them and they make so much noise and slobber. Often, I just turn away from these requests and find somewhere else to escape.

"Maybe we should find *you* an assistant," Emil grumbles, eyeing me from the kitchen.

I prop my chin on my fist.

"I resent that," Drake says, shaking his spatula at Emil. He sets it on the counter and moves toward me.

My stomach flips madly as Drake steps around behind me. The heat from his body radiates through my clothes. When his hands fall on my shoulders, my whole body tenses. Then the tips of his fingers work out the knots along my neck and shoulder blades. I groan again, this time with relief. Slowly, I relax beneath his touch. This is a gift. Maybe not the Powered kind, but a gift nonetheless. Drake's hands work magic on the tension in my neck, shoulders, and spine.

"See. I can fulfill whatever need he has." Drake's amusement makes me smirk against the tabletop. The implication of his words does a number on my blood. Not that his hands help. I'm clay for him to sculpt.

Maybe not any *need*. I would do anything he asked at this moment.

Emil grunts. "This should be ready soon. I have to check in with Ally before I turn in for the night. She's worried about how some of the other Elders are reacting to the retaliation against the mines."

Drake leans closer and whispers in my ear. "Look at him. He's lit up like the sun. I think someone has a crush."

I bite down on my lip, fighting off the urge to do something stupid as Drake's warm breath rolls across my ear. But I can't hold back the shiver. He quickly pulls back, dropping his hands away. I almost moan in disappointment.

But Drake's words hit me like a hammer. *Lit up like the sun.* Those were the same words Paige used when she talked about Emry. I need to tell him. I can't bear it any longer. I've been so busy there hasn't been a chance.

"Emil, wait." I hate the words as they slip out.

Emil lingers close to the door, eyeing me curiously. These past few weeks have lit a new fire in Emil. While he's still gruff, there's a softness to him now. A purpose. What I'm about to tell him could undo all of that. I hope he's made of stronger stuff than me.

"I..." Suddenly I don't know how to explain how these dreams with my sister work. "Have you had Dreamers in the Haven?"

He cocks his head, brows furrowed together. "Not in a really long time."

This doesn't surprise me. The gift is rare, even in Elpis.

"My sister is a Dreamer." *Among other things.*

"I've gathered as much."

Drake moves toward the kitchen and busies himself cleaning the cooking mess. The ruse fails miserably. Though he pretends to focus on his task, I know he is listening.

Emil crosses his arms impatiently. "And?"

"She has been living in the palace in the Kingdom for months now," I explain. "As long as I have been here, nearly."

His spine stiffens.

"She met your sister."

Emil's face lights up, jaw slack. He takes a moment to recover his wits. "Emry?"

I nod.

Before I can say more, Emil rushes toward me, kneeling and taking my hands. "How is she doing? Tell me everything."

My grip on his hands tightens. The truth, or some version of the truth, must be written on my face. The hope in his eyes flickers, then wanes.

"She did not marry the King, but she fell in love." There's no easy way to tell him this. I stumble over the right words. "They had a son. Zephyr. He's—"

Emil lurches. Where it not for my grip on his hands, he would have withdrawn completely. His words are sharp, laced with disgust. "I know who he is."

"Who is he?" Drake asks.

Emil glares at Drake, though the anger isn't directed at him. "Captain of Tides. The same jerk who attacked us in old St. Louis, I would wager."

I nod.

Drake pales, grunting a few expletives.

"What about my sister? Is she well?" Some outside force pulls the words from Emil. Deep down, he already suspects what is coming next.

My throat clenches. Tears well in my eyes for his loss. "I'm sorry, Emil."

He yanks his hands away, stumbling to his feet.

"It was no one's fault," I add quickly. "She had a Power-related illness, and their doctors didn't know how to stop it. They could only slow it and ease her pain. But Paige told her about you before she..." I can't force the truth past my lips. Saying that one word is as good as ripping out Emil's heart, and it won't allow a breath from my lungs. I swallow. "She was so happy to hear you are alive and well. Paige said she lit up like the sun."

Emil's eyes water. He blinks furiously, clenching his jaw so tight the veins in his neck pop out. Without a word, he pivots and storms out of the apartment, slamming the door shut like thunder.

I crumble at the reaction, though I knew it would happen. He handled it better than I would have. Still, I can't hold back my own tears. For his pain, for the pain I could suffer as well, mirrored in him.

Drake rushes toward me, easing into a nearby chair. He pulls my hand toward him, folding it tenderly in his own. Those dark eyes meet mine with intense sorrow. "He will come around. You've given him a gift. He just doesn't see it yet."

I shake the sorrow away, but it only crashes harder over my heart. Because this isn't just about his sister. It's about mine, too.

Chair legs scrape against concrete as Drake pulls his seat closer, then pulls me against him in a fierce hug. "If your sister is a fraction as strong as you, she will be fine." Drake knows my heart, my worries. Of course he does.

"I have to get to her, Drake." My voice is thick with unmeasurable grief.

"We will."

We. Drake is with me in this, no matter where it takes us. I can't thank him enough for his friendship. Without Drake, I would have collapsed in on myself long ago. He is my rock. My strength. My breath.

And one day that will break me, too.

30

PAIGE

I'M NOT SURE WHAT'S worse: facing Mom and Dad with the news in my dreams or facing Queen Elena. She made herself perfectly clear months ago. King Cypress would never choose me; I would never be his queen. I hadn't cared much at the time because I didn't want to be. I still don't. But King Cypress insisted we not waste a moment sharing the news. The sooner the people see their king settling into his role, the sooner we can begin the actual work. Part of me wonders if he is rushing the announcement to trap me in this cage before Easton or Zephyr can show up to change my mind.

Lack of sleep burns behind my eyes. At King Cypress' insistence—*Cypress; call him Cypress*—I returned to my room to get ready for the day.

Mariah is over the moon with the news, prattling on and on about how she knew it from the start. Despite the early hour, she is bright-eyed and eager to select the perfect dress for the day—not to mention the wedding dress she will design. It will be beautiful, no doubt. And a useless waste.

Her mother works my hair into perfect curls in silence, smirking at her own thoughts as if she, too, expected this. The twins gush, already talking about how they will make up my face for the wedding.

But there won't be a wedding. I can't marry Cypress. Somehow, I have to find a way out of this that won't hurt his position or his heart. I close my eyes as Maddy works eyeliner in place. It's too late to save his heart.

The quartet of maids work efficiently to ready me as quickly as possible. In less than a half an hour, I head back to Cypress' suite. He wanted me to return as quickly as possible, before his mother arrives.

Each step feels like a funeral march, heavier and more emotional than the last. How I will hold myself together through all of this, I don't know. But Bella will no longer hold Easton over me. With this move, she loses all her leverage. And hopefully her chance of overthrowing Cypress. I can't save his heart, but I can save his crown.

Voices rise in argument from behind his closed doors. I hesitate upon emerging from the nearby elevator. Cypress and Queen Elena.

"I know I'm not what you wanted." Cypress' voice is muffled by the door, but I hear his pain clearly. "But this burden has fallen on me and at some point you will have to trust that I know what I'm doing."

"How can I when you do things like *this*?" Queen Elena's voice is as sharp as a whip. "We are holding this throne together by our fingernails, and you have just spurned the daughters of *two* of the most influential lords in the Kingdom! Do you have any idea what you have done?"

My feet itch to flee. Queen Elena is right. Cypress is making an impulsive, selfish choice. While I wouldn't trust Bella not to try killing him the second she had her crown, Nora is a different story. I doubted her before, but now wonder if that was Bella working her manipulative magic to case doubt in my mind. Nora was the safest choice. The best choice.

"I do." The certainty in Cypress' voice makes me wonder what I've missed. For some reason, he believes I'm the best choice. It isn't just selfish. The absolute conviction in those two words reveals the truth. He has a plan. I need to have faith that his plan will work. If only he would tell me what it is so I can help him.

Two guards standing vigil on either side of the door bow to me as I approach. As one of them opens the door, I straighten my spine and do my best to avoid revealing the terror spreading throughout my body.

Queen Elena steps away from her son the second I enter. He cowers from her as if prepared for a slap that never lands. The moment passes swiftly. As soon as I cross the threshold, he draws himself up with full regal bearing. She dips her head slightly as she backs up, as if deferring to him. But I know what I saw, and what I heard.

"Lady Paige," she says with sugary sweetness. A warm smile plasters her face. The act would fool anyone else. Not me. Not after what she has said to me in the past. "My son has just given me the news."

I move with confident strides to his side, sliding my hand into his. Cypress squeezes it, then laces our fingers together. A smile just as fake as her own blooms on my face. "Yes. We spent a great deal of time talking through a few things early this morning and have come to a mutual understanding and respect."

"Among other things," he says, raising my hand to his lips. As he brushes them against my skin, chills roll up my arm. His smile is warm and charming, filled with an affection I can't share.

"I can't say I'm not surprised by the engagement," she says smoothly. Her hawkish, icy gaze sweeps over me, stripping me down to my bones in seconds. "I heard your heart was elsewhere."

"A misunderstanding, Mother." Cypress doesn't give her an inch to latch onto. Nor does he give me an inch to hang myself with. I should be grateful, but I'm broken inside. Bleeding from a wound no one else sees. "One I plan to remedy. Zephyr will return to his post."

"You can't give him back his position as Captain." Queen Elena's eyes widen ever so slightly. It takes me a moment to recognize the masked fear in her eyes. "It will weaken you."

Cypress doesn't miss a beat. "He and I will talk first. But I disagree. If anything, it will show that I will accept council and admit when I'm wrong. The other lords should appreciate that."

Another argument springs to her tongue, but dies on her lips as the door opens and Prince Dominic strolls in, hugging a bundle of papers. Admiral Baron is close on his heels. Both immediately notice our joined hands. Prince Dominic's brows shoot up his forehead in shock. Admiral Baron clenches his jaw, scowl deepening. *Why is he angry?*

"Shall I see to sending the other two girls home?" Prince Dominic asks.

"Not yet. I would like to speak with both, first. In fact, please don't say anything to anyone until I've talked to them. It will be done. Today."

"Is there a rush?" Admiral Baron's voice is as hard as stone. He doesn't like me. I can't think of a single interaction the two of us have had where he has shown any warmth.

"No. But I see no need to string the other two along, either."

"A fair decision," Prince Dominic adds.

"Baron, I want you to track down Easton and see him safely to the palace today," Cypress continues. As he speaks, he glances at Prince Dominic from the corner of his eyes. "If anyone else so much as lays a finger on him without my permission, I will cut off their hands."

"If that's *your* wish, it will be done," Baron says. He eyes me curiously now. I don't miss the emphasis he placed on that sentence, as if he suspects I've manipulated the King somehow.

Cypress nods, turning his full attention on his brother as his hand clings tighter to mine. "Dom, I wrote up a list of tasks for you. I need all of this today." He reaches into his pocket and pulls out a sheet of paper. "Tell no one else what's on that list, present company included."

"What?" Queen Elena's eyes widen. She shifts closer to the prince to peer at the paper, but Prince Dominic snaps it closed and nods to Cypress.

"Mother, you have quite a lot to do today," Cypress presses on. "I would like you and Wyn with Paige all day. We will send word to her family, and once they arrive, I want everything ready."

No waiting around for this guy. Will he push for the wedding as soon as my family arrives? With any luck, my message will warn them of the truth about this island and the royal family. The idea of spending the entire day with Queen Elena makes my head spin. Will we both survive until sunset?

Cypress steps into my line of sight, bringing my hand to his lips. "Everything will be as we discussed, Paige. Trust me." Something glints in his eyes as he says those last two words.

Trust him. His requests sound innocent enough, but he has a plan. If he would bring me along, I could help. Instead, he has shuffled me off to his mother and sister for the day.

I flush as he edges close enough for me to feel the heat of his body through our clothes. His hand slides up to cup my face, and his featherlight kiss on my cheek sends shivers down my spine. "Trust my mother and no one else," he whispers.

Then Cypress pulls away and marches out the door with his brother, leaving me terrifyingly alone with his mother.

How am I supposed to trust the woman who hates me to her core?

Maybe this engagement is what Bella wanted from me all along. She pushed me toward Cypress. I thought I was bucking her plans, but what if this *is* her plan? *It doesn't matter. Zephyr will return. Easton will be safe. I will see my family.*

31

DRAKE

SCREAMS TEAR ME OUT of sleep, but I'm used to it now. Gavin has nightmares often. Usually about what the Minister did to him and Pippen. I throw back my blankets, smothering the grief over my friend's death, and pad to Gavin's room. I can't let myself think about Pippen anymore. I just can't wrap my head around why her father did that to her. Gavin tried to explain it to me, and it isn't that I didn't understand *what* he did as much as *why*. It's the why that haunts me.

I rub the sleep from my eyes, peering toward Emil's room. The door is wide open and there's no light on. He hasn't returned since Gavin told him about Emry. I'm worried about him. Not that I will tell Gavin as much.

I shuffle into Gavin's room. He thrashes at his blankets, whimpering in agony. The sound rips at my core. I denied who I was for so long. When I met Gavin, I constructed a wall around myself to keep out the blasphemous emotions that overwhelmed me. He changed me in ways I can never, ever tell him. I think Emil suspects, but he hasn't said anything.

I perch on the edge of the bed, making soothing sounds. "Shh, Gavin, it's a nightmare. It isn't real."

Tears roll down his temples. I press a cool hand to the side of his face, unable to resist wiping the tears away.

He meets my gaze in the dark. His stone-gray eyes are haunted, but shockingly gorgeous. After he takes a few measured breaths, Gavin closes his eyes. A second later, he whimpers, no doubt remembering something from the nightmare.

"It was, though. It was real. He really..." Gavin's voice trails off, unable to finish.

The events at the temple that horrible day left me questioning my faith. How could something so horrifying be acceptable? The burning, the torture, the murder. Weren't those sins? Even if done in the name of the greater good, of the Prophet, were they not evil? And then, to learn what they have been doing behind closed doors beneath the temple to those poor acolytes... I don't know what to believe any longer.

Gavin takes a moment to collect himself. His eyes locked on me. It makes my mouth dry when he looks at me like that.

"You're fine," I reassure him. It eases some of his tension.

Something passes between us, as it so often does. A forbidden longing, locked away. Neither of us has the courage to speak of it, to act on it. He has some ghost from his past that haunts him. I'm just terrified of what people here will do if they learn the truth.

Gavin sighs. His tears linger on his temples. Without meaning to, I brush them away with the back of my hand, gentle, afraid of touching him. Afraid I will lose my final ounce of self-control. Gavin means more to me than anyone or anything. I won't lose him over something stupid; something forbidden.

His speech about love and longing and safety in that terrifying breeding room grabbed hold of me. I've turned the words over as I've studied him in the days since. Was there someone else back home? Someone besides his sister and family he was eager to get back to? There must be. How else would he know exactly how I felt?

Gavin leans into my hand, eyes closed. My heart seizes. My head spins. My feelings for him constantly fight to break free. Controlling myself gets harder by the day, but I must. I can't lose his friendship. It would destroy me utterly.

When he cracks his eyes open again, he notices my gaze before I do. I'm staring at his lips. I can't help it. I've done this so many times when he wasn't looking, but now, so close, the pull is magnetic. His Adam's apple bobs.

I can't handle this. I draw my lower lip in and bite down to fight off the sinful urge.

"Drake..." The intensity in his voice makes my stomach flip. If he does that again, this is over. I'm done for.

"Don't say my name like that," I whisper, unable to speak in any normal way. I close my eyes so I don't have to see the disappointment on his face.

"Like what?" Goodness, he is gloriously oblivious...or very good at this. I would place my bet on the former and not the latter. Gavin often misses emotional cues.

"Like you want..." I swallow. *Don't say it. Don't say it.* "...me." *Curse you for an idiot, Drake.*

Gavin's face warms beneath my hand. He turns his head away, forcing me to relinquish my tenuous hold. "I'm sorry." *Shame. He's ashamed.* "You should go."

Those three words rip out my heart. I feel like I'm drowning in only inches of water, unable to push up to save myself.

He does this so often, closing me off whenever he thinks he is hurting me. I wish he wouldn't. "Don't do that," I beg. My voice cracks. "Don't shut me out."

"But you said..." He turns his gaze to me, perplexed. His eyes dart back and forth, from one of my own to the other, as if calculating something or weighing me. I'm terrified to hear the result and I know I have to say or do something to avoid a total disaster.

"What I want and what I can have are two very different things," I say. I can't touch him, so I fidget with my hands in my lap. Touching him will ruin our friendship. I've been flirting with him relentlessly for weeks. If he doesn't know how I feel by now, I'm not sure what else to do. But I can't tell anyone else. No one can know. It would put us both in danger.

If he could just see, understand... *No.* That wouldn't matter. The end results would be the same, just like they were for my friend Inka two years ago.

Gavin continues studying me like I'm a puzzle he has to solve. I need him to know what my statement implies, that I want him, but we can never be together. Maybe I shouldn't have said anything at all.

"Why?" he asks, voice tremulous.

My gaze snaps to Gavin. I clench my jaw. Direct. I should have seen that coming. I knew better. Gavin can't read my emotions like most people. It's worked out in my favor for weeks—months. I want to tell him, but can't say a word. Instead, I shake my head and surge to my feet. The sooner I get out of here, the better. This was a huge mistake.

"Drake, wait!"

I want to refuse, to keep moving, but his words freeze me surely as a fist gripping my nerves and rendering me helpless.

He throws back the blankets and races after me in only his boxers and t-shirt. My gaze flicks down his arms and chest and an ache opens up inside of me to run my hands over his skin. *No, no, n o.* I try to shuffle away, but can't move.

I hold out a hand. "Stop. Please. If you care about me at all, just...stop."

Confusion draws his brows together. He slows but doesn't stop. *Please stop!* The gap between us shrinks. *Run, Drake. Run!* But I'm rooted in place. My mouth goes dry and my heart hammers against my ribs like war drums.

"Gav, I can't... I can't take it." Desperation and desire war for control, bleeding into my voice.

And then recognition passes through his stone-colored eyes. His lips part ever so slightly, as if he only just connected the dots. *He knows. Curse me, he knows!*

"It's taken me years to build this wall." My voice shakes with him so close. It lowers an octave of its own accord, and I curse my body for hating me so much. "But...you..."

Gavin's feet nearly touch mine. He studies me with so much hope and fear and curiosity that I know I'm completely screwed. He has never studied me so clearly, with such apparent purpose before.

"What am I doing?" I murmur.

Some new resolve emboldens him. He leans closer, then hesitates. I can't help drawing in a sharp breath. I should run. *Run!* But I don't. I've wanted this since our conversation on the boat, since we shared that blanket and talked about the stars. I've used any excuse I could to touch him. A reassuring pat on the arm or shoulder. A calming hand squeeze. The back rubs...well those might have been too much, but I couldn't resist, and he didn't seem to mind.

"I don't want to ruin our friendship," he whispers. His lips are so close. I don't just feel his words cross my skin. I can taste them, like a summer lemongrass, sharp, tangy, and horribly addictive. He has given me a chance to step away, but I know with absolute certainty that I won't.

"Me either," I breathe. Compulsion forces the sinful confession past my lips. "But I'm absolutely crazy about you."

I barely finish my sentence before our lips press together. I don't know if he kissed me, or if I kissed him. It doesn't matter. All that matters to me is this moment of acceptance. His lips are soft, deliberate, testing the waters. My fingers slide up into his thick, short hair. The kiss is even more glorious than I ever imagined, and I don't want it to end.

"Why can't we have this?" he asks when we come up for air.

I stay close, clinging to Gavin as desperately as he clings to me. "It's against the laws of nature." I close my eyes, pressing my forehead against his just for another fraction of skin contact, a connection. "It's forbidden."

"Says who?" He slides his hands over the thin fabric of my t-shirt. It sends a wave of overwhelming desire through me.

"The *Book*. The Minister." My eyes flutter open, peering at Gavin as if I can consume him with a look alone. Because it could be all we ever have. "The punishment is death by cleansing."

Gavin's thumb slides along my lips. I almost groan in delight. Then he says, "The *Book* says no such thing." A shock rocks through me at yet another lie brought to me by my faith. "And if they have a problem, I dare them to punish us."

I can't help but chuckle, remembering how they tried to burn him already—an event that still gives him nightmares. He could do it. He could protect us. With Gavin, I'm finally safe, finally free to be myself. The last piece falls into place, solidifying my feelings for him.

"I'm serious." He draws back, flipping the door shut so firmly it rattles in the frame. But his gaze never breaks from mine. It burns with a longing I've never seen before, and everything inside of me melts. "This position of mine comes with a few perks." He kisses my jaw, and I'm his to bend to his will. I tense a little at first, then wrap my arms around Gavin, pulling him tight against me as his lips heat my neck. His fingers brush under the hem of my shirt, shooting electric excitement throughout my chest. He shivers in delight.

Gavin draws back again, and I groan in irritation. Why does he keep doing that? Hunger flares in his stone-gray eyes. "But you are my favorite perk by far."

"You talk too much," I tease, desperate for his lips again.

And he lets me shut him up.

32

ZEPHYR

I WAKE BEFORE DAWN, a nervous energy keeping me from getting further rest. Instead, I set to work outlining everything I can think of about each of the island lords. Who owns what land? Who has the most to gain by seizing the crown? Which houses align with whom? Lord Greene's leering at Paige the night of the ball resurfaces. I grit my teeth and scratch his interest under his name. The pen nearly rips through the page.

More and more signs are pointing his way. I don't want to jump to any conclusions, but he seems like the obvious choice. That could either make him a scapegoat...or guilty. So how can I find out before it's too late?

Easton naturally rises early, usually long before I do, so a stunned expression crosses his face when he steps out of the room and sees me hunched over the coffee table. He says nothing until he holds a cup of coffee so pale, I wonder how he can taste it through all the cream. He calls island coffee sharp and bitter. I prefer it that way. That's how I know it's working.

"Have you been up all night?" he asks, eyeing the notebook as he settles next to me.

"No. A couple hours, though." I drop my pen and scrub a hand over my face, then pinch the bridge of my nose and draw in a deep breath. "This is harder than I thought."

"How so?" He pulls the notebook toward him.

I had to draw him a map of the island yesterday. An unruly thing with harsh lines between each lord's sector, population density, and a tangle of arrows where I attempted showing him who aligns with whom. It turned out to be a mess. He whistled, then commented on the disorderly organization of the social structure.

"No wonder people are overlooked," he had said.

Now, he reviews the names, scanning them with sharp attention to detail.

"Four of the major lords stand to gain something from Cypress' downfall," I point out. "All of them have backing from several lesser lords. A few lines cross, which makes it easier for them to rally behind a new king." I pick up my coffee and grimace as the cold fluid hits my tongue. Cold coffee is not my favorite.

Easton glances sideways at me with a smirk, as if to say, *told you it's too bitter*. The moment passes quickly, and he returns his attention to the pages. Focus draws his brows together. We sit in silence as he studies my scratches.

We exchange confused glances when a knock on the door startles both of us. Who would visit so early?

I shuffle toward the door, running my fingers through my hair.

Baron stands on the other side, his face grim, as usual. But something in the slope of his shoulders sets my teeth on edge.

"Zephyr, we need to talk."

"Why?"

"Please." His dark eyes bore into me, pleading in a way I've never seen before.

I step aside to allow him inside.

Baron stalks in, shaking the cold from his coat, but the draft from outside isn't so bad. Spring will arrive soon. I'm running out of time to help Cypress. "Easton, can we have some privacy? Don't go far. I need to talk to you, too."

The other boy raises his brows but nods curtly and takes his coffee back to his room. I don't like the tension following in Baron's wake. *Am I too late to help Cy?*

"You're making me uneasy." I sink back into my seat, closing the notebook.

Baron pulls a chair across from me and settles, leaning forward and resting his thick arms on his knees. "I've put this off long enough. There are things you need to hear, whether you want to hear it or not. Because it's important that you understand the truth. Today."

I groan, pressing my back into the sofa. "Again?"

"Zephyr!" The sharpness mingled with urgency catch me by surprise. "Things are moving quickly now. You may not want me to act like your father, and tides knows I don't deserve it, but it doesn't mean I don't love you. Or that I don't want to protect you with every fiber of my being. I owe you an explanation."

"You don't owe me any—"

"I do." His anxious energy sets my own nerves on edge. *What has happened?*

"Is Cypress okay?"

"For now." Baron examines his hands. "I just...need you to understand. Because you and I are not so dissimilar, and I don't want you to follow in my footsteps." He sighs, rubbing fingers into his eyelids. It takes a moment for him to collect himself. I don't enjoy seeing him this way. Baron is *never* this nervous. "I loved your mother before she ever met my brother. Her energy and spirit were magnetic. I didn't need your magical ability to know that much. Presenting her to Alric ripped me apart. A feeling I think you understand."

Paige. He's talking about Paige. It didn't rip me apart, but it felt horribly unfair.

If Baron notices the twitch in my limbs, he gives no sign. Instead, he barrels onward. "Alric was drawn to her just as certainly as I was, but it was already too late for him. Emry wanted me. She chose me. She begged me to choose her. I tried. I confessed my feelings to my brother, but instead of understanding, he flew into a jealous rage. He sent me on a horrible mission, promising me that, if I proved my loyalty by carrying out his orders, he would let her go."

"But he didn't," I say. That much is obvious.

Baron shakes his head. I've never witnessed so much sorrow, regret, and shame in one hulking form before. Baron positively bleeds with ghosts. "To win Emry, I had to go back to her community and..." He closes his eyes, wincing at the memories. When he opens his mouth to continue, nothing comes out.

Not that he needs to tell me. The king ordered him to wipe out her community. Baron did it just so he could be with the woman he loved. But something went wrong. I don't want to hear his excuses, but I need answers. I need the words to come from his mouth.

Baron must sense my need because he presses on. "By the time I returned, he had already selected Elena...*and* Emry. He knew she would never really love him, so he chose a queen who would offer him power. And he refused to let Emry go out of spite. I'm ashamed to admit that I didn't fight for her. Instead, I distanced myself from them in a self-inflicted exile, licking my wounds. I left her to his devices." His throat bobs and his voice thickens. "Two years passed before I found out how he treated her behind closed doors." His fingers lace together until his knuckles turn white. His jaw twitches.

Knowing what the king did to me, I don't even want to think about what that monster did to her. What did my mother suffer at his hands before I was born?

"I went to Emry, begging forgiveness." Tears glisten in his eyes. I don't think I've ever seen Baron cry. *Except when Mom died.* "Your mother, in her infinite patience and mercy, insisted I had nothing to be forgiven. We unburdened our regrets on each other that day. She wanted me to marry and find happiness, but I couldn't. Not while she was living in his shadow, a toy to his devices."

My nails dig into my palms. I don't even realize I clench my hands in fists until the pain pierces the cloud of rage building in my heart. *His devices.* Those two words make clear enough what my mother endured at the king's hands. And all to send a message to his brother.

"We couldn't marry. Alric would have killed us both. But I swore myself to her all the same, mind, body, and soul."

The king would have killed them, but they would have died together. Wouldn't that have been better than what they suffered? Mom told me a little of her story of woe the night of the ball before the truth came out. Before she and Holly died. *"When you realize you love her, you will risk everything to have her, hold her, protect her. Don't make the same mistake I did. Fight for it."*

I'm backed into the same corner she and Baron found themselves in. But Cypress isn't as cruel as his father...*is he?*

"He knew I wasn't his son," I say. The grief in my voice makes it thick, foreign even to my ears. Not grief for my dead uncle, but for the life I could have lived, had my parents fought for each other. For the mother I lost. For what could have been and never was.

Baron nods grimly. "Alric couldn't have the court knowing the truth. It would make him appear weak. He used you against the two of us. If we tried to leave, he would have killed you. If we told the truth, he would have killed you. And he promised to make us live long lives, knowing it was our fault."

Anger burns in my veins. Tears of frustration and pain well in my eyes. No matter how hard I blink, I can't force them down. I was their curse. "But you didn't stop him from abusing me. I suffered at his hands for years. He beat me to exert his absolute power over you. And you never stopped him."

Tears roll down Baron's cheeks, face drained of color. "I know. I tried to stop him."

"Once!"

He shakes his head, desperation in his dark eyes. I see it now; how much I look like him. Shame that his desperation reveals it. "No. More than once. The first time, he shipped me off on a mission to the mainland to think about my position in his court. Each time I tried after that, he would..." Baron's voice trails off, his eyes glazing over as he remembers some distant horror. "He poisoned himself and made her heal him."

The revelation makes the floor drop out beneath my feet. Her illness progressed because she cured the king of toxins. He knew exactly what he was doing to her. Because of me. Her illness and death are my fault as much as the king's.

"Why now?" I ask, voice weak, trembling. "Why today?"

Baron scrubs away the tears and takes a moment to collect himself. When his eyes meet mine, the sorrow is as well-aimed as any of my dead uncle's punches. "I can't let you suffer as I did. As she did. I can't allow you to relive our mistakes."

My anger bubbles over. "Baron!"

"Cypress made his choice this morning."

My mind reels. He says Paige's name, as I expect, but the sound is distant, muffled by the slow thumping of my pulse in my ears. Everything inside of me shuts down.

33

EASTON

*P*RIVACY. I CLOSE THE door behind me, but the second Baron settles into his story, I crack the door and listen. Every piece of information about this court and these people helps me plan Paige's rescue and our escape from this place. Already, I've figured out how to steal a two-person kayak. A homestead along the western shore has several propped up against a shed wall near the water. All Paige and I have to do is get to it and paddle away with no one noticing.

It's high time we leave this place before the powder keg blows. Tonight. I will slip out when Zephyr passes out and get her. I've learned enough from Zephyr to know where her room is. In and out through the servant's exit.

Baron's story is twisted. A few times, his voice drops off to such a low pitch I can't make out his words, but I get enough to piece it together. The old king was a dirtbag with absolute power. *Which is exactly what is wrong with systems like this one.* I've been trying to tell Zephyr this for weeks. The stubborn fool is so blinded by his own traditions he can't see the truth plainly in his face.

I peek through the crack. Baron's back is to me, and he's hunched over as if a great burden presses him toward the floor. Zephyr's face shifts through a wellspring of emotions so quickly I have a hard time keeping up. The complex web of deceit is hard to track, but I do my best.

As Baron talks about the mission to wipe out Emry's community, I recall our trip toward old St. Louis. We came across a bridge mended in haste as people fled slaughter years ago. My fists clench. Slaughter at Baron's hands, all because he dared to love one of their own. Another piece clicks into place. *Emil*. The guy from the Haven who had been looking for his sister, taken by the Kingdom. He was from that community. Emil is Emry's brother. I almost laugh at the absurdity of it all. Zephyr attacked his own uncle the day he captured Paige.

Zephyr's anger booms through the living room. I jump, startled by the outburst.

Then Baron confesses the true reason for his visit. The king chose Paige.

I can't wait in the shadows any longer. I throw the door open and storm into the living room. "Paige will never go along with this."

Baron glowers at me, probably guessing I listened to the whole sob story. "She already has."

I shake my head, grasping for the Power just out of my reach, thanks to Zephyr. "This is a trick. He has something over her. I know Paige. She would never agree to this."

Zephyr remains as he was on the sofa, hands clenched in fists in his lap, eyes staring at the coffee table with a far-off look. He's checked out. It was only a matter of time, I suppose.

"I was there when they broke the news." Baron challenges me. "Are you calling me a liar?"

"No. I'm calling you blind."

"She was smiling. He was thrilled."

"Blind." I cross my arms over my chest, a position I can usually flex with my Power to make me more imposing, but again Zephyr's presence cuts me off. I can't believe this is true. I can't accept that Paige would go along with something like this. "She is playing him. She must be."

Baron waves me off, returning his attention to Zephyr. He rises and moves toward his son, kneeling in front of the catatonic Zephyr. It takes a moment for him to unclench one of Zephyr's fists, revealing tiny incisions on his palm from his nails. Beads of blood prick his skin. Baron ignores the blood, taking his son's hand.

"If you love her, don't make the same mistake I did. Fight for her."

Zephyr blinks slowly, pulling himself from his daze.

"Do you love her?" Baron asks.

Zephyr's lips part, but it takes a few seconds for words to pass. "Love has nothing to do with it." His voice is hollow, devoid of emotion, a black hole of nothingness. He *does* love her, and this news has hollowed out what little was left of him. "Love fades into resentment and distance."

Baron shakes his head, crestfallen. "No."

"Cy loves her. She's better off."

I want to slap some sense into him. Into both of them. *Love. Who cares about love?* Paige is trapped and we need to rescue her. Don't they see that?

"Zeph..." Baron's voice begs for understanding.

Zephyr gives him nothing. He jerks his hand out of Baron's, shoulders coiling tight like a predator preparing to strike.

Baron flinches away. "You're wrong, son."

"I'm not your son."

"My love never faded. I love your mother more now than I ever did before. Alric set a poor example. He loved nothing but his crown and his heir."

Zephyr lumbers to his feet, staggering toward the cupboards in a daze. *Did I miss some of his hidden bottles?* If he drank himself to oblivion before, he will drink himself into a grave now.

Forget all notions of love and who loves who and who the hell cares. I need Zephyr ready to leap into the fire to get Paige out of there *now*. And I know exactly how to do it.

I push past Baron, trailing after Zephyr. Baron tries to stop me, but one well-aimed glare makes him draw back.

"Zephyr, listen to me. Paige doesn't want this. I know her. She is getting something out of this. A ticket home, maybe."

"It has something to do with you, I would bet," Baron says from the sofa. I half turn to find him peering at me, not Zephyr. "King Cypress asked me to bring you in."

I shake my head. "No. Not yet." It's a good way to get into the palace, probably the safest, but everyone will be watching me. Paige and I will never make it out. For the moment, I need to stay the course.

Zephyr slams cupboard doors as he rummages, searching for a stray bottle, no doubt. His hands tremble violently with each jerky movement. "You saw her that day in town, falling over him all smiles and charm."

"An act." It had to be.

"A good one."

My fingers grip his collar, jerking him around to face me. I glare at him, hoping to ignite a fire in his dead eyes. "If you won't fight for her, I will."

His jaw twitches. It's the only sign of life, the only warning before he blindsides me with a punch that sends me reeling. I work my jaw, blinking stars from my vision. Rage burns in Zephyr's eyes. His entire body vibrates with it.

I smirk. "That's better."

34

PAIGE

THE DAY TUMBLES INTO chaos faster than I can breathe. Cypress breaks the news to Nora and Bella alone. He believes it's better that he faces them without me looming over his shoulder. I wish I could see the look on Bella's face when he tells her. And I want to talk to Nora about this. She is one of the few people in this place I've trusted. Is my trust misplaced? Will she be angry? No doubt she will take his rejection with grace—as she does with everything—but that doesn't mean she won't be upset by the news.

Despite being dismissed while Cypress attends to the day's business, I'm not given a moment to myself. Queen Elena marches me to Princess Bronwyn's suite—it seems Cypress' request to keep this quiet does not include excluding the royal princess, and he did ask her to keep me close at all times.

Princess Bronwyn's face lights up and she hugs me close, calling me sister. That word sends a rod of sorrow through my heart, reminding me of Gavin. No one else has ever called me sister. While I like the princess, and I've never had a sister, I worry she will grow too attached when the inevitable happens. I agreed to this, but I will find my way out. I feel like I'm stealing something from her.

Immediately, the queen and princess whisk me down to the kitchens to speak with the head chef, then the salon, to "see what we can do about this hair"—even though their stylists have already had their way with it—then to the gardener, and a hundred others I had no idea even existed. It feels as if they are planning the wedding for the next day with the eager urgency they place in every decision.

"I won't marry without my family here," I tell the two women. "No matter how long that takes. Cypress agreed with me."

The princess waves the comment off. "It won't take that long."

But it will. Easton is the only one I trust with this message. And Gavin is part of my family. He has to be here as well. That's more moving parts than these two women are aware of.

Hopefully, Cypress or Baron can get a hold of Easton before Bella exacts her vengeance—assuming this is not what she had planned all along. I can't stop worrying about Easton all day. *The heart comes next.* Cypress asked to keep the letter and the box with the eye. While I didn't want to keep them, I don't know why he would.

Dinner ends up the tamest part of my day. If you can call sitting with Cypress, Queen Elena, and Bronwyn tame. We're just waiting for Dominic. Cypress sits back in his seat, staring at the door as if willing his brother to stroll through. He drums his fingertips against the tabletop. I remain silent at his right side, hands folded in my lap. My stomach growls with a vengeance. Something about the way Cypress clenches his jaw the longer he glares at the door has me worried.

Queen Elena remains statuesque on his left, the very image of patience. Except for the glances she sneaks my way. We haven't had a second alone yet, and I'm terrified of the moment she corners me. But I won't tremble in her presence. Whatever hold she thought she had over her son was clearly not as absolute as she thought.

Bronwyn studies the napkin folded in her lap, eyes occasionally flicking to the empty seats that family members used to occupy. Alric. Lady Emry and Zephyr. Cypress occupies the former King's seat. Admiral Baron's and Prince Dominic's seats are vacant as well, though either of them could stride in at any moment to claim their place. Still, three vacancies and four losses in the family must be difficult to bear. Especially for someone as kind as the princess.

Her gaze lingers a moment on Zephyr's seat. Sadness shines in her blue eyes, though she remains expert as keeping it from her expression.

"My brothers wouldn't miss me, but Bronwyn would be crushed," Zephyr's voice haunts me. He and the princess were close. How is she really handling his exile? Does she know what Cypress and I agreed on, that Zephyr will return to his family, where he belongs? I wish I could tell her, but Cypress said he would handle it. Can I trust him to keep his word?

You *won't*, I remind myself. The moment I can break this engagement, I will. Cypress must know that. Perhaps Zephyr's pardon is conditional on my following through.

I'm certain of one thing. If I don't keep my distance from Zephyr, his family will lose him all over again—maybe for good. Cypress has placed me in a beautiful cage, but a cage nonetheless.

"We shouldn't wait any longer," Cypress announces, a sharp edge in his tone. "Who knows how long his work will keep him away." Without further preamble, he digs into his dinner, a juicy red steak with steaming mashed potatoes and lightly steamed vegetables.

They remove the cover from my plate, and my mouth waters in anticipation. But instead of steak, a tilapia salad waits.

"We need to keep you lean for the wedding," Queen Elena explains, as if remarking on the clear blue sky and not my weight. I silently fume. The first blow is struck.

I won't give her the satisfaction of knowing how her comment infuriates me, so I keep my response simple before diving into the salad as if it were a steak. "My Powers require more calories to burn. I'm not too worried about keeping trim."

"Perhaps a few etiquette lessons before the engagement reception are in order as well," the queen says flatly.

My future in this family immediately becomes clear. The queen will pick me apart skin, nerves, and bone, molding me into what she thinks I should be. And Cypress won't stop her.

"Does Vincent teach etiquette?" I ask, hoping to sound perfectly innocent in my question.

Cypress freezes. His fingers tighten around his fork. Steak juice drips down his fist and into the white cuffs of his shirt. He's oblivious. "Vincent *Greene*?" He says the name through his teeth.

My heart stutters. Greene. Lord Greene. Bella Greene. Vincent Greene. I remember him now... from the ball. He looked so different that night, or maybe I was too distracted to really notice him.

Cypress and I lock gazes. Something dark passes through his blue eyes. The reaction fills me with dread. If Lord Greene is working against Cypress, and just his name caused such a reaction, does that make Dominic an accomplice...or is he being used? My mouth dries as I try piecing everything together. I need to know where Dominic stands before it's too late.

Before I can open my mouth to respond, Dominic strides in, each step full of purpose. Cypress' jaw twitches before he drops his fork on his plate and wipes his hands on a napkin. I quickly reach over and wrap a hand around his wrist.

"Cypress..." I whisper, hoping he senses my urgency.

A hurricane brews in his blue eyes—pure and dangerous. But it isn't directed toward me. With a slight nod of his head, I let go, watching him in fear as he crosses the dining room. Each step is like thunder.

The two exchanged clipped words, their voices low. Whatever Cypress says to Dominic, the prince tenses, but his sharp response seems to send a rod down Cypress' spine. He doesn't move, doesn't blink. The only signs that he hasn't frozen dead on the spot are a twitch in his tight jaw and the subtle clenching of his fists at his sides.

"Staring is rude, Lady Paige." Again, Queen Elena's voice sends a wave of rage through me.

Without meaning to, I shoot a glare at the queen before turning my attention to my extremely inadequate dinner. Using peripherals, as I was taught at the Department of Security, I observe as the prince shows Cypress something on a page, then whispers urgently in Cypress' ear.

The king closes his eyes and takes a deep breath to center himself. Even Queen Elena watches now.

Cypress draws himself up to his full height and turns to the three of us. His gaze sweeps the empty seats before settling on me. "Paige, I'm sorry." He doesn't sound sorry. "I made you promises I'm not sure I can fulfill."

The world tilts. My Power surges despite the bracelet, hammering against the wall blocking it out. "Is Easton...?" I can't finish. Grief already clenches my throat tight.

It takes too long for him to catch on. Long enough for tears to prick my eyes. *Bella did this! I will kill her slowly.*

"No." Cypress takes a step toward me, but his movements aren't as fluid as usual. Whatever Dominic has whispered to him has Cypress on edge. "He's fine for now. But your friend seems to have become an unfortunate pawn in a much larger game."

I breathe a sigh of relief, irritated that he led me to believe Easton died at all. Shouldn't a king know how to choose his words better? Then understanding hits me. The larger game. The reason for our agreement. The traitor working with Bella. I flick my gaze to the prince, but Dominic looks...sad. His face has mottled in some sort of grief. *Zephyr?*

"I'm sorry to cut dinner short, ladies," Cypress says, and he sounds like he really means it. "But Baron has some questions to answer."

Neither of the women beside me catch on. Do they even know someone is working against Cypress and the crown? *No. Not someone. And certainly not Baron...* But what do I know about the Admiral? He doesn't talk to me. He doesn't seem to like me much. And Cypress sent him to retrieve Easton this morning. So why isn't Easton here yet?

What does Baron have to gain if Cypress falls? Would he be next in line for the throne?

I can't ignore Cypress' reaction to learning that Vincent was the one training me. Dominic knows that. Cypress must have questioned him...or he should. Why would Domonic use someone he knows his brother clearly mistrusts?

It must be Vincent. He would be a fantastic inside man for Bella, who just so happens to be his daughter.

I rise to go after them, but Queen Elena snatches my hand and pulls me down.

"Don't overstep your boundaries on the first day, girl. Sit and finish."

I no longer have an appetite.

Trust my mother and no one else. Can I even trust her?

35

GAVIN

R AYS OF SUNLIGHT SHINE through the open ceiling of the temple. I stand in the warmth, basking in it for as long as possible. Winters around these northern lands are harsh and bitterly cold. I don't enjoy the sharp wind that rips my breath from my lungs. The need for a protective barrier against the elements became apparent within days of my display in front of the entire community. With the help of a few more experienced acolytes, we create an invisible barrier that keeps the elements away while allowing natural light in.

I flex my fingers on the stage, remembering the high of raw Power that pulsed through me that day. How I conjured so much, I still don't understand. I've used pieces of it since then, but nothing so strong. Something tells me I will need to learn to harness this Power not only for my protection but also for the sake of everyone. While I may not have faith in prophecies and omens, I understand evolution. My Powers result from a new need in the world. A need I'm terrified to discover.

Weeks of grueling campaigning for the open Elder council seats have finally drawn to a close. Today, the people will cast their votes to fill the vacancies.

The night I spent with Drake distracts me when I least expect it. It was the most beautiful night I've ever experienced. If anyone suspects the two of us, they don't give any sign. I don't think Emil would care. Not that he has been around to notice. Emil vanished after I told him about his sister. I've asked around the Haven. He's around, mostly with Ally. Which means he's avoiding me. It hurts. I hadn't meant to hurt him. He deserved the truth.

Creating a government is harder than I expected. Even with a foundation from which to work. I have studied systems from ancient worlds—long before the war and collapse—as well as those that followed. I know the pros and cons of each type of government inside and out, as well as what caused their eventual collapse. One would think that, with all the knowledge locked in my brain, I would have no trouble with this task. On paper, I don't struggle. But it isn't just about balance. It's about people. Keeping them healthy and happy, equal. I can outline a perfect government but can't read the people within it. If only Dad were here to help balance me out. He would know what to do. He's done this before.

Except the Haven is nothing like Elpis. Nor are the people. Their needs are vastly different. If the infighting here doesn't reveal that truth, I don't know what else will.

The tickle of matter brushes my fingertips, then creeps across my palm. I reach out carefully with my heart and mind, focusing on the sensation of so many elements and how they blend. Using elemental matter mutation isn't as simple as changing one thing into another by manipulating the molecular structure. A Naturalist needs to understand how various elements work together—or don't. The wrong combination can be lethal in a million different ways.

The first time I used my Naturalist Power to transform matter, it created an explosion that left a small crater in the backyard. Dad sat me down and explained the importance of control and understanding my Power. The next day, the school had me enrolled in a class that teaches students to use that exact Power. Messing with matter is highly volatile.

I've come a long way in the last eight years—nine, almost. I've memorized every known element, their interactions, reactions, and hypothetical applications. My touch is much smoother than it was when I was eleven.

The temple stage ripples around my feet, slithering up my legs like wooden armor, smooth and seamless. But this is child's play compared to what I did before.

I raise my gaze to the sunlight once more.

Havenites come and go from the temple to bask in the natural light—something most of them have lived their entire lives without—but they still see this place as sacred and treat it as such. They only come when they need to atone or when they see me and think I'm about to take up the Minister's mantle. They always leave bitterly disappointed.

None of them touches the stage, afraid it's akin to touching the birthplace of God. The notion makes my skin crawl. And here I am, wrapping the stage around me like a comforter.

The wood whips away from my legs like dancing flames. For a moment, I can't breathe. The memory of agony, of fire and heat and burning flesh arise. I fall to a knee, gasping for air as if suffocating on smoke and pain all over again. I have nightmares about being burned alive while my family watches, or while no one is there to witness my gruesome death.

It isn't real, Gavin, Drake's soothing voice echoes in my head.

I flick a hand away from me, and the dancing wooden flames transform into waves of wooden water, flowing outward as if washing away the memory. The nightmares aren't real, but they are founded on fact. A fact I can't get over.

These people burned me alive. They lauded me a creature of destruction, fit for death, in one breath, then praised me as their savior in the next...after I saved myself. What will they do if they learn about Drake and me?

Gramps was there the day they burned me. I've never met him. He died when Dad was younger than I am now. But there is no doubt who it was. He thrust me from death. I can't wait to tell Dad and Gram, but it scares me, too. Because it means telling them what happened to me here, on this very stage.

Wood transforms before my eyes, creating a flawlessly smooth image of Gramps—albeit made of wood. He strides toward me, broad shoulders stooped. Then he wraps his arms around me, dwarfing me in his embrace. In a half dozen embraces. All wooden recreations of my family, huddled in a mass. A reunion of grain and grief.

I cry in the center of the huddle, sheltered by the arms of my family, invisible to the naked eye among the five of them. I let it all out. All the sorrow and fear and loneliness. I miss them so much it tears my heart in two. Will I become bitter one day, like Emil, never to see my sister again? He's avoided me ever since I told him about his sister's death. Another painful, festering wound I can't heal.

Clouds gather overhead, casting shadows over my wooden family, mirroring my mood.

"Gavin?" Drake's voice is soft, patient.

The family circle opens, allowing Drake space to step in and join them. He eyes the wooden, stringless marionettes with unease. Instead of joining the circle, he disrupts it, taking my hand and pulling me away. They disburse and become part of the stage once more. I eye Mom as she vanishes.

"Hey." He takes my face in his hands, forcing me to meet his eyes.

"Why do I not just leave, Drake?" It's the logical thing to do. No one would dare stop me. I could go home and never look back. "Why do I stay?"

"I would like to think I have something to do with that." He offers a weak smirk. The joke is lame. We both know he would come with me if I left.

"You do."

Drake brushes away my tears, just as tender as always. And like I have since we gave in to our true feelings, I lean into it. I want to kiss him, but we are here in the open. Even this touch is risky.

"I got something for you," he says.

I follow his gaze to see the mountain rope bracelet in his open palm. My cheeks heat as he slides it on my wrist. That's when I notice he's wearing the other one of the crashing wave. It feels like something momentous just happened between us. And if anyone sees...

I pull back and his hands reluctantly drop to his sides.

"I'm not built for this sort of thing," I admit. "I'm an idea guy, a creator. Not a leader."

"Some people don't get to choose. No matter how much they want to." Drake turns away, tilting his gaze toward the open sky above. He stuffs his hands in his pocket.

"I'm going to screw this up."

He purses his lips thoughtfully, then shakes his head. "I don't believe that. I have faith in you."

Faith. I hate that word. I want to burn it from existence. "At least someone does."

I'm not immune to the warning of Charles that the people would turn against me, nor the whispers. I ignore them because I can't change anything. And certainly not like these people want me to. I won't be their Minister. I don't even want to be a leader. Once this election is over and things settle down here in the Haven as they should, I will take an offer of alliance back to Elpis, then go get my sister and bring her home. If the Havenites and acolytes knew I planned to leave them, they would turn against me today.

For a moment, Drake and I bask in the sunlight in agreeable silence, standing close enough that our arms touch. This moment is one perfect fragment in a shattered kaleidoscope of chaos. I breathe it in, absorbing as much as possible.

"The votes are in," he whispers, knowing his words will shatter the illusion. He senses the perfect tranquility of the moment, how I sometimes revel in the silence with only my thoughts. "Final counts should be just about done."

I groan, shoulders sagging. I step toward the massive arching doors as a flash of color disappears on the other side. "Okay. Let's get this over with."

Drake slides his hand out of mine the second we walk out of the temple. I miss the warmth and comfort it provides instantly. But holding hands in public is out of the question here. It breaks my heart that we must hide who we are in the Haven. It shouldn't matter.

"If we were in Elpis, no one would care," I say softly, only for his ears. "No one would even look at us twice."

Drake is silent for a few steps, hands stuffed in his pockets. Finally, he sighs. "How long until you leave?"

I glance at him. The tightness in his jaw and the sadness in his eyes make me ache. "Come with me, Drake. You'll never be happy here." I swallow, averting my gaze. "And I'll never be happy if you stay."

Drake stops, grabbing my arm to pull me to a halt as well, forcing me to face him. "Gavin, you must realize by now that I would follow you to the end of the world. I'm absolutely mad about you." His voice drops. Not because he's ashamed of the words—I know that now—but because he is worried someone else will hear his confession.

The words make my head spin in a way I've never experienced before. It fills me with pure delight, but scares me as well. How long can it last?

He shifts like he wants to move closer but doesn't dare. Not in a hallway where anyone could see us. "I would rather die at your side today than live a single breath without you."

I can't help snorting and rolling my eyes, making light of the moment. "A bit dramatic." I'm deflecting. I share his feelings, without a doubt, but can't get the words out. Instead, I resort to my dad's tactic of making light of a serious moment.

Drake bites his lip, drawing my attention to it. "Gavin..."

"We have a job to finish here, Drake." I can't focus on this now. I need to finish what I set out to do here. "Let's get it done. Then we can talk about the future."

"I just told you I love you."

"I know."

"And you can't say it back?"

Is he angry with me? "Do I have to say it?"

Drake's dark eyes flick back and forth, like he can't choose which part of my face to focus on. His brows crease. Finally, he sags and shakes his head. Drake won't say it, but I've hurt him. Expressing my feelings has never been a strong point. I feel things just like anyone else does, but when it comes to putting those feelings into words, I fail. Because I can never find the *right* words to truly express myself. It's like they don't even exist.

"Let's go." Drake turns away and shuffles toward the square where everyone will gather for the announcement.

Before we arrive at the square, the noise reaches us. A cacophony of shouts and stomping feet, punctuated by screams.

"What in the name of the Idols?" Drake mutters.

Instinctively, I move closer to him and pull at my Powers, letting them flood through my body. Electrical pulses of energy. Tingling sensations from the natural materials around us. My heart races, causing sweat to bead on my brow.

"Stay close," I say.

Drake swallows, then nods stiffly.

Together, we step toward the mouth of the hallway opening in the square and are greeted by chaos.

36

PAIGE

CYPRESS HAS BEEN GONE for *hours*. The sun set long ago, despite his promise to see me before bed. What is keeping him? Does he understand the danger he is in? Do I? I don't love Cypress by any stretch of the word, but I do care about him. He holds a special place in my heart. I pivot on my heel, wearing a hole in the rug.

The knock on my door sounds like an alarm in my eardrums. I rush to the door and thrust it open, stumbling back to find Bella waiting.

"You certainly don't waste time," she says as she pushes past me, assuming an invitation.

I grit my teeth, holding the door open as a clear sign she is to leave. Bella doesn't care. She slides her fingers along the purple gown I wore all day, now hanging on the bathroom door, admiring Mariah's handiwork.

"I believe I have the authority to remove you from the palace grounds now," I growl.

"I believe you don't have nearly as much authority as you think." Bella drops the sleeve of the dress and rounds on me, hands on her wide hips.

"If anything happens to Easton, Cypress will know it was you. I told him everything."

She snorts, rolling her eyes. "I'm not afraid of a prince pretending to be a king."

"He knows about your father." I can't help the smugness washing over me. *Let her swallow that!* "And Baron."

"Does he, now?" Bella's plastered smile makes my insides twist. Why is she smiling? "Perfect."

The smugness flushes away. I clasp my hands around the door so she can't see me shaking. Though with worry or rage, I'm uncertain. What does she mean by *perfect*? Unless... "You set Baron up."

"A little information in the right place can make all the difference."

I turn to rush out the door to stop whatever Cypress is doing to his uncle. Hopefully, nothing that will haunt him. He needs to know before it's too late.

Before I step past the threshold, the door rips out of my hand, slamming shut in my face. Vines whip up around the frame, locking it shut. Bright yellow flowers bloom, assaulting my senses. I stumble backward.

"Thank you, Paige, for keeping the king distracted. It was far more than I could have hoped for."

"You *wanted* me to do this, to accept his proposal and tether myself to him so I could continue being your pawn. But I'm done with your game, Bella." I stalk toward her, feeling the familiar heat of my Power as it sets my nerves on fire. How I would love to burn her face off! And I could. Easily. But that fire might consume the room, or the palace, without a firm grasp on the wild Power.

"I don't care if you agree to marry him. None of that is of real consequence. Your role is to keep him distracted, and you did it marvelously." Bella touches the surface of my dresser. Part of the wood transforms into a sharp wooden dagger as white as bone. Her bracelet is conspicuously absent from her wrist.

Why does she need me to distract Cypress? What did he tell me...? *"I've suspected her of something for a while now."* So why did she need me to distract him if he was already on to her? That doesn't make sense. I told him the whole truth, everything I remember about her from the moment I arrived in the palace, and she doesn't seem the least bothered. Nor did he seem very surprised.

"It's too late…" I breathe the words, unable to hide my trembling any longer.

The door handle rattles. The door thumps against the frame. "Paige, are you alright in there?"

Nora! I throw my Power at the door, shattering the lock on the bracelet. The vines burst into thin flames, then flutter to the floor in ashes. I rush forward to open it, but Bella grabs my hair and yanks me back. Her knife presses to my throat.

"Shh…" She hisses in my ear in what she must assume is a soothing sound.

I swallow, feeling how sharp the blade is against my throat. Can I destroy the wooden blade as easily as the vines without hurting myself?

"Paige, I heard commotion," Nora calls through the door, her voice muffled. "Are you okay?"

I squeeze my eyes closed, worried about what Bella will do if Nora walks in. *Please leave. Please leave.*

Power rages to life inside me. I try to ride the waves as I did in training with the prince, but I can't seem to grasp the flow. It slips through my fingers like water, coating me but never allowing me control.

"I'm coming in," Nora announces.

"No!" The blade slices my neck, cutting off my protest. Bella didn't even hesitate.

I try to call out a warning to Nora but can't do anything more than fall to my knees, clutching the wound in my neck. Blood flows through my fingers. My vision dims.

"Paige! What—?" Nora steps through, only seeing me on the floor.

I reach a shaking hand out to stop her, but it's too late. Bella moves like a viper, shoving Nora out of the way with a mass of tangled vines as she bolts into the hallway.

Nora rushes to my side, pressing her warm hands to the wound. "I should have known," she mutters.

The pain in my neck abates, though the dizziness remains. Nora's Power has something to do with Hematology. She's healing me.

"Cypress..." It's all I can say as the breath rushes back through me.

Nora understands well enough. She throws a hand toward the hallway, at Bella's retreating form. The other girl pitches forward as if shoved from behind. In a matter of seconds, Nora has Bella lifting off the ground until her toes scrape the carpet. Bella's skin mottles. She struggles against Nora's Powered grip, but it's no use. Nora is stronger. Even as she stitches me up, she pulls Bella's blood to the surface of her skin like a magnet.

Bella screams, shouting for help, shrieking in agony. Her fingers splay outward on either outstretched arm.

I feel the shift around us, but don't understand what is happening until it's too late.

A spear of wood shoots out from my dresser, lancing Nora's back through her heart. She immediately slumps over the spear as the blood drips on the floor, dead before she knew what was coming.

Tears prick my eyes. I brush a shaking hand over Nora's sleek hair. *Dad was right. I'm not ready for this.* He warned me I couldn't handle watching a friend die. Nora deserved better. She *was* better...than all of us.

Bella coughs, gasps, and scraps in the hallway. I wish I could take a moment to absorb this moment with Nora, to honor her death as she deserves, but Bella is free.

And Cypress is in danger.

Instincts honed by a year of training kick in. I launch to my feet, stumbling through the waves of dizziness, fighting for control of my Power. I race into the hallway after Bella.

She's on her feet at the elevator door, hitting the button repeatedly. My bare feet thunder over the floor. She glances back, eyes widening, then abandons the elevator for the stairs.

As she rounds the corner with me closing in on her, Bella collides with Prince Dominic. He wraps his arms around her to steady her.

"Nora!" Bella gasps, clinging to the prince.

His blue eyes sweep over her, taking in the blood, then at me. I skid to a stop to avoid colliding with both of them.

"Why are you both covered in blood?" he asks.

Bella plays the part of a maiden in distress unnervingly well, pressing her advantage before I can get in a word. "Nora attacked me. She attacked both of us with her Bloodart."

"She killed Nora," I say, hoping to pin Bella while the prince has a hold of her. Will she kill him as easily as she killed Nora?

"In self-defense," Bella whimpers. "She tried to pull me apart."

I open my mouth to protest, to explain, but the words won't slip past my tongue. I try to use my Power to rip at her feet, to feel the glorious satisfaction of removing her ability to run ever again. But something yanks on my Power like a helpless dog on a leash. I yelp, brushing my bloody hands over my throat as if the leash is real. As if I could burn it away. *Who is doing this to me?*

Prince Dominic *tsks* as he peers past us toward my open door, sadness etched on his long face as he sees Nora's body. I don't dare look back and see Nora's sightless eyes or blood on my floor.

"Cypress is in danger," I say, unable to do anything else. Someone is Controlling me somehow. I don't understand. Gram's wall should keep everyone out.

"Come with me." Prince Dominic ushers both of us away from the floor. I trudge along, if for no other reason than to ensure Bella doesn't spear him like Nora. We stop outside the door to his suite on the top floor.

"What are we doing? Dominic, we need to help Cypress!" I halt outside his door as he swings it open, digging in my heels. Every second we waste puts Bella close to her goal.

"And I will." Prince Dominic rests a gentle hand on my shoulder. "But you need to stay safe."

I want to scream at him, hit him to make him see what's right in front of his face. How can he be so blind? "I can fight."

"I know."

"Bella... she..." *Why can't I tell him?* Every time I start, the words strangle in my throat. A growl of frustration climbs up my throat.

Behind his shoulder, Bella clings to the prince's arm, smirking at me.

"Paige, inside." Prince Dominic dips his head into his suite, firmly insistent. "I will deal with Bella."

I want to refuse. I'm trained for these situations. I can help. But my steps are forced, as if someone else controls me. *What is going on?* I can't control my body. I can't say what I want to say. I can't use my Power.

I'm helpless.

Prince Dominic eases the door closed, offering me a weak smile, as if it makes up for turning me into a prisoner. "Stay."

"I'm not a dog."

But the door closes, sealing me in. The lock clicks into place. *"Trust my mother and no one else."* Cypress' warning comes unbidden as the horrifying truth slams against me.

Prince Dominic. He brought Vincent to those training sessions. When I couldn't control my Powers, Prince Dominic stepped in to calm me, reassure me. He convinced me to open up to his Influence. But this... this feels different. He can't control me, which means it must be Vincent. He slipped in when Dominic had my mind open like a book. He rewrote the pages to gain future access. Now, even without my bracelet, I can't seem to grasp my Powers. They slip through my fingers like water, unwilling to respond to my coaxing. Tears well in my eyes.

Cypress suspects more than he let on. He must. He warned me, *"I...need to check something for myself before I cast suspicion further."*

Oh, Cypress, what have you learned?

On shaking limbs, I stalk toward the window. Maybe I can find a way out. But the prince's suite doesn't have a balcony like the others. Just numerous bay windows that peer out at the grounds and lake beyond.

Shadowy forms move in formation around the palace, taking up positions. *An army.* Are they here to help Cypress, or Vincent? What part does Dominic play in all of this? I can no longer assume his innocence. He knows more than he's let on.

I scream in frustration, pounding a fist against the thick glass.

A boom resounds somewhere deep in the belly of the palace, shaking the floor. As I sink onto the sofa, tears stream down my face. I need help. I need out of here. I need my Power.

Zephyr would help me if he were still here. His Power would free me from this hold.

The thought strikes agony in my heart. Cypress was going to bring him back. *Too late to be of real help.* I bite my lip and close my eyes, willing his stupid, stubborn face to appear before me.

37

ZEPHYR

E ASTON GETS ON MY last nerve. He won't stop pacing and peering around the corner toward the fort entrance. My jaw hurts from grinding my teeth. We've been waiting for nearly a half an hour for Baron to return.

Cypress requested Easton's safe escort into the palace, and Easton plans to make full use of the invitation to warn Cypress that Lord Greene is working against him. But Baron must sneak me in at the same time so he and I can rally the soldiers to defend the king. No one can see me go in. If Lord Greene knows I'm back inside the palace walls, it might warn him we are on to him. Surprise is our ally.

But Baron was supposed to be back for Easton already.

I can't lie to myself, even if I lie to the others. I'm not okay. My reasons for storming the palace are entirely selfish. The idea of Paige and Cypress married has broken the last of my resolve. I don't know what I expected. Of course Cypress would choose her. She's powerful, smart, and beautiful. I don't care what Easton says, Paige chose this. Cypress has looks and charm in spades. Without me around to distract her, he probably had no trouble winning her over.

Anger bubbles up. I close my eyes and take a deep breath. In. Out. Repeat.

"Something is wrong," Easton mutters. "He should have been here a long time ago. A few minutes late, sure, but this..." He peers around the corner again, tensing. "Your friend is coming. Fast."

I join Easton. Sure enough, Nat sprints to where we wait, his face flushed as if he ran quite a distance to get here. Baron must be indisposed and sent Nat in his place to slip us in. He dips around the corner, grabbing my hand as he goes. And he doesn't stop. Nat jerks me along, still sprinting away from the fort. Easton remains on our heels.

"Nat, what—?"

The question dies in my throat as I watch the fort gates open. Regimented lines of troops march out. My heart sinks.

"We're too late," Easton says, echoing my conclusion.

"Baron was arrested for treason, Zephyr," Nat says around gasping breaths. "They are saying he conspired against the crown to seize control."

I shake my head. "But he was—"

"Helping *us*. I know." Nat nods grimly. "But they have evidence against him. He won't survive the night."

The world tilts and spins. The lines of troops turn west, heading toward the palace. We watch the troops with growing unease. Are they going to help Baron or Cypress?

"I barely got out before they spotted me," Nat says. He leans back, gulping down air. "They're wrong, right, and he's been set up to take the fall? I mean, we know Lord Greene is tied to this somehow."

I suspected Baron, at one point, and told Dominic as much. Unless he's very good at lying, there's no way Baron is guilty. *But he did hide the truth about being my father from me my entire life... Stop it Zephyr, you're being an idiot. It isn't Baron. It can't be.*

Easton gapes at me. "No, Nat. I've seen the guy who..." He cuts off, as if unable to say any more. Easton's fingers drift to the eyepatch. Why won't he tell us what he knows even now? "It isn't Baron."

I groan, wishing for a hearty drink to calm my nerves. Instead, I settle for scrubbing my hands over my face.

"What about the prince or princess?" Easton asks. "Maybe the King's selection has forced them into action. If they are aiming for the crown, having a queen at the king's side can't play into their plans very well."

Nat chuckles, shaking his head. "Bronwyn and Dominic? Not a chance. I would suspect the queen of turning against her son before either of them."

Easton lifts his brows as if he just proved some point. "An overlooked princess and the youngest prince have nothing at all to gain here. Right. I'll eat my boots if that's true."

I shake my head. "Nat's right. And Queen Elena hates me, but she adores her kids. Even if she has an odd way of showing it. Maybe she had something to do with her husband's death, and Alric was an accidental casualty, but she wouldn't harm her kids."

"I don't believe any of this for a second," Easton grumbles. "And if you do, you've been blinded by some foolish sense of nobility."

The words are as good as a knife in my heart. He's right. I've been blind to some secrets in this family for years. The Strongs are so fractured by greed and ghosts it's hard to trust anything. But a Strong will never turn against a Strong. *Cypress turned against me*.... No. In the end, we always stand together.

"Look, we know Lord Greene is up to something," I say, but the rest of my speech is cut off as magic slams against me. The familiar sensation of Paige's magic that sends me staggering into a brick wall as if she shoved me into it herself.

Easton clenches his fists and pivots. He knows what just happened. "Enough talk. I'm going to get her the hell off this island."

Nat jumps forward, snatching Easton's arm and jerking him backward. "Wait. You can't storm the palace when it's heavily guarded."

Easton sneers, jerking his arm free. The well-aimed fury in his dark eye bores into Nat. "Watch me. I have an invitation to come unharmed."

"Nat's right." I sigh, hating the words, but knowing what I need to do next. Before Easton can throw himself into a rant, I cut him off. "The game has changed. We don't know if those guards will honor the invitation. We don't know who they serve... We have to sneak in."

Nat shakes his head, eyes wide. "Zeph, if they catch you, Cypress will kill you. His orders were explicit. Kill on sight."

"Then they better not see me." I stalk away from the marching lines of troops to swing wide, nodding for Easton to follow.

Fight for her.

I don't want to fight Cypress; I want to help him. I don't want any of this, but I can't leave Paige trapped in that den of vipers. And I can't leave Baron to die.

38

GAVIN

THE HAVEN SQUARE HAS become a writhing mass of bodies moving and screaming in chaos. The final count has been announced, and Drake and I missed it, but whatever the results, the people aren't happy.

I can't make out most of what the people are shouting, but I catch enough bits to understand the sentiment. The division between those who support the Elders and those who are eager for change has erupted, making the previous fights look like toddlers throwing a tantrum by comparison.

Menlue and his supporters fight their way to the front of the square, to the platform. I skim the frantic mass of bodies, moving in all directions as they fight. It's like watching a swarm of flies with no apparent destination in mind—only constant motion. And the noise. Guardians and acolytes shout commands at the Havenites. Those who don't obey are dragged into place or subdued with Powers. But I can't make sense of anything. Panic spiders out through my nerves. I've never been good with crowds, but this...

I release a shaky breath.

A familiar voice resonates over the din. "A false idol has deceived you, marching through our halls, our Haven, spreading his seeds of doubt, sowing discontent. We must gather and repent, or else face punishment."

Charles.

I clench my jaw so tight it aches, and my hands curl into fists at my sides.

Charles stands on the platform, surrounded by several Guardians and a few acolytes. He has support...from those who are allegedly following me. He warned me, but I foolishly assumed he simply wanted to get under my skin. *"You refuse your Call and it worries them. They question your true divinity... How long before the acolytes and the Elders rise against you again?"*

"Gavin?" Drake breathes.

My hammering heartbeat swallows his voice. The noise engulfs me. I can't think straight, can't collect my thoughts. The madness of the crowd combined with the realization that Charles knew all of this was coming, warned me, and I ignored him, overpowers my senses. Back home, situations that overwhelmed me like this would force me into a corner to block everything out until matters settled.

But this is my mess. Something tells me this won't settle until I step forward.

How did Charles get out of his cell? How did this happen? But I know the answer. The right guards who believed his lies and considered me a false Idol would set him free to stop me.

"Gavin!" Drake calls to me.

A Psionic force field slams against the ceiling, raining dirt, then it forces part of the crowd back, herding them out of the square...straight toward us.

I tremble, turning to Drake, only to discover the Guardians blocking the door have noticed us. They wrestle Drake's arms behind his back and drag him away, back toward the temple.

"Drake!" I snap out of my trance as fear pulses through me. "Let him go!" The words roar out of me as I thrust my Powers at the Guardian holding Drake captive, unaware of just what I'm doing and too panicked to think straight.

Blood drips from the Guardian's nose. He drops his hold. I surge forward. Drake breaks free as the Guardian drops to his knees. Hematology Power. I used it somehow, but don't really understand. Not at the moment. All I can think about is getting Drake to safety.

The floor shakes violently. Two Strongarm acolytes are locked in battle. I can't tell who is fighting for whom as Ally joins the fray with a handful of Guardians. Flames leap toward the ceiling as bodies are flung toward the Psionic barrier using Telekinetic Powers.

"Submit to me," Charles calls above the din, his voice ringing with startling clarity. "And I can absolve you of the false Idol's influence! We can no longer allow him to poison our lives!"

Poison! My blood runs cold.

Drake manages a few steps toward me before Charles calls for his capture.

"Seize Drake! He has been dragged beneath the veil of the false Idol's shadow. We must free him!"

Menlue has pressed toward the platform—though with a few less supporters—and is not locked in a heated argument with Charles that I can't hear as the roar of battle and screams of the Havenites reach a crescendo.

What happened while I was in that temple? How did everything turn upside down?

As I spin, the crowd herded by the Psionic field presses between Drake and me, separating us. I crane my neck to find him over the heads of the people pushing past me. They bump my shoulders, knocking me to and fro. A few grab hold of any part of me they can reach—my arm, hand, shirt, shoulder—begging for me to save them, to help them. The turmoil has my mind swirling. I can't make sense of the chaos.

Panic grips my heart, making my pulse slow the longer it takes for me to spot Drake. I grab bodies, nudging them aside, calling out to Drake.

"Gavin!" I hear him, but can't spot him anywhere.

"Drake!" This is too much. I need space.

My Power coils around me, blue and pulsing with frenzied life. People no longer press near me or reach for me. The sea of bodies parts as if afraid of my Powers, which surges bolder and brighter with each passing second. The lights buzz loudly, then pop. Citizens scream and block their bodies with their arms. They fight against one another, against the acolytes and Guardians. *I don't understand. I don't understand!*

Tears roll down my cheeks.

Then the square plunges into absolute darkness. The only pin-point of light comes from my blue Power. I whimper Drake's name, trying to find him.

Large arms wrap around me, pinning my arms to my sides. Before I can react, something pricks my neck. My vision blurs. I shake my head, attempt pulling away, but the arms hold me firm. Then my knees give out as my vision darkens.

39

ZEPHYR

I T LOOKS LIKE EVERY soldier in the fort has come out to surround the palace. Easton, Nat, and I crowd behind a line of shrubs across the street, near the tavern. My eyes stray to the locked doors, hands shaking for a drink.

Easton follows my line of sight and grumbles under his breath. The distaste for my habit is clear, but he moves on quickly, returning attention to the troops. "A siege."

"What?" I peer over the shrubs alongside him. He's right. These troops aren't here to keep people out. They have regimented all the lines strictly—and all facing the palace. They are there to keep people in.

"They will have every entrance blocked," Nat hisses. "We can't get in. This is suicide."

He's also right. Greene has organized the troops carefully. Even the trees around the cottage are under watch. If we want in, we are likely to end up dead.

"You don't have to come with us," I tell Nat. "I won't blame you for sitting this one out."

Nat snorts.

A boom shakes the earth, something created by magic deep inside the palace. Easton tenses, glancing at me as if looking for some warning sign. I know what he wants and shake my head. "That didn't feel like her."

His lips move as my head swims and my vision darkens. Pressure against my skull makes me weak.

One moment I'm crouching behind shrubs with Easton and Nat, the next I'm crouched in Dominic's suite. *How...?* The room isn't empty. The crying catches my attention first. It twists a knife in my heart.

Paige huddles in a chair near the window, knees drawn to her chest and arms wrapped tightly around them. Her sorrow bleeds into me. Is this real? Did I just teleport, or is this a dream? I rise slowly, eyeing my limbs as if they have answers.

"Paige?" I approach slowly.

Her eyes shoot up, reddened by tears and wide as she meets my gaze. Then she launches to her feet and throws herself at me, wrapping arms around my neck. I grunt from the impact of her body colliding with mine. Despite my confusion about this situation and my anger at her for agreeing to marry Cypress, I can't help but hold her tight.

"We need to help your brother," she cries into my shoulder.

The plea sends a shock down my spine. I stiffen. Cypress. She's worried about Cypress. This reaction has nothing to do with me and everything to do with him. Jealousy flares in my gut. For weeks, I've imagined this, holding her in my arms. I pictured what I would do, how I wouldn't hold back any longer. But she doesn't want me. She wants him. And I have to be strong enough to step back and let her have her happiness.

I should let go, but I can't. My arms are stone, protecting her, clinging to her. If this is the last time I hold her, I'm not ready for it to end. I press a cheek to her smooth ebony hair and breathe in the scent of roses.

"Where is he?" I ask, the words drawing out painfully.

"I don't know. He left dinner to question Baron. But it wasn't Baron. I know it wasn't him. You need to believe me." Paige pulls back but doesn't let go. Not completely. I want her to let go. I want to cling to her forever. "Bella... She's been using me, sending me pieces of Easton as a warning. Cypress was supposed to summon him to the palace to protect him today, but he never came." Her body trembles against mine. "I'm worried about him."

"Easton..."

Paige barrels on, "We don't have much time, Zephyr. She is working with someone else. I don't know who—her dad, maybe?—but she has been using me to keep your brother distracted and using Easton as bait. I think she means to kill Cypress. Tonight. You need to get to him before it's too late."

My fingers trace the lines of her face absently. I don't mean to do it, but I can't help myself. I've waited so long to touch her, and it may never happen again. I focus on memorizing everything.

"Easton is safe," I reassure her. "For the moment, anyway. He's outside the palace right now. I...was with him. Then I was here."

"That's a relief." Her shoulders sag. "I'm sorry. I don't know how I do this." Her hands slide along my neck, cupping my face. "I just needed you, and here you are."

A lump lodges in my throat. Her umber eyes draw me in like two black holes intent on devouring me whole. She searches me, as if reading the truth in my heart, in my soul.

I swallow thickly. "Cypress..."

She shakes her head. A slight motion. "I don't love him. I did what I had to do to protect him. To protect Easton. And you." Her thumbs caress my cheeks. My heart hammers. A hundred protests rage in my mind, all the reasons I shouldn't allow her in. All the reasons I should pull away. All the reasons this is wrong when she is engaged to Cypress. Mother's confession brands itself on my heart. *"You may not recognize love. You may even try to deny love. When the right girl comes along, she will slip through the cracks in your walls."*

Paige hasn't slipped through the cracks. She has created gaping fissures through which she simply strode.

"Will you please say something?" she whispers.

But I can't. I don't understand these emotions raging through me. I don't know how to put any of this into words. I told myself I wouldn't hesitate again. Instead of choosing words, my lips crash against hers, terrified that she will pull away.

She doesn't. Her hands grasp at my face, holding it against hers. Heat pours off her body as she presses against me. My arms slid around her, crushing her body against me, desperate to feel her close. I slide my fingers through her hair. This is hardly the time for passionate kisses, but if this is it, I won't waste a moment.

The earth trembles. Glass breaks nearby. None of it compares to the thudding of my heart as Paige folds into my embrace, giving in to the moment wholly. Is this kiss even real? Her lips taste sweet, her mouth like honey. I've kissed other girls before, but nothing like this. Not just a want or a need, but the pulsing of my heat throughout my body and the ache in my chest that only she can create. I tumble end over end into her orbit. She is the sun. The center of the galaxy, and I gravitate helplessly around her.

When our lips finally part, her hot breath washes over my face. Both of us gasp for breath. Still, I can't let go. Our foreheads touch. Our noses, too.

"I need you to find Bronwyn," I whisper as dust rains from the ceiling. "Tell her I will be in my favorite hiding place."

Her lips reach for mine, brushing with urgent need. If the earth weren't trembling beneath our feet, I might give in utterly.

"How do I get out of this room?" she asks breathlessly.

"No prison can hold you." I drink her in like whiskey. It works, calming my nerves, clearing my mind.

"Someone is Controlling me, Zephyr." Her voice trembles. "I can't use my Power. I can't even touch the door handle."

Fear rips through me. An Operator? This only confirms what the rest of us suspected already. Lord Greene is behind all of this.

My voice quivers as I cling to her. "Okay. We are coming for you now."

Paige blinks at me. Once more, tears sparkle in her umber eyes like stars against a night sky. "Find Cypress first. Please."

Cypress. Invoking his name only reminds me how she and I can never be. But I can't stop these feelings from engulfing me. I kiss each cheek, trying to summon the courage to speak the words I've spurned my entire life.

She gasps gently as my lips touch her skin. The sound sends a thrill through me. The world is crumbling, and all I can think of is spending these last moments with her.

"Paige."

"Zephyr." Her breathless voice sends my stomach into a mess of excitement and fear.

Just as suddenly as I was thrust into the room with her, I'm ripped out.

40

PAIGE

ZEPHYR'S ARMS HOLD ME with desperation. We both know this moment won't last, and just like me, he clings to it like a drowning man to a sinking life raft. The intensity in his dark eyes as he peers at me lights something in my soul; a need I've never known before. His breathless voice sends a call straight to my heart.

Then he is gone in an instant. I didn't send him away. Not knowingly. I blink at my empty arms, turning my palms up as if expecting to see him there still. But I'm horribly, utterly alone.

"Paige Powers," a melodious voice emanates from the surrounding air. It's everywhere and nowhere at the same time.

My stomach drops. The surrounding room vanishes, replaced by an endless expanse of shining stars against a swirling sky of deep colors. I turn slowly. *Where am I?*

"You play with an energy you don't understand," she says, then materializes out of the air. Dark ringlets frame a pale face. Her dress is made of stars, glittering as they fall over her in waves. Piercing emerald eyes shine like the sun brilliantly against the darkness. She is the most stunning woman I have ever laid eyes on, made of the cosmos themselves. "Dreaming is a dangerous endeavor. It becomes a trap. The more you pull them in, the harder it becomes to let go. It alters their lives, bending them around your fate."

Something about her tickles in my memory. We step around one another, circling like two animals preparing for a fight. But she doesn't seem eager to attack. If anything, the air of calm around her radiates peace.

"I needed to see him." Pulling Zephyr to me had not been intentional. I had a need only he could fulfill, and then he was standing there.

She holds her palm up. The fingers of her other hand dance over it, creating a swirl of light. Am I capable of something like that?

"You have already witnessed potential fates," she says calmly, focused on her hands. "His and yours. The more you pull him into these dreams, the more certain your fates become. But which one is out of your control."

The visions. The dreams about my Power and the end of the world. About Zephyr being there with me, trying to stop me. Will my Power be the death of him?

"I can't be responsible for his death." Terror grips me at the very notion that I might be the reason he dies.

The light in her hand transforms into a symbol I know all too well. A looping infinity the same as the one in Tribute Park, back in Elpis. A single star moves along the scooping curves.

"This is his life. It loops infinitely, just as everyone else does. Interactions. Passages. Moments of birth and death aligned." Her words make little sense to me, but I watch the star, captivated by the notion that it represents Zephyr.

She lifts her other palm. Another symbol appears, but the entire form shifts and wavers as if unable to maintain its shape. The star that follows this path pulses with bursts of light that break apart pieces of the track, leaving behind grooves like dents in armor. I don't need her to tell me who that is. My lips part in agony.

"Each time you pull him into your orbit, it changes his." She shifts her palms sideways, arching fingers cradling the two symbols until they become one highly volatile track. The tracks splinter as the stars glide along with increasingly frantic movements. When the two stars touch, the speed increases like frenzied atoms eager to break free of one another. Polar opposites. My star burns brighter, larger, consuming, breaking. Then the two stars collide. The track shatters outward. Both stars wink out.

My weakening knees give out. I bury my face in my hands as grief overwhelms me as the message hits home. I won't just kill *him*. I will destroy everything.

Cold arms wrap around me. She strokes my hair and makes soothing noises that do little for my shattered soul. I should be furious with her, eager to burn her where she stands, destroy her utterly. But this isn't her fault. She is only the messenger.

"Who are you?" I ask. My voice is thick with grief.

"I am called Astra." She tips my head back, wiping away my tears like Mom does. The warmth in her smile wraps around my aching heart. "But you would know me by another name."

And then I remember the story. A hysterical laugh bubbles up through the lump in my throat. "Celeste. Dad knew you were alive somewhere."

"Alive is a flexible term, given my perspective. I am neither alive nor dead. I *am*."

"Is there no hope for me? For...for him?"

"I am so glad you asked." Relief sags her shoulders, as if she couldn't tell me this unless I asked. "There is another."

She kneels beside me, holding up her hand, revealing a new infinity symbol. Where Zephyr's track is thin but steady and mine is misshapen and breaking, this one is thick, strong, and steady. The light pulses just as bright as my own, but instead of weakening the track with each passing, the loop thickens, growing stronger by the moment.

"He walks a dangerous path, but he is learning. The choices he makes right now will determine whether you ever cross paths again. If he chooses the correct course, he will be ready."

"To save me and Zephyr."

She shakes her head. "To save *everyone*." Her body tenses and her fist snaps closed around the new loop. Something dark passes through her eyes. "You must go now, Paige. Be careful of your Powers. Without proper care, you will never reach him in time." She fades, leaving me kneeling alone among the stars.

But her voice carries. "Give your father my love, should you choose the path that brings you to him again."

Then she vanishes completely, and I am kneeling on the floor of Prince Dominic's suite once more.

41

EASTON

ONE SECOND ZEPHYR IS beside me, ready to launch in a series of commands. The next, he passes out cold on the ground. Nat blinks dumbly. But I recognize this for what it is. Paige. Her Power punched him out again.

The rumble in the ground makes me anxious. We don't have time for this. Thankfully, I always come prepared. I rip the smelling salt out of my pocket, tearing it open and thrusting it under his nose, muttering about this stupid link he has with Paige.

Zephyr's eyes snap open and he smacks the salt away. He's disoriented. That's a new development. He usually bounces back quickly, but this time, he seems confused about what happened.

"We don't have time for naps, Zephyr," I snap. "Pull yourself together."

He sits up, rubbing his head, then brushes his hand over his lips. For a moment, he seems elsewhere. I'm about to slap some sense into him when his eyes light up.

"We were right. It's Lord Greene," he says. The heel of his palm rubs against his chest, and he winces.

Nat's lips part in an "o", as if something has just dawned on him. I don't know him well enough to understand the importance of his revelation. "I probably should have mentioned this before, but he has been spending a lot of time with some officers lately. Only a select group, though."

"The ones connected to his house, no doubt," Zephyr grunts as he gets his feet under him. Whatever Paige did to him this time, it did a number on him. "His daughter is in the palace wreaking havoc, from what I hear."

"Hear?" Nat frowns.

"With me out of the picture and Baron being questioned for treason, which leaves Lord Greene to take over the military," Zephyr explains. "Baron's arrest thrusts Greene into position. If Greene and his daughter get the upper hand in there, and he uses his magic..."

My eye darts back and forth between them. "What can he do?"

"He's an Operator, able to control the actions and thoughts of others," Zephyr explains.

"Operator?" My eyes widen, shoulders drawing tense. "He can Control people? Why did you not mention this before?"

"I didn't think about it!" Zephyr snaps. "He hasn't used his magic in a long time. Not since he and my uncle got into a fight when he used his magic on us kids during training. Greene barely held on to his title."

"Motive," Nat mutters.

Fear rips down my spine as the earth shakes again. I turn my gaze toward the palace, still holding strong regardless of what is happening inside. "Paige. You said someone was training her."

Zephyr's dark gaze is grim. His lips thin into a tight line. He only nods once, sharply.

A string of curses slips past my lips. "That settles that. It's him. So, we just need to get our hands on him. Where will he be right now?"

Before they can answer, the rumble of fighting inside the palace falls utterly quiet. The world is still.

Except for Zephyr, who shoots to his feet. His face crumples and his shoulders fall toward the earth, as if the fight has gone out of him utterly. I follow his gaze to the palace as red and blue lights bloom to life along the front columns.

"No." Nat's voice is weak, strangled. Even he seems defeated.

I grit my teeth, completely clueless, and I don't like it. "What?"

"Those lights only mean one of two things," Nat says soberly. "They crowned a new king, or..."

Zephyr completes the sentence, misery in his voice. "The king is dead."

As if spurred on by some signal, the lines of troops move in on the palace. This is no longer a siege. It's a takeover.

"Greene is in the palace," I mutter. And we're too late to help the king hold on to his crown.

42

DRAKE

I'VE HEARD THE WHISPERS for weeks, but never really accepted that the people would ever turn against Gavin. Why would they? Did they not see what I saw when I looked at him? Did they not feel his strength? Yet the chaos in the Haven square has driven a wedge between the two of us, and I'm ripped away from him.

Even after the guard holding me collapses, the tide of fleeing bodies washes me away. I struggle against the flow, but am helpless, pushed farther and farther from Gavin, deeper into the belly of the square as the masses bottleneck the exit.

On the platform, the Minister continues preaching about the false Idol. Some people protest—Menlue among them—but others align with the Minister, throwing fists as freely as insults. An intense hate pulses through the square.

Our fears have manifested into reality. Insurrection. Gavin worried about it from the beginning. He knew, somehow, that this would happen. Still, we were confident in our safety, in our new positions in the Haven. We let that confidence blind us to the truth.

The Minister always had a plan.

He warned us, warned Gavin, that the people would turn against him if their faith waned. Gavin had been so certain that his plan to give the power to the Havenites would bring about the balance we needed. We thought, hoped, that time would be all we needed to make them see the truth before the Minister's warning could come to fruition.

Fools. All of us. We exposed Elder secrets, peeled back the veil of deception to give the people just a peek at what lies behind it.

The Elders never would have let it pass. Nor would those in charge of that horrible set of programs below the Haven. Gavin warned me that absolute power corrupts those holding the reins, that they never give in quietly.

We thought we had more time...

An explosion of fire supercharges the air just feet from where I press against the flow of the crowd. Gifts are wielded like weapons against acolytes, Guardians, and Havenites while the Minister continues calling for submission, for Gavin's capture...and mine.

My heart stops. I crane my neck, hearing Gavin calling out to me. He's taller than me by several inches. I should be able to see him, but the press of bodies is too intense.

"Gavin!" I call back.

The ground trembles.

Screams erupt from the crowd of fighting bodies. A gap opens through them like a fissure in stone. I spot Gavin in the center, pulsing with brilliant blue light. My heart lifts, then plummets as a Guardian wraps him up in massive arms. I reach out, shoving bodies aside, hoping to reach his pulsing blue light.

All the lights go out, plunging the square into screams of terror and chaos. Only Gavin is lit up like a beacon.

I've hardly done more than throw one person out of my way before Gavin's body gives out. And with him goes his light.

No. Nononono. What will they do to him this time? Panic climbs my throat. I wash out all other noise with my gift, casting Silence over everything but him, hoping to follow his trail.

The lights flicker, then turn back on.

Gavin is gone. I drop my Silence, sinking to my knees as momentary grief overcomes me.

On the platform beside her husband, Mrs. Garraty observes what remains of the chaos with a calm that sends a jolt of fear through me. She is blind to everything around her, immune to the pain of her own people. She is so serene.

Then her gaze falls on me. I surge to my feet, ready to rush to the door, but some magnetic power pulls at me, freezing me in my tracks. My blood heats; my pulse slows. I collapse to my knees again, unable to hold myself upright, too weak to stand on my own.

Rough hands seize my arms, dragging me toward the platform as the chaos dies down. My legs drag on the ground behind me. My chin lolls against my chest. I have no strength left to do anything.

Mrs. Garraty stands proudly at her husband's side, clinging to his arm as she stares intently down at me. For a moment, no one says anything. All is silent. Is my gift still stifling the air in the room?

Boots click against the platform steps, then Mrs. Garraty's icy fingers hook under my chin and force my gaze onto hers. Once warm, inviting eyes burn with cold fury. Some strange sensation pulses through my veins. We have made a grave error, assuming she held no gifts of her own. I can feel it now, corrupting my blood, controlling the slowing beat of my heart.

Her lips twitch. "The false Idol has tainted him," she declares. "Bring him to the temple stage. Perhaps we can still save his soul."

"Gavin...?" I can hardly utter his name.

Emil. Where is Emil? Maybe he can help us. *Unless they already got to him.*

43

ZEPHYR

*C*YPRESS IS DEAD. THERE can be no other explanation for those lights, no reason for a new king to be crowned. My legs grow weak, but my resolve turns to fire. I clench my hands into fists at my sides. Vincent Greene will die for this. I will rip out his spine.

Unless...

Perhaps Cypress isn't dead yet. Maybe Greene made his move, forcing Cypress to abdicate using his Operator magic to control my brother—*because he is my brother, whether or not by lineage, he is my brother*. Was Greene responsible for the rockslide that killed King Alric and my oldest brother? Cypress was with them. He was a target as much as they were. But my oldest brother's heroism saved Cypress' life.

Pieces fall into place. Pieces I was too blind to see. But now I do. King Alric's anger at the way Greene trained the royal children to use their magic. The agreement the two of them struck in the aftermath—that he could never use his magic again, but in exchange he would be given more land and power, and a chance for his own line to take control of the military should there be no royal heirs to do it. My idiot uncle set Greene up for this. He handed everything over, then died because of his own arrogance. After all, who would dare move against the royal family?

Troops storm the palace, securing Greene's takeover. I watch, but don't truly see. My mind is too busy spinning Greene's web.

I had to go, obviously. The mutiny was supposed to do it—eliminate me before I could return home to stop Greene's orchestrations. It nearly worked. But he couldn't account for Paige's magic.

Instead, he trained her and harnessed her. He wrapped his mental leash around her throat, choking off her magic.

Which means he can force her to use it to destructive ends as well. She is a weapon. A terrifyingly deadly one.

Fury makes my entire body quiver. My magic pulses, growing. My jaw twitches in rage. I can stop Greene, and he knows it. I just have to get close enough to smother him with my magic.

Baron was another obstacle in Greene's way. As long as Baron controlled the military, Greene couldn't command the troops to take the palace in his name. So, he planted his daughter inside the palace to keep tabs on the family. Perhaps Bella even planted some of the evidence now used against Baron to condemn him. It would explain why Bella insisted Paige keep Cypress distracted. It can't be coincidence that the very day Cypress announces his engagement is the same day Baron is accused of treason.

If it's too late to save Cypress, is it too late for Baron, as well?

Easton and Nat are locked in urgent conversation, probably planning their next steps. Their body language indicates an argument they are hoping for me to settle. I leave them to their plotting.

I don't need a plan. I have pure, righteous vengeance on my side.

And no one knows the passages of the palace as well as I do.

"Get Bronwyn out of the palace," I growl. Greene could force her into marriage to further legitimize his claim on the throne. I will not allow him to touch her.

Whatever Easton and Nat were arguing over dies on their lips at my command.

I step out from behind the bushes, stalking toward the lines of troops with their backs to me. My companions call after me, but their pleas fall on deaf ears. I slip into rank with the lines. No one seems to notice me at first. Are these troops under Greene's control? He can't be that powerful. Even he has limits and I've sensed nothing as strong as that.

Paige wants me to find Cypress first, but I can't allow Greene to maintain control over her. Not when she can be so dangerous to everyone. Paige is my priority now.

In the Dream—if I can call it that—she was in Dominic's room on the top floor, far west wing. A service door at the back of the palace should send me right up the service steps and into the west wing. I need to get to her before Greene does. Then I can break his control over her and storm the throne room to stop him.

The strategy could end in death, but I can't stand around talking anymore. My family needs me.

Paige needs me.

As I infiltrate the soldier lines, a ripple of grunts and gasps move outward in my wake. I cut their magic off fifty yards or more from where I stand. Dozens of them feel the loss acutely. A few foolish, brave idiots turn their attention on me, drawing swords. It's their only defense against me without magic to vault in my direction.

One soldier wraps his hand around my arm, attempting to jerk me to my knees. Instead, I use the momentum to wrap my hand around his sword hilt. As he pulls me down, I yank it free with an upward stroke. I try not to think about the blood as he collapses.

Another catches me from behind, wrapping an arm around my neck and pulling back. But not before my fingers find the knife in the first soldier's boot. I capture it as I'm pulled away. Without hesitation, I thrust it back with all my might. A squelch is followed by release of the grip and more blood. I don't look at his face when I pull the blade free and wipe it on his coat. I trained most of these men. I don't want to think about who I must kill to get inside. I would rather not kill any of them, but I'm outnumbered...*significantly*. A few I could incapacitate, but dozens of them are beyond my skills. They will just come after me.

The arch leading to the back entrance is close. Ten soldiers stand between me and my means of entry into the palace. At least two dozen, if not more, crowd around me, edging cautiously closer now that they've seen me kill two of their own. Smart to be wary. And stupid. It gives me more space, more of a chance to succeed.

The ring stops moving inward. I assume a defensive stance, sword in front of me and knife tucked in my belt loop. "I would rather not do this, but if you don't let me pass, you leave me with no choice."

They shift anxiously, but don't move. All of them have seen me fight before. Some have fought me in the sparring ring. They know what I'm capable of.

A boulder soars through the air, straight toward me. As the projectile edges closer, I push out my magic. The magical grip moving the boulder dissolves away. It tumbles to the ground fifteen yards away, crushing or killing several soldiers in a sickening scream. Then it rolls, bowling several more over. The momentum carries it within inches of my boots.

I don't flinch, glaring at the ten soldiers blocking my path, sword still raised.

"Step aside."

Another boulder rises seventy yards away. Someone hasn't learned. Before it travels five yards, a thunderous crash drops it in place. A hole opens around the soldiers responsible. In the center of the hole, Easton moves with practiced ease, breaking legs with sweeps, launching soldiers at one another like bowling pins. Nat fights at his back, each movement of unused energy stored for a further, larger impact. His ability to Absorb momentum impresses me every time. Once he learned to fight, Nat became an unstoppable force.

The corner of my lip twitches upward. They will create a diversion, but they can't join me. Not if they intend to use their magic as a weapon.

The commotion distracts the soldiers blocking my way forward. I lunge toward them, slicing one across the calves to bring him down before spinning to slice off the hand of another who tries grabbing me. The others step back, but it's too late. A hole is made and I surge through.

They race after me, boots pounding against the pavement. One is swift enough to catch me, but foolish to try stopping me. As he grabs my jacket to yank me off my feet, I dip the sword beside me, plunging it into his gut. His grip slackens, then falls off.

The door hides behind a thick tree trunk. They added the door years ago, as a service entrance, but also as an escape for the royal family, should the worst happen. *I'm living the worst*. But none of my family runs through. Not Dominic with Bronwyn in his arms. Not Cypress, bleeding but alive. Not even Elena. I would take her horribly icy stare and hate over the alternative.

Alone, I peer back over my shoulder as I hit the door at a full sprint. The rest of the soldiers are on my heels. I have seconds. Without hesitation, I pull the door open and tumble through. It slams shut with a clang that echoes as I engage the lock. The moment I'm out of range, they will break through, but it gives me time to get away. By the time they open the door, I will be gone.

I pause momentarily to breathe, gripping the sword like a lifeline. The soldiers hammer at the door and my teeth ache at the pounding. Deeper in the palace, the sound of fighting is distant. The takeover is not heading anywhere near me. My entrance into the palace is on the lower level, and Dominic's room is on the top floor, so I have a lot of stairs to climb.

With a final glance at the closed door, I creep silently toward the nearest staircase. An elevator would cushion me from surprise attacks on the way up, but anything could spring on me when the doors to the elevator open. I would be a sitting duck in the elevator, ripe for destruction. At least the stairs give me open space to move.

I take each step slowly, listening for signs of danger with the sword down, blade out—just in case. Will Greene order the servants killed or captured? The idea makes my stomach churn with anger. Often, the servants disappear for the night, but the insurrection started before they would have gone for the day. Who knows how many are left?

Signs of struggle litter the main level as I round the corner and peer along the hallway. A servant lays face down in a pool of blood, a knife in her hand. She tried to fight back. Bless her, the poor thing. A few of the doors are blasted away.

I continue upward. When I reach the first floor of suites, I can't help edging toward Cypress' door. *Please be here.*

The door remains open. On silent feet, I creep inside, checking his bedroom first. Nothing. The bed is made. No sign of struggle. I abandon the bedroom to check the office on the far side of the suite. The door is open a crack. I tip the toe of my boot against the bottom gently. It eases open on silent hinges. Shuffling carefully, I edge into the space to make a quick visual sweep.

A knife darts out at me. I barely have time to jump back and raise my sword in defense to avoid a nasty cut on my face.

Queen Elena pants, clutching the knife with manic eyes, heaving breaths. "You," she snarls.

I rush a few steps backward as she jumps at me with her knife again. "Stop. Elena, I'm here to help you. Where is Cypress?"

Her blue eyes harden. She studies me for a lie, but her magic doesn't work on me. Doubt tips her mouth down and she looks ready to lunge again.

"I swear on my mother's grave, Elena. I'm not entirely clear on everything that's going on, but you can be damn sure that as soon as I get the family out of here to safety, I will find out. And I will put an end to it."

Elena studies me for so long I nearly growl at her. She is wasting time. Finally, she grimaces and lowers the knife. "Fine. But only because Cypress was ready to bring you back."

The news sends a jolt through me. *"I did what I had to do to protect him. To protect Easton. And you."* Paige struck a bargain with Cypress, just like Easton predicted.

"Where is he?" I ask again.

Tears brim her icy eyes, and she shakes her head. "I don't know." Grief clenches her throat. I'm not sure I heard grief from her even when her husband and first son died. "I don't..." She runs her hand through her silky black hair, eyeing the door. "He went down to interrogate Baron and never came back up. Then we were under attack. And now...the lights."

I grimace. "I saw, but I won't believe he is dead until I find him. There's a chance he was forced to abdicate."

"Who... who would dare?" Her hands shake. This attack has struck her, shaken her to the core. Nothing rattles Queen Elena. Easton was wrong, it seems. There's no way she's part of whatever's happening.

"I think it's Lord Greene."

She closes her eyes to steady her own thoughts. "Bella." Her shoulders sag. "Cypress dismissed her this morning, but she and Nora were going to stay until after dinner." A harsh laugh rips out of her. "If my son is dead, I will gut that girl in front of her father." Then her eyes alight on me. She has connected something else. "If it *is* him, you can cut off his magic." She takes my arm, clinging desperately, begging. Another first. "Zephyr, I will give you *anything* you ask for if you stop him."

Anything...like freeing Paige from Cypress' grasp? I can't ask. Not when I can't be sure he still lives. It would be like pouring salt on a cannonball wound and grinding it in.

"Right now, I need you to focus on getting out of here," I say. I can't work knowing any of them are still in the palace. Their magic is useless with me around. This falls on my shoulders and I won't risk anyone else in the family. I've always been the expendable one. "Find Wyn, and Dom if you can, and get out of here. The emergency passage is under siege. You will need to fight your way out. Nat and Easton are battling off soldiers on the east road. Go to them. They will get you all to safety."

She nods, a stiff motion for her under such duress. "Baron might still be alive. If he is, and Cypress was wrong about him, the two of them will probably be together in the basement." It's an olive branch. Elena knows about my parents.

"Baron will defend him to his last breath, Elena. Now go. I am leaving Bronwyn in your hands." I pull out the knife and offer it to her. "It's all I have at the moment. If you can find more weapons, grab them." Both she and Bronwyn have mind magic, but it won't be much good in a fight.

Elena wraps her hands around the hilt and nods.

Before she can say any more, I slip out the door, checking the hallway before I go.

The lower level is a war zone, flooded with soldiers on both sides. I will go into the belly of the beast to find them, but not until I have Paige out of Lord Greene's control.

44

PAIGE

CELESTE'S WARNING HAUNTS ME. I can't shake it. As I fight off the bone-chilling fear that grips my bones, I curl up on the sofa in Prince Dominic's suite, arms around my knees. Tears roll down my cheeks, blazing a hot trail along my skin. It doesn't matter. I can't leave this room. I can't reach out for help. I can't even use my Powers to help myself.

I don't know how long I sit and cry, listening to the thunder of battle somewhere below. Cypress is likely dead by now. Bella is attacking with her conspirators. Is Prince Dominic still alive, or has he fallen in the fight as well? What if Zephyr's body lies on the stairs, dead before he can reach any of us? And the horrible, nagging doubt...what if Dominic is in on all of this somehow?

The what if's stack up too high for me to handle, smothering me in layers of helplessness and fear.

The door opens slowly. I lift my chin, hopeful that Zephyr has arrived. Or even Cypress or Prince Dominic—*I'm wrong about him; I must be!* Any of them.

But the face that peers through sends a wave of rage through me.

Bella.

I launch at her, but before I can wrap my hands around her throat, something within me freezes me in place. I can't attack her!

A smug smile splits her face. Her dark eyes sweep over me, and she grimaces. I'm still in my pajamas and covered in blood. Though I scrubbed my hands clean in the bathroom sink, I did nothing about my clothes.

Bella drops a filmy red dress on the chair by the door. "Change into that. Now."

I clench my jaw and raise my chin stubbornly. I refuse to be put on display.

Her brow quirks upward. "Would you rather stay here until everyone you care for is dead? Dress. Now."

I hate the fear that rushes through me. If I can get out of this room, maybe I can help the others. The acknowledgement in her eyes means she knows I will do as she commands. In haste, I strip out of my pajamas and into the dress. It clings to my curves, the material nearly sheer. Black sparkles beneath the red with each step.

The door opens further, and she motions me out. A twitch in my jaw gives away my irritation, but I obey. I just need to bide my time for a chance to escape before they can stop me.

Silence has settled over the palace. The battle is over. Does that mean Bella has won her fight? My skin crawls as I step into the hallway. "Where is Cypress?"

She gives no answer.

Vincent waits near the door, dressed in military blues that remind me of Baron's uniform. A bloodied sword rests on his hip. The memory of Cypress' suppressed anger at the mention of Vincent's name makes my steps hesitant. And I see it clearly now. The way he presented himself to me at training was so different from this formal, collected man. *This* version resembles the man I met at the ball.

Either Vincent is oblivious to my distress, or he doesn't care. He holds out his arm as if waiting to escort me into a ballroom and not to my doom. His lips twitch in irritation, the only sign that he is not completely at ease.

In training, Vincent was often at my ear, whispering encouragement, guiding my technique. Did I unknowingly hand over control of my mind to him? He must be the one Controlling me. I opened myself to the prince, not him. Perhaps the proximity was all he needed to seize his opportunity. I let him in without knowing it. Did Dominic know? I still can't decide whether Dominic was in on all of this, or if they used him. Maybe he was no more in control of himself than I am now.

My arm slides through Vincent's, making my skin turn ice cold. He places his free hand over mine and starts toward the elevator. I have no control over my own choices. I join him, with Bella trailing on our heels.

The elevator doors slide closed, sealing the three of us inside. I can't breathe. The space is too confined with the three of us together. I can't pull away either, no matter how desperately I want to put distance between myself and these two.

"Why are you doing this?" I ask, each word strained through my teeth, forced out as another influence tries to prevent me from speaking at all.

Vincent keeps his eyes trained on the elevator door. The corner of his mouth twitches upward. "When you have children, you will reshape the world into anything they want or need it to be. I only want my daughter's happiness."

Bella beams at him, pride shining in her dark eyes.

"What is it she wants?"

"You will learn soon enough," he says calmly.

I see the resemblance now. The same sharp chin and dark eyes. While she is thin with wide hips, he has broad shoulders. But their faces resemble one another. I can't believe I never put those pieces together myself. *Idiot.*

"Sadly, these ignorant kings—arrogant to their last breaths—think they can keep her from her deepest desire." He turns his dark eyes on me. Eyes just like Bella's—cold and determined. It gives me chills. I feel foolish for not having connected these two sooner. "You were the key. Nothing else we tried worked out. But you changed everything, Lady Paige."

The elevator door slides open on the main floor. I dig in my heels, refusing to move. Then they move of their own accord, controlled by another mind. By Vincent.

"I won't help you." I would rather die.

"You already have, dear." Vincent almost sounds sorry. "It's too late for your conscience now. You were willing to use King Cypress for your own ends. We all know you wouldn't have married him. Not so long as that *bastard* lives."

Fury burns hot under my skin. It sends a crack up through the Control forcing my steps. I jerk back. The motion isn't firm enough to escape, but it surprises Vincent. He halts. I latch onto the Power, fighting for control of it.

"Resist all you wish, Lady Paige. But the fight is already over."

Zephyr, where are you? If he drew close enough, it would cut off this Power over me. I don't need him to rescue me. But I do need him to help.

45

DRAKE

WHIMPERS AND SOBS OF fear penetrate the darkness shrouding my mind before my vision slowly comes into focus. Jeers greet me. Anger, disgust, cries for cleansing. My stomach drops out. Tears blur my vision before I get a good look at my surroundings.

But I've been here thousands of times in my life. Enough to know, even through blurry eyes, where I am.

In the temple.

On the stage.

I'm on my knees, but upright, held in place by my arms. I shift, but my wrists are bound by thick twine that chaffs at my skin. I'm tied to a pole on the stage, on a bed of straw, for all to see. Fear pulses through me. I blink furiously to clear my vision, searching for signs of Gavin, for anyone to help me.

Calling this hammering of my heart, the sensation of my pulse in my veins fear would be a gross understatement.

One word repeats from dozens of lips, thrown in my direction: *Cleansing*.

They know. They know about my relationship with Gavin.

My gaze sweeps the temple, searching for the key to my heart, the other half of my soul.

Where *is* Gavin? What have they done to him? Is it too late? Burning didn't work last time. They would need to try something else with him this time. Something more drastic and final. I shudder to think what that might be. I squeeze my eyes closed and pray to the Idols, or whatever higher power might exist, if there even is such a thing, to spare him. Agony rips at my heart. I'm about to die, and I know it. I can even accept it. But not if Gavin dies. I would give myself a hundred times over a thousand if it saved him just once.

A sob climbs up my throat, but I choke it down.

"Drake." The Minister's voice sends a cold spike down my spine.

I blink my eyes, unable to stop the flow of tears.

The Minister kneels in front of me, filling my vision. False sympathy shines in his eyes. I want to punch him right between the eyes. This is an act. All of this. I clench my jaw and raise myself as much as I can, glaring at him in defiance.

"You have been such a dedicated servant to the Haven and the temple all of your life," he says. His words are meant for the crowd, as if he means any genuine sympathy for my plight at all. This isn't about me. It isn't about my relationship with Gavin. This is about my taking Gavin's side, supporting him in opposition to the Minister and his teachings. Probably about the secrets I still harbor regarding what happens to the acolytes, too.

Gavin was right. The truth burns, but I can't deny it any longer. The Elders only want their power, and they are using the *Book of the Prophet* for their own evil means. How much of the *Book* was fabricated to keep us in line? They taught us that being gay is a sin, but Gavin told me the *Book* said no such thing. What else have they lied to us about?

"The false Idol has corrupted you," the Minister continues. "He has tempted you with his power, corrupted your faith, and seduced you into sin."

"No." I glare rebelliously at him. The Minister can tell these people whatever he wants, but none of this is Gavin's fault. And he certainly didn't corrupt me. He set me free.

"It's okay, Drake." He places a hand on my shoulder. "You can still be forgiven if you repent."

I shake out of his grip, then spit in his face. *Let him burn me.*

The Minister jerks back in alarm, then slowly wipes the spit from his cheek. He heaves out a dramatic sigh. "It's too late to save your mortal form, then. But we can still cleanse your immortal spirit."

I raise my chin and give him the most hateful glare I've ever given anyone in my life. This isn't about who I chose to love. It's about who I chose to follow. No matter what I say, they will still burn me.

He rises to his feet, dipping his head to someone else. I follow his line of sight to see Mrs. Garraty standing in the center of the stage wearing pure white robes.

"The Haven rises today!" Mrs. Garraty announces. "Those who follow the false Idol will be given one chance to repent."

My mouth goes dry, but my palms sweat. While they aren't looking, I carefully work the twine binding my wrists to the pole. It chaffs, cuts at my skin, but if I don't get out of this, I'm dead.

"Bring them forward," she commands.

Her husband gives a signal, and the doors to the acolyte chambers open. Dozens, hundreds of Havenites, Guardians, and acolytes are forced to line the front of the stage. Men, women, and children whose only crime is believing in Gavin like I do, in not allowing the corruption in the Haven to blind them. I identify many of their faces. Teachers who helped me learn to read and write. The doctor who fixed my broken arm after my dad died. Families who voiced firm support for Gavin. Candidates for election, whose only crime was working for a better future for the Haven and voicing their concerns about Elder corruption.

Ajax. Our gazes meet. Shame floods his chiseled face. Shame and sorrow, but something else. A fire burns in his eyes. A defiance against these people. At least he remains loyal to Gavin.

Menlue glares at the Garratys in open rebellion. As hundreds of others bow their heads in fear or shame, he holds his high.

"Menlue," Mrs. Garraty says. Her tone reminds me of a bitter winter breeze. "We will start with you. Repent. Beg forgiveness for being fooled into following the false Idol, and we will free you and your family."

He glances at his wife kneeling beside him, then at the twin girls clinging to their mother. His words won't just determine his fate.

If he refuses, they will all die. I see this realization pass between him and his wife. She gives a subtle shake of the head, then raises her chin.

Menlue straightens his spine, glaring at the Minister and his wife, then he takes in the others supporting the Garratys. The rest of the Elders, included. He won his seat at their table, and they rejected him.

"There is only one false Idol here," Menlue declares. "'The true Idol of Creation will rise again'!" Menlue projects his voice clearly, quoting verses from the *Book*. "'The non-believers will fall when he comes. For they cannot see the light. Their fall will herald the coming of the Days of Glory!' I have seen his light and triumph, even in this dark hour of falsehoods. All things come with purpose. Even the end."

Pride swells inside of me as Menlue condemns these leaders for their actions. I glance at them from the corner of my eyes, blinking back tears of pain as the twine continues ripping into my wrists. But it is loosening. Little by little.

The Minister hangs his head. His wife grimaces, then raises a hand toward Menlue and his family. "Your blood will be cleansed of corruption," she declares.

Menlue's lips part in agony, but no sound escapes. His body tenses, pales, then shrivels.

She's a Bloodmage!

A cry of horror slips out of Menlue's wife, but it cuts off as the same gift claims her life before her husband even hits the floor.

I buck wild against the bonds now. Burning alive is horrifying, but this blood manipulation scares me even more.

A cry of terror rises from those still kneeling. A few attempt to escape, but they don't make it off their knees before they collapse in a bloodless heap. Mrs. Garraty continues her horrifying work, claiming innocents in the name of cleansing the Haven of the false Idol.

I close my eyes, struggling to break free. Where is Gavin? He will come.

46

ZEPHYR

NOT EVERYONE SLIPPING THROUGH the shadows in the palace is on Lord Greene's side. I pass a few servants as I make my way to Dominic's suite who inform me Baron is in the sub-level of the palace. No one has been allowed down there since he was escorted to a cell, except for the royal family and certain members of the royal guard.

Baron isn't guilty of treason. With my mother dead, Baron has little else besides his family to fight for. He wouldn't turn against us.

I can't head down to the sub-level yet. First, I need to reach Paige. She will be a vital weapon against anyone who opposes Greene. *Please still be in Dominic's room.*

The hallway is remarkably silent. All signs of the fight are over. *For now.* I'm not foolish enough to think this is over. I just hope my family is still alive.

I peer around the corner from the back stairs. No one is around. Gripping the sword at my side, I ease down the hallway. Each of the creaking floorboards is familiar to me. I spent a fair amount of my childhood creeping around the palace, avoiding the king. Weak floorboards plague the building, old as it is. The actual age of the building is unclear. At least two hundred years.

I carefully measure each breath to keep my heartbeat steady. Adrenaline pumps in my ears. She is so close, but I can't feel her. Not like I expect. Her magic is in the building, yet it feels so distant. I try wrapping myself in the familiar embrace of her strength—brutal and beautiful.

The end of the hallway is only twenty yards, but already I see the open door to Dominic's suite, nestled in the corner of the palace. I should have known. I can feel her, but not here. My lips part and I fight for control of my breath. *I'm too late. No. Please, no.*

My steps hasten toward the open doorway. I toe it open wide, sword ready in my hand. I have to check. "Paige?"

Silence. Deafening, complete silence.

I shuffle deeper into Dominic's suite. No signs of struggle. The main parlor is clear. I check the bedroom, spotting Paige's pajamas on the floor. But no Paige. I call to her again, hissing her name, not expecting a response. Whoever came for her made her change clothes. Why?

Her absence creates an ache in my gut. I can feel her magic still in the palace. What will Lord Greene do with her? Fear for her life—and for my brothers—rips through me.

I dart into the hallway and rush for the stairs. Baron will help me. I'll free him from the sub-level cells, and we can end this together.

The stairway is no longer vacant. Men in tactical gear flood the base of the steps. Calls of warning rise when they spot me. I'm far enough away for them to grip their magic, creating walls of flame and stone, blocking my passage. The sensation of my magic, of the complete silence it creates within, spreads through me as desperation takes hold. These guards are blocking the sub-level where Baron is a prisoner. I can't stop. Not now.

The magic swells like the tides, consuming me, pressing outward against the others as I continue descending toward the wall. What are the odds I can dispel the stone and take them by surprise? Not great. I don't think I've ever done it before. But I've also never harnessed so much before. Most of the time, the magic pours out of me like breath or heat from my body of its own accord. I don't have to focus on using it anymore. It simply is. Unless I'm making direct skin contact with someone. Then I can push the magic through them to cut them off for a time.

But these guards aren't dumb. They know me and they know what I can do. They all hide behind the stone wall. Flames lick along the floor at the base of the wall, keeping me just out of reach of the stone. Thick vines climb up the stone, reinforcing it like a net.

Heart hammering, I step into the flames, pushing my barrier magic into my boots. Then I hold my breath and pray.

Flames flick up the leather, dancing like hungry beasts, making my feet and legs sweat. But they never make contact. Even so close, I can feel it burn. The fire wants to consume. I close my eyes and try something I've never attempted before. With everything in me, I focus on my barrier magic, sliding a palm along the flat of my sword blade to spread it across the surface.

"I don't want to fight," I call to the guards beyond the wall. "Stand down before it's too late. Don't force my hand."

Whoever built the wall must be further down the staircase to prevent my magic from blocking them off. The vines will remain without someone controlling them, but the wall and flames need a mage to maintain.

I open my eyes slowly, blinking at the thick vines. Holding my breath, I pray this will work. The sword cuts through the vines like a knife through soft butter. When metal hits the stone wall, it shrieks loud enough to hurt my ears. Somewhere beyond, I hear a scream.

The flames climb higher, reaching for my limbs. Sweat beads on my brow. The edge of my clothes singe, but the flames cannot even kiss my skin. How long that will last is uncertain.

Pressing the heel of my palm against the flat edge of the blade, I push it against the stone, trying to force the sharp edge into the rocky wall. Another scream pierces the air. I continue pouring my magic into the sword, straining to pull it from the rest of my body. The flames burn away the hem of my pants at the boot, searing my flesh. I grit my teeth against the pain. With one more burst of magic into the sword, I lean everything I have into the blade.

The wall shatters. I stumble forward, taken off balance. The fire vanishes as I fall to a knee. Dozens of hands grasp at me, yanking my arms, prepared to seize me. I struggle against their grips, but they aren't using magic to hold me.

One guard wrenches the sword from my grip. It clatters against the tiled floor. Then they drag me down the stairs, clasping my arms behind my back.

They are taking me right where I need to be.

"Cover the stairs," one of them orders as four escort me down. "No one in or out."

Who gave those orders?

Another level down, two bodies lay unconscious on the steps, both pale-faced and barely breathing. Is that what the screams were? Did I do that when I attacked the wall?

We emerge in the sub-level prison hallway. I blink at the blindingly bright lights. Why are they so bright down here? Heat from the overhead lights amplifies the sweat trickling down my face. Not only are the lights too bright, but there's a green hue to them that makes me sick to my stomach. Why are they green? The guards don't like it either. They move with quick efficiency toward a cell.

"Zephyr?" Baron's weak voice reaches out to me from a cell as I'm dragged past.

"Dad?" Some reserve of strength comes to life inside of me. I kick outward at the guards leading the way, using the momentum to push back against the two behind me. They lose their footing and tumble to the concrete floor. I land on them in a heap, arms no longer restrained. Before they can grab me again, I push away, launching to my feet.

One guard grabs my ankle, but I reach instinctively, kicking out at his head. It connects with a sickening crack. I avert my gaze quickly, having no desire to see what happened to him.

The two I kicked recover quickly. I could put a name to their faces but force myself not to see them. Not if I must fight them; not if I must kill them. My gaze flicks at the sword one of them holds. *My* sword, stolen off a different guard. None of their magic will work against me. This is a fist fight. Fists and a sword.

The last guard on the floor sweeps out at my legs. I push my barrier magic out, uncertain what it will do—if anything. Grasping at my magic makes my stomach heave. *What is going on down here?*

The sweep misses me by a breath, close enough that I feel the breeze in its wake. Vomit climbs up my throat as the two standing guards edge toward me, weapons in hand. Still, I reach a hand back, thrusting my magic into the one on the floor, pulling his force toward me. His magic is weak—a three compared to my five—and the speed of it rushes through me. My adrenaline pumps so hard I feel electric. The man groans in agony, a horrible gurgling sound that reminds me of the rattles of death. But I don't relent. His magic spreads through me.

Then he falls silent.

Even though my head spins, I clench my fist in wonder. I didn't just stop him from using his magic. I stole it from him.

The other two guards hesitate, eyeing me, then their fallen comrades.

I launch at them, dizzy with sickness the likes of which I've never felt, certain I will vomit all over the concrete floor. My body vibrates in agony. It hums with magic. A whole new sense of the world around me pulses through my body. The electrical veins of the building. The buzz of the lights and outlets. An Electron. He can control electrical currents. I knew it in some back drawer of my brain when I felt him.

But this kind of magic...

The overhead lights fill me to the brim with power and sickness in a deadly dance. I crouch, watching the two guards in front of me. They take a step backward. Then another. Electricity snaps between my fingertips as I touch the stone floor.

They turn and run, unable to fight my might. But I can't let them go. I can't allow them to warn the other guards, let alone Lord Greene. Pulling the lingering current from the overhead lights, I shoot electricity out across the concrete toward their boots. It strikes, winding up their legs. Both guards fall in screaming agony. Then silence.

I vomit on the floor, unable to hold it back any longer. The lights overhead flicker, spark, and die, plunging the sub-level into darkness, broken only by the glowing red exit sign at the staircase. The entire contents of my stomach hurls out on the floor.

"Zephyr," Baron calls feebly through the bars, worry lacing his voice.

Sweat drips on the floor as I tremble on my hands and knees. As the sensation of sickness slowly dissipates, I wipe my sleeve across my mouth and grimace, turning away from the mess on the floor.

Baron clings to the bars of his cell. "It's the lights."

I peer up, but they remain dark. How could the lights make me feel so wretched? Is it a recent development, brought in by Lord Greene?

I'm horribly cold, shivering in my marrow like I've contracted some illness. I push myself to my feet and stumble into the bars, eyeing the lock. Would the keys be on one of these guards?

"You can't stay down here," he says. His knuckles are white, face drawn and hollow. He looks ill as well. "Go."

I shake my head. A grievous mistake, with my vision swimming toward recovery. Then I spot Cypress hunched over in the next cell, face buried in his hands. *He's alive, though!*

"Cy!" I lurch toward his door, testing it even though I know it's locked. "What are you doing in here?"

He peers up through his fingers. A dark shadow passes over his face. His expression is that of utter defeat. I shake the bars pointlessly; they won't open.

"You win," he mutters.

I sneer, baring teeth, "What?"

"I have no crown, no throne, no power." His voice is hollow. I don't know who this is, but he is a shell of the Cypress I know. "I can't give her anything she wants anymore."

"What happened?"

Cypress opens his mouth like he wants to tell me, but nothing comes from his lips. Greene has somehow locked away their ability to give anyone specifics. Cypress' lip twitches in an animalistic snarl, but he makes no sound. Then his head is in his hands again.

"He was captured and forced to abdicate," Baron whispers, eyeing Cypress.

Forced to abdicate. Just like his mother predicted. *But he's still breathing*. "By whom?" I ask.

Neither answer. No doubt, they can't.

"How about we get you out of here and Paige can decide for herself what she wants?" I ask.

Cypress moans and shakes his head. I think he mutters something like, "no point."

I throw a fist at the bars. "Hey! Pull your shit together, Cy. You are King. You can't crumble at the first sign of defeat."

Rage colors his neck. Cypress surges to his feet, struggling with his own limbs worse than I am. What did those lights do to us? "Did you not hear him?" he roars. Spittle flies from his mouth. "I am not King!"

I jump back, startled by his outburst. Cypress throws a punch into the wall. I hear a crack, but he gives no sign of pain. He doesn't even shake out his hand. He just drops his bloodied knuckles to his side as he falls back on his cot again.

"Listen to me, Cypress." I keep my voice even, pressing importance in each word. "She is in danger. He is controlling her mind, which means he can also control her magic." I shake, wiping sweat from my brow. "I lied. Paige isn't a seven. She is off the charts. I don't even have a number for her strength. She can destroy us all in the wrong hands."

His blue eyes glitter as he peers at me, weighing my words. Again, he sneers at me, "You lied to me. From the beginning."

"I panicked."

"If you had told me the truth, all of this could have been preventable!"

I wince. He's probably right, but there's no going back. We can only go forward.

"Zephyr." Baron's calm voice is like a soothing balm on fraying nerves. He's collected as much as one can be while imprisoned. "If that's true, you need to leave us and get to her now. Stop wasting time on us."

"But—" I can help them. I can find the key, and we can storm the throne room and take down Lord Greene together.

"Go." That one word is spoken with such calm, but such command that I pivot on my heel and march toward the exit, peering back over my shoulder at them. "I'll be back soon."

Baron calls out a warning to me, too late. Something hard hammers against my skull, knocking me out cold.

47

EASTON

C OMBAT IS NO FOREIGNER to me. I've fought in battles of a variety of scales in a variety of settings and scenarios. I've studied strategy and learned to lead my team to success. But this is different. A whole other kind of beast.

Men and women fight brutally on both sides. The streets around the palace have become a battleground. Bloody and without order. It's nearly impossible to tell the enemy from an ally when soldiers fight against one another with civilians taking up arms on both sides as well. Leadership is unclear. It's utter chaos no Specialist training simulation could have prepared me for.

Bodies litter the street. Some people are simply knocked unconscious. Some are dead, crushed beneath the weight of someone else's Power or sliced open with knives or swords. A few have been speared through the gut or neck and left to bleed out on the concrete. These people don't *need* guns to kill.

This differs from the simulations in the Department of Security. There, I could ignore the death, the killing. Those were simulated people. These are living, breathing humans. Powered and non-Powered. Every fatality digs into my skin, into my brain like another cut. Soon, the brutality of so much killing will flay me alive. My emotional stability holds on shaky ground.

Who do they think they are fighting for? Do they even know? *Do I?*

Nat and I have collected a few men he knows from the fort—officers I've trained with there. Jeff and Ody. Cante. A handful of others. We work like demons to press the lines and break through.

One thing is for certain. Despite the chaos of battle, we're being pushed further from the palace walls.

We're losing the fight.

Losing an eye has created a whole new set of challenges in combat. Adapting to a new depth perception has cost me a few cuts that will probably become scars, and I'm pretty sure I've broken a big toe. But I can't stop. I've adjusted and am getting a crash course in modifying to my new vision.

Exhaustion seeps into my bones. Sweat beads on my brow. As I swipe it away from my one good eye, a tree shoots out of the ground, straight through the woman standing two feet away from me, spearing her through. For a moment, I freeze, watching the blood drip from her body and roll down the bark as her sightless eyes turn toward the sky. Then the tree rips out, disappearing back into the ground as if it never existed.

I yank on Nat's arm as he throws a fist into the ground. The impact of his Power creates a ripple into a closing crowd of hostiles. We stumble a few steps back with the knot of men fighting with us. Rock shards shoot up, dark and horrifying in their multitude as they spear the people standing over them. Dozens of shards. Just like the tree, they vanish as quickly as they appear.

Zephyr disappeared inside some time ago. I'm not sure how long it's been, but I pray he found Paige. I can't get close enough to any of the doors to get inside and help. Her fate is in his hands. It makes my skin crawl.

Using my Strongarm muscles, I launch off the ground, straight up in the air. My boots thump against the roof of a bar across the street from the palace. It quivers beneath my weight, but holds, thankfully.

A bolt of lightning rockets toward me. I dodge easily enough, but the follow-up shot glances by my arm, slicing through my jacket and shirt. I grimace, but pain is no stranger to me.

My gaze sweeps the white palace walls, shining with the red and blue glow of the lights against the darkness—apparently, they signal a dead king or new one. Neither bodes well for Zephyr's family.

A knot of people fight their way through the mess of soldiers and civilians. Under normal circumstances, I might ignore such a group, but the fighters protect two people in the center. I squint into the darkness, holding my breath and praying it's Zephyr and Paige.

Two women with dark hair and fine clothes huddle tightly to one another as the guards and servants around them cut a path for their escape. Not Paige or Zephyr, but royals for sure, judging by their clothing.

"Nat!" I point toward them.

He glances up, then follows my direction. Nat hops up and down on his toes. I thought it odd the first time I saw him do it, but now I know better. He's storing energy for an attack. Sure enough, a few seconds later, Nat picks up two nearby construction barrels and launches them with impressive force. They zip along the lines of fighters, creating a path between us and the royals. It forces the soldiers locked in combat to either stumble back or be crushed.

The knot of guards darts through the gap straight for us. Straight for Nat, where he crouches low, fingers tapping the earth, absorbing the energy others are throwing through it with their Powers. I've seen no one fight with energy absorption Power before. It's extraordinary. He can draw Power from *anything*, like a finely tuned machine.

The younger noble woman breaks through the knot of guards, throwing her arms around Nat's neck as he rises to his feet. She cries for something. He rubs at her back even as he eases her out of the way. No doubt, he stored the impact of her hug for future use.

We are hardly in a safe zone.

From the corner of my one eye, I spot a massively muscular man—even bigger than me—throwing people aside like they weigh nothing. He marches straight toward the young noble woman beside Nat. I launch off the roof, landing on his back as he reaches for her arm. Her sleeve slips through his fingers.

The two of us tumble to the ground. The impact knocks breath from my lungs as I land on my back with his back pressed like a ten-ton weight against my chest. I wrap an arm around his neck and use my legs to pin him in place. He attempts to thrust his immense weight against my body to crush me, but I flex my Powered muscles and resist. Still, his efforts leave me breathless. It's everything I can do to hold on as he rams the back of his head into my nose. The world spins into doubles, then triples. My grip snaps as tight as I can manage, knowing he will kill me if he breaks out.

I release a growl as I pull hard and tight on his neck. Something snaps. His head moves at an odd angle. His body goes limp.

Nat calls for me through the fray, but I hardly hear him as my head swims. Blood pours from my broken nose. I gasp agonizing breaths, unable to draw more than a fraction of what I need with the Strongarm's weight on me.

I killed him. I only meant to incapacitate, but his thrashing and resistance forced my tightening grip at the wrong angle.

The tang of blood coats my mouth, then air rushes through me. The body is hauled off. The young noble woman kneels beside me—two of her, then three in a sickening swirling movement. She motions someone else forward. Warm hands press against the side of my face, then a shot of cold healing surges through me. A painful pop snaps my nose back into place and the bleeding stops. All my wounds from battle are erased. I'm about to ease myself into a sitting position when the healer presses me back.

"You have several broken ribs and a concussion," he says. "Don't move until I'm done."

Concussion. That explains why I'm seeing a strange kaleidoscope of faces hovering around me. Ice rockets through my chest, making me certain I'm about to turn into an ice sculpture from some warring Power. The multiplying, shifting world solidifies on one image.

A stunning young noble woman with freckles bridging her nose peers at me with worry shining in her honey-colored eyes. Dark hair falls in waves over her shoulder as she peers down at me. She raises a brow at me, as if waiting for some answer to a question I never heard. Her glossy lips move, but I'm oblivious to her words.

"What?"

She holds her hand up over me. "How many do you see?"

"Three. Four." I smirk. "You changed it."

I rub at my head, letting her soft hands help me sit upright on the ground. The healer kneels on the other side of me, checking for further injuries. He won't find anything he can heal with his Power. My other wounds are mental. Unless he can grow my eye or pinky back...

The sounds of the battle are muffled, as if beyond a wall. I glance around our tight knot of survivors. *It* is *a wall!* And a roof. We are cocooned in a Power-made building.

Nat towers behind the young noble woman, his limbs quaking with unused energy. "That was close," he says, raising an eyebrow at the dead Strongarm. "He almost had the princess."

I turn my gaze the other way. I don't think I can stomach seeing his dead eyes staring at me.

"You saved me from a horrible fate," she says.

The princess. Of course, she is. "We aren't safe here." I eye the surrounding structure.

Then I get a good look at the older woman towering over everyone else. The queen, without a doubt, judging by the way she holds herself.

"Have you seen Dominic?" the queen asks Nat.

He shakes his head. "Zephyr went inside to help."

"I saw him. He's going to find Cypress."

Nat sucks in a breath. "He's alive?"

The Queen's regal mask cracks, as does her voice when she speaks. "I don't know."

Something about the Queen sends chills down my spine. I rise, backing a few steps away on unsteady feet. The princess holds her hands out, ready to help me if I fall. I don't.

The Queen's ice-blue eyes strike me like a sword through the chest. I know those eyes. They haunt my nightmares. But not from her. From an unnamed man.

In a panic, sucking down desperate breaths as if I'm drowning on land, my gaze sweeps the surrounding guards. None of them are *him*.

"Dominic must still be inside," Nat says to the Queen. I've missed part of their conversation, but the pieces being falling into place.

My words are little more than a whisper from my lips, but I feel them deep in my core with absolute certainty. And it's enough to freeze everyone in place, staring at me as if I've gone mad.

"It's him."

48

GAVIN

THE THROBBING IN MY head pales compared to the sensation of nausea that threatens me. I shift as I wake, hands scraping the dirt and stone beneath me. My limbs tremble, threatening to give out. I squint into the darkness, hoping to get a handle on where I am.

A candle flickers a few feet away from me. The wax has only slightly melted, so I haven't been here more than an hour or two, assuming I can trust the candle as any sort of sign of the time. I crawl toward it on my hands and knees, unable to stand.

A great weight presses down on me, exacerbating the sickness rising in my throat. I swallow repeatedly to hold it down. My hand shakes violently as I reach for the only source of light and hold it aloft.

Flames dance along the uneven stone walls, casting an eerie light on the space. I shift onto my backside and raise the candle as high as I can, scanning the walls and floor. A sinking feeling hits me as the light makes the gemstones in the wall sparkle. I draw in ragged breaths, tasting sulfur and damp stone. I can't hold it down any longer. The vomit climbs up my throat. I barely get the candle safely on the cavern floor before the contents of my stomach empty.

I heave on all fours until nothing remains, then shuffle to the other side of the cavern.

The space isn't enormous. Perhaps only ten by twenty feet. But the weight pressing down on me, the headache and weak limbs, the nausea, are all familiar.

The gemstones in the wall are Power stones.

This is the mine.

Desperation and panic claw at me. After my display of Powers before, the Elders didn't want to take any chances. They possibly assumed their Power-dampening cells wouldn't hold me and they are most likely correct. But down here, buried beneath who knows how much Power stone, even I can't fight back.

"Drake?" I call to him, my voice cracking and weak.

I already know he isn't here. What happened to him? What happened to *me*?

As I fight off the weakness in my body, I inspect the mine. They got me down here somehow, which means there must be an exit. I'm distracted by the chaos I witnessed in the square. By Charles.

His escape from the Power-dampening cells indicates just one logical explanation. Someone turned against me and let him out. Acolytes who questioned my validity, most likely. Charles warned me this would happen. He told me that if I didn't accept my place and take the right action, people would doubt. *And gullible, naïve Gavin believed in the best in people.*

I refused to believe him. I needed to believe these people wanted their voices heard, to be accepted as equal. But they are so ingrained in their religion, and I took from them the one crutch they had to lean on.

Drake warned me, before any of this began, *"The only thing that gets us through that darkness is faith. Our hope that one day things will be better."* I close my eyes, picturing Drake's face. My heart aches. I hope he's okay.

Have I made a grave error in judgment? By refusing to accept this role the people wanted—*needed*—me to fill, did I make them turn to Charles for help? I spurned their faith openly, refusing to accept my titles, to bless children, rejecting my position. I hid from their faith because it scares me. That fear doesn't stem from my rejection of organized religion.

I run a hand along the cavern wall, holding up the candle as my only source of light. There must be an exit.

My fear is that they are *right*. Their Prophet had the gift of future sight. If he saw my arrival, and how I can change and shape the world—which I no longer doubt might be possible—then a heavy burden rests on my shoulders. A burden I don't know how to bear. And if I am their prophesied Creation…who is Desolation?

A brush of cool air strokes the tips of my fingers. I hold the candle close and the flame flickers. *A breeze!* There must be a way out of this way.

I set the candle on the ground and place both hands against the cold stone wall. The role the Prophet saw me accept in his vision does not require me to believe in their faith. I recall a verse from the *Book of the Prophet*. A verse Drake once quoted to me, though he used slightly different phrasing. *That which can be proven does not disprove that which is believed. Both are essential to survival.*

"Just because I can explain things doesn't make the Prophet inherently wrong." A bittersweet smile touches my lips.

If he is right about me, if Drake's faith isn't misplaced, then nothing—not even this Power stone mine—can stop me.

I reach for my Powers, and they slip through my fingers like sand. I try again, pressing palms to the stone wall. I fail. Again. And again. But Drake is up there somewhere. What will they do to him? What is happening to those people in the square who were fighting back?

Determined to help, to fix this horrible mess I've made once more, I grit my teeth, pushing against the wall as I grasp at my Powers. They slide over me like oil, coating my skin but unusable. Sweat rolls down my temples. I only need a little Naturalist Power to get out of here. A fraction of it would be enough to open a gap to slip out. The harder I fight for control of my Powers, the harder it becomes.

A growl of frustration climbs out of me. I throw a fist into the stones blocking the passage, drawing blood across my knuckles. They think they have sealed me in this Power-leaching tomb. I will not quit. I won't be trapped down here while they seize control and exert their authority over the innocent Havenites.

Desperate, weak, and angry, I close my hands into fists and hammer them down toward my sides like yanking on an invisible chain attached to the mine walls.

The ceiling rains dirt on my head. My Powers pulse for a moment in hungry anticipation, then slip away. I run my hands over my arms as if I can collect the oily coating the Powers leave on my skin. Then I try again.

More dirt.

And again.

A crack forms.

Again.

The walls tremble as small rocks fall from above.

I know what I must do. The only way to break free from the Power stones around me is to destroy this mine. Will this make the Haven vulnerable to the Kingdom? Or was that another Elder lie fed to the acolytes?

I focus on the cracks in the ceiling and the holes in the walls, drawing my Powers in and coiling them tight around me like thick ropes. They wrap around my arms, my chest, my legs. I raise my palms to the ceiling, pushing out with everything I have as a scream rips apart my throat. The Powers climb up and off my body like snakes, then rise into the cracks overhead. I expand the cracks outward in all directions with a thrust.

Any moment, my Powers could give out, but I can't stop. I continue pushing and pulling and will continue until I'm free or my body gives out completely. Sweat stings my eyes. I blink furiously to clear my vision, refusing to lower my arms as small rocks turn into larger ones, then boulders. The cavern doesn't collapse around me. It implodes in slow motion. The walls and ceiling break apart, moving inward.

The utter exhaustion threatens to consume me. My vision blurs. My legs and arms give out. I collapse to the floor.

As my vision dims, I raise my weak head.

And I see light.

"G AVIN?"

Water splashes over my face as someone tries pouring it into my mouth. I grasp at the bottle and take greedy drinks. I'm on the ground, with something soft rolled up under my head.

Emil crouches next to me, his brows drawn together in fear and worry. It's the first I've seen of him since telling him about his sister. What happened to him?

"Get yourself together, quickly," Emil orders.

I tremble as I push myself upright. My clothes are covered in dirt with a few rips where stones probably did some damage.

"Drake?" I ask, surprised by how much my throat hurts. Did I scream so much?

Emil shakes his head. "Ally warned me something was happening before I left. By the time I came back to the Haven, it was stone cold silent. And the square... it was a mess."

I focus on my breathing, trying to gather my strength. "Charles turned the Haven upside down."

"I noticed." Emil glances over his shoulder, then rises, pulling me up with him.

I stumble against his side, knees trembling horribly.

"I don't know how it started, but I know how it's ending," Emil says. "And if we don't hurry, a lot of people will die."

A cold shock rushes through me. "What?"

"They have everyone gathered in the temple and are *cleansing* your supporters. I think they mean to burn Drake."

No! I will tear this place to the ground before I let them hurt him. No one and nothing in this place are as important to me as he is.

"Let's go," I say, continuing to lean on him as I gather more strength. "We can form a plan on the way."

49

PAIGE

THE THRONE ROOM HAS never felt so ominous. I march through the wide doorway with Vincent and Bella, my mind screaming for anyone to help me. But all the words I want to speak are trapped in my throat. This sensation of being Controlled is deeply unnerving, like slime over my skin. I want to scrub myself clean, but it wouldn't do me any good. The Power coats my mind, not my flesh.

Prince Dominic paces the dais like an agitated animal. *Run! Help! Hide!* A dozen warnings spring to my mind, but nothing passes through my lips. He pauses when he sees me, but I can't get a read on him.

Vincent releases his grip on my arm with a slight shove.

I stumble toward the dais, where Prince Dominic catches me in his arms. When I peer up at him, there's no anger in his expression toward Vincent. "*Trust my mother and no one else.*"

More and more of the pieces are pointing toward the prince's involvement, but I can't accept it. He's been so kind, so compassionate and friendly.

The lights flicker, then hold steady.

"Stay here," Vincent says. He pats Bella on the shoulder. "You, too. I will go deal with this."

Bella nods stiffly. She watches her father stalk out the door, then peers at the prince from the corner of her eyes.

"Paige." Prince Dominic's breath slides over my forehead. I don't know whether I should take comfort from his presence or attempt fleeing now, while Vincent is gone. "Patience. This will be over soon."

"What will?" I ask.

Prince Dominic just gives me another reassuring squeeze before pulling away. He edges toward Bella. I want to stop him. Had I any control over my body I would tear her apart, turn her inside out with my Powers.

She slides her hand into Prince Dominic's, then melts against him. Her show makes me sick to my stomach. He holds her, stroking her back, her silky hair, and presses a cheek to the top of her head, murmuring reassurances.

Every nerve in my body vibrates with rage. If I could burn her alive with a look alone, I certainly would have done so already.

Then Bella tilts her head up. Prince Dominic cups her face in his palm. My stomach twists in sickening knots as the truth slams down on me just seconds before their lips meet.

I edge back one step, then another, and another as the world drops out beneath my feet.

It was him. Prince Dominic fooled me with his innocent act, with his friendship and kindness. I trusted him. Gavin warned me not to trust him, but I did it anyway!

Bella never wanted Cypress.

She wanted Dominic. Weeks ago, after my first encounter with her, I saw her speaking with someone in the elevator. I assumed at the time it was Cypress. But it was Dominic. It was him all along...

I turn while they are engrossed in their kiss, ready to bolt toward the door.

Something yanks at my body like a leash, jerking me to a stop even as Prince Dominic's smooth voice cuts through my nerves.

"You aren't leaving, Paige."

My body trembles violently. I turn, meeting his shining blue eyes. Bella looms over his shoulder, smirking at me. Her eyes shine with joy. I wish I could claw her face off!

Then the doors creak open. Vincent marches back in, a contingent of guards on his heels dragging...something. Someone. My heart skips in terror.

Vincent steps aside, motioning for the guards to drop their prisoner on the floor. They do. And I get a good look at Zephyr's bloodied face. Is that his blood, or someone else's? I attempt to rush to Zephyr's side, but I hardly manage more than a step before that invisible leash pulls me back again.

"He was breaking prisoners out of their cells," Vincent says, waving a hand at Zephyr's unconscious body.

Manacles tether Zephyr's wrists together. Steel laced with glowing green stones not dissimilar to the Tribute bracelets. They blocked him from his Power. I'm alone in this fight.

"Let's wake him and get answers," the Prince says, motioning toward Zephyr.

Yes, let's wake him up!

Vincent kneels beside Zephyr, placing his hand against the back of Zephyr's neck. As he uses his Power to force Zephyr awake, Prince Dominic settles in a seat. Not just any seat.

The throne.

Zephyr groans as he comes around. My heart thuds.

I can't tear my gaze from Zephyr's face. He blinks slowly, likely fighting for some kind of focus. When he sees Vincent, Zephyr's entire body tenses. He lunges but falls, unable to get his feet under him, not expecting the manacles confining his movements. He glares at Vincent as full of fire and fury as I did at Bella minutes ago.

Then his eyes sweep the room. Zephyr and I lock gazes. I scrape my teeth over my lip, wishing I could say something or give some sign. All I can do is shake my head.

Zephyr's dark eyes flick to his brother, perched on Cypress' throne. Confusion creates a subtle line between his brows, but it passes quickly as Vincent stalks toward Prince Dominic. Zephyr's body coils like he's preparing to strike.

"Dom..." Zephyr's warning dies on his lips when his eyes dart to Vincent's hands.

In the one, Vincent holds a knife. In the other, a crown I know all too well. It used to rest neatly on Cypress' dark, wavy hair as if made for him. A whimper slips out. Cypress is dead. He must be. How else would Vincent have gotten a hold of that crown?

Bella's hungry gaze alights on the crown as her father marches closer. She warned me that Cypress wouldn't be king for long, that she had more in mind than being his wife. She wanted it for Dominic!

Zephyr's breaths are ragged as he struggles against his guards. He thinks Vincent is after Dominic. He doesn't realize what's really going on yet.

Vincent stops at the base of the dais, only feet from Prince Dominic. Then Vincent kneels, holding up the crown toward the Prince.

Zephyr gasps.

Prince Dominic's lips curl upward as his fingers slide around the ring of gold. "It's about time."

50

ZEPHYR

No. No, this can't be right. Dominic is the softest of all of us, the gentlest and kindest. My heart thuds in agony against my ribs as my head spins out of control. None of this makes sense.

But Easton saw it. All of it. He predicted this without having stepped foot inside the palace. How blind have we all been? How long has this been happening?

"Why?" It's the only question I can manage in my confusion, betrayal, and rage.

Dominic snorts in disgust, sliding the crown on his head. He sinks back on the throne, hands casually gripping the arms. "I should think that's obvious. Father saw me as weak."

"Soft," I growl. How wrong his father had been. "That's the word he used for you. Dominic is too soft to lead."

The corner of his mouth curls up in a nasty grin. "I wonder what he would say now." For a moment, the throne room plunges into silence as he considers this. Then he shrugs it off. "Too bad you have those manacles on." He flexes his fingers. "You would feel my *true* power."

I do sense it, like something in the corner of my eye that I can never actually see, but I know it's there. For years, Dominic has displayed little magical ability. His rank was three, at best. Gifted, for certain, but not overwhelmingly so. But now, that strength flares brighter in my periphery. Without a good look, a good feel, I can't be sure how strong he really is. It's at least double what I had thought. *He hid it so well.*

"I've worked so hard to hide it from you," Dominic admits, as if reading my thoughts. "Dancing around this family was easy. I had to choose my words carefully around Mother for years. Cypress could read my past, but never my future. Still, I had to be wary of how my past actions looked to him. So, I held back all the time, except under Vincent's stellar tutelage." He nods at Lord Greene in appreciation. Greene smiles and nods back like a proud father.

"And Bronwyn... sweet, dear Bronwyn. I allowed her to see only the best, most loyal and dutiful parts of my mind. Her understanding of my thoughts is little more than a misguided vision, distorted versions of the truth masked in the life she expected of me. She never second-guessed a thing. And if something slipped through the cracks, I simply layered my magic over them to make them forget."

Dominic leans forward on one elbow, eyeing me. "But you were not so easy. I could never use my full magical might in these walls when you were around. Cypress sending you away was a blessing. It gave me more freedom to do what needed to be done to prepare for this day. And Bella..." He holds her hand up, peering affectionately at her in a way that makes me angry. "She played Cypress and Paige off one another beautifully."

The confession makes my skin crawl. With the manacles on, I can't touch my magic, nor can I reach out to his. Looking at Dominic makes my stomach churn. I can't meet his icy gaze any longer. He looks like his mother now, but much more terrifying. A monster lurked beneath those innocent eyes for years.

On the dais, Greene stands to the side, watching me with a hard look in his eyes.

"What do you get out of this?"

"An alliance. A new title. *Vindication*." The last word is emitted with a snarl. Dominic's father humiliated Greene when he found out the sort of magic Greene used against us in training. Dominic was the one who cried to his father about the brutal training—the mind control. Did this go so far back? Did Dominic put Vincent in a position to want vindication so desperately he would turn to treason?

I don't need to ask to know what the alliance entails. My gaze darts to Bella, standing at Dominic's shoulder, beaming with pure adoration at Dominic. She rests a manicured hand on his shoulder. Dominic reaches up and takes her hand, bringing it to his lips.

Paige stands at his other shoulder, body shaking as if she wants to react but can't move. Are they controlling her right now? Fury pulses inside of me, alongside a deep desire to free her, to protect her from them—and herself. My heart aches when I attempt shifting to my feet, ready to run to her aid, but strong hands clamp down on my shoulders. My knees slam into the wooden floor with a crack that rattles my teeth.

"That, right there!" Dominic leans forward like an eager dog with a bone, stabbing a finger at me. "That fire and desire and *need*. I'm human. I feel it too." He thumps his palm against his chest. "But I was forbidden because Father thought I was too *soft*." His lips curl around the word in disgust. "Cypress should have had your job as Captain. I told you that before. He should have been Captain, and *you* should have been Keeper."

I remember the conversation Dominic and I had at the ball. He watched Cypress dance with Bella, crowing about how Cypress was selfish and would keep all the girls for himself. I see now that he was jealous of Cypress' relationship with Bella—even if it was never real. Dominic told me exactly what he just confessed, with the added barb about my legitimacy in the family.

"What better way to punish me than forcing me to swear off women and never produce offspring?" I parrot his words back at him.

Dominic nods, as if his words are genius. "Instead, he cursed *me*. It should have been you." He shifts. Bella remains at his side, looking terribly pleased with all of this. "Oh, I was angry at first when he chose you as Captain instead of Keeper. Cypress and I spent several months in commiseration. He was angry that Father had overlooked him completely. Father even called Cypress weak right to his face. Too weak for service. But you were strong. Broken yet unbreakable, Father called you. We hated you for it."

I was fourteen the first time I stepped into the fort to train with the soldiers. It wasn't serious training. That came later. My uncle had insisted I toughen up. I refused to be weak around him, even as he beat me, so I did as he wanted. I hardened myself. If he saw me deserving of the title of Captain of Tides, it's because I worked for it while Cypress lazed around the palace playing games with his brothers and taking his life for granted.

"I was weeks into my training as Devotee of Tides, working closely with Uncle Cole, when everything changed." Dominic's gaze flits to Bella, and a softness passes through his eyes. My heart sinks. This isn't just an alliance. *They're in love.* "At the holiday ball, Bella and I found one another. Like two souls drawn together." As he returns those unnerving eyes to me, he snarls. "I begged Father to change his mind, to make me Captain. When pleading didn't work, I turned to the only person he ever listened to."

"Alric," I mumble. The Crown Prince. Kind, compassionate Alric. Saying his name aloud draws a sneer from Dominic.

"Alric," he growls in agreement. "Oh, he sympathized with me. I thought I had an ally who would fight this battle with me. I don't know what he said, but Father called me aside the next day in a fury. He said he would hear no more talk of marriage, or he would send Bella to the mainland, and I would receive the ultimate punishment for breaking my vows. After all, what good is a Keeper of Tides who is not willing to keep tradition? Do you know what the punishment is?"

A chill runs down my spine and my mouth goes dry. But I'm also not surprised that King Alric would make the threat. "Castration."

Dominic's blue eyes brew in a wild storm. "The rules surrounding the Keeper are archaic."

My heart sinks. The motivation for all of this makes much more sense to me. The rockslide wasn't an accident. Dominic somehow caused it. He set up the king.

"So you killed him."

"What choice did I have?" A child-like sadness creases his face. It only lasts a moment before he resumes his anger. "He threatened me. He refused to be moved."

I snort. "He wouldn't move if the world crumbled beneath him."

The corner of Dominic's mouth twitches upward. "I'm aware."

My stomach curdles. I cannot reconcile this Dominic with the boy I grew up with. This monster before me is *not* my brother.

"Uncle Cole caught Bella and me kissing behind the pool house one night," he carries on, oblivious to my internal struggle. "He vowed to tell Father about it first thing in the morning."

Uncle Cole died in his sleep. No one could explain what happened. He was so young it came as a shock to everyone. Dominic, in particular, took the loss hard. He was inconsolable for weeks. Whether it was an act to cover his tracks or true guilt over killing his uncle, I will never know. And I won't ask. "You killed him in his sleep that very night."

His casual shrug sets my teeth on edge.

Something else strikes me and I work my jaw, forcing the words out. "You tried to kill Cypress, too. He was there when your father and brother died. Alric saved him."

Dominic's fingers twitch. "An unfortunate mistake. This would have all been so much easier had Cypress died with them."

I remember Cypress in the cell, far below us, beaten but still breathing. "So why not kill him now?"

Paige gasps, eyes widening as she glances at Dominic. Her face is horribly pale. Engrossed in piecing all of this together with her lingering in the shadows silently, I had almost forgotten her there. She didn't know Cypress was still alive.

"I'm not completely heartless, Zephyr." The words are so honest I would almost believe him, were we not in this situation. "Cypress is my brother, and he has never stood in my way. Not until he had that crown on his head." He spits out those last words with intense disgust. Dominic's eyes glint with mischief. "But you..."

I swallow hard. He knows we aren't really brothers. And if he knows, will that change his mercy? Perhaps I'm dead already. "Where is Queen Elena? Your mother would be ashamed of you."

Dominic's jaw tightens so firmly his teeth grind. That storm continues brewing in his blue eyes. "I didn't do anything, Zephyr. *You* did."

My lips part as a breath escapes like a punch in the gut. He will blame everything on me, then laud himself the hero of the Kingdom. And Queen Elena will believe him. Everyone will. What a perfect mess he has made.

"Opening the Tribute season early was your idea, wasn't it?" I ask. "You played off Cypress' weakness, his need to prove himself worthy of his new position, and his trust in you." My gaze darts to Bella. "Then you planted her among the girls."

Dominic sneers, "It wasn't exactly hard to convince him it was the right thing to do. And once he decided it would happen, he was determined not to be pushed over by anyone. Baron included. Cypress is nothing if not predictable."

"Where are the other girls? The missing mainlanders Cypress dismissed."

"You've been busy." His jaw cracks, hands tightening into fists. But he refuses to answer my question. Dominic nods at someone behind me. I twist against the hands holding me on my knees.

Baron marches in, head held high despite the manacles and guards surrounding him, as if they follow his command and not Dominic's.

"Zephyr, I tried to make this easier on everyone," Dominic continues as they march Baron forward. "Smuggling away supplies to feed my army. Employing physicians to find ways to exploit magical abilities."

Easton's experiments... He refused to talk about what happened.

"You have an army?" I can't help myself. Where is Dominic hiding an army?

Dominic clucks, his shoulders sloping in satisfaction. "Oh, cousin, I have far more than an army." His gaze flicks on Paige.

My stomach flips in wild rage. My fingers itch to wrap around his neck.

I track Baron's movements through the throne room. He glares at Dominic with a vengeance I've never witnessed in him before.

"You were always going to be a complication," Dominic tells me. He holds out a hand to his left, then points at my father.

Paige whimpers, tears rolling down her cheeks but steel lacing her eyes. She steps toward Baron.

"It isn't Greene," I breathe. "It's you. *You're* controlling her." When did he gain Operator magic? I always knew he could Sway—a tool he no doubt used to his advantage. "Let her go."

"You have nothing to bargain with in exchange for her." He waves me off, turning his attention to Baron. His tone becomes all business, laced with a hint of sadness. Whom does he think he is acting for? "Uncle, I'm afraid the evidence against your treason is irrefutable."

"No! Dom, blame me!" I struggle against the guards. A growl climbs up my throat.

"I do." He doesn't even bother looking at me.

Baron raises his chin, defiance fortifying his posture. His dark eyes don't waver a moment as he glowers at Dominic.

"We have evidence that you orchestrated the death of my father and brother," Dominic announces. The lie is obvious to everyone in the room. Baron doesn't flinch. "And a witness, should the need arise, to verify your guilt."

A witness? That must be another fabrication. Or Dominic planted the impending confession in his scapegoat.

"You made an attempt against the life of the Captain of Tides, encouraging men to mutiny against him."

I shake my head. "Lies."

"When that failed, you coerced King Cypress to exile the Captain, using his jealousy to fuel his actions."

My gaze darts around the room. Bella and Greene, smug and happy as can be. The guards, either controlled by Greene and Dominic, or sworn to them.

And Paige. Her tawny skin a sickly shade of green. For a moment, our eyes meet. Her anger and sympathy and understanding for my plight shine in her umber gaze. Fear also shines there. Her fingers arch and she closes her eyes, fighting off whatever war rages beneath the surface. A sob climbs out of her, cut off with a sickening choking sound.

"Baron Strong, you are found guilty of treason and sentenced to death," Dominic announces.

Red mist springs to life in Paige's hand. Her neck turns bright red as she struggles to stop herself.

Grief catches in my throat as I realize what he is forcing her to do. "Please, Dom, don't make her do this. *Please.*" I can't let her suffer the guilt of killing against her will. I must stop it. The next words rip out of me. "I'll do it."

Paige freezes in front of Baron, her hand in the air as the red magic crawls along her limbs like an eager serpent. Dangerous magic that I know she fears.

Dominic leans forward, smirking at me. "Now that's interesting." His cold eyes flick between Paige and me in some mysterious calculation. He raps his fingers against the arm of the throne.

"Very well. Zephyr, you will carry out your father's execution. Here and now."

My hands tremble violently as the guards yank me to my feet. We stumble toward Baron as Paige moves to the side. Greene unsheathes a knife, slapping it into my hand.

"Try anything, and I will skewer you myself," Greene hisses in my ear.

Baron meets my gaze as I stop in front of him. A hurricane of emotions passes through his eyes. Understanding. Acceptance. Forgiveness. Sadness. And an undercurrent of something more. I hear his words in that gaze. *"Fight for her."*

He offers me a subtle nod. "Steady, son."

Had I not already emptied my stomach in the sub-level, I might vomit here in the throne room.

51

GAVIN

O
UR PLAN SOUNDS SIMPLE enough, but I know that nothing ever goes according to plan. Emil will slip into the temple while I create a spectacle to distract the Elders and the Minister. Once I have their attention, Emil will get as many people away from the fight as possible. It means I need to stay out of reach. I think I can handle avoiding Powers, but if they touch me and knock me out again, we will lose our only chance to save these people.

Despite the plan, the screams from inside the temple as we draw near the doors evaporate all logic.

One scream, in particular, rips into me. The pure agony of it sends my mind and heart into a tailspin. "Drake..." I'm too late. *No! I don't want this Power if I can't have him.*

"Get as many to safety as you can," I say.

"Gavin..." Emil lunges for me as I rush the temple doors.

I slip from his grasp. Desperation pulses through me. Despite over a thousand bodies between us, I can see Drake on the stage at the head of the temple, surrounded by flames. Everything inside of me shatters into a million pieces.

Without thinking, I launch myself upward, using the air itself to hoist me above the heads of everyone. Did I not do enough, sacrifice enough for these people already?

I gather those shattered pieces of my soul like shards of Power. Elements bow to my will as the ground opens and the mass of jeering onlookers—people condemning those brave enough to stand up for me and for themselves—all fall into the earth. Hundreds of them, devoured by the ground.

With a flick of my wrist, the flames consuming my love, my heart, my *everything*, spread across the stage like a hundred desperate, starving predators. Julia, Carmen, and Luke stumble backward on the stage, seeking escape. But they won't find it. The fire will win. I grind my teeth as their shrieks replace Drake's as the hungry flames eat away at them.

Drake's body thumps against the ground. I rush toward him, soaring over everyone and everything in my way in a bound of air.

As if my arrival signals a charge, hordes of people on the ground surge to their feet—those who supported me and stood up for themselves—taking advantage of the distraction I've provided by attacking their captors. Emil herds them toward the exit, only to be blocked by dozens of massive Guardians. The people begin the fight for freedom, aided by acolytes and Guardians like Ajax.

My pulse slows as something tugs at me, yanking me off course. I tumble to the stage at Mrs. Garraty's feet. My head hits the wood, stunning me momentarily.

Then my lungs collapse, and my heartbeat slows. Tears of pain and sorrow and frustration and grief roll down my burning cheeks as I flip over on my back. I fight against this strange Power taking hold of the blood in my veins.

"My daughter is dead because of you," Mrs. Garraty growls, baring her teeth like she wants to suck my blood dry like some mythical vampire.

The timid ghost of a woman I knew has transformed into something terrifying. How does she command so much Power? Where did it come from? Did she always have this?

She flicks her wrist and my body rises at her command. My toes scrap at the ground. My Power slips from my grasp as she tightens her hold on my slowing heartbeat. A nearby Power stone pulses against me, just as angry and hungry as the woman in front of me.

Mrs. Garraty edges closer, providing me with a closer look at her eyes. The veins are thick and scarlet, as if ready to pop. The formerly dull brown of her irises are now a deep shade of crimson. This Power of hers is consuming her, destroying her from the inside out. I wish I could leave her in misery, allow it to run its course and destroy her, but all I can think about is Drake. His body. His death at their hands.

Her hot breath smacks my face. So close, she doesn't see my arm move as I reach up behind her and place my hand over the Power stone embedded deep in her neck. So deep no one else would have noticed. Somehow, they have given her a Power with this stone. Who did they steal it from to give it to her? Who died so she could become this monster?

"I took something you love," I hiss, playing off her own accusation. "And you took something I love."

Her gaze flicks at Drake, then her lips curl in disgust. But the distraction is enough. I check to be sure Emil is doing his part. People stream toward the exit I created outside the temple walls. It's best if no one remains underground for this.

I slap my hand over the stone in her neck, grasping my Power at the same time. The suddenness takes Mrs. Garraty by surprise. Before she can react, I thrust Naturalkinesis into the stone. The solid becomes liquid, bleeding into her veins. While she can control the blood of others, Mrs. Garraty is helpless to control her own. Her screams split the air, hurting my ears. Her grip on me vanishes instantly as she claws at her own veins in a pointless attempt to remove the liquefied stone.

The scarlet in her eyes flashes bright green, then she falls to the floor in a heap.

I stagger, sickened by what I've done. I killed her. I killed all the Elders. Their charred remains are positioned around the stage in various stages of agony. I close my eyes to block it out, but still vomit up bile.

One Elder remains.

Ally trembles in fear, cowering in a corner away from the destroyed temple floor and burned bodies. She gags on the scent and taste of burned flesh, just as I do.

"I tried t-to s-stop them," Ally cries. She hugs her knees to her chest and rocks back and forth. "I tried. I tried." Tears leave clean streaks down her dirty cheeks.

I believe her. I believe her because Emil trusts her. "Go."

Ally scrambles to her feet and darts toward the exit.

I turn toward Drake. What remains of him.

A sob climbs up my throat, and once the dam breaks, I can't control my grief. It spills out in horrifying, gut-wrenching sobs. The agony of kneeling beside his burned body is far worse than anything I've experienced before. I can't think, can't move, can't breathe. He died alone, without me. Was he waiting for me to come save him? *I have faith in you.* But I failed him. When Drake needed me most, I failed him.

I curl over his body, allowing my grief to bury me here beneath the Haven as I lash out with my Power and bring the entire underground society crashing down. The thunder of collapsing tunnels in the distance rumbles through the earth. The world is crumbling, and I don't care. I can't. I've been hollowed out.

"Gavin!" Ally's scream reaches through my haze of grief.

I sink back on my heels as snow and earth fall around me from above.

Charles thrusts a knife at my neck.

Without thinking, in the blink of an eye, the falling rocks solidify around him, turning Charles into stone—knife and all.

I scoop Drake's body in my arms and turn away from Charles, staggering with Drake's weight leaving me unbalanced. The massive head of one of the stone statues cracks, then tumbles down. It crashes into Charles, shattering the stone, grinding him to dust.

Dirt creates a fog in the surrounding air. I don't know where I'm headed with Drake's body, but I won't leave him here where they tarnished him.

Stairs appear in front of me, one at a time, until I reach the surface. All the while, my focus remains on Drake, even if I can't bear to look at his ruined face.

I emerge from the belly of the Haven, stepping out of the fog of debris, clutching Drake desperately. My Powers pulse with life, and I hate them for failing me. For failing to save him. I crouch on the ground, and a crowd gathers around me, watching, waiting to see what I will do next.

Emil pushes to the head of the group, clutching Ally close to his side. She must have just escaped before the final collapse. Emil's jaw tightens as he stares at Drake. I can't look. I close my eyes and lean over Drake, pressing my face to his chest, clutching his burned shirt in my fists.

Once more, the grief overwhelms me. I cry and no one stops me. Time ticks by so slowly. I try desperately, pointlessly, to force some of my life into him, but there's no fixing this. The best Healers in Elpis couldn't bring him back.

I thought I hated the Kingdom for taking my sister from me. But it's nothing compared to the hate in my heart for the people who did this to Drake.

"Gavin." Emil's voice is tender as he eases me back. I try pulling away. "Gavin, give him space."

"Space?" I blink furiously, unable to see anything clearly. Why would Drake need space?

Murmurs ripple through the Havenites gathered around me. Shock and awe. It makes me sick to my stomach.

I squeeze my eyes closed, willing this nightmare to end, willing Drake to come back to me.

A hand closes around mine. Cold, but familiar.

The murmurs of the crowd are no longer hushed, but cries of alarm and astonishment.

I blink to clear my vision, but it doesn't happen fast enough.

"I knew you would come." Drake's weak voice breaks through my fog.

He's pale, and a few scars remain on his neck and chest, making the skin puckered and gray. Light shines in his dark eyes. His chest, covered with new skin, rises and falls.

I gasp. "What...how...?"

Drake's grip is weak, but he's alive. *He's alive!* "Because you are *him*. Gavin, I've been telling you for months. You are Creation."

I would argue the point, but how can I?

Emil stands behind us, eyeing the collapsed ground where the Haven once hid. "What now?" he asks.

Drake smiles, and it lights up my world. "We go home."

Home.

52

EASTON

"YOU CAN'T HONESTLY BELIEVE my son would do all of this." The Queen has lost patience with me already. That can't bode well for my odds of survival.

"Why not?" I stand alone in *this* battle, facing down royalty, their trained guards, and servants. Each of them stares at me as if I've gone mad. I wish I had. "I don't know Dominic at all. Not like you do. Which gives me an unfiltered perspective on all of this."

"He wouldn't turn on his family," the Queen snaps.

Princess Bronwyn watches me as if attempting to read me or calculate something in my posture. "Read him, Mother."

I flinch. If she can read minds, she doesn't want to see what I've seen about her son. I draw back another step. "Listen to me...please. I've been used to keep Paige in line since we arrived. He took my finger—well, not him. A doctor who was working for him." I shudder at the memory. "Those blue eyes. Your eyes. He had mine surgically removed."

"Why?" Bronwyn asks.

I lick my lips. Every muscle in my body is tense as these people glare at me. I could easily die in this circle. I'm no idiot. "To send a message to her. That's why Baron smuggled me out." Well, part of the reason. "Blue Eyes was forcing experiments on me, then healing me so I could go back to training. And I...something blocked me from saying anything up to this point. I don't know how, nor do I understand why I can talk about it now." But I do. There's nothing we can do at this point, so what does it matter if I tell the world?

The Queen pales. Her lips tremble and tears make her blue eyes shine. She shakes her head in denial, but something tells me she already knows the truth. Bronwyn holds her palms up, taking a placating step closer.

"May I?" she asks, nodding at her empty hands.

My jaw twitches. I don't want to relive what Dominic did to me. I don't even know that I want a name to match those horrifying blue eyes. Yet, the princess has such a calming effect I place my hands over hers before I realize what I've done.

Her skin is warm, soft, smooth. Her touch is gentle. As she cradles my hands in hers, her eyes glaze over. It only lasts a moment, but she jerks back with a gasp. Tears roll down her cheeks. She can sense it somehow. Psychometry—the ability to read things through touch? Or Telepathy, maybe?

The truth has shattered her just as certainly as it did the queen. Both women are broken by what I know, what I've seen and suffered.

"Wyn?" Nat asks softly.

"How did we not see this?" Bronwyn whispers to no one in particular.

"I'm sure this is hard to deal with, but we don't have time to linger on what has already happened." I hope I sound gentle, but tact has never been my strength. "Zephyr and Paige are still in that palace. If the king or Baron still lives, they are trapped in there, too. We have to regroup and plan an extraction. Time is working against us. Every second we waste, Dominic and his followers gain strength."

They all flinch when I say Dominic's name. Though they begin to accept the truth, there is still denial lurking in all of them. Even Nat.

A servant steps forward, though her mother tries pulling her back. "He has Paige. The Prince. He ushered her away from her room after Nora died. To safety, he said."

"Nora?" Nat breathes her name, sorrow creating deep lines on his forehead. I don't know who Nora is, nor do I care at this moment.

"If the Prince already has Paige, Zephyr and all of us are in even more trouble," I say. "We are wasting time."

The queen draws herself up to regal bearing once more. Something like steel laces through her as she raises her chin, and her eyes harden with resolve. "We need to seize the fort and whatever remains of the soldiers. Without a defensible base, we are vulnerable."

Outside our dome of protection, all is silent. The battle for the palace is over.

And something tells me we just lost.

53

PAIGE

MY MIND THRASHES WILDLY against the Control Dominic has over my actions and my Powers. His Power has been woven for weeks over my mind, a delicate, intricate web of lace and steel I can't fight free from.

Gavin warned me about the prince. He questioned why Dominic wouldn't just have Baron check in on Easton, why he would be the one to handle things. I hadn't questioned it at the time because I trusted Dominic. *I trusted him.* Betrayal rips at my core, my heart, my soul, shattering the pieces I barely held together already. I did this. I trusted him and let him in, giving him the access he needed to create this web of Control.

Dominic is a monster. He in no way resembles the prince I thought I knew.

The layers of everything Dominic confesses, everything Zephyr responds with, make my head swim. It's too much for me to piece together so quickly, but one piece shines with crystal clarity.

Several times, Dominic calls Zephyr cousin, hints that he isn't his brother. Zephyr doesn't seem the least bit alarmed by the news. He must have learned the truth after leaving the palace.

My Power springs to life as I move with stilted steps toward Baron. His hard jaw—so like Zephyr's—softens on me even though he must know what they are forcing me to do to him. Something about the way he meets my gaze tells me he isn't angry, that he understands. Not that it makes any of this easier for me.

Zephyr bucks against his guards, begging Dominic not to make me do this. Tears well in my eyes. I can't look at Zephyr. I can't stand the idea of seeing the agony that surely shines in his dark eyes.

"I'll do it." Zephyr's declaration sends a bolt of fear and sorrow through me. No. Dominic can't let him. He won't. He wants Zephyr to see me suffer.

Dominic agrees, ordering Zephyr to kill his father.

My gaze darts to Baron.

Baron is Zephyr's father? Agony tears through me. Agony that mirrors in Baron's dark eyes. His teeth grind. *No, Zephyr. Don't do this.*

As Zephyr approaches, my Power winks out. There must be some way to break out of this Control... Some way to stop Dominic.

Vincent slaps a knife in Zephyr's trembling hand. I shake my head, imploring Zephyr to look at me, to understand that I don't want him to do this. I don't want him to make this sacrifice to spare me the burden. He shouldn't have to. He shouldn't be forced to kill his own father in my place. Why would he? I wouldn't do it for him. Does that make me a horrible person?

Tears roll down my cheeks unchecked as I struggle against the web blocking me from controlling my Powers. I can feel it, sense it as surely as the pulse in my veins, but it won't answer to me. I tremble, weak in the knees. Were it not for Dominic's mental grip over my body with his Power, I would crumble to my knees.

Baron murmurs something to Zephyr that strikes Zephyr to his core. His shoulders sag and his back straightens. The grip on the knife tightens as he steadies his nerves, then he murmurs something back. An apology, I think.

Please, stop! I want to scream at the top of my lungs. Instead, only hot tears stream down my cheeks as I watch Zephyr place a hand on Baron's shoulder. He raises the other and the knife catches in the light.

I buck and kick and fight at the Control holding back my Power. Dominic grunts behind me, a clipped sound, and the only sign that he is fighting to maintain his Control over me. If I could just harness a fraction, I could end all of this. But Dominic's strong. His grip over me is firm, laced around my nerves as tight as well-spun silk.

Baron tips his head back, exposing his throat. My stomach heaves.

Zephyr strikes the blade quickly. I squeeze my eyes closed as if it can block everything out. But nothing can block out Baron's gurgling, nor the strangled sounds of agony from Zephyr. The thump jolts me like a current through my bones. I jump, eyes snapping open.

Baron is in a heap on the floor. Zephyr sinks to his knees, folding himself over the body as the knife clatters to the wooden floor. His shoulders shake with sobs, though he makes no sound. I want to hold him, comfort him, remove his pain in any way I can. He killed his own father so I wouldn't be forced to do it. I can never thank him for sparing me the pain. Nor do I ever expect him to forget that he did it because of me.

Dominic has driven a wedge between us, and he knows exactly what he did. His iron grip on my limbs yields, freeing me to move as I wish for the first time since I attempted bolting for the door.

With this newfound freedom, I consider lunging at Dominic to rip out his throat like he just made Zephyr do to his own father. Or maybe kill Bella so he can feel the agony of loss. Can he feel anything at all?

Zephyr's grief rips at my heart. All I can do is sink down beside him, ignoring Baron's pooling blood around us, and pull Zephyr into my arms.

Zephyr's arms slide around me, clinging to me like I'm the only thing keeping him afloat. I reach for my Power, ready to lash out at everyone in the room for him, but something yanks it out of my grasp. Dominic *tsks* behind me, a clear warning. His moment of reprieve will only go so far.

I close my eyes, holding Zephyr close as he buries his face against my collarbone. His tears soak into my skin. I murmur an apology, knowing it's worthless.

"How touching," Dominic drawls. "It's nice to know this hasn't broken your bond. I will need that in the weeks to come."

Zephyr stiffens, drawing back. His bloodshot eyes flare to life, red hot with wrath. "Take these manacles off and we will see who breaks first." His growl sends a chill down my spine.

My arms remain around Zephyr, afraid of letting go. Afraid of being forced to let go. He must share the sentiment because his grip tightens around me as well.

Dominic clucks. "I think not. I may be strong, but I'm no fool."

"What's wrong, Dom? Scared of the little *bastard*?" Zephyr hisses, shooting an obvious challenge at his cousin. I know what he's doing. If Dominic removes his manacles, Zephyr can cut him off from his Power, thus freeing me from Control. In a fistfight, Zephyr would be the clear winner. But if I know this, Dominic does as well. If tonight has proven anything, it's that Dominic isn't stupid.

"Enough." Dominic leans forward. "Say your farewells."

A chill runs down my spine. *Farewells? No. I'm not ready to let go.*

"The harbor will be ready in a few days." Dominic's lips turn upward as Bella's hand closes around his. "Then I will keep the promise Cypress made." His frost-blue eyes fall on me, plunging me into an ice bath. "I'm taking Paige home."

Home. Elpis. It's all I've wanted since arriving on this island, but something tells me it won't be to release me. Dominic wants something more. He wants the city. I'm not sure what he learned from Easton over these past few months. He can't honestly dream of defeating or conquering Elpis. He doesn't have the military strength to do it. *Does he?*

Dominic appears sickeningly satisfied with himself. Does he know what I'm thinking? "I will bring my most powerful weapons. I had never dared to dream of such a thing before. But with a weapon like Paige... Just imagine what I can do with that much magic under my control. The Kingdom is about to become an empire."

I clench my jaw, finding my voice for the first time in an hour. "I won't attack my people. And I won't take you there."

"I think you will."

Zephyr takes my face in a bloody palm, turning me away from Dominic. His eyes speak volumes. Love and agony and understanding. I know, in that moment, the depth of his feelings. It speaks to my heart. I never would have imagined, when he captured me months ago and ripped me away from everything, that I would dare to fall for him. If anything, I would have laughed at myself. He doesn't speak the words. Neither do I. But we both understand.

Then he places a brief, tender kiss on my lips. It ends far too soon. Zephyr strokes my cheek, spreading Baron's blood on my skin, but I hardly notice as he presses his forehead to mine.

"This isn't over," he whispers, only for me to hear. His reddened eyes burn with determination and grief.

I understand the sentiment. The true fight has only just begun.

Dominic sighs. "Yes, I thought so."

My limbs betray me, slipping out of Zephyr's embrace. I yelp at the suddenness, my body moving at Dominic's will.

Dominic motions for the guards to take Zephyr. "You will take me to your homeland, Paige. And to ensure you don't resist, that you remain loyal to me even when I don't hold you in my grasp, I think I will keep your lover-boy under lock and key here in the palace. Should you refuse, we will deliver pieces. I believe you are familiar with the exchange."

Everything crashes around me. My stomach churns in agony as my heart breaks. I've only just gotten Zephyr back, and already he is ripped from me. But even worse is the horrible truth.

I can't exchange his life for a city of innocent people—for my family—even after he has just done it for me.

As they drag him out of the throne room, Zephyr glances at me over his shoulder. He casts a look of understanding and defeat back at me. A sad smile perches in the corner of his mouth. He nods.

Because he knows as well as I do that he will die.

Elpis cannot fall.

Curious what Ugene uncovered to make this mission possible? Wondering about the barrier?
Download the prequel, Revelation, only available at Starr ZDavies.com.

Ready to find out what happens next? Get your copy of *Invasion* and let the adventure continue!

I hope you enjoyed Paige, Gavin, and Zephyr's story. If you did, please consider leaving me a review. I love hearing what people liked about the book.

ACKNOWLEDGMENTS

I OWE CYPRESS AN apology. You suffered so much, yet I still dragged your heart and soul through the mud. I wish I could say it gets better, but we both know you can't have what you want. The best I can do is promise you will find peace in your soul before this is done. And Gavin, keep your chin up. Sometimes we have to destroy something before we can build something better.

Celeste, it's good to see you again! I didn't know if you would have a part to play, but it turns out Paige might need you.

As always, a special thanks to my husband. We had so many projects to complete around the house and you did your best to understand my need to meet a series of tight deadlines. You give me the space to do what I love and I will do my best to hold up my end of our bargain. To my kids: I know you hate cleaning bathrooms and doing dishes, but your help around the house lets me breathe a little easier every day. And again, to my daughter, Easton is still alive. The guy is remarkably resilient.

This book wouldn't be where it is without the dedication of my beta readers: Kevin Mackie, TaniaRina Perry, Asher Jones, Jared Goldman, Kris Shotts, and Jennifer Garcia. Nor would it have been fit for print without the steady hand of my editor, Maddy, who always has the best suggestions, advice, and praise alike. Thanks for taking multiple passes through this book to make it as clean as we can manage as a team. The support from my fellow dystopian authors in the Dystopian Author League have helped me launch this series. You should read their books, too. I promise they're all amazing!

To Cole R. Eubanks, thanks for giving these characters *amazing* voices for audiobook lovers to enjoy. I know I do!

And of course, I want to give a big thanks to you, my dear reader. Because without your support, my books would go unloved and unnoticed.

POWERS TRILOGY SERIES

A POWERS UNIVERSE SERIES

A SUPERPOWER DYSTOPIAN SCI-FI SERIES
FEATURING DIVERSE CHARACTERS,
FOUND FAMILY, DYNAMIC FRIENDSHIPS,
AND POLITICAL CORRUPTION

WWW.STARRZDAVIES.COM/POWERS-UNIVERSE

ABOUT STARR Z. DAVIES

 STARR Z. DAVIES is an award-winning au-
thor of over 20 tales that span dystopian
realms, epic fantasies, and echoes of forgotten
histories. Dubbed the "Character Assassin,"
she weaves stories where heroes are tested by
fire—both emotional and physical.

From her woodland home in northern
Wisconsin, she crafts worlds while surround-
ed by her greatest allies: a supportive husband, two imaginative
children, and a curious menagerie of robotic pets. When not con-
juring new adventures, she dabbles in home enchantments, swims
like a siren, battles through video game quests, and devours books
like ancient tomes of power.

If you want to become friends with Starr, dark chocolate, Doctor Who, Parks & Rec, The Office, and the MCU are all fantastic
ways into her heart. That or a love for fantasy books by indie
authors.

Learn more about Starr and her books.

Keep up with Starr by signing up for her newsletter.

Want to be part of her community? Follow Starr on social media.
facebook.com/szdavies
instagram.com/s.z.davies
threads.com/s.z.davies
tiktok.com/starrzdavies